CHAMELEON

BOOKS BY WILLIAM DIEHL

Sharky's Machine
Chameleon

CHAMELEON

WILLIAM DIEHL

RANDOM HOUSE 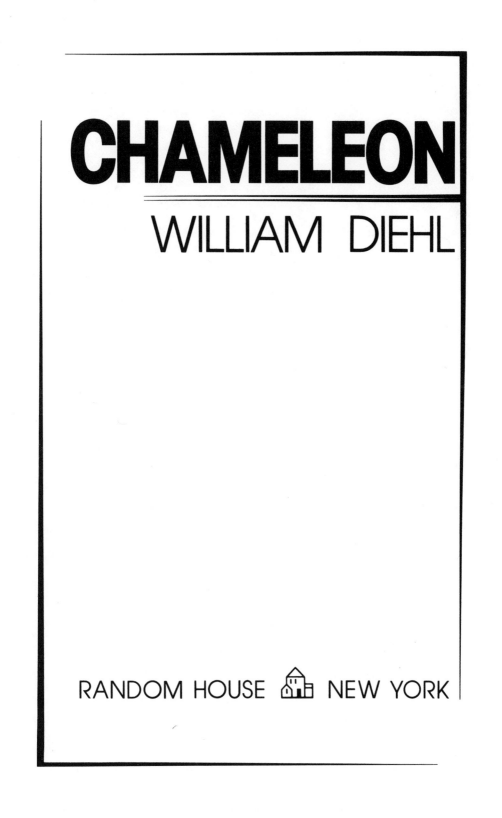 NEW YORK

All rights reserved under International and Pan-American Copyright Conventions.
Published in the United States by Random House, Inc., New York, and
simultaneously in Canada by Random House of Canada Limited, Toronto.

Library of Congress Cataloging in Publication Data

Diehl, William.
Chameleon.

I. Title.
PS3554.I345C5   813'.54   81-40228
ISBN 0-394-51961-2   AACR2

Manufactured in the United States of America
2   3   4   5   6   7   8   9
FIRST EDITION

For Virginia—
And the poetry of her spirit
Arigato, *Lizzie*

ACKNOWLEDGMENTS

With gratitude.
To Mom and Dad, Cathy and John, Stan, Bill and Melissa.
To Temple and little Katie.
To Michael and Marilyn, Michael and Mardi, Irving and Sylvia, Carole,
Don and Rose, David, Mitch and Cobray, DeSales, Bobby Byrd,
Missy, Joel, Ira and DeeDee, Peter and Cathy, and Betty and
Dr. Sam Gray.
To George, Eddie, James, Chuck, Paul, and the News department of
Channel Five, Atlanta.
To Betsy Nolan, Tommy, Ed, Sidney Sheldon and Burt.
To Marc Jaffe and Random House, and Nat Lefkowitz
and William Morris.
To an inspiring editor, Peter Gethers.
A wondrous agent, Owen Laster.
And finally in loving memory of the old bear, Townsend:
So long, Stromboli, wherever you may be.

PROLOGUE

*History is an account,
mostly false,
of events,
mostly unimportant,
which are brought about by rulers,
mostly knaves,
and soldiers,
mostly fools.*

—AMBROSE BIERCE

HE HAD BEEN WATCHING her for almost an hour. She was absolutely stunning as she moved gracefully through Bloomingdale's, carefully pondering each gift before buying it, then checking it off her list before moving on to the next department. An elegant and exotic creature, tallish, trim, chic, wonderfully stylish in black Jordache jeans, Lucchese cowboy boots, a pale-blue silk blouse and a poplin jacket lined with rabbit fur.

The clincher was the hat, a black derby, cocked almost arrogantly over one almond-shaped eye with just a trace of black veil covering her face.

He moved with her, a counter or two away, fifty feet or so behind her. She methodically did the store. Her shopping bag was full by the time she reached the first floor, and as she stepped off the escalator, suddenly picking up speed, heading toward the Lexington Avenue entrance. In a few more moments she would be outside. And that would be that. If he was going to make a move, now was the time.

He slipped into his leather coat as he hurried along a row of blinking Christmas trees, past a red and white banner that said: "Merry Christmas, from all your friends at Bloomingdale's" (and under it, a commercial prod: "only 4 more shopping days left"), down the stairs from the mezzanine and below a balcony where a group of timid high school carolers were almost whispering their version of "The Little Drummer Boy." Then he almost lost her. An army of resolute shoppers, fleeing before the wind and wet snow, charged through the revolving doors, forging relentlessly into the store. He was a temporary victim, caught up in the momentum of the rude assault.

He side-stepped and angled his way through the mob, shouldered his way free, lurched forward, and almost ran into her. They were face to face, almost touching, and then, just as suddenly they were apart again.

Her move away from him was so graceful he sensed rather than saw it. Before he could apologize, she recovered her composure and quickly appraised him. An older man, forty-five or so, and handsome, although his face was beginning to show the strains of the good life and his brown hair was peppered with gray. His dress was impeccable: tweed jacket, slate-brown wool slacks, a wide-striped shirt and Cardin tie.

He stared straight back at her, smiled, motioned her into the door and gave it a shove when she entered the glass triangle. Was she Oriental? Polynesian? A mixture? Mexican and French, perhaps. She seemed a bit tall to be Japanese.

Outside, cold wet snowflakes raked Lexington Avenue, dancing over the subway grates before the harsh crosstown wind swirled them up Fifty-first Street. They flagged the same cab, dodged the same shower of slush as it pulled up, and since most of the cabs had either vanished or gone to lunch at the first sign of bad weather, they decided to share it.

That was the start of it.

He suggested a drink. She stared at him for a moment from under the rakish brim of the derby and, to his surprise, nodded. They stopped at the Pierre and she played it just right. One drink and she was gone. While he was paying the bill, the maître d' came to the table and handed him a note. Her phone number was scribbled across the slip of paper.

Perfect.

They had lunch the next day at La Côte Basque, spent part of the afternoon browsing through a new exhibit at the Museum of Modern Art, had a drink at Charley O's and went ice-skating at Rockefeller Plaza. She went home to change and met him later at the Four Seasons for dinner. She was wearing a severe black suit with a white silk Victorian blouse trimmed in Irish lace, its high collar tucked just under her chin and always a hat, its veil adding a constant touch of mystery. She said very little, and when she did speak, the conversation was impersonal. As it often goes with fledgling love affairs, they skirted personal questions, keeping the mystery alive as long as possible. After dinner, caught up in the spirit of the season, they listened to the Christmas carolers in front of Rockefeller Plaza and they window-shopped along Fifth Avenue.

It began to snow again but the wind had died down and the thick powder began to drift on the sidewalk. Several cabs went by with their "Off Duty" lights on. Then the street was bare except for an errant carriage that had strayed several blocks from the Plaza at Central Park, its horse clopping forlornly through the snow while the driver, a young woman wearing a stovepipe hat with a silk rose in the band, huddled under a blanket. He flagged her down, in the middle of Fifth Avenue, and she agreed to take them to Sixty-third Street.

They huddled under a warm blanket too, and he put his arm around her, drawing her to him, moving her face up toward his with a gentle nudge from the back of his hand and she, responding, kissed him very lightly, the tip of her tongue tracing the edge of his lower lip. They kissed again. And then again, exploring each other's faces with their fingertips, their tongues flirting, back and forth.

Fifth Avenue was empty when they got to her apartment. The wind had blown itself out and the snow was falling almost straight down, filling the ruts in the street. A gentle hush had settled over everything. He gave the driver three ten-dollar bills, jumped out of the cab and gallantly swept his lady out over the soggy curb and under the apartment awning, and she took his hand and led him into the lobby. Behind them, the crack of the young woman's whip was swallowed up by the snowdrifts. When they entered her apartment she immediately excused herself and went into the bedroom.

Her apartment, which was on the fourth floor overlooking the Park, was a small but tastefully decorated one-bedroom flat with an open fireplace in the living room. But there was something missing, and it was a few moments before he realized there were no personal effects in the room. No pictures, no mementos. It was almost as if the room were a showcase in a department store.

He stood and appraised the apartment for another moment or two, then stepped into the guest bath and closed the door. He lowered his pants. A leather belt was strapped high on his left thigh with a sheath on the inside of his leg. The handle protruding from the sheath had been planed until it was flat and narrow, and then it had been grooved out to fit his fingers. He wrapped them around the handle and drew out a wood chisel, the kind used by sculptors. He inspected it. The curled edges of its gutterlike shaft gleamed with evil promise. The blade had been cut off about five inches from the handle and honed to a needle point. He tested the point with a forefinger, barely touching it before it broke the skin. He sucked a bauble of blood from his fingertip, pulled his pants back up, and reaching around his back, slipped the awl into his belt. He checked himself out in the mirror and returned to the living room.

A radio was playing softly in the bedroom. She called to him and he went in. The lights were out, the only illumination coming from a half-dozen candles flickering in the room. She was seated in the middle of the bed, leaning forward with her head lowered, her long black hair cascading down almost to her lap, a lacy gown thrown over her shoulders. He squinted his eyes, trying to make out details in the dark room.

No mirrors behind him.

Good.

Approaching the bed, he slipped off his jacket and threw it over a chair, unbuttoned his shirt and started to pull out his shirttail, moving his hands around his belt, freeing the shirt.

As his hands moved around to his back, she sat up abruptly and shrugged her shoulders. The gauze gown fell away. The sight startled him and he hesitated for an instant and as he did, she swung her right arm up and held it straight out in front of her.

She moved so fast that he didn't see the gun, only the brilliant flash from the muzzle, and he felt the awful blast of heat on his face a moment before the bullet blew his brains out.

As Colin Bradley fell, he gasped a single, final word:

"Chameleon?"

BOOK ONE

Murder may be done by legal means,
by plausible and profitable war,
and by calumny,
as well as by dose or dagger.

—LORD ACTON

1

IT WAS STILL DARK when Marza awoke—that last minute or two before dawn when the sun was still caught behind the church spire out on Venezia and the first sanguine fingers of the day stretched out between the buildings and reached across the lagoon toward them. His wife lay beside him, asleep on her side, her flaming red hair fanned out on the yellow satin pillowcase, and for several minutes, his eyes half open, he admired her as she slept.

Hey, Marza, you lucky bastard, he thought. You have it all and this time it is all working. It is a good time for you, the best time of your life.

His eyes caught a glimpse of the silk nightgown lying on the floor where she had thrown it the night before, and he laughed very quietly to himself. They had been married for ten years, and she still surprised and delighted him with her recklessness in bed. Milena de la Rovere, the tempestuous actress, the red-headed tigress who had driven every director in Europe and Hollywood crazy, yet with him, after ten years, she was still his temptress and his lover.

Looking at the tattered nightgown, he remembered her kneeling over him on the bed, yelling raucously, at the top of her lungs, all the English "feelthy words" he had taught her, and then popping the thread-thin straps at her shoulders and pulling the champagne silk gown down slowly, painfully slowly, over her breasts, until finally they could be held no longer and burst free, the nipples erect and waiting for him as she continued taunting him, patiently wiggling out of the gown and letting it drop around her knees, swinging one leg free and straddling him with it, then tearing the gown from the other leg and throwing it carelessly across the room.

"Three hundred thousand lire," he had bellowed, laughing, "and she treats it like a Holiday Inn towel!"

"The sheet Holeeday Eenn," she yelled back and started to laugh too. Then she leaned over Marza, and taking one of his nipples between her teeth, she began to move very slowly around, and he felt it get erect in her mouth before she began to suck it and then she looked at him.

"*Va bene?*" she asked mischievously.

"*Molto bene . . .*"

She slowly ran her tongue from his nipple down to his navel, ringing it with her tongue. "*È permesso . . . ?*"

It was a whisper, and she concentrated on his stomach while awaiting the answer.

Marza groaned and then said, almost as quietly, "Don't mention it."

He lay on his back and smiled at her for a long time, feeling the tips of her fingernails, as light as butterfly wings, stroking his abdomen. Then her tongue, just as vague, a sense rather than a feeling. This was for him. It was a thing she loved to do to start things off. Then her lips brushed across the tip of his penis and he rose to her and then she enveloped him and began humming, a deep monotone, and Marza was lost. She seemed to be everywhere. With her tongue, her fingers, her lips. He began to move in rhythm with her, an almost involuntary response to her erotic overture. He could feel his heart pulsing in his throat. His fingers searched her hair, then she began to move her head and the moaning increased and he could feel the deep rumble in her throat vibrating against him as he grew harder and harder.

"*Il tempo si è fermato per me*"—"A small death," he breathed. "Time has stopped for me."

And she answered, muffled, "Time does not exist."

And then there was no more talking, and finally, when he felt he was about to explode, he slid down, pulling her up toward him as he did, and he ran his hand lightly down her stomach, felt her hair, then he squeezed her between two fingers and began moving his hand in slow circles and then both of them were moving and she was stroking him, still, drawing him closer and closer to her until he felt her fire envelope him. Her arms slid around his back and clutched him and as he was about to burst inside of her he chanted, over and over, "I give it up . . . give it up . . . give it up . . ." and finally, "I love you."

When they were married, the international gossips had given them a few months, a year at best. She was twenty and had been one of Italy's brightest movie stars since she was seventeen. Marza was thirty-eight and was making a comeback. He had just won his third race in a row after having been written off as a washout by most of the sports writers and sponsors in the business. For three years he had been considered unbankable, a failed driver at thirty-five.

Then Noviliano, the great automobile maker, had come to him and offered him a fresh shot. A new car, experimental, temperamental, but insanely fast and stable. "It needs a man of experience," Noviliano told him. "I cannot trust this machine to some youngster."

It was the beginning of the most successful relationship in racing history. Noviliano and Marza and the Aquila 333, a revolutionary automobile with heated baffles on the rear deck to "boil the air" for stability, a cutback design, and a unique alcohol jet-injection fuel system that gave the car a fifty-mile range on everything else on the track, reducing its pit stops by at least a third.

It was a bitch, make no mistake, and Marza drove it like he was part of the frame. Nobody could touch him, and he was absolutely fearless, a man who scorned death. In an interview he once said, "I have seen death, two, three times, sitting on the fence waving at me. I say, 'Fuck you, man, not yet. You don't get Marza this time.' I think, If you are afraid of death, you should maybe be a cashier. This is not your game."

When he met her, he was still on the way back up, and they were saying he would quit or be dead in a year, and besides, she was only twenty and how could he hope to keep her when every male between puberty and senility wanted her?

Marza and the Aquila 333 made racing history, and the car was to spawn one of the most exciting automobile ventures in modern times.

The faster her star rose, the faster he drove. For every hit film she made, he took another checkered flag. There was no competition between them. He delighted in her success and she saw in Marza what few others were ever permitted to see, a champion in every way, who loved her and respected her and treated her as a friend and a lover, not as a movie star. Others were intimidated by her beauty and her success. "Intimidation" was a word he did not know. It was not part of his vocabulary. For Marza, intimidation was unthinkable.

And she adored him for it.

He drove with frightening skill, a man possessed, until Milena finally asked him to quit. He was rich beyond all dreams. There was nothing else for him to prove. And besides, Noviliano wanted him to work on a new idea, a new car that would have speed and grace and drive like a champion with a remarkable jet-injection engine that would triple normal gas mileage. Not a racing car, but a street car employing all the commercially practical aspects of the racer. Marza's job was to test it and test it and test it until it was perfect.

The car was to be called the Aquila Milena because, as the Professor —the great Di Fiere, its designer—said, the car was like a rare and beautiful woman. It was a tribute to Marza, having the car named after the thing he loved most in life. And what a car it was—it just might revolutionize the industry. The patent on the injection system alone could make them all millionaires again.

So he quit racing. And she quit acting. He found the perfect place for their new home, a knoll outside Malcontenta, on the edge of Laguna Veneta, overlooking her beloved Venezia, and he built a Greek villa for her, just twenty miles from the factory at Padua.

Turning his head, he gazed through the arched doorway, beyond the terrace and across the lagoon, toward Venezia, watching the sun edge from behind the church spire and slowly bathe the room with a translucent red glow. The best time of day for him. Always had been. He felt good. Today would be the perfect day to test the Milena. After all, he was taking its namesake to Monte Carlo for New Year's Eve. Running the initial test would be his New Year's present to himself.

She moved beside him, rolling over on her back; the satin sheet fell away and she lay sleeping before him, naked. He marveled at her body, as he always had, longed for it again, but dawn was definitely not her time of day. A chill draft swept through the doors, moving the lace drapes in slow motion, as though they were underwater. He pulled the sheet gently back over her so she would not get cold.

Ten years she had given him, and there was not a moment he was sorry for. *"Grazie,"* he said softly. *"Tante grazie."*

He leaned over and kissed her gently on the cheek, and then, after one final look at the blazing sunrise, went in to take a shower and dress. And before he left he went back and leaned over her and kissed her once more on the cheek and she opened one eye and smiled up at him and said, in her imperfect English, "Doan drive too fass."

II

When Falmouth was first assigned the job by his section chief, he made a list. It took him several days. First he wrote out his objectives, then he broke the job down into segments: on one side of the paper he listed the segments in chronological order; on the other side he listed the same segments in the order of the risk involved, starting with the high risk first. Then he very carefully edited them, combining both lists into what he felt was the safest and best way to execute the assignment.

They had provided excellent intelligence reports. Everything he had asked for. Plans of the car. A detailed map of the plant showing all the security positions. Photographs of the track itself. M.O. sheets on Marza, Noviliano, Di Fieri and the three relief drivers, sheets which emphasized their personal as well as their work habits. And a rundown on the town of Padua: picturesque, highly provincial, known not only for the Aquila Motor Works but also for the basilica of Sant'Antonio and the Giotto frescoes, which attracted visitors from all over the world.

That was good. A tourist place. And there would be pilgrimages there, to start the New Year right. Much easier to operate, and it provided good opportunity for a cover.

It had taken them a month to put all that together. He planned the operation in Paris, in a small tourist hotel on the rue Fresnel, just below the rue de Longchamp and half a block from the river. It was near the heart of things but still quiet. He converted the flat into a private war room, with maps on the walls, train and plane schedules, photographs of the principals, plans of the car and the factory and the town.

He began by studying his road maps and transportation schedules. Falmouth put first priority on getting in and out of a place. Like any good intelligence agent, he put self-preservation on top of the list. After that he would concentrate on the job itself.

From Paris he could fly to Nice, then take the night train along the coast and across to Milan. There he would get a car and drive to Padua, a distance of perhaps one hundred and twenty-five miles.

Getting out would be more ticklish. Once the job was done, he would have to move fast without attracting too much attention. He would drive to Verona, take the train north through Trento and the Brenner Pass to Innsbruck and from there to Munich. Then he would fly back to Paris.

The only risky part would be the drive from Padua to Verona. But that was only forty-five miles, an easy hour's drive. Hell, it would be an hour before the shock wore off, and if the job went the way he planned, nobody would be looking for him anyway.

He fed it all into the computer in his head, letting it simmer, revising the list each night, then memorizing it and destroying the written copy, and starting his emendations in the morning. Each time he revised the list, he memorized it and then destroyed it. Falmouth had been in the business a long time; he did not make mistakes.

It took ten days to devise what he felt was the perfect plan.

The toughest part of the job was getting to the car; plant security at Padua was impossible. Oh, it could be done, but the risk factor was high. There had to be a better way. He sat for hours studying the blueprints of the factory, then poring over the plans of the car itself, examining every part of the machine and the list of subcontractors.

And suddenly there it was, the perfect answer. An elaborate electronic computer system had been devised for the test runs. Instruments built into the dashboard would immediately provide digital readouts on every key part of the automobile, with the same readings transmitted to a board in the control tower at the track. Memory for the system was contained in a mini-computer the size of a small stereo tape deck located between the firewall of the car and the cockpit. At the press of a button, the digital readout would reveal speed which could instantly be converted into miles per gallon, miles elapsed, average speed per mile, gallons remaining, oil pressure, even stress on certain parts of the car, like the suspension system, the transmission and the front and rear axles.

It was a sophisticated system but not particularly revolutionary. General Motors had offered similar digital readout computers on its larger cars for more than a year. This computer was being modified to provide specific information on the Aquila Milena and was subcontracted to a small electronics specialist in Marseilles. There was little security in Marseilles. Nothing the firm was doing was a secret. It was relatively easy to get a schematic of the General Motors system from a dealer in Paris. For weeks, Falmouth pored over these plans until he knew the system perfectly.

The memory was contained on wafer-thin boards eight inches high and thirty inches long. Each of these boards contained dozens of electronic chips no larger than a fingernail. Now Falmouth put his knowledge of explosives to use. He designed and then made a series of tiny C-4 bombs, of what the French call *plastique,* which were no larger than the head of a match and flat and could be attached to the memory boards, and dabbed with paint. He interconnected the explosives by thin wires to the wires leading to the digital counter. He made up several long strands of wire containing a very thin phosphorus fuse that would run from the mini-computer to the gas tank and to the sensors in the roll bar and tie rods of the front axle. They were set to explode when the speedometer hit 90 miles an hour. At that speed the tie rods, which kept the front wheels in line, would be blown apart and the car would go out of control. The gas tank, too, would go a second or two later.

It took Falmouth more than a month to get the explosives ready. It was dangerous business, even for an expert like him. But getting into the small factory and planting the bombs on the memory boards was a piece of cake. He flew into Marseilles on the evening plane; shortly after midnight he picked the lock on a skylight, lowered himself into the plant and found the boards, lined up neatly in the testing room. The check slips told him what he needed to know: all of them had been approved and were ready for delivery but one, and it was not critical to his operation.

It took him hours to complete the job. He left the plant at a few minutes before five and returned on the morning flight back to Paris.

So far, so good.

He settled down to refine the overall plan. He had three more weeks. He grew a mustache and had his hair restyled, but he did not like it. Not long enough. He bought a shaggy black wig to cover his red hair, and the night before he left, he dyed the mustache black. He chose only casual clothes, the kind a free-lance photographer would wear: a pair of tan corduroy slacks, a white turtleneck sweater, a suede jacket, and hiking shoes with platforms and interior soles that added almost two inches to his normal five-eleven.

He was feeling good, very good, the morning he left.

When he arrived at the terminal in Milan, Falmouth went straight to the American Express office. A young gigolo in a formless jacket, with a narrow tie hanging from his open collar, peered at him through aviator sunglasses and said, *"Si?"*

Falmouth smiled, his casual, boyish, photographer's smile. *"Buon giorno, signore. Scusi, c'è una lettera per me, Harry Spettro?"*

The creep sighed and said in a bored voice, *"Un momento,"* pulled open a drawer and leafed leisurely through the letters.

He looked up at Falmouth. "S-p-e-t-t-r-o?"

"Si."

"Identificazione, per favore."

Falmouth produced a fake driver's license and passport. The young man's eyes flicked back and forth between the picture in the passport and Falmouth. Satisfied, he nodded and handed the letter to him.

"Mille grazie," Falmouth said with a grin and, under his breath, added, "You little prick."

"Prego," the kid said—Don't mention it.

He went outside and tore open the envelope. Inside was a key and a brief message: "Locker 7541."

He found the locker, took the heavy, flat leather case that was inside and placed it in his own suitcase and then went to the men's room, where he checked the contents of the case. Everything he needed was there, including the car keys and another simple message:"Black Fiat 224, license XZ 592, terminal parking lot, row 7, section 2, ticket under spare tire." So far, it had gone well. He drove straight to Padua and checked into a small hotel.

It took him several days, longer than he had planned, to find a vacant room with a clear view of the ten-kilometer concrete test rink. He had almost decided to abandon the project until after New Year's when he spotted the house from a pub. It sat up on a rise, back from the road, a three-story building facing due east.

High enough and aimed right. Now all he had to do was arrange to get a room on the backside. That was tougher than he thought. It was finally arranged only after some heated negotiations with the woman who owned the place, a fiery Italian widow who at first slammed the door in his face, then threatened to call the police if he persisted. But when he told her that he was there to photograph the basilica for *Paris-Match,* and that the local hotels were full, and then offered her what must easily have been ten times what such a room normally would rent for, she finally relented.

Her son was skiing in Austria for the holidays. Perhaps his room would be suitable. But she demanded quiet—no radio after nine o'clock and no visitors. She was a good Catholic and would not have the neighbors talking.

The location was perfect, less than a mile from the track with a completely unobstructed view, and although the room was fairly small, it was comfortable and clean, its walls covered with photographs of skiers, skiing posters, maps of famous ski runs, and patches from famous resorts. The son was more than an *aficionado,* he was a fanatic.

A dormer window faced the track. That was good, Falmouth thought. It would be almost impossible for anyone to see him from the street and it provided a small shelf to work from. He locked the door and immediately went to work.

The case he had brought from Milan contained a Bausch & Lomb Discoverer telescope with a $15\times$ to $60\times$ constant focus zoom lens and a minimum field of forty feet at a thousand yards. It weighed less than six pounds with the tripod and was only seventeen and a half inches long.

The rifle was even more impressive. He had never seen one quite like it. It was nothing more than a barrel and firing chamber with a skeletonized aluminum stock, and it was thirty-three inches long, including the flash suppressor and silencer. The tripod was also aluminum. It was fitted with a laser scope he knew to be pinpoint accurate up to fifteen hundred yards. A five-shot clip dropped down below the firing chamber, fully loaded with 7.62-mm. steelpoint explosive shells. The whole rig didn't weigh more than ten pounds.

Hair-trigger. The heat from his finger almost popped it.

Neat. Everything he had asked for, plus a little bonus. The rifle was strictly for backup. If the C-4 explosives didn't work, he would have to make the shot—and what a shot it would be. Six hundred yards at an automobile moving 90 miles an hour on a ninety-degree path.

Sure, Falmouth.

He laughed to himself and shook his head. What the hell, it was strictly insurance anyway.

He set up the tripod and zeroed it and zoomed in on the entrance gate to the track. He could read the hinges on the gate, a helluva scope. He set up the rifle beside it, calibrated its scope and sighted it, and watched it change focus as he slid his aim up the track.

Beautiful.

I hope to God I don't have to use it.

Now all he had to do was wait.

III

The office was empty when Marza arrived. It was a little after seven and the staff usually did not arrive until eight. He made a pot of coffee and checked the weather. Then he went to his office and changed into his racing gear: cotton long johns; a black fire-resistant jump suit with a red slash down one sleeve and the number 333 in blazing red across the back and the Aquila patch over his heart with the single word "UNO" under it; white sweat socks and Adidas jogging shoes. He stuffed a pair of pigskin racing gloves in the knee pocket of the jump suit. And when he was ready he walked down the hall from his office to the private door to the garage and went inside.

The odor was an aphrodisiac to Marza. It wasn't the smell of gasoline and alcohol and engine oil, it was what they represented, and he stood in the dark for a minute or two, his mind gliding back in time. There had been a lot of great days in his life and he savored the fact that today would definitely be another one. Finally he turned the lights on.

The car sat alone in the middle of the garage. It was spotless, waxed like a mirror, and absolutely stunning, a low-slung sedan that was a masterpiece of styling, an aerodynamic marvel, its hood tapered and louvered, the top swept back, to avoid what Di Fiere called the *aspetto di carro funebre,* the look of the hearse, and the lines rolling gently back from the front fenders to the Ferrari-type rear deck. Di Fiere had not tried to improve on that. "One does not improve on perfection, one accepts it," he said.

The instrument panel was filled literally from door to door with electronic gadgets. That would be Di Fiere's job, operating the various control buttons which would give the observation tower's mirror computer an instant readout of the car's performance, one which would be printed simultaneously on a paper tape.

It gleamed like a jewel, even under the fluorescent lights, its jet-black coat disturbed only by the two thin bright-red racing stripes down either side because those were Marza's colors and this car would be his someday and because ultimately he would be the one who would say, "It is ready," and they would go the market and find out just how good they were.

Marza walked slowly around the car and swept his hand lightly over the roof, patted it affectionately and whispered, *"Va bene, signora, siamo soli—lei, io e il Professore. Facciamogli vedere qualche cosa!"*— Okay, lady, it's just you and me and the Professor going to be out there, let's show them something!

Then he went out into the brisk, clear, cold morning. There was just a breath of wind and that pleased Marza. In an hour or so, there would be none at all. Conditions were perfect. He rubbed his hands together and then started what had become a ritual. He walked the track, just as he had walked Le Mans and Raintree and Monza before every race, looking for cracks in the pavement, slick spots, picking up pebbles and branches and throwing them over the inside wall. The ten-kilometer walk usually took him about an hour. Marza didn't like surprises.

Signora Forti, Falmouth's temporary landlady, awakened him at seven o'clock with coffee and a roll, the least she could do for what he was paying.

"Grazie. Scusi, non sono vestito," he said, apologizing for not being dressed, and holding the door just wide enough to take the tray.

He put on pants and a T-shirt and then took the telescope and rifle out of the closet, setting them up on the tape marks he had laid out on the dormer sill. He put a tablet of graph paper and a small pocket calculator beside the scope. He had already calculated and programmed the distance between two marks on the back stretch of the track going into the far turn. By simply punching the calculator when the car passed the first mark, and then hitting it when it passed the second mark, he'd get the calculator to read out the exact speed. If the car topped 90 and nothing happened, he would have to do the shot. He took a sip of coffee and casually loosened the set screw on the rifle tripod and sighted through it.

He switched to the scope and zoomed up to full power, saw the familiar black jump suit with the splash of red on the sleeve. He could even read the word under the Aquila patch: "Uno."

And the face—that dark, intense face with the granite-hard jaw and the unruly shock of black hair—Marza!

According to latest information, Marza would be in Monte Carlo with his wife until after the New Year. The first few tests were to be done by the relief drivers. Falmouth's hand began to tremble slightly as he realized that he was about to kill Marza—the idol of every woman, the hero of every daydreaming schoolboy, the fantasy of every man in Italy. Marza was a national hero—no, he was an international hero. Someday there would be statues of him in town squares. Everywhere he went, crowds gathered to see him, touch him, to chant: *"Marza, Uno . . . Marza, Uno . . ."*

This wasn't part of the deal. This was definitely not part of the deal.

What was it Jack Hawkins kept saying in *Bridge on the River Kwai*? "There's always the unexpected."

Jesus, was that a parable! After twenty years in the business he should have known it was going too well. Anyway, the car was programmed for destruction, and that was bloody goddamnwell that. But if the C-4 failed, if he had to take the shot, that was different. It was a tough enough shot, and with Marza behind the wheel . . .

He lit a cigarette and watched the racing king walk briskly all the way around the long track. And when Marza was through and had gone back into the factory, Falmouth dismounted the rifle. That was it. If the bombs failed, Marza would walk away from it.

Hell, Marza was one of *his* heroes, for God's sake. He was not about to kill him with a gun. In fact, after twenty years in the business, he was hoping that, for once, for just this once, he would fail.

Giuseppe di Fiere, who had so masterfully designed the Aquila 333 and the Milena, arrived at seven-fifty, his white hair tangled from the wind. Di Fiere was seventy-one years old and he drove his modified Aquila Formula One with the top down, rain, shine or snow, every day, the eighteen miles from his *casa di campagna* to the factory.

He had never been a driver. It was a failed dream, and it had died hard. He had started racing motorbikes when he was fourteen. By the time he was sixteen he was already making a name for himself. Then one Sunday afternoon on a dirt track at Vincenzion, coming out of the esses, he lost it. He could feel the bike going out from under him and he was down before he could react, his right leg trapped under the rear wheel, the bike, its engine still growling as it skittered crazily along the hard-packed track, dragging him along for fifty yards, grinding the leg into a formless, boneless mass before it began tumbling over and disintegrating insanely around him.

The doctors in the field tent took off the leg just below the knee, what there was left of it.

It had cost him his leg and his taste for driving, but not his love of racing, that was a part of his psyche, a blood dream, and so he did the next best thing, he began designing race cars. He studied engineering, became a mechanic for a while, studied aerodynamics and worked in the design department of the de Havilland airplane factory in England. While still in his twenties, he knew every nut and bolt and design element on every winning automobile ever made. He scoured Europe for old relics and began restoring them. Before he designed his first successful car at the age of thirty-four, he was already an automotive genius.

And his cars won. He designed for the best—Ferrari, Maserati, Porsche. Now he had gone full circle with the greatest of them all, Noviliano.

Marza was very special to Di Fiere. Perhaps he saw in Marza the son he never had or the driver he never was. Whatever. He agonized every time Marza was on the track, suffered every injury with him, vicariously won every time Marza won. He had educated Marza as a father would a son. For three years he had shared with Marza—and with nobody else, not even with the *padrone,* Noviliano himself—every agonizing detail, every heartbreak, every breakthrough, every triumph and failure in his pursuit of the perfect car. When he described it, even before it was committed to paper, it was as if he were talking about the woman he loved, describing her temperaments, her joys, her displeasures. He even told Marza how to talk to her, out there on the track, so she would obey him and perform properly.

It was his fantasy come true: to have the resources of the finest automobile maker in the world to build his baby, and the best driver to test it. And because they were both passionate men, Marza understood the old man and knew that this car was no bitch, no flashy tramp; this car was a lady—elegant, beautiful, the perfect champion. So Di Fiere had named it Milena, after the one thing Marza loved more than racing.

Noviliano arrived last, and predictably so. He was a man of tradition, disciplined and habitual. He arrived at the factory, six days a week, at precisely nine o'clock, a large man, almost six-five, his weight wavering around three hundred pounds. Yet everything about him was impeccable. He wore an impeccable blue three-piece suit, with an impeccable red carnation in the lapel, and an impeccable white shirt with the perfect blue-and-red Countess Mara tie. His steel-gray hair and beard were trimmed impeccably. Nobody had ever seen Noviliano in anything less formal, or his hair mussed or his tie pulled down.

Elegance was Noviliano's trademark. He was the perfect playboy, and was, in his own way, as good an advertisement for his cars as was Marza.

He was carrying a wine cooler in one hand and three champagne goblets in the other. He didn't say a word, he just came in, put the bucket on a workbench, took the bottle of Dom Pérignon from it and popped the cork. He filled each of the glasses, handed one to Marza and the other to the Professor. A hint of a smile played at the corners of his lips but it was almost obscured by his beard.

Marza turned to the Professor. "Did you see that, signore? Hunh? I think it was a smile. Yes, by God, it was definitely a smile. The great *padrone* has finally smiled." Laughing, he raised his glass. The three goblets chimed as they tapped.

"*Salute,*" Noviliano said, "*e grazie.*"

Marza and Di Fiere each took a sip and put their glasses back on the workbench.

"I'll be watching from the control booth," Noviliano said.

He slapped Marza on the back and kissed Di Fiere on the cheek, then the two men got in the car and buckled up. Marza turned on the ignition and cranked it up and pulled the stick down into "D," and the Milena rolled smoothly out onto the track.

"What do you say, Professor?" Marza asked.

The old man leaned back, smiling with great contentment. "Ready. Finally ready."

Marza dropped it into the "1" position and started off. "We'll take her around once just to get warmed up," he told the tower.

The Milena moved out smoothly, the green lights on the digital reader changing constantly as the Professor punched buttons, checking speed, mileage, engine heat, stress. Marza took it around the track at 35 miles an hour. The engine had been broken in on the bench and it cruised quietly, responding instantly to Marza's commands. He let go of the wheel for a moment, marveling at its stability, then did the back stretch of the track, driving with one finger on the wheel. He jiggled the wheel, felt the car respond, stopped and felt it settle back almost instantly.

"It drives itself," he said.

The Professor smiled. *"Grazie."*

They started the tests. The car performed magnificently twisting through the slaloms at 35, 40 and 45. Marza was amazed at the stability of the passenger sedan. Di Fiere had made the conversion from racing car to street car with immaculate precision, losing as little as possible in the transition. The Professor was keeping a running tab on the mileage, and the car was averaging better than 60 m.p.g., dropping off to 45 or 46 when accelerating. On the straights at 50, the digital counter zipped up to 70.

"Buonissimo," he said with great satisfaction as he continued to push buttons and carry on an almost whispered conversation with the tape recorder, making suggestions which he would later evaluate when he listened to the tapes. He noted a tremor in the front suspension at 40 m.p.h. which he attributed to a slight overbalance for torque; he suggested increasing the alcohol mixture in the injection system to increase the mileage three or four m.p.g.; he made note of a whistle in the window of the right door, which developed at about 52 m.p.h.

Occasionally it was Marza who threw in an observation: "We should think about softening the springs on her, they're too tight now. She rides a little too hard."

But mostly he drove and talked to the car under his breath and silently reveled in the fact that he was the first person to drive a car which might someday be driven by millions of people.

Then he felt the Milena was ready to show some stuff. "I'm a little bored with this," he told the tower, "we're going to try some accelerations."

"Good, let's see what she's got!" Di Fiere said.

V

Falmouth was glued to the superscope, his fingers punching the "Start" and "Stop" buttons as the Milena passed the markers, his eyes flicking from the eyepiece to the calculator, checking the speed. It had gone as high as 40 once, then dropped back down.

Jesus, isn't he ever going to let it out? he thought.

Then he thought, Maybe he won't. Maybe he'll just do some preliminaries and save the fast tests for someone else.

Sure.

This is Marza, remember, the fastest driver in the world. He's going to open it up. Before he's finished today he's going to have that son of a bitch wide open.

The car pulled to a stop at the far end of the track, pointed toward Falmouth. It suddenly took off, pulling out smoothly. It passed Falmouth's markers and he checked the speed.

35.

Okay, he's into acceleration tests. That would have been zero to 30. He's getting restless.

Falmouth watched the car move around the track to the start. It slowed to a stop again. Maybe this time, Falmouth thought. Maybe now he'll go for it, push it on up there, over 85 m.p.h.

Falmouth was chain-smoking now and there was a thin line of sweat high on his forehead, along his hairline.

The car moved out again. This time Marza did zero to 40. Then he seemed to pick up speed going around the near curve. Falmouth checked it out on the back-stretch markers. He was doing 65 and seemed to be picking up speed as he approached the far curve.

Marza drove the Milena through the far curve of the track at 70 miles an hour, and it felt as if he were driving on the flats.

"*Fantastico!*" he exclaimed, pulling into the straight. "Let's goose her up a little—what do you say, Professor?"

Di Fiere beamed. "You bet! Let's pinch the lady's ass, shall we? Slowly, now—don't force her!"

Marza raised an eyebrow, as if to say, "Are you telling me how to drive a car?" and when the Professor pulled his head down into his shoulders in embarrassment and said *"Scusi,"* Marza laughed and assured him, "No offense, my friend, it's the excitement."

Di Fiere stared at the digital readout as Marza began to let the Milena loose, watching it climb fast by tenths of a mile.

75.5.

80.

80.6.

82.

85.

85.7.

88.

89.

On the front stretch, Falmouth had checked it out at 62.8, watched it zap through the near turn without even dropping a tenth of a mile an hour, and then zoom into the back stretch.

Now he watched as the digital readout climbed over 80.

Good God, he's going for it.

The back stretch swept under Marza and Di Fiere as the car moved out, climbing steadily without faltering, the digital reader flicking faster and faster.

82 . . . 85 . . . 87 . . .

Falmouth's mouth turned to cotton as his fingers nimbly punched away at the calculator. Sweat dribbled down the side of his face and, annoyed, he swept it away with the back of his hand.

89.9.

"È stupendo!" Marza yelled.

They hit 90 and the C-4 went off on order.

When it exploded, the main force of the blast was directed down toward the ground, lifting the front of the car and instantly separating the tie rods that held the wheels in line. They popped apart like brittle sticks. The wheels went haywire. At the same time, the phosphorus wire fuse sizzled straight back along the frame toward the gas tank.

Marza was heading into the turn, leaning with the car, his arms extended almost straight out in a classic driving position, when he felt the blast in front of his feet. The fire wall shattered and a hot burst of gas rushed into the cockpit. A moment later the wheel was wrenched from his hands. The car went wildly out of control as he grabbed frantically for the steering wheel and tried to get it back. It swerved, ripping into the inside wall of the turn at about forty-five degrees, and the left front side of the car shattered. The fenders peeled back with the agonized scream of tearing metal. The engine was torn from its mounts and the air bags under the dash whooshed full and jammed Marza and the Professor into their seats.

The car careened off the wall and a moment later the gas tanks exploded. The Milena was catapulted across the track toward the other wall when Marza felt the rear blow out, felt the sudden, ghastly rush of heat and then the flames boiling through the back seat, enveloping both him and Di Fiere, and then the air bags burst.

The old man screamed once as the fire rushed into his nose and mouth and scorched his lungs. Then he was dead.

For Marza, it seemed to take forever, although it was no more than a second or two. As the car spun crazily across the track he saw his old enemy, that grinning, obscene apparition he had seen so many times before and shunned, sitting on the wall straight ahead of him, wrapped in flames, motioning to him, drawing him on, and as the car crashed headlong into the wall, Death opened his arms and the driver rushed to his embrace.

VI

Falmouth did not relax until the train was out of Verona station and well on its way north toward the Alps.

His heart was rapping at his ribs and his shirt was damp with sweat when he found his compartment and sat down. He leaned back, closed his eyes and hummed to himself, slowing everything down. He clocked off the list in his head, making sure it had gone right.

He was certain no one had seen him leave the house. The drive to Verona had gone off smoothly; he hadn't even seen a policeman. He parked the car and checked the case in a locker, from which, he assumed, somebody had already claimed it. He looked at his watch.

Hell, by now someone in Verona was probably melting down the barrel.

He felt the train lurch under him. As it moved out of the station he went into the bathroom, took off the wig, combed his red hair and shaved off the mustache. Then he burned the wig, driver's license and passport issued to Harry Spettro and flushed them down. By the time the conductor tapped on the door, he was Anthony Falmouth again.

The ticket man, a short paunchy little fellow in his sixties with watery eyes, took his papers. "You are *inglese*?" he said in a hushed, quivering voice.

"*Si*," Falmouth replied.

"And have you heard our tragic news?"

Falmouth did not want to hear it. Dumbly, he shook his head.

"Marza is dead. Our great champion. The greatest sportsman in Italy since Novalari. *Numero Uno è morto.*"

A chill moved up Falmouth's back. He said, "I'm very sorry." Then, after a moment, he added, "And how did he die?"

The conductor punched several holes in his ticket and then said, rather proudly, "In a car, of course," and went on.

When the conductor was gone, Falmouth sagged. It all went out of him and suddenly he was drained and overcome with sadness and he felt tears beginning to sting the corners of his eyes.

Hell, he said to himself, I'm getting too old for this kind of shit.

2

HARRY LANSDALE PAUSED while making his customary rounds, leaning against the bulkhead of the towering *Henry Thoreau* and staring grimly through the porthole at the deck of the largest oil rig in the world. He had seen storms before, in every part of the world, but this one, this one was going to be a killer.

It was nearing midnight, and the sea was running $-3°$ to $-4°$ Celsius and dropping. A harsh Arctic wind had been moaning down from the Beaufort Sea and across the barren grounds north of the Brooks Range since the night before. The temperature was still falling, the sea continuing to grow colder as the sun cast its gray, persistent dusk across the frigid north Alaska wastelands. The wind cried forlornly through the stub pines and grasslands, and the white foxes, foraging for lemmings, lamented their skimpy hunt with mournful dirges to the constant twilight. Chunks of ice were beginning to appear, drifting down from the

Arctic Ocean into the Chukchi Sea, where the misting whitecaps tossed them about like wafers.

Now the winter gale, sweeping with fury across the open sea, assaulted the floating oil rig, one hundred and twenty-two miles from land, screaming through its rigging and snapping at its guy wires.

Lansdale was not concerned about the rig. It was built to take anything the Arctic furies could toss at them. From the air the *Thoreau* looked like a giant bug, with its four enormous steel legs dipping down deep into the thrashing sea. The rig was a monster, twice the length of a football field, its deck sixty feet above the water and the superstructure rising almost five stories above that. Its spidery legs thrust down two hundred feet below the surface of the sea and were anchored to the bottom, two hundred feet farther down, by steel cables.

Lansdale held the flat of his hand against the wall. Not a tremor. Not even the six-foot waves and the brutal winds could shake his baby.

The *Thoreau* was indeed Lansdale's crowning achievement; the largest semisubmersible rig ever built, a floating city, its towering concrete blocks containing apartments for the 200-man crew; three different restaurants, each serving food prepared by a different chef; two theaters showing first-run movies; and a solar dish that beamed in ninety different television channels from around the world to 21-inch TV sets in every apartment.

Everything possible was provided for the crew to make the endless days bearable, for the structure sat off the northwest coast of Alaska, one hundred and forty miles northeast of Point Hope, at the very edge of the polar cap, possibly the loneliest human outpost in the world. And it sat on top of one of the richest oil strikes ever tapped.

Lansdale was not only chief engineer and manager of the project, he was its creator. For eighteen years he had dreamed of this custom-built Shangri-La at the edge of the world. It had taken him four years of planning, of fighting in board rooms and lobbying in bars and restaurants, to convince the consortium of four oil companies to take the chance.

What had finally swayed them was the man himself. Harry Lansdale knew oil; knew where to find it and how to get it. He was as tough as the Arctic and as unshakable as the rig he had built, a man who had devoted his life to pursuing the thick black riches bottled up beneath the earth. He had worked on rigs all over the world and, to prove it, had a list of them tattooed proudly down his right arm, like the hash marks on the sleeve of an old-line Army top kick—from Sweet Dip, the old Louisiana offshore rig, to Calamity Run in the North Sea, to the endless, sweeping desert fields of Saudi Arabia they had nicknamed the Sandstorm Hilton.

Oh, it had taken its toll, all right. At forty, his leathery face was craggy with hard-work lines, his hands sandpapered with calluses, his shaggy hair more salt than pepper. But to Lansdale, it was worth every line, every callus, every streak of gray. He smiled, raised the coffee cup and, tapping the porthole lightly, growled in a voice tuned by cigarettes and whiskey and not enough sleep: "Happy New Year, storm."

Even at fifteen fathoms the sea was rough, its swells rolling beneath the six-foot waves on the surface. A thin sliver of light pierced the dark sea, followed by what at first might have appeared to be four banded seals struggling in formation through the grim waters. They were four men in winter wet suits, lashed together like mountain climbers by a nylon band, and pulled through the dangerous sea by an underwater scooter. A box the size of a child's coffin was attached by nylon lines to the scooter.

The man leading the small pack held his wrist close to his face mask. He had only one good eye. The other was a grotesque empty socket. He checked his compass and depth watch, constantly adjusting their direction. The narrow beam from his flashlight swept back and forth as he directed the beam into the dark sea. Then one of the men spotted it and his eyes widened behind the glass window of his face mask: a giant steel column sixteen feet thick and still as a mountain, defying the turbulent ocean, as flotsam swirled around it and then rushed on.

The leader steered the scooter uptide from the column, keeping a safe distance from it, for one heavy swell could throw them against it and destroy both the men and their underwater machine. They hovered twenty feet away as the leader prepared a speargun and fired the spear so that it slashed through the water past the steel leg before losing its momentum. The tide swept the cable around the column. Then the driver guided the scooter in three or four counterturns around the shaft, forming a taut line between them and the leg before steering the scooter into the tide, keeping the line taut.

The three others detached the coffinlike box and inched down the line toward the column.

Lansdale, making his swing through the installation as he did every night before going to bed, stepped inside the control room and stood watching the skeleton crew at work. It looked to him like the set of some sci-fi movie, its rows of computer readouts flashing on and off as the ingenious station pumped oil from several undersea wells within a thirty-mile range into storage tanks built into the perimeter of the rig, and from there, through a twelve-inch line that ran along the bottom of the Chukchi Sea to a receiving station near the village of Wainwright, a hundred and twenty-two miles to the east, where the Alaskan badlands petered out by the sea.

It was a revolutionary idea. And it was working. For three months now, the station had been cooking like a greased skillet. Lots of little headaches, of course, those were to be expected. But nothing major. Now the *Thoreau* was operating with a skeleton crew of 102 men and 4 women, a hundred people fewer than normal, all of them volunteers who had passed up their Christmas furlough to work the station during the holidays.

Slick Williams, the electronics genius who ran the computer room, was sitting at the main console, his feet on the desk, sipping coffee and watching the lights flashing. He looked up as Lansdale came in. "Hi, Chief," he said. "Slumming?"

Lansdale laughed. "In this sixty-million-dollar toy?" Around him was possibly the most sophisticated computerized operation ever built. "Keep an eye on the stabilizers, it's getting rough out there."

"Check," Williams said. "Tell Sparks to let me know if it gets too bad."

"Shit," Lansdale said, "I sat out a hurricane on the first offshore rig ever built. A goddamn wooden platform fifteen years old. You could fit the son of a bitch in this room. Only lost one man. Silly bastard got hit in the head with a lunchbox flying about ninety miles an hour. Broke his neck. Otherwise, all we got was wet."

Williams nodded. He had heard the stories before.

"I'll either be in the bar having a nightcap or in my apartment," the Chief said and left, walking down the hall to the weather room. Radar maps covered one wall, their azimuth bars sweeping in circles, covering a four-hundred-mile radius. The weatherman was just a kid, twenty-six, skinny, acned, long-haired, with glasses as thick as the bottom of a Johnnie Walker bottle. But he was good. Everybody aboard was good or they wouldn't be there.

Below them, the heavy seas thundered mutely against the pillars.

"We got a bitch comin' up, Chief," said the youthful weatherman, who, for reasons of his own, had nicknamed himself Sparks, after the old-time radio operators.

"What's it look like?"

"Hundred-mile winds, sleet, snow and big, I mean *big*, seas. And it's already running four degrees below freezing. Anybody takes an accidental dip tonight, they got about five minutes in that water."

"Anybody takes an accidental dip tonight'll be in Nome before we get a line to 'em," Lansdale said.

"These storms gimme the creeps."

"We been through worse, kid. Why don't you knock off and catch a movie. They got that Clint Eastwood picture showing, the one with the ape." The theaters operated twenty-four hours a day.

"I'm staying here. There's no windows and you can't hear much. I'll sleep on that cot if I fade out. Besides, I got Cagney keeping me company." He pointed to one of more than a dozen monitor screens near the radar maps. The sound was turned down, but there was Jimmy Cagney, running through an oil refinery, shooting up everybody in sight.

"There was a man," Lansdale said. "He makes those macho assholes today look like a bunch of Ziegfeld broads."

Now Cagney was on top of one of the huge refinery globes and the FBI was trying to pick him off.

"Watch this," the kid said. "This has got to be the biggest ending ever."

Cagney was surrounded by flames, riddled with bullets and still fighting back. "Made it, Ma!" he yelled. "Top of the world!" And *blooie!*—there goes Jimmy and the refinery and half of Southern California.

"Neat," said the Chief.

"Neat," echoed the kid.

"What are you pickin' up?"

"WTBS in Atlanta, Georgia. They show movies all the time. There's a Japanese station that's pretty good, too, but all the flicks are dubbed. It's weird seeing Steve McQueen talking chinguchka."

"Okay, kid. Ride it out in here. I like devotion to duty."

"Shit," Sparks said, "if anybody had told me I'd end up here when I was taking meteorology at the University of Florida, I'd have switched to animal husbandry."

"You can't make two hundred bucks a day getting cows to fuck, Sparks."

"No, but it's a helluva lot more fun."

The Chief laughed. "Well, if you get nervous, gimme a call. I'll come hold your hand."

The lights on the computer readout began to flash.

"Here comes the report in from Barrow now," Sparks said. He

punched out the word "TYPE" on his keyboard and the report immediately flashed on one of the monitor screens.

"Jesus, Chief, they're reading winds up to a hundred and eighty knots. And waves! They're running twenty to thirty feet along the coast. Temperature"—he whistled through his teeth—"forty-one below. Freezing rain. No shit, freezing rain. What do they expect, a fucking spring drizzle? This goddamn rig is gonna look like Niagara Falls by morning."

"Your language is getting terrible, Sparks," Lansdale said. "I may have to write your mother."

"You do and I'll tell her who taught me."

Lansdale laughed. "Lemme know if anything serious pops up," he said and left the weather room. Walking down the tunnel toward the bar, he could hear the heavy seas thundering at the steel legs below him and the wind shrieking in the rigging. He liked the sound and feel of the storm. The *Thoreau* was as sturdy as a pack mule and as indomitable as Annapurna.

He took the elevator to the second floor and went to the bar. Willie Nelson was lamenting on the jukebox, and there was a poker game in one corner under the head of a giant caribou one of the riggers had bagged on a weekend hunting trip to the Yukon. Lansdale loved it. It was the Old West, the last frontier, it was John Wayne and Randy Scott and Henry Fonda and the O.K. Corral all rolled up into one. He looked down the bar and saw Marge Cochran, one of the four women on the rig, a red-haired lady in her early forties who was a hardhat carpenter. Hard work had taken its toll on her, as it had on the Chief, but there was still the echo of a young beauty in her angular face and turquoise eyes. The work had kept her body lean and young. But despite the seams of her tanned face, she was a handsome woman, earthy and boldly honest.

The Chief kept watching her for a long time but she paid him no mind. Finally, as he bore in with his stare from the end of the bar, she turned briefly and a wicked little smile flew briefly across her lips.

Tough lady, he thought. Yeah, tough. Like a steel-covered marshmallow.

He ordered a Carta Blanca beer and gulped it down as a handful of technicians strolled in from the evening shift.

"How about a game, Chief?" one of them asked.

"Rain check," Lansdale said. "I need some shut-eye." And he left and went to his apartment on the third floor.

II

One hundred and fifty feet below Lansdale's feet, the four men continued their perilous task. As the driver kept the scooter aimed uptide, one of the scuba divers snapped the cable of the box to a clasp on his belt and shortened the line to twelve inches or so. He was obviously the most powerful swimmer, his biceps straining the thermal suit as he moved down behind the leader.

The swell was sudden and monstrous, striking without warning out of the murky and violent sea, the tail of a twelve-foot wave on the surface ninety feet above them. It seized the scooter, flipping it up so that, for an instant, it seemed to stand on end, pointing toward the surface, before the driver got it under control. The line slackened for one deadly moment and then snapped tight again. As it did, it jerked out of the hands of the man with the box. The angry sea snatched him away from the line, sweeping him, end over end, and tossing him, like a piece of seaweed, toward the column. He thrashed his powerful arms against the treacherous, silent tide, but he was like a child caught in a deadly undertow, and the giant column was like a magnet. He spun end over end through the water and smacked against the column upside down, his head cracking like a whip against the enormous post. His body shuddered violently, a death spasm, and a burst of red bubbles tumbled from his regulator and wriggled toward the surface.

The leader glared through his good eye and hauled in the limp form by the life line and peered through the face mask. The injured man's eyes were half open and only the whites showed. Blood, gushing from his nose, was filling the mask. He shook his head toward the other members of the team and, unhooking the box, let the lifeless form go. The dying man was swept to the end of his life line by the harsh tide.

The leader swung his flippers toward the column and let the sea throw him up against it. The other diver joined him. Together they worked their way down the column until they found a welded joint. Struggling against the vicious sea, they lashed the box to the steel leg while the driver of the scooter tried to keep the machine aimed into the tide. When the box was secured, the leader pulled a handle on the side of it and the top popped off. He aimed his light into the opening in the box. It was a timing device. He set it for four hours and then he and the other diver worked their way back up the column to the steel line.

The third diver hung grotesquely below them, his body battering the column. Bubbles no longer came from his regulator.

When they reached the scooter, the leader cut the line holding it to the column with a pair of aluminum wire cutters, and it lunged forward and the three huddled together, their companion, tossed by the undersea waves, dangling behind them at the end of the life line, as the leader checked his compass and pointed the flashlight into the darkness, guiding the scooter away from the deadly column.

They disappeared into the black sea, pulling their macabre bundle behind them.

III

A bank of monitor screens along one wall gave Lansdale a closed-circuit view of the control rooms and the exterior of the *Thoreau.* Sleet was sweeping through the rigging and almost straight out across the deck.

The wind's up to a hundred and ten, maybe twenty, knots already, he thought. Gale force and picking up.

There was a tap on the door.

"It's open," Lansdale said.

Marge came in and closed the door and smiled at him for a couple of seconds and then snapped the lock on the door without taking her eyes off him.

"You're downright shameless," he said.

"There's no such thing on this barge," she said.

"Barge! Jesus, that's sacrilegious!" He laughed. "You're just going with me because I'm captain of the football team."

"Naw. I wanted to see if hardhats really make love with their socks on."

"Depends how cold it is."

"It's about twenty below out there and falling."

"Then maybe I'll keep them on."

"The hell you will."

She walked across the living room, stopping for a moment at his bookcase. Shelley, Coleridge, Shakespeare, Franck's *Zen and Zen Classics,* French and Spanish dictionaries, copies of *Red Harvest* and *Blood Money* by Dashiell Hammett. Through the porthole she looked out over the gray, bleak, endless sea, the waves lashed by sleet and wind.

"It's scary," she said. And then she turned her back on the window. "God, I'll be glad to get back to civilization where it's light in the daytime and dark at night."

He made her a rum and Coke and carried it across the room to her. "Why the hell did you stay out here for the holidays anyway?" he said. "It sure as hell wasn't the bonus."

"It helps. Sixty-two fifty a day on top of a hundred and twenty-five. That's almost a thousand dollars for two weeks. Anyway, one of my sons is someplace in Vermont with the college skiing team, and the other one is at his girl friend's house in Ohio. What's to go home to?"

"That's it?"

"Well . . . you're here, too."

"I thought you forgot."

"Not likely."

"Are you divorced?" he asked. They had never talked about personal things before.

"Widowed. Married at twenty-two, widowed at thirty-seven."

"What happened?"

"He worked himself to death. Forty-two years old. One day he went off to the office and the next time I saw him he was lying in a funeral home with some creep dry-washing his hands over him, trying to sell me a five-thousand-dollar casket."

"A little bitter there."

"A little bitter? Maybe. Just a little. It sure turned my life around."

"Did you love him?"

"Oh, I . . . sure. Sure I loved him. He was a nice man."

"Christ, what an epitaph. Here lies Joe, he was a nice man."

"His name was Alec."

"It's still a lousy epitaph."

"Well, he wasn't a very exciting man. He was . . . comfortable. Alec was wonderfully comfortable."

"So how come you end up a carpenter? On this barge, as you put it."

"I was into restoring antiques. It got out of hand. Next thing I know I was a full-fledged hardhat. How about you? A master's degree in engineering and an armful of tattoos. That doesn't fit, either."

"You can thank an old bastard name of Rufus Haygood for that."

"Rufus Haygood?"

"Yeah. I was finishing my thesis at the University of Louisiana and these hotshot interviewers from ITT and Esso and AT&T and Bell Labs were giving me all this steam about how good it was gonna be workin' for them, and one day old Rufus comes up to me and says he's ramrodding a wooden jack-up rig out in the Gulf and he says, 'I'll give you ten silver eagles an hour, which is more than you can make dancin' with those goddamn lard-ass bastards, and I'll teach you everything there is to know about the oil game and you can teach me about books'—and I find out, you know, he never went to school. So for the next seven years I dragged around with him from one rig to another and he'd give me shale and blowholes and rigging for an hour or two, and I'd give him Shelley and Coleridge and Hammett for an hour or two back. But I learned about oil, yessiree."

"Where is he now?"

"He's with your Alec, wherever that might be. Drowned. Fishing in some dipshit lake in Florida. Got drunk and fell out of the boat. The old bastard never did learn to swim."

Outside, the wind wailed past the window, peppering it with sleet.

"Wonderful night to stay in," Marge said. "We could build a fire and snuggle up."

"If we had a fireplace."

"We can make believe," she said.

"I haven't been laid for three months."

She held up four fingers. "Gotcha beat by a month," she said.

"You've got a reputation as the *Thoreau* virgin," Lansdale said.

"Been checking up on me, hunh?"

"Well, it's my job, make sure everybody on this rig is happy. We can't afford morale problems."

"I've got one you can take care of right now," she said, closing in on him.

Lansdale said, "You are shameless."

"Yeah," she said, "ain't it a kick in the ass."

He laughed, a big laugh, and nodded. "Ain't it, though," he said.

And laughing too, she ripped open her workshirt. She was not wearing a bra. Her breasts, firm from the hard work on the rig, stood out, the nipples already signaling her desire.

Lansdale stood near the wall, staring at her. He shook his head. "Incredible," he mumbled, tearing off his shirt and throwing it on the floor.

She was still seven or eight feet from him. She zipped down the fly of her jeans very slowly.

"Need some music?" he asked.

"Unh unh."

He sat down on the bed, leaning back on his elbows, watching every little move she made. She was swaying back and forth as she slowly slid the jeans over her hips and let them fall away. A curl of black hair peeked over the top of her bikini panties. She turned away from him, still swaying, and began to tighten and loosen her buttocks. She had an absolutely incredible ass.

"Hard work sure becomes you," he said.

She hooked her thumbs under the edge of the panties and slipped them down partway, still moving, still swaying to the music in her head.

He zipped down his pants and pulled them off. He was rock-hard and bulging against his Jockey shorts. She looked at him over her shoulder, began moving backwards toward him, turning as she reached the edge of the bed and sliding her hand under her panties, caressing herself as she looked down at him. He could hear her fingers sliding through her lips. She knelt between his legs on the edge of the bed and began massaging his hard penis through the shorts, then finally she slipped her hand under them, pulled them down to his thighs, and began stroking him. He jerked, involuntarily, surprised by her callused hand. But she had a special talent, rubbing the underside of his penis with the palm of her hand while her fingers stroked the top.

Lansdale closed his eyes. "Christ," he said, "you ought to patent that."

"Just the beginning," she said, and leaning over, sucked him into her mouth, her teeth nibbling at him. He leaned forward, reached out, and took one of her breasts in his hand and caressed it with his fingertips, letting the palm of his hand barely touch the nipple. Her tongue darted and traced the length of him and he sat up a little more, sliding his hand down to her hard belly, his fingertips just touching the edge of her panties. She began to hunch, moving against his hand. He could feel the moisture through the silk, feel her distending clitoris as he stroked the length of her vagina.

She started to laugh, but then the laugh became a soft moan. "Goddamn," she cried out. Her legs began to tremble and she fell on her side next to him, grabbed his head and thrust it between her legs. He ripped her panties off and sucked her hard clitoris into his mouth, moving his head in tight little circles and flicking his tongue.

Her fists tightened in his hair, guiding his head as she moved with him. She began to tighten all over. She sucked in her breath, held it, then let it out in short spurts. And again. And again. She rose against him, hooking her heels behind his hips.

The tempo increased, her breaths coming shorter, the movement faster. Then all the muscles in her body seemed to freeze, her head moved slowly back, her legs straightened, her breathing stopped for a moment, and then she began to cry out and thrash her head back and forth and she came.

"Oh God," she cried, "enough," but he didn't stop and she felt it building again, felt the trembling, the fire streak down her nerves and envelope her entire body and she began coming again and she could not talk and her breath seemed to be caught in her throat and then suddenly it all burst out at once.

He rolled over on his back, slipped his arm under her waist and dragged her to him, lifting her so she was lying on her back on his chest and she reached down, found him and shoved him into her, while he stroked her breasts with one hand and masturbated her with the other.

"No . . . more," she gasped, but he couldn't stop. He thrust harder and harder, faster and faster, his fingers fleeting over her mound and as she tightened around him, he finally exploded with a great cry of relief and then he began to laugh, and a moment later she came again. He raised his knees and pressed down on her thighs and stayed in her as long as he could as the storm howled past the window.

IV

Lansdale awoke sharply from a deep, untroubled sleep. He lay on the bed for a moment, blinking his eyes, wondering what had awakened him so abruptly. The lights in the bedroom were still on and Marge lay beside him, sleeping soundly. It was 3:05 A.M. He sat up and grabbed the hot-line phone and punched out the number of the stabilizer control room. It only rang once before someone answered "Hello."

"This is Chief, who'm I talkin' too?"

"Barney Perkins."

"Everything all right down there?"

"I'm not sure."

Lansdale was stunned by Perkins' response. He jumped up, cradling the phone between his shoulder and ear, and grabbed clothes from the floor, chairs, wherever they had fallen a few hours before.

"What d'ya mean, you're not sure?"

"We got a . . . uh . . . like a tremor, Chief."

"Tremor?"

"Yeah. There was like . . . I dunno, it was like . . . the whole rig shivered . . ."

"Shivered? What the fuck is that supposed to mean?"

Lansdale was watching the monitor as he spoke, looking at the exterior of the *Thoreau,* draped with ice, like some primitive ice castle. Searchlights played the seas around the rig. The waves were battering the legs, smashing small ice floes to bits.

"I think maybe . . . uh, maybe we took a hit from . . . maybe a small iceberg or something."

" 'Or something' my ass. There's no 'or something' out there, for Christ's sake. I'll be right down."

He slammed down the phone. Then he picked it up and punched out the number for the radio room.

"Radio room. Harrison."

"Harrison, this is Chief. Check the area for surface craft right now. Find out if we got anything in the area."

"Jesus, what's—"

"Don't fuck around, do it! Call me back."

Marge turned over, eying him sleepily.

"What is—" she began, but he cut her off abruptly. He was across the room, pulling life jackets and thermal suits from the bottom of a closet. He tossed them to her. "Get this on fast and come on."

The phone rang again and he snatched it up.

"Yeah?"

"Chief? It's Harrison again."

"What've ya got?"

"A Greek tanker, running the troughs at quarter speed."

"Where?"

"Hell, if the weather was clear we could see it. About three miles northwest, heading toward the Strait."

"Listen to me, Harrison. Something may have bumped us. Call the tanker and tell her we may need help."

"You want me to give her a May Day?"

"Just do exactly as I said, tell her we may be having trouble and we'd like a courtesy call. I'll get back to you from Stabilizer Control."

He was still watching the monitor, then he felt it again, it was a tremor, like a light earthquake. Glasses jingled on the bar. Then it settled again.

She was pulling on the thermal long johns and there was panic written in her earthy features. "What's happening?"

"I dunno," Lansdale said. "Maybe something hit us. I got to get down to Control. Ready?"

He was dressed only in long johns with a life jacket over them.

"Can I put some clothes on?" she asked.

"No! Let's get going—now. Right now."

At 3:04:58, the thermal explosives attached to the north leg of the *Thoreau* had gone off on schedule. There were actually two blasts. The first was an implosion, which rent the welded joint of the steel leg and split it open. The second was more formidable. The shock wave from it rippled the water despite the raging waves. It almost finished the job, but not quite. As the terrifying power of the second explosive was released, it split the leg, the crack edging up the column, ten or twelve feet. Air bubbles poured from the wound. The air seal, meant to provide additional buoyancy, was destroyed. The sound was largely drowned out by the storm, but the explosion itself telegraphed up the leg and jarred the rig. The leg, although buffeted by the heavy seas, held valiantly at first. But the joint began to oscillate as the twenty-foot sea wrenched it back and forth. Then it separated, and another tremor riffled up to the station. Still it held, flexing before the storm, the welded seam gradually tearing around the girth of the steel shaft. Above, the wind wailed torturously at the buildings, adding extra stress to the already shattered leg. Then with the agonizing screech of metal tearing, the leg finally surrendered to the sea and separated. It seemed poised for a moment, this spidery shaft tossed by the sea, and then the twenty thousand tons of steel and concrete above it, urged on by the wind, leaned into the ruined column and it plunged, like a needle, toward the bottom, four hundred feet below.

On the surface the *Thoreau,* mortally wounded, yielded to the storm and as the north leg collapsed it listed, bobbed back and was immediately struck by a mountainous wave. Steel cables snapped like twigs. Its wintery shroud crumbled and shards of gleaming ice, caught in the wind, whistled through the air. Then the *Thoreau* tipped over. Its north perimeter plunged into the sea and the tower collapsed, smacking the waves and shattering immediately, bits and pieces of it washing back over the partially submerged deck. As it keeled over, the eight lines pumping crude oil into its tanks were torn loose, twisting in the wind like snakes, spewing crude into the wind. Electrical circuits exploded like fireworks, and the raw oil flooded through the cavernous room where the system converged. When the oil reached the hot lines, the room exploded. The six men on duty were roasted as the room blew up in an enormous mushroom of fire that filled it and burst through the side of the building before it was swept away by the wind and sea.

Inside the stricken rig, men were tossed about like toothpicks, crushed under furniture, thrown through smashed portholes. The lights went out. Most of them, trapped in darkness, died in panic and fear.

The *Thoreau* lay on its side, held momentarily by the other legs, as the sea pounded it and the waves crashed against its five-story superstructure, which now lay sideways in the water.

Lansdale was standing in the doorway of his apartment, urging Marge to hurry, when suddenly the earth seemed to tip crazily underfoot.

"My God, we're rolling over!" he screamed as the floor bounded up at him. When he fell, his legs dangled through the open doorway. He clutched frantically at the walls, which now, insanely, had become the floor, trying to keep from falling back into the apartment. As the *Thoreau* tipped, there was a crescendo of destruction. Glasses, furniture, anything not tied down, poured through the hallways of the five-story building.

As Lansdale struggled to pull himself out of the gaping doorway he could hear shrieks echoing up through the corridors of the dying structure. He turned back, looking down into the apartment. Marge lay crumpled in the corner, covered by furniture and debris. She was unconscious. Lansdale needed a line to get down to her. Then he heard the oil explode and felt the whole structure tremble. At the far end of the corridor the force of the oil explosion tore the door off and blew away half the wall. Frigid, damp air rushed through the hall. The lights went out. Lansdale turned his flashlight down into the ruined topsy-turvy apartment. The porthole, now submerged in the raging sea, could not withstand the pressure. Its rivets suddenly began popping like champagne corks. The round window burst open and a geyser of freezing water gushed up through it. Lansdale jumped to his feet and started down the hallway. Then the rig rolled again and this time he was thrown against the ceiling, now the floor, of the hallway. And then the sea rushed through the doorways and he saw the mountain of water pour down and engulf him.

The shock of the below-freezing seawater numbed him. He held tenaciously to his flashlight as he was swept along the hallway by the torrent. He clutched at an open doorway, but his fingers slipped away from it and he was trapped in the submerged corridor. His lungs were bursting as he frantically felt the walls, trying to find an opening, anything to get free of this watery trap. But the frozen sea was already taking its toll, and the shock of the icy water robbed him of breath.

My God, I'm drowning, he thought.

And then he was in a glistening underwater wonderland, numbed beyond pain or caring, his lungs wracked with spasms, and as the flashlight slipped from his fingers and tumbled away, its beam diminishing to a pinpoint, he opened his mouth, like a fish in a bowl, and the sea flooded in, and his life, too, blinked out.

The *Henry Thoreau* lay upside down. The cables that had held it firmly to the bottom were either uprooted or had snapped. Its once mighty legs pointed straight up. Buffeted by the storm, they bent before the gale and then were torn from their mounts on the deck. Their air pockets burst. The escaping air hissed out. And the *Thoreau* plunged straight down, four hundred feet, leaving in its wake a trail of bubbles, debris and bodies which bobbed upward, like innocent toys from a stricken dollhouse, toward the raging surface of the Chukchi Sea.

V

The Greek tanker, plowing through the gale, arrived on the scene forty minutes after the *Thoreau* had gone down. The tanker's searchlights swept the area, picking out one life raft with three bodies lashed to it. Three men, all frozen to death. For more than two hours the tanker lay in the troughs of the pounding waves while several volunteers recovered one corpse, then another. When the captain finally decided to abandon the search, they had fished fifteen men and a woman out of the sea. There was no sign of the *Thoreau.*

By eight o'clock the next morning the storm had passed, and the sea, although still running high, had lost its muscle. The storm clouds raced onward, sweeping south toward the Bering Strait and Nome. Winds were down to twenty to twenty-five knots. Three more bodies were recovered. The captain sent a simple message to the Air Force rescue station at Point Barrow, two hundred miles northeast of the disaster area:

"*Henry Thoreau* down in 70 fathoms. Location: 72 degrees north, 165 degrees west. Nineteen bodies recovered. No survivors. Holding position. Please advise."

The Russian air station at Provideniya, just south of the Bering Strait, offered assistance, but three Air Force rescue planes arrived on the scene forty minutes after the tanker's message and reported no signs of life or the fated oil rig. They thanked the Russians but declined help. One of the planes swept low over the tanker and wiggled his wings in a final salute to the *Thoreau* and its crew.

"This is Air Force 109," the pilot radioed the tanker. "Please drop a marker and you are relieved. Thank you and Happy New Year." He banked sharply and joined his formation and the three planes headed back toward Barrow.

On the bridge, the man who had led the scuba-diving team the night before peered through powerful binoculars, watching the three planes leave. He had been there all night, watching the rescue attempt. Now he lowered the glasses. There was a patch over his right eye now, and a deep red scar ran, from his hairline to the edge of his jaw, down the right side of his face. He nodded to the captain, left the bridge and went to the radio room, where he sent a simple message:

"Mission accomplished. Scratch Thornley. Le Croix."

That afternoon, eight hours before the beginning of the New Year, the man whose neck had been broken planting the explosives on the leg of the *Thoreau* the night before, was buried from the deck of the tanker as it plowed southward toward the Bering Sea.

3

EDDIE WOLFNAGLE WAS ON TOP of the world. It was a gorgeous day, the temperature was in the mid-eighties, and the sun was blazing, except for an occasional downpour that started suddenly and stopped just as suddenly. He guided the rented Honda along the Hana Road, which had started out as a respectable two-lane blacktop and now had petered out into a dirt road, barely wide enough for two cars to pass. As the road got narrower, the forest got thicker, so that before long he was driving under a canopy of mango, kukuis, African tulip blossoms and pink Rainbow Shower trees. Hidden among them, parrots squawked indignantly and ruffled the rainwater out of their feathers, and to his left, a hundred yards below, the Pacific Ocean was putting on quite a show, smashing at huge boulders with twenty- and thirty-foot breakers.

Paradise.

Everything was paradise. The night before, he had scored some unbelievable Maui grass. He had been shacked up at the Intercontinental Maui at Makena Beach for three days with a gorgeous model from London. In eight hours he was flying first class to L.A. The next day he had tickets on the thirty-yard line for the Rose Bowl game, with an even thou down on Michigan plus ten over Southern Cal, the biggest bet he had ever made in his life.

And here he was, in a rain forest on the back side of Haleakala, the ten-thousand-foot volcano that dominates Maui. He had read all about the Seven Pools of the Kings, which was supposed to be a sacred place where the Gods lived and where, centuries before, princes from all the Hawaiian islands had come in their outriggers with their entourages to be coronated king.

Eddie felt like he was in an old Dorothy Lamour movie he had seen on television when he was a kid.

He got out of the car and lit a cigarette. He was wearing a fringed suede jacket, Tony Lama boots, which lifted him to nearly five-nine, Polo jeans and a Stetson cowboy hat. Shit, it was bouncing his way. And about time. He watched a high school kid as he dove from one clear pool to the next, working his way down the mountainside until he reached the pond at the bottom. The kid rolled over on his back, spat water two feet in the air and closed his eyes as the spray from the surf splashed up over the rocks.

Eddie had come a long way from swimming in the Harlem River when he was a kid. God*damn!* He was feeling good. And why not? He could afford all this now, could afford trips to paradise and London motels and pot at four hundred dollars a lid. In less than an hour he, Edward (NMI) Wolfnagle, once cashiered out of the Marines in disgrace, was going to be worth a cool hundred grand. What would Vinnie and the bunch back in Canarsie think of that?

Hey, Vinnie, lookit me, ain't I hot shit, cruising through paradise and tonight I'm flying first-fucking-class to L.A. and tomorra I'll be watching the Rose Bowl from the thirty-yard line and in a few more minutes I'll have one hundred big ones in hard-fucking-cash in my two-hundred-dollar-fucking-hat.

He yelled out loud, a good solid Texas geehaw.

"Way to go, Eddie," he shouted to nobody in particular.

He got back in the car and drove deeper into the forest, past other rented Hondas parked haphazardly around the small bathhouses near the road. A heavyset Hawaiian in a red print shirt and wash-and-wear pants stepped into the road and flagged him down. He showed Eddie a badge.

"State police," he said in precise English. "May I see your license, please."

"Sure," said Eddie. "Anything wrong?"

"No, sir, just checking. I see you're from the mainland. Better be careful if you leave your vehicle. Take all your valuables with you. There's a lot of car theft in the islands. Young punks, y'know. Grab and run. That's why none of the locks on these rentals work. They just bust 'em open."

"Thanks, Officer."

"Yes, sir. We don't want anybody goin' home mad." He smiled.

"Am I headed right for Mamalu Bay?"

"Straight ahead another ten miles or so. You can't go anyplace else. You'll have to turn around there, though. There's a road through the Haleakala lava field but it's just for Ranger use. Very dangerous."

"I was planning to do just that," Eddie said amiably, and went on.

Hinge parked his car before he got to the bridge at the Seven Pools and hiked up the mountainside to the edge of the Haleakala lava field, then followed it down to the bay at the end of the road. It was an easy hike, going over the ridge that way, not more than three miles. And although it was hot and the humidity was high, Hinge did not sweat. Hinge never perspired.

A few yards from the road he turned and walked back into the thick foliage. He sat down and took a paper bag from his coat pocket, spreading the contents on the ground: a cigar, a thick ball-point pen, a small package of cotton, a thermometer, a hypodermic needle.

After removing the ball-point cartridge, he broke both ends off the pen, then slowly augered the shaft through the center of the cigar. He blew out the tobacco and sighted through it: the tube of the pen formed a perfectly clean shaft through the cigar. He roughed up one end, concealing the hole. Next he broke the thermometer, and holding the hypodermic needle between his fingers, he carefully dribbled two or three drops of mercury into its aperture. Next he took a wooden match out of his pocket, lit it, blew it out and twisted it into the opening of the needle, trapping the mercury inside. He wrapped the end of the match with wadded cotton and then inserted the handmade dart into one end of the cigar. He put the other end in his mouth, stuffed his trash in the paper bag and put it in his back pocket. Then he leaned back against the tree.

The forest got thicker and the road narrower. A sudden downpour thrashed the trees. Wild birds yelled back. It got so dark that he turned on the lights. Then, just as quickly, sunrays swept down through the trees, pockmarking the road ahead. A few miles farther on, he suddenly drove out of the woods. The lava field lay ahead, and to his left the Pacific Ocean, as far as he could see.

The place was deserted.

Eddie Wolfnagle got lonely.

He got out of the car and looked around. There were no other cars. Nothing. Nothing but the ocean, the forest behind him and the awesome, black-ridged river of petrified lava ahead, sweeping down the mountainside straight into the ocean, the outfall of a volcano that once, thousands of years ago, had inundated over half the island, leaving behind a crater bigger than the island of Manhattan. The gray-black plateau stretched ahead as far as he could see. To his left it rolled gently down toward the sea, then suddenly fell away, dropping a hundred feet or so down to the ocean.

"Jesus!" he said aloud.

A barrier closed off the road. The sign nailed to it read:

DANGER! LAVA FIELD. ROAD UNSAFE.
THIS ROAD IS PERMANENTLY CLOSED.
TRESPASSERS WILL BE PROSECUTED.
HALEAKALA NATIONAL PARK
U.S. RANGER SERVICE

A twig cracked behind him; he turned and saw a man coming toward him. He was about the same height as Eddie and was using a branch as a walking stick.

Eddie was a little surprised. If this was Hinge, he looked like a real square. Butch haircut? A polyester suit? Jesus, where's he been? And he was younger than Eddie had imagined, and fair-skinned. For some reason, Eddie had expected Hinge to be dark. Maybe even with gray hair. This guy—hell, this guy was hardly thirty.

"Hinge!" Wolfnagle called out to the man, who smiled vaguely and nodded. "Hey, all right! I'm Eddie Wolfnagle."

They shook hands and Hinge said, "Let's get in the car, in case somebody comes by."

"Good idea," Eddie said.

They got in the Honda.

"Where's your car?" Wolfnagle asked.

"I'm camping out," Hinge said. "Up the draw there, a mile or so."

"Oh." Wolfnagle began feeling anxious. This was the moment he had been dreaming about for two months. Now it seemed too easy. "Uh

. . . maybe . . . uh, you should show me something. You know, some identification."

Hinge took a brown manila envelope out of his breast pocket and dangled it from his fingertips. "This should be enough," he said. "You have my goods?"

"Right here." Eddie took a roll of 35-mm. film from his coat pocket and held it up with two fingers, but as Hinge reached for it, Eddie let it drop into his fist. "Well . . ." He rubbed his thumb and forefinger together and grinned.

For just an instant Hinge's eyes went cold, but it passed quickly and he smiled. He handed Eddie the envelope. Eddie gave Hinge the film and opened the envelope. Packets of nice, poppin-fresh hundreds. He riffled them with the dexterity of a Vegas croupier.

Hinge took a jeweler's loupe from his pocket, and pinching it in front of his left eye with his eyebrow, unspooled a foot or so of film, which he held up toward the light.

"Whaddya think?" Eddie said, still counting.

"So far, so good. You have close-ups of everything?"

"You're lookin' at it, old buddy. Plans *and* the actual installation. Just what the doctor ordered, right?"

"Yes."

"All here," Eddie said and giggled like a kid. "I can't believe it, man. A hundred grand. You know something? I don't think my old man made a hundred grand his whole fucking miserable life."

"Congratulations."

Eddie took off his Stetson, dropped the envelope in it and put it back on. "Look," he said, "you need something else, I'm your man, okay? I can steal the crutch off a cripple, he won't know it till his ass hits the ground."

"I will be in touch."

"I started boosting when I was nine. Stole my first car when I was twelve. Could hardly see over the steering wheel. I did, shit, coupla hundred jobs before I was sixteen. Never got caught. Never seen the inside of a slammer."

"You're lucky."

"It's talent. A little luck, maybe, but mostly talent."

"I mean you are lucky never to have been in prison. How did you manage this job?"

"Right place at the right time. Security on the rig was nothing. The plans? That was a break. They had them all out one night, checking something in the transfer station. When they was through, they asked me would I run 'em back down to engineering. I sez sure, no problem, then I just stop off in my room on the way, whip out the old Minolta, bim, bam, boom, I got myself an insurance policy."

"Just off the sleeve like that? No planning?"

"You got it. You stay alert, things pop your way. Look, I knew I had something, see. I knew somebody, somewhere, would like a shot at those plans. All I hadda do was find the somebody. Then you pop up. What a break!"

An amateur, Hinge thought. Just a blunder. But it was lucky the word had gotten to him first. "How can I be sure you don't have copies? You could be peddling this material to our competitors."

"Look, that'd be dumb. I wanna do more business with you guys. I wouldn't cut my own throat."

"That's acceptable," Hinge said.

"You have the drop in Camden, New Jersey, right? It's my sister. I'm tight with the bitch."

"Yes."

Wolfnagle winked. "I'm gonna be travelin' awhile."

"You deserve a trip."

"Yeah, right. Well, uh, anything else?"

"Yeah. Got a light?"

Did he have a light? Bet your ass. He had a fucking Dunhill lighter, that's what he had. He took out the gold lighter, flipped it open, struck a flame and leaned over to light the cigar. He heard a faint *poof,* saw ashes float from the end of the cigar and then felt a sharp, stabbing pain in his throat.

At first he thought a bee had stung him. He brushed frantically at his neck.

Something bounced off the dashboard and fell on the floor.

He reached down and picked it up. It was a dart of some kind. He stared at it.

Dumbly.

It was going in and out of focus. His skin began to tingle. His hands had no feeling. His feet went to sleep.

Then the tingle became pain, sharp, like pinpricks, then the pain got worse. His skin was being jabbed with needles, then knives. He tried to scratch the pain away but he could not move. A giant fist squeezed his chest. He gasped for breath. Nothing happened.

He turned desperately to Hinge, and Hinge was a wavering apparition, floating in and out of reality. Wolfnagle looked like a goldfish, with his eyes bugged out and his lips popping soundlessly as he tried to breathe.

It had been a good shot, straight to the jugular. The mercury worked swiftly, thirty or forty seconds after hitting the bloodstream, and when Wolfnagle began to thrash, Hinge grabbed him by the arms and jammed him hard against the car seat. Now he went into hard spasms and Hinge almost lost him. He was stronger than he looked. The seizure lasted a minute or so, then Wolfnagle's teeth began to rattle, and then they snapped shut. There was a muffled rattle deep in his throat. His body stiffened. His eyes rolled up and crossed. Hinge heard him void.

Hinge held him for a few moments more, then released him. He seemed to shrink as he sagged slowly into the seat. His chin dropped suddenly to his chest. Hinge tipped Wolfnagle's hat and the brown manila envelope slipped into his hand. He reached over and took the dart from Wolfnagle's stiffening fingers. He pressed two fingers into Wolfnagle's throat. There was no pulse.

Hinge got out of the car. The wind blew up from the sea, rattling the palm fonds and sighing off into Haleakala's crater. A bird screamed and darted off through the trees. Then it was quiet. So far, so good.

He went around to Wolfnagle's side of the car, released the brake and pushed the car in a slight arc until it faced the ocean. There was nothing between it and the sea but a couple of hundred yards of black, ridged, petrified lava. He looked around again. They were still alone. He started the car and the engine coughed to life. He raised the hood and pulled the automatic throttle out an inch. The engine was roaring. He went back to the driver's side and pressed in the clutch with his walking stick, dropped the gear shift into first, held the door with his free hand and then jumped back, releasing the clutch and slamming the door. The rear tires screamed on the hard surface. The engine was revving at almost full speed. The car lurched forward, picked up speed, struck the edge of the lava bed and leaped over it. It wove erratically toward the sea, then turned and started back up the incline, teetered for a dozen feet or so and flipped, rolling side over side, until it reached the drop-off. It flipped over the edge, soaring down, down, down, and smacked into the ocean. A geyser of water plumed up and was carried away by the hard wind. A wave washed over the car, then another, until finally Hinge could only see its trunk. Then a heavy swell shattered it against the lava wall. The ocean foamed and receded. The car was gone.

Hinge hurried back into the woods, walked to the top of the ridge and sat down for a moment. It was quiet, except for the wind and faraway boom of the surf. He smiled to himself, realizing that the cigar was still in his mouth. He crumpled up the cigar and held out his hand, watching the tobacco blow away, then burned the paper bag containing the rest of the paraphernalia.

Hinge was feeling good now. It had gone off without a hitch. So much for the little thief. He took out the roll of film, held his lighter under one end and watched the flames devour it. Then he went back to his car.

Hinge did not make the call until he got back to the Honolulu airport. He dialed the 800 number and was surprised at how fast the call went through.

"Yes?" the voice on the other end said.

"Reporting."

"State your clearance."

"Hinge. Q-thirteen."

"Tape rolling."

"Jack be nimble, Jack be quick, Jack—"

"Voice clearance positive. ID positive. State your contact."

"Quill."

"We are routing."

He was on hold for almost a minute before it was picked up.

"This is Quill."

"I made the connection. The information was retrieved and destroyed."

"Excellent. And the connection?"

"Terminated."

"Good. Problems?"

"No problems."

"Sorry you had to interrupt your vacation."

"It worked out fine. I'll be back at the Royal Hawaiian by dinner."

"Thank you. Happy New Year."

"The same to you. Aloha."

4

IT WAS AN ENORMOUS ROOM, menacing in its darkness, the hand-sculpted molding around its ten-foot ceilings vaguely discernible in the eerie shadows cast by one small Oriental lamp in a corner. Bare hardwood floors glistened like the surface in an ice-skating rink; corners were pools of shadows. The only windows in the room, lining one entire wall, had once been exterior French doors, now glassed in to reveal a windowless hothouse filled with tropical ferns and flowerless leafy plants. The three or four small grow lights on the floor of the hothouse accentuated its greenery but succeeded only in creating ominous silhouettes of what little furniture there was in the main room.

The temperature in the room was exactly 82 degrees; it was always exactly 82 degrees.

The place was as quiet as a library. Except for the incessant ticking, like a time bomb ticking away the minutes of someone's life.

Near the door was an ensemble of leather furniture: two large easy chairs and a seven-foot sofa separated by a low teak coffee table. The end tables were made of matching teak, and each held a Philippine basket lamp. The coffee table was empty except for a single oversized Oriental ashtray.

Two of the other three corners were bare except for antique temple dogs that squatted angrily under tall leafy ferns.

The other corner was dominated by a large oak campaign desk with eight hard-back chairs in front of it. The top of the desk was bare except for an old-fashioned wooden letter file, a large ashtray, a leather-bound appointment book and an elaborate red Buddha lamp with an old-fashioned fringed lampshade and a pull string.

And the box.

It was a plain white box about the size of a large dictionary. There was a red ribbon around it with a large frivolous Christmas bow.

The chair behind the desk loomed up like a throne, its giant back rising into the darkness. A cloud of smoke eddied out from the dark tombstone of the chair. The only lamp on in the room was the Buddha lamp. It slanted an eerie light over the desk, casting the white box in harsh shadows. Its heat sucked the smoke away from the chair, sent it swirling in little whirlpools, up through the lampshade.

There was a sound in the box, a scurrying. The top moved slightly, then was still again.

The man in the chair moved forward. His long, narrow, skeletal head was topped by thin strands of white hair, carefully brushed from one side to the other. His cheeks were deeply drawn, each line and wrinkle accentuated by the light from the single lamp; his jaw tight, the veins standing out along its hard edge like strands of wire. It was a face from the past, from history books and old newsreels and magazines, a stern, hawklike face, promising victory while defeat was still sour in his mouth, a vengeful face that conjured memories of the wrath of Moses and the zeal of John Brown.

General Hooker. The Hook. He had been called a military genius, compared by militarists and historians to Alexander the Great, Stonewall Jackson and Patton. Hooker, chased out of the Philippines by the Japanese early in the war, becoming the architect of the Pacific War, plotting every strategic move, studying every island as he edged closer and closer to the Japanese mainland.

Hooker had almost become a legend.

That son of a bitch, he said to himself. He was thinking about Douglas MacArthur. Dugout Doug, who had run the war from Australia while the Hook plodded wearily from one bleak atoll to the next in the bloody march toward Japan. True, the old bastard was quick with the praise as Hooker scored the victories, but he knew just what to say to the press, and when to say it, and ultimately the mantle of victory fell on MacArthur's shoulders. There was no way to top the son of a bitch. On the day Corregidor fell, one of the blackest days in American history, while everyone else was in a panic over how to tell the public, the old bastard had turned the melee into a personal victory chorus with his goddamn "I shall return." It had become a slogan, a war cry, the "Remember the Alamo" of World War II. But, even the Hook had to hand it to the old s.o.b., it was also a promise of victory, said with such stalwart authority that no one ever doubted him. And when he did get back, with that "I have returned" shit, everybody knew it was all over. The photographs even made the old bastard look like he was walking on water, just in case there were any heretics around.

So MacArthur became the legend, and the Hook became a mere folk hero, along with Wainwright, Chennault, Stilwell, and a few others.

After that, there was nothing but disaster ahead. Hooker could see it coming. People were tired of war. MacArthur got the sack in Korea. A hot war was brewing in Indochina. And the Hook knew the Orient, knew that Vietnam, as it would come to be known, was no place to be.

Screw it.

Let Westmoreland or some other daisy take the rap for Vietnam. The Hook hung it up and retired. There were other things to do.

Two years later the rigors of those years claimed their toll. A massive coronary almost killed Hooker. The ticking in the room came from deep in his chest; a pacemaker, flawed yet effective, and much too dangerous for doctors to replace. It was a constant reminder of his mortality and would one day be a harbinger of his death. When its ominous note stopped, for that fraction of a moment before everything stopped with it, Hooker would know he was a dead man. In the meantime he continued to defy the odds; he was pushing seventy-five, but he still had the brilliance and the obsessions of a man much younger.

There was a knock on the door.

"If that's you, Garvey—come!"

The voice, too, was unforgettable. Deep, commanding, authoritative, intimidating and yet paternal; a voice that engendered every word with reassurance. A war correspondent had once written: "To know what God sounded like, one need only hear General Alexander Lee Hooker speak."

The door opened and Garvey entered the room. He was Hooker's oldest friend as well as his closest wartime aide, and although both had been retired for at least fifteen years, Garvey, who was a year shy of sixty, still carried himself with the ramrod posture of a Marine honor guard. He stood at attention in front of the desk. Hooker and Garvey, two men, born to the khaki, their hearts and minds shaped inexorably by the cry of the bugle, retired into an alien world of peace lovers where they still fantasized about that one last battle to ride out to, even though the dream had died years before; two men whose friendship stood second only to the charade they continued to play.

"Good evening, General," Garvey said. "Happy New Year."

His eyes strayed to the box.

Hooker's harsh blue eyes stared with hatred across the long Irish clay pipe he was smoking and focused on the box.

"Thanks, Jess. And you. At ease, have a seat."

"Thank you, sir."

"Let's deal with pleasant things first." He reached behind him, into the gloom, to the bottle of champagne nestled in a silver bucket on a small table behind his chair. He poured two glasses and handed one to Garvey.

"To the Division," he said. Garvey echoed the toast and their glasses rang in the solitude of the room. Garvey took a sip, smacked his lips and leaned back, staring up into darkness.

"Taittinger, definitely." He took another sip, pursed his lips, let the bubbles tickle his tongue. "Uh, 'seventy-one, I'd say."

The older man laughed. "Can't fool you. Never could. Well, here's to the years. Been a long time, Jess."

"Forty years exactly, General. I joined your staff at Hickam Field on New Year's Eve, 1939. I was a nineteen-year-old shavetail."

"Best I ever saw. I used to tell my officers, 'That Garvey, he can be another Custer. He'll have a star before he's thirty.' "

"Didn't quite make it by thirty," Garvey said.

"Hmmp. There were a lot of disappointments in that war. And the rest to follow. Goddamn that old son of a bitch, playing politics at the last minute. He should have fought Truman over Hiroshima. They should have let us go in there and do it right. We deserved that shot. Damn, we *deserved* it. He got to do his act in the Philippines. We earned the right to Japan."

It was a complaint heard frequently when the two men were together.

He looked down in the glass, watching the bubbles tumble to the surface. "What the hell," he said finally, "it's all just history. Kids sleep through it in classrooms. They're all gone now, anyway. Bless 'em all. At least we won it. It's the last goddamn war we won." And he raised his glass again.

"May I smoke?" Garvey asked.

"Of course, Jess. Smoking lamp's always lit for you."

Hooker reached into a desk drawer, took out a box wrapped in silver paper and slid the package across the desk.

"A little something to start the new year off right, Jess. With thanks for all the good years."

It was a tradition with them, exchanging gifts on New Year's Eve. Garvey handed a slightly smaller package to Hooker.

"And Happy New Year to you, General."

He stared back at the box for a moment, then watched as Hooker opened his present. It was a watch fob, a replica of the insignia of the First Island Division, The Hook's old regiment, forged in gold with the motto "First to land, first to win" inscribed across the bottom of two crossed bayonets.

Hooker was visibly moved.

"By God, old man, that's something to cherish. Yessir, I'll be wearing that when they put me away."

"Thank you, sir," Garvey said and smiled with satisfaction.

There was a sound from the box. A scraping sound. Garvey cast a nervous glance toward it but said nothing.

"Well, sir, your turn," Hooker said, and Garvey tore the silver paper from around his gift. It was a pewter wine goblet, hand-crafted, with the artist's name etched in the base, and inscribed on its side were the words "Major General J. W. Garvey, U.S. Army (Ret.)."

Garvey held up the chalice by the stem. "Beautiful, sir. Has a great feel to it."

"Well, I know your love for the grape, old man. About time you had a proper goblet."

There was a more urgent sound from the box. The top moved again, just a hair.

Hooker struck a match and relit his pipe. "It came about an hour ago," he said, without looking at the box. "Done up like a goddamn Christmas present, that bloody heathen."

He opened the center desk drawer and took out a knife, a malicious stiletto with a curved blade and a hand-tooled leather handle. He slid its razor edge under the string, turned the box slightly and snipped the string off. With the point of the knife he lifted the lid and slid it slowly back.

They heard it before they saw it. Scratching, slithering along the bottom of the box and up the side.

Hooker saw its horns first, the two tusks protruding straight out from over its eyes, the third, like a needle, between them. Then its head peered over the side of the box.

It was bright-green to start with, its eyes lurking under hoods of wrinkled skin, its tail switching slowly back and forth.

Eighteen inches long or so, he guessed. Hooker knew the species, all eighty kinds of *Chamaeleontidae.* For thirty-six years now, he had been studying them. This one was the *Chamaeleon jacksoni.* African, most likely, although it might have come from Madagascar, its eyes moving independently, looking for prey before they focused together and the tongue struck. And arrogant—they were all arrogant.

It crawled down the side of the box and very slowly across the desk to the base of the lamp and then just as slowly up over the belly of the Buddha. It changed slowly, its eyes picking up the change in the light rays of the new color, signaling down the nervous system to the pigment cells in the skin, first mud-brown, then beige, then pink, then blood-red, like a salamander. Its tongue continued to work the air, its head turned, its stony eyes studying the darkness beyond the desk. Then it switched again and moved on to the letter box.

Hooker watched it turn again, this time to the color of teak.

He reached in the box and took out a note. His hand trembled as he read it.

"What's it say?" Garvey asked.

Hooker handed it to him. There were three names on the slip of paper:

AQUILA
THOREAU
WOLFNAGLE

"He's everywhere," Hooker croaked, "he's like the mist, like some foul fog." He tilted the box, looked inside and paused for a moment before reaching in and taking out a man's gold watch. He turned it over and read the name engraved on the back.

"We've still got Bradley," Garvey said. "He's one of the best assassins in the world. If anybody can terminate Chameleon, he can."

"Afraid not," Hooker whispered and his voice quivered with rage. "This is Bradley's watch."

BOOK TWO

*A true friend always
stabs you in the front.*

—OSCAR WILDE

1

THE FRIGID FEBRUARY WIND SWEPT in off Boston Bay, and Eliza Gunn and George Gentry huddled in the arched doorway to avoid the stinging snow that was swept along with it. The car was half a block away. James, the sound man, a latter-day hippie who was only slightly larger than Eliza, would be sitting in there with his cowboy hat pulled down over his eyes and the heater on, listening to the Top Forty while they froze their onions here on Foster Street.

It had been four days since they started following Ellen Delaney, making like the FBI, changing cars twice a day, keeping in touch on CB Channel 11. So far, it had been a waste of time. But by now George knew better than to bitch. The minute he did, the Delaney dame would do something dumb. And they would score. It always turned out that way. Eliza had strange instincts, but they worked. So he kept his mouth shut and turned the collar of his jacket up a little higher and pulled his head down into it. "I'm catching pneumonia," he said. "Somebody ought to put a sticker on your butt. It should say: 'Caution, the Surgeon General has determined that Eliza Gunn is dangerous to your health.' "

"A big guy like you, complaining," she said. "You should be ashamed."

"There's three times as much of me to get cold," he growled.

George Gentry was over six feet tall, and his weight ranged between two-twenty and two-fifty, depending on how well he was eating. Eliza Gunn was barely five feet and weighed ninety-eight pounds, no matter what she ate. Mutt and Jeff, freezing their onions in a doorway because Eliza had a hunch.

"How come James always gets the car and I always get the street?"

"He drives better than you do."

"I'll be goddamned!"

"Now, Georgie—"

"Don't gimme any of that sweet-talkin' shit."

"Trust me, Georgie-boy. My instincts are going crazy. All my systems are on go."

"The last time this happened," George said ruefully, "I had four Mafia torpedoes baby-sitting me while I shot your exclusive interview with Tomatoes What'sisname."

"Garganzola."

"Hell, his name isn't Garganzola. Tomatoes Garganzola sounds like something off a Mexican menu. I thought at any minute you were gonna ask the wrong question and we were all gonna end up in the foundation of some bridge somewhere."

"But I didn't. Besides, Tomatoes was cute."

"Right. The DA's after him, the Feds are after him, everybody but the goddamn Marine Corps was on his ass, for every felony on the books—and you, fer Chrissakes, think he's cute."

"It won us an Emmy, Georgie."

"I work for wages, not glory."

"Oh, bullshit."

And George started to laugh. He always laughed at her profanity. It was like hearing a child cuss.

She ignored the cold, watching the office building through binoculars.

"If we had—" he began.

"George!"

"Hunh?"

"There she is," Eliza said.

"Lemme see."

She handed him the binoculars. "Coming out of the bank building, in the mink jacket."

"How about the blond hair?"

She took the glasses and zeroed in on the Delaney woman—tall, over five-ten, and stacked. Eliza checked her out again, especially the legs, the walk. It was Ellen Delaney, all right. She was positive. "It's a wig. Look at the coat. I'd know that mink anywhere. She was wearing it the day Caldwell disappeared. Must have cost ten thou at least."

"You know how many mink jackets there are in the city of Boston?"

"Not like that one. That's a sweetie-pie mink, George."

The woman, holding her jacket closed with gloved hands, started up Foster toward Congress.

"That's just the kind of coat the head of the biggest bank in Boston would give his honey," she said, still watching.

"Now what?" George asked.

"She's hoofing it toward Congress," Eliza said. "Gimme the walkie-talkie. I'll follow her; you go back to the car with James and stand by, just in case she decides to make her move."

"Which you're convinced she will."

"Sooner or later. She's a lady in love, George, and I know how a woman in love thinks. She's going to want to see her man."

She grabbed the walkie-talkie and took off on the run, her short legs propelling her along the snow-swept street, her short black hair dancing dervishly in the wind. George walked around the corner to Eliza's car, a dark green Olds whose front end looked as though it might have been used, on more than one occasion, as a battering ram. He climbed in and flicked off the radio.

"You're not gonna believe it," George said to the sound man, "but she actually spotted the Delaney woman."

"Oh, I believe it," James said and laughed. "I been wrong too often not to believe it."

"You know how she spotted her?"

"Tell me."

"The mink coat."

James laughed again. "Neat," he said, "if she's right."

"Five more minutes in that goddamn doorway, I woulda been in intensive care."

Eliza followed the tall woman in the mink coat along Foster to Salem to Congress. The woman entered a drugstore and went straight to the prescription counter in the rear.

Eliza crossed the street, looking at the posters in front of a theater, her back to the store. "This is E.G., you reading me?" she said into the walkie-talkie.

"Gotcha," George answered.

"Salem and Congress, across from the Rexall drugstore. Get in close."

"On the way."

Ellen Delaney got a package, signed the slip and came out. She started up Congress again, then suddenly veered across the street to Eliza's side, flagged a cab, jumped in and headed back down Congress in the opposite direction.

"Oh, shit!" Eliza said to herself.

The green Olds appeared seconds later and she jumped in.

"U-turn! She's in the Yellow Cab heading back that way," she yelled.

James swung the Olds in a tight turn, cut in front of a truck, almost went up on the curb, and screeched off after the taxi. "Is she on to us?" he asked.

"Nah," said Eliza, "she's just seen too many James Bond movies."

"They're headin' for the tunnel," James said.

"Shit, Caldwell wouldn't be caught dead in North Boston," George answered.

"That's probably what he hopes everybody thinks," Eliza said. They followed the cab through the tunnel and out into the north side. It moved slowly, weaving through the trucks and vans that choked the narrow streets of the market section.

"That slowed her down," James said.

The cab turned into a quiet street of restored town houses and stopped. The woman got out, looked around and went inside one of the houses.

"He's in there. Betcha a week's salary."

"Instinct again, Gunn?" George said skeptically.

"Guessing," she said. "We've been on her for—what, four days now? Caldwell's a diabetic. I'm betting she just picked up his insulin for the week."

"Wanna cruise down past the place?" James asked.

"Let's just cool it and see what happens. I don't see her Mercedes anywhere."

"Lemme see the glasses a minute," George said, and began to appraise the street. He focused on the house she had entered.

"It's got a garage built in," he said.

"So much for the missing Mercedes."

"Where's the equipment?" Eliza asked.

"Back seat on the floor, in case we need it fast."

"Good."

"If he's in there, he's not coming out," George said.

"We're dealing with a sports freak, George, he jogs five miles a day," Eliza said. "How long can he stay holed up without coming up for air?"

"If he's in there," George said.

"Yeah," said James, "and if he is, what's to say he hasn't been jogging every morning? Nobody's looking for him over here."

"Well," George said, "at least it's someplace new. We sure know all her other haunts."

"I got that feeling," Eliza said.

Fifteen minutes passed. Twenty. Thirty. Nothing. George casually checked out the street again through the binoculars.

James said, "Mooney's gonna have all our asses if we don't come up with something, soon. Four days following this maybe girl friend around."

"She's his girl friend. No maybe about it."

"She's probably got the flu, picked up some nose drops," James said.

"Maybe not," George said. "Lookee here."

The garage door was slowly rising.

"Take it," Eliza said. "Block the driveway so she can't get out."

James threw the Olds in reverse and backed crazily down the street. He screeched to a stop in front of the driveway just as the Mercedes started out. Eliza was out of the car on the run.

Jonathan Caldwell was in the car with Ellen Delaney.

Ellen Delaney put the stick in reverse and headed back into the garage, but Eliza ran alongside the car and into the garage before the door swooshed shut.

There they were. A Mexican stand-off. Caldwell, who had once been a middleweight boxer at Harvard, glared at her through the windshield, his ice-blue eyes afire with anger. Eliza glared back.

"You're trespassing," he said finally, his voice trembling with rage.

"Mr. Caldwell, do you know who I am?"

"I know who you are," he said flatly.

"Mr. Caldwell, nobody's heard your side of this mess. I'll make a deal. I'll give you five minutes. You can say anything you want."

"And if I refuse?"

Eliza stared at him and said nothing for a moment. Then she smiled. "You wouldn't do that. You're too smart to pass up five minutes of free air time."

He nodded toward his girl friend. "She's out of it. It's just you and me."

"You got it."

When the garage doors opened up again, a minute or two later, the boys were facing it. George had the video camera on his shoulder and James was plugged in and they were ready to shoot. They knew their Eliza very well.

2

AT THE SAME TIME that Eliza was interviewing Caldwell, it was night in Japan.

Kei guided the old Toyota up a gravel road, winding through a row of wind-bent pine trees, and when he peaked the mountain, the city of Tokyo twinkled below them, fifteen miles away, like a constellation reflected in the sea. They were in a parking lot filled with Mercedes and Rolls-Royce sedans, American limousines and, here and there, a Z series Datsun. The building was round and triple-tiered and very contemporary, constructed of teak and redwood that had been steam-curved, with balconies that spanned half its circumference and jutted out over the cliffs, facing the city. The main entrance was on the opposite side of the building, and as Kei pulled up, the largest Oriental that Gruber had ever seen emerged from the entrance, itself a massive twelve-foot-high teak door, several inches thick and trimmed in royal blue. The doorman, who helped Gruber out of the back seat, was built like a prize fighter and dressed in a classic *gi* of black silk.

"I park, come right back," Kei said, and drove around to the side of the building, squeezing the four-door in between two large black European limos. He was slender and agile and handsome in a stoic way, and he wore American jeans, Nike sneakers, a dark-blue raw-silk blouse, and a black headband to keep his thick black hair in place. He was maybe twenty-seven or -eight and crowding five-six.

When Kei returned, Gruber was standing in the shadows near the entrance. He was obviously angry. Gruber was a large man who kept himself in perfect physical condition, his waist tight and trim, his back as straight as a post, his graying brown hair neat and militantly close-cropped. Kei felt tension emanating from Gruber like an electric charge; his skin was as gray as lead and one could almost see, reflected in his lifeless eyes, a lifetime of killing without remorse or feeling.

"Look, I don't like the vay dis iss sizing up," Gruber said in a low, flat monotone, barely concealing his German accent. "You understand my meaning? Don't leave me alone like dat. I am on alien ground."

"Hunh?" Kei said.

Goddamn, Gruber thought, fighting his thin temper, it's always difficult dealing with Orientals. "You, me, stay togedder, now on. Okay? You understand dat?"

"Sure," Kei said. "Now, you understand this, this is private club, some Japanese, mostly Americans and Europeans who live in Japan. I have guest letter, very hard to get, pay twenty-five thousand yen, you gimme fifty bucks American, that's twelve thousand yen, so you owe me another thirteen thousand, right?"

"I told you, if dis girl knows Chameleon and I get vat I need, I'll triple what you get, eh. Three times, okay? Dat's anodder thirty-nine thousand. But only if I find Chameleon. If it is a vashout, nutting."

Kei nodded. "Agreeable. You listen good now. There is show on inside, but we have no time for that."

"What kind of show?"

"I tell you there is no time for show. You wanna see show, we come back some other time, you must go to the baths, take steam bath to prepare you for the massage. The *maiko* who massages you, she will be the one."

"*Maiko?* Vat the hell's dat?"

"She is training for geisha."

"An amateur, eh. Does she have a name?"

"Her name is Suji. She knows what you want. She will start the talk, *hai*? So you will know it is her. You just listen. But must hurry, before show is over. There may be crowd after show. Suji will not talk with others there."

"So, vy de steam bath? I do not even like de steam bath."

"This is very traditional club, even though pretty crazy, too. It would be an insult, to skip the steam."

Gruber muttered something in German and followed Kei into a small, low-ceilinged anteroom that was simple and elegant. The muted lighting came from a globe lantern that hung over either end of a priceless antique desk, its façade covered with hand-carved scroll work. An Oriental rug lay before the desk, and in the *tokonama,* the small alcove behind it, was a magnificent floral arrangement. The geisha who sat behind the desk was just as elegant, a diminutive woman, no more than twenty, a single jade ring on the small finger of her left hand, her mouth a splash of red in her chalk-white painted face, her night-black hair braided to one side and held in place by a splinter-thin pin with a delicate jade handle. She wore a kimono of pure white silk with a startling, blood-red obi that matched, perfectly, the color of her lips. And when she spoke, her voice was as delicate as wind chimes.

"*Konbanwa.*"

Kei nodded and returned her "Good evening."

She smiled and nodded back. "*Tegami o onegai itashimasu.*"

"*Hai.*" Kei produced a letter and handed it to her.

"*Domo arigato gozaimasu.*"

"*Do itashimashite.*"

She read it slowly.

Somewhere in the vastness of the club, behind walls and doors, Gruber could hear the slow, solitary beat of a *taiko* drum, and there was a delicate scent of incense in the air. And while Gruber tried to keep his mind on business, he found himself uncontrollably stirred by the place, by a sensual promise he could not ignore.

This is business, he said to himself. The pleasure can wait. And yet the odor, the slow rhythmic thump of the drum, the beauty of the young geisha, kept chipping away at his concentration.

When she finished the letter, she looked at Gruber for a moment and then asked Kei, *"Kochira wa Gruber-san desuka?"*

"Hai."

She folded the letter and slipped it into one of the desk drawers, looked briefly at Gruber, and with the vaguest of smiles, nodded toward another door, pressing a button under her foot as she did. The door clicked very quietly. Kei opened it and ushered Gruber into Takan Shu.

The only light in the enormous space seemed to come from near the ceiling, but it was so subtle, so subdued that it took Gruber a few moments to adjust before he could study the interior of the club. It was an arena, a plush arena in a large circular room towering sixty feet to its flat ceiling. The core of the main floor was a small stage and, stretching out from it, like ripples in the water, were tiers, circular rows, like giant steps rising one above the other, to a point perhaps halfway to the dome. There were no windows. Each step accommodated several bays separated only by small tables. There were no lamps and no lights on the walls, and in each of the bays were deeply piled *futon*, thick down quilts normally used for sleeping. Most of the alcoves were occupied, some by a single couple, some by as many as six people. Their faces were hazy apparitions in the dim light.

The music, a Japanese love song, was being played by three geishas who sat on the stage in the center of the room. When Kei and Gruber entered, the only sound had been the slow rhythm of the *taiko,* and a murmur of anticipation from the crowded room. But then the drum had been joined by the samisen, the three-stringed Japanese guitar that always sounds slightly out of tune, and then, a beat or two later, by a flute.

Gruber, despite his profession, had managed through the years to acquire an element of taste and had once played the role of interior decorator as a cover. He thought, The place is a marvel of naked elegance; everything in the room is essential. And: Those goddamn Japs, you must give it to them, they have impeccable taste.

It was a few moments before Gruber was aware that everyone in the room was staring up at the ceiling, sixty feet above, at a large plexiglass disk, at least twelve feet across, that was being lowered slowly. It was perfectly balanced by four velvet ropes attached, ten feet above the disk, to a single strand that rose to a winch hidden somewhere in the false ceiling.

Colored lights faded up slowly as the clear disk was lowered. He was looking up through the disk. It was occupied by two men and a woman.

The men were both Japanese but quite disparate in age. One of them was no more than twenty or twenty-one; the other in his forties. Both looked like athletes, their muscular bodies enhanced by oil. They wore loincloths. The woman was Caucasian with perhaps a strain of Polynesian, young, not yet twenty, and small, although her body was almost perfect, her breasts not too big, her legs not too short. She wore a loose, sheer tunic that draped to mid-thigh. Both men were blindfolded with black silk. She was not.

And he thought, Ah, even the show will be a study in elegance of style.

Pornographic? Of course. But never obscene.

As the disk came down, very slowly, it began to revolve just as slowly. And the two men began to caress the woman, each in his own way. The younger man was more impetuous, his touch was more urgent, his moves more direct. The older man began to stroke her with his fingertips, starting at the tip of her fingers and moving slowly up her arm, fondling the hollow where her arm and body joined, moving down her side to her knee, then as he started back up, he slipped one hand along the inside of her thigh. Her head fell back and her long black hair draped across the back of her legs. She began to move her head back and forth with the beat of the music.

"Must go now," Kei said.

The German had begun to sweat, very lightly, just under his nose. "In a moment," he snapped under his breath without taking his eyes off the revolving disk.

The tempo of the music began to pick up, and with it, the emotions of the trio. The younger man began to slow his pace as the older one increased his. The woman was being touched by four hands that seemed to explore every inch of her body, caressing her ear lobes, her eyelids, her lips, her throat.

She was swaying back and forth and the men moved closer and began weaving with her, their hands overlapped, the tempo of the music increased and she moved with it. The faster the music, the more frenzied she became.

Gruber appeared to be transfixed. He stared up at the disk. His lips were dry and now drops of sweat appeared along the edge of his hairline.

Everything is possible here, he thought. It is hard to tell where reality stops and fantasy begins.

The older man's hand slid up under her tunic and began rubbing her stomach while the younger man's hands encircled her breasts, never quite touching them, but tracing the outline of each through the thin gauze. She leaned back on her arms and looked down at her body and she rose slightly so the older man's hand could slide low on her belly and he turned the hand so the fingers pointed downward and slid his hand lightly between her legs.

She moaned and the audience reacted immediately. A murmur of whispers flooded the room.

Gruber was hooked. Kei, standing nearby in the darkness, studied his reaction, his dry lips, the sweat on his face, his eyes, gleaming as he watched the performance.

She moved in unison with the hand of the older man, sliding forward on it, rising slightly, letting him taunt her with his palm just barely touching her hair. The younger man finally brushed a hand across one of her nipples, then the other, and finally she reached up and pulled the straps of her tunic loose and it fell away. And then she straightened up and began stroking both her lovers and they grew under her touch.

Kei touched Gruber's elbow and whispered, "We must go now. Show over soon."

"Rate dey are going, dey vill be up dere for weeks," Gruber said. His blood was pounding in unison with the music.

"We can come back later, see another show. Maybe tomorrow night."

"A minute more," Gruber whispered with irritation.

"Okay, pal, it's your grave."

"The expression," said Gruber without moving his eyes from the disk, "iss funeral. It iss your funeral, dat iss the expression."

All three of the performers had become extremely vocal. The woman put her hand on the older man's hand, guiding it deeper and deeper.

Kei was not watching the show. He stared off across the room somewhere into a dark corner, waiting.

The disk was now below the line of sight of the people in the top row. The young woman's moves were becoming spastic. Her tight jawline was etched in the spotlights. Every muscle in her body was taut. Suddenly she tore the older man's loin cloth away and he sprang free and she began stroking him and both men eased her down and they lay down beside her and began kissing her breasts, her stomach, her thighs, and a tight scream burst from her clenched teeth.

"Pretty soon too late," Kei whispered.

"All right, all right," the German growled, and Kei led him to a doorway at the side of the arena. They entered what appeared to be a large closet with a single blue light in the ceiling. A second door faced them.

"Vait a minute," Gruber whispered. "Vere are you taking me?"

"It's okay," Kei said. "Health club right there, other side of door. Don't want light in the club, okay."

He pulled the door shut. The music continued achingly in Gruber's mind, although the door was thick and he could really only feel the beat of the drum now. But his concentration was shattered and he was having difficulty making the transition from fantasy back to reality. Kei opened the other door and light flooded the small room. A half-dozen steps led down to a narrow hallway which was painted a dazzling white. Its indirect lighting was so bright it was hard to tell where walls and floors joined. Now even the beat of the music was a memory. But the scene was etched in Gruber's brain and he could not dismiss the fantasy that continued to play out in his mind.

Kei led the big German to one of the doors and ushered him into an immaculate dressing room with six teakwood lockers and a long teak bench. Kei pointed to a door directly across the hall. "Steam bath. Door on other side of steam room leads to massage room, okay?"

Gruber was getting nervous again.

"Vere are you going?" he demanded.

"When you finish, Suji will show you exit door. I will wait for you there," Kei said and was gone.

The little son of a bitch, Gruber thought, he is probably going back up to see the end of the show.

Gruber took off his clothes, hanging them neatly in the locker, and draped his shoulder holster over a hook in its side and wrapped a towel around his middle and tucked it in place. His body was hard and his skin tight and there were two round scars in his side, .38-caliber scars, constant reminders that once, in another time and place, he had become dangerously reckless.

He stared at himself in the mirror for a few moments and then looked down at the scars. His mind was like the blip in an electronic game, bouncing back and forth, from the arena above, to the woman on the other side of the steam bath who supposedly would lead him to Chameleon.

Almost as an afterthought, he took the .25-caliber Beretta from the shoulder holster, held the small gun in the palm of his hand, and checked the clip, then tucked it into the towel at his waist. He draped a second towel over his shoulders, letting it fall at his side to conceal the pistol. He entered the steam room.

It was like being lost in a cloud. He had never seen steam so thick. Gruber groped his way along the wall to the benches on one side and sat down. Driblets of sweat trickled down and began to gather at his waist in the tuck of the towel. He took the Beretta and laid it on the bench beside him.

The room was larger than Gruber had expected. He could vaguely make out its perimeters from the haloed glow of the lights recessed in the walls.

God, he thought, it must be a hundred and twenty degrees in here. I'll give it two or three minutes and then get the hell out.

He took the towel from his shoulders and dipped it in a bucket of ice that sat melting on the floor near the wall and wiped his face with it.

The sound of a sudden shower of water, followed immediately by a harsh burst of steam, jolted him. It came from across the room. Some-one had just pulled the cord and released a water shower on the hot coals that were obviously over there somewhere on the other side of the room.

The mist swirled and grew thicker.

To his right, he heard the other door open and *thunk* shut.

His hand edged closer to the Beretta. He was jumpy, his pulse still hammering from the opening minutes of the show in the arena above.

Then the mist on the far side of the room seemed to clear for a moment and he saw briefly, as though through gauze, the shaggy figure of a man, staring at him.

It jolted him. He sat upright, instantly alert. But the steam immedi-ately obscured the figure. He took the Beretta in hand and stood up and took a few cautious steps across the slippery tile floor toward the figure. Was he large or small? Fat or thin? Gruber wasn't sure.

He sensed, but never actually saw, the figure. It materialized for an instant, tore off his towel and vanished back into the mist. The Baretta clattered on the floor. Gruber stood in the room, naked. Panic began to gnaw at his stomach. He bent his knees and lowered himself slowly down toward the gun, peering into the thickening mist.

Another hiss of steam from across the room. It distracted him for a moment. The kick came from nowhere, a sudden jarring pain from out of the mist, *bang!* Just like that.

He didn't see who kicked him, didn't even hear it coming. But he felt the heel rip into his side, felt the ribs crack and the tendons tear loose. His feet thrashed from under him and he went down on his side, sliding across the tiled floor, and hit the wall.

All of his finely tuned systems went haywire for a moment. Then he twisted his body, ignoring the fire in his side, got quickly to his knees, and waving the pistol in front of him, pointing at everything and nothing, he stood up, keeping his back against the wall.

He hardly had time to appraise the situation.

The second time it was the toes, hard as a cake of ice, that came from nowhere into the pit of his stomach, digging up deep into his diaphragm, slamming him into the wall. He gagged as the air gushed out of him, and the back of his throat soured instantly with bile.

He jackknifed forward, caught himself with his hands, the Beretta still clutched in a sweaty fist, and rolled away from the wall, seeking the sanctity of the thick steam himself.

As he started to get up, he caught a fleeting glimpse of something, a specter that seemed to materialize just long enough to shatter the right side of his jaw, before it was enveloped once again in mist.

The pain screamed out along his nerves and flooded his brain. This time he screamed, but as he fell, he swung the Beretta up and got off one shot, its flat *spang* echoing off the walls.

Karate.

Traditional.

Okinawan.

What was the best defensive stance possible under the—

Whap!

He felt his wrist snap, saw the black pistol spin away into the fog, heard it smack the floor and slide into a corner.

He spun quickly in the direction of the blow.

Nothing but swirling clouds of hot steam.

He was beginning to shake. Sweat was gushing from every pore in his body. His breath came in labored gulps. He turned and lurched for the door.

His feet were swept from under him, soundlessly, effortlessly, invisibly. He fell flat on the wet floor, his broken jaw smacked the wet tile, fire raged in his ribs, his ruined hand was folded uselessly under him.

Groaning uncontrollably, he was fighting to stay conscious. He decided to stay down until he could get some strength back. The ice bucket was a few inches from his good hand.

He rolled slowly on the other side and inched across the floor until he got a grip on the handle and rose very slowly to his knees, his eyes darting fearfully in their sockets, his ears straining for any sound of warning. Pain warped his judgment.

He had to get out of the room. The door was behind him and perhaps six or seven feet away, lost in the haze. Gruber backed toward it, swinging the ice bucket in wide arcs, growling like a hurt animal.

The chop came from behind and separated his left shoulder. The ice bucket soared from his hand and hit the benches nearby. Ice showered down around him.

He was helpless, his left arm and right hand useless and needled with pain, his jaw hanging crookedly, his side swollen and red.

"You son of a bitch," he groaned hoarsely, partly in English, partly in German, "show yourself." But he was washed up and his nerves began to short-circuit and then everything went, and shaking uncontrollably, he collapsed against the bench.

From the other side of the room a voice said, in perfect English: "Be out of Japan by five tomorrow afternoon."

The Beretta, from out of the fog, slithered to his feet. The clip was gone.

Gruber heard the door open, felt the cold rush of air from across the room.

"Bon voyage," the voice said, and the door banged shut.

3

IT WAS FOUR-THIRTY in the afternoon and the news room was, as usual, the capital of Pandemonia. One of the editing machines was down and Mooney was getting a rubber ear from listening to all the complaints and excuses, and the phone rang and Mooney snatched it up and snapped, "Forget it!"

Eula, his secretary, wisely replied, "Unh unh."

And Mooney said, surprised, "Unh unh?"

And Eula said, "It's God."

Mooney groaned. "Aw shit!"

Just what he needed. God, of all people. The Hare Krishna of all Hare Krishnas, owner of the moon, the stars and the rest of the universe, as well as the Boston *Star,* five radio stations and three TV affiliates, including the one for which he, Harold Claude Mooney, was Director of the News Department. Not News Director. Director of the News Department. Big difference, especially at Channel 6 in Boston. God, otherwise known as Charles Gordon Howe, among other things, was a fanatic about chain of command and titles. To Howe the title was almost as important as the job. Howe had once explained this philosophy at a rare meeting of his executives: "People are immediately intimidated by titles. It takes them a while to size up a person. But the title, the title gets 'em every time. It says 'Here's the power,' bang, just like that."

Well, Howe had the title. The Chairman. Not chairman of the board. *The* Chairman. An hour and a half from showtime, ninety minutes until the daily Circus Maximus. The Six O'Clock News had a stick in his mouth and was staring down his throat and who's on the phone? The fucking Chairman.

He put a smile in his voice before he answered. "Mr. Howe? Hal Mooney here."

"Mr. Mooney, I know you're probably wishing some kind of strange voodoo curse on me for calling you right now, but I want five minutes of your time. Then I'll let you get back to work."

"Five minutes, sir? Okay, shoot."

"I want five minutes on Eliza Gunn. Sum her up for me. I'll time you."

"Right now? Are you starting the clock this minute?" Mooney said and chuckled, although he knew Howe was probably sitting on the other end of the line with a stop watch in his hand.

"Right now."

Mooney glanced idly at the clock over his office door, thought for a few seconds and started. "One of the best investigative reporters I've ever known. She uses it all, whatever it takes. She can be adorable if getting it takes adorable. She can also be serious if it takes serious, or funny if it takes funny, or heart-warming, or cold-blooded, or meaner than a goddamn cobra with tonsillitis, if that's what it takes. Point is, she gets it. She's Joe Namath his first year with the Jets. Every throw's gotta be a winner.

"The first thing comes to my mind is the cross-eyed tiger. She called it a hunch. I call it instinct, pure instinct, without which a reporter's a dancer with a broken leg.

"Thing is, it took me little while at first, y'know, to see it. At first I figure she's just cute, a little ditzy. I used her on light stuff.

"But that tiger story, that was a doozie. The rest of the stations were treating it as a humor piece, y'know, a kicker. I mean, what the hell, how else you gonna treat a story about a cross-eyed tiger named Betsy Ross who's getting her eyes uncrossed? So everybody gets stuff on the tiger going into the operating room and the doctor talking about the operation, like that. Then they split.

"Not her. She hangs in there. I even told her to leave the damn zoo. There was stuff fast-breaking all over town that day.

" 'I got a hunch,' she says.

" 'Whaddya mean?' I says.

" 'You know what a hunch is, for Chrissakes,' she says.

"I feel like a dodo. I got this five-foot, ninety-eight-pound twenty-two-year-old asking me do I know what a hunch is and me in the business—what, twenty years? Almost as long as she is old.

" 'Look,' I says, 'I got shit busting all over the place, I'm the news director, get your ass in the van and get over to—hell, I don't even remember where.

"Now, she's on staff maybe two, three months at the time, she's a goddamn receptionist before that, I'm the expert, she's nothin' short of an intern, so who's the boss, besides, what does she know, right?

"Wrong.

"She says, 'I don't trust these assholes'—she talks like a longshoreman by the by—and I says, 'What assholes?' and she says, 'The vets,' and I says, 'Isn't this like three expert tiger doctors they got out there?,' and she says, 'I don't give a shit if it's the top vet, he's got a funny look in his eye. Trust me.'

" 'Trust me'!

"I'm looking the Six O'Clock News dead in the eye three hours away and she wants to tie up a camera crew, herself and a van on a hot news day because the tiger doctor has a funny look in his eye.

"I make a little joke. I says to her, 'Not as funny as the look in the tiger's eye, ho, ho, ho,' and she gets pissed, starts giving me all this jazz about this tiger, how it's real valuable because it has white under the black stripes instead of yellow and how they're just doing the operation to make the tiger even more valuable and then the zoo's gonna sell it to some Arab king for some enormous amount of money and on top of that the vet's in for some big fee.

"A tiger, for God's sakes.

" 'Get your ass outa there now,' I says, and she says, I swear to God, she says, 'Bullshit!' And she kills the connection. Not only that, she leaves the damn phone off the hook and I'm ready to kill her and I'm dictating a memo canning her ass and at five-thirty she bombs in the door and the tiger is dead on the operating table and this big-time vet has fucked up royally and the zoo people are freaking out all over the place, and she's got this hotshot doctor with his balls hanging out trying to get off the hook explaining why the tiger died and all they were trying to do was fix its eyes, and there isn't another newsman within twenty miles and the next thing I know Cronkite's people are on the horn looking for a national pickup and we get more phone calls from that one goddamn story, for Chrissakes, than anything I can remember.

"That lady has instincts. And that's the name of the game. I have never argued with her since. And she's never let me down."

"She seems very good at finding people," Howe said quietly. "People who don't want to be found, that is."

"It's far from the first time. Take Tomatoes Garziola. Just before that mess between Garziola and the Feds blew up. In fact, she kind of fired the first shot in that war. An assistant DA named Flannagan had made some comments at a luncheon about Garziola and everybody was looking for him, except Garziola wasn't that anxious to be found.

"But Lizzie decided, by God she was gonna find him, so she pulled his package and was going through the stuff and found a reference to Garziola's mother. Lo and behold, it's the old lady's birthday. So she and a crew head down to Providence, which is where the old lady lives, and Lizzie cruises up to the door, and sure enough, there's Tomatoes with half a dozen of his gorillas, having dinner.

"Thing is, she kept calling him Tomatoes to his face. I mean, the last time anybody called Garziola Tomatoes to his face, they floated up under the Atlantic Street pier. Did you see the original tape? Here comes Garziola out of his old lady's front door with a look on his face would make the whole front line of the Dallas Cowboys wet their pants and he stares down at her and says, 'I don't pick on ladies, okay, particularly they don't weigh twenty pounds soakin' wet, but I could make an exception in your case, sister.'

"She looks up with that fifty-dollar smile, says, 'The DA, Flannagan, is making a fool of you, Mr. Tomatoes, I just thought you'd like to get your side of the story on the record,' and he starts laughing and he turns around to these four apes behind him, says, 'Mr. Tomatoes!,' and he's laughing so, of course they all start laughing, too, and then he says, 'Whaddya talkin' about?,' and she says, 'Mr. Flannagan has publicly accused you of graft and kickbacks and hijacking and even a little murder here and there,' and Garziola looks down at her again and says, 'Why, that little son of a bitch, on my mother's birthday, too,' and she says, real tough like, 'Yeah, on your mother's birthday,' and then without even a breath in between she says, 'Why do they call you Tomatoes?,' and the next thing you know, Garziola's sitting there on his mother's stoop telling her all about how it was on the docks in the old days when he was getting started and how they used to hold up off-loading the produce until the tomatoes were rotten and finally the owners started knuckling under and that's when they started getting a living wage and that is where the name Tomatoes came from.

"Forty-five minutes later he's still talking and then he puts the cork in the bottle and says, 'Look, little lady, when it comes to kickbacks and the old payola, the first one's got his paw out is that little *schmuck,* Flannagan. You want a story, I'll give you a story,' and his lawyer's standing there trying to shush him up and he's telling everybody get lost and he gives her book, chapter, verse on what turned out to be one of the juiciest scandals in years. I'm not saying she broke the story— I mean, in the long run it all had to come out—but we got it first, and that's the name of the game. Your papers got most of the mileage out of it, but you saw it first on Channel Six and she's the one started the river flowing. That time it took adorable . . .   She was adorable. See what I mean?"

"Sum her up in one word."

Mooney thought for a few moments. "Tenacious," he said.

"Thank you very much, Mr. Mooney."

"Anytime, sir. She's not in trouble, is she?"

"If she were, Mr. Mooney, she wouldn't be anymore. Not after that accolade. And by the way, congratulations on being number one in the ratings again this period."

"Thanks. Thanks a lot."

"Goodbye, Mr. Mooney. Thank you for your time."

Click.

Just like that. What in the hell was the old bastard up to? If he steals her away from me for some other station, Mooney said to himself, I think what I'll do, I'll go over his house and kill the son of a bitch.

II

She got off on four, a floor below the studio, and ran down the hall to the editing room. Eddie, the best editor at the station, was waiting for her. Good old reliable Eddie.

"You're a dream," she said and kissed him solidly on the top of his bald black head.

"Anytime. What've you got?"

"An exclusive interview with Jonathan Caldwell."

"Are you kiddin'?"

"It's all right there," she said, pointing to the video cassettes.

Eddie whistled softly through his teeth. "How in hell did you swing that?"

"I nailed him, Eddie. I've been following that cute little girl friend of his for four days, and today she led me right to him. What time is it?"

"Four forty-five."

"Shit, just a little over an hour . . . Okay, let's put together five minutes and I'll bend Tubby's arm to get the extra air time."

"Okay, but I better leave you a thirty-second outtake, just in case he holds you to your usual time. That way we won't have to make any last-minute cuts."

"He can't do that . . . this is a hot break. Everybody in town's been after Caldwell since he got indicted. And I've got him . . . exclusive."

"Hey, baby, you don't have to convince me. You got to convince Tubby Slocum."

By five-ten she had her show together and was ready to write the intro and close. She went up to the fifth floor and found Vicki, the floor manager, talking to a human mountain.

Tubby Slocum made even George look like a dwarf. He was six-four and weighed somewhere in the neighborhood of three hundred and fifty pounds, a great deal of it resting dead center. His enormous belly sagged over his belt, his pants hung as full as an Arab tent from his global stomach, his neck swelled out over a shirt that had to be opened three buttons down to accommodate it. His thinning hair, combed in strands from one ear to the other, was always damp with sweat, and when he spoke, his voice, squeezing up through that enormous hulk, wheezed out, like a chipmunk in a Walt Disney movie.

Slocum had inherited his bulk with his job. He had always been ample, but he had become obese in the past four years. Those who disliked him attributed his five-year tenure as producer of both the six and eleven o'clock news to the fact that he was a shameless sycophant to Raymond Pauley, the station manager. Fat or not, sycophant or not, he was still the toughest, hardest-driving and best news producer in Boston. Channel 6 had dominated both time slots since he took over. And as long as he stayed number one, Pauley didn't give a damn how fat he was.

Eliza looked up at him like Hillary appraising Mount Everest. "Tubby, I've got a hot one," she said.

"You always got a hot one, Lizzie. What is—"

"It's E-liza, Tubby."

"Right. So what's so hot?"

"I've got Jonathan Caldwell on tape. Five goddamn good minutes, Tubby . . ."

"Your spot's five minutes, kiddo," the big man said, walking laboriously toward the control room. "Not four fifty-nine or five-oh-one. Five minutes. Now, if you can run it without any intro and close—great."

"Listen to me, Tub. It's really strong stuff. I've got him saying that the only way to do business with the Arabs is through bribery. I've got him admitting to several flagrant violations of the Fed banking laws. He says he's a victim of the times and he says he expects to go to jail and that all the banks do the same thing and the Federal Reserve people are just making an example of him."

"Sounds like dynamite. You've got five minutes."

"Dammit, Tubby . . ."

"Hey, you got problems? I got a lot more, okay. I got three teenagers dead out in Lynn in a head-on, a former Secretary of State lost at sea on his sailboat, a Harvard doctor who thinks he can cure cancer with a mixture of prune juice and asparagus, and I haven't even started on what's going on outside Boston. You got five minutes, E-liza. Five." He held up five chubby fingers and vanished into the control room.

She called the editing room.

"Well?" Eddie asked.

"That son of a bitch."

"Four minutes on tape, right?"

"Yeah, I guess. I need at least thirty seconds to get in and thirty to get out of the interview."

"No problem, lady. We got two thirty-second options we can pull out."

"I hate to lose that stuff—where he's talking about being a victim of the times—but everything else is so good."

"Go write your stuff; it's twenty of. I'll edit the tape and get it on Max." Max was the nickname given to the computer that controlled all the tape feeds on a program.

"Thanks."

She went back to her office and started writing.

Ten minutes. There was never enough time. She scribbled out a first draft, threw it away, and started pecking out her intro and close on the typewriter.

The phone rang. It was the monitor typist. She needed copy.

"Two minutes," Liza barked and hung up.

She went back to the typewriter and finished the second draft.

The phone rang again. She snatched it up and said, "On the way," pulled the sheet out of the typewriter and ran down the hall to the crib setter.

"Sorry," she said.

The gal who set the type for the monitor was never in a hurry. "It's okay, you got the tag story, just before the editorial. I got plenty of time."

As Liza was leaving the room, a secretary called to her, "Phone call, Liza. It's urgent."

"Not now, Sally, it's two minutes to six. I can't take it, get a number, please."

"I think you'll want to take this one . . . it's Mr. Howe."

Charles Gordon Howe, two minutes before air time.

She went into Sally's office and picked it up. "Hello?"

"Miz Gunn, this is Charles Gordon Howe."

"Mr. Howe, it's less than a minute to air time and I've got a very hot story working and I really don't have time right now to—"

"I'm aware of the time. I wouldn't be calling if it wasn't a matter of urgency. It *is* my station, Miz Gunn."

"Right, Mr. Howe, but it's my career. Call me back at six thirty-one. Bye."

She started back out the door. "Thanks, Sal."

"Sister, you got more guts than a gladiator," Sally said.

Eliza headed for the studio.

III

It was out. He was going to fight. The Gunn interview would leave little doubt about that.

Caldwell stared out the window of his office, a bright, cheery room, its walls covered with abstract paintings, and watched the shells, thirty floors below and half a mile away, gliding across the placid Charles River, and his mind drifted back to one glorious day when he had helped row Harvard to an unexpected victory over Yale. But the dream passed quickly and he took off his suit jacket, pulled down his tie and wearily climbed the circular iron stairway that led to the penthouse apartment on the floor above.

He would write a statement and tell the whole story in his own words. For days he had been writing and rewriting it in his head. The allegations were false, but if the examiners dug deep enough, there were other things.

The penthouse was much warmer than Caldwell's office. Two bedrooms, two baths, a small kitchen and a large living room, with floor-to-ceiling windows that gave him an unrestricted view to the north, east and south. The apartment had been decorated by Tessie Caldwell, who knew her husband's taste well. The furniture was strictly antique, the drapes yellow and white. Plants abounded, and against the wall between the bedroom doors was the only painting in the room, a six-foot-high Jackson Pollock, its dizzying colors dominated by yellow. A secretary dating back to Daniel Webster stood near the sliding glass doors leading out to a wraparound balcony.

Caldwell was so engrossed in deep inner conflict that he did not see the visitors until the older one spoke: "Hello, Johnny, you had us worried."

The voice was soft, textured by the South but not of the South, a voice that Caldwell knew could be reassuring one minute and patronizing the next. It belonged to Senator Lyle Damerest, a grandfather of a figure with white hair that flowed down over the collar of his tweed jacket, a bow tie and a gnarled shillelagh to support a game leg from a slight and unpublicized stroke. He was the senior Senator from Virginia and the country's ranking congressman in terms of longevity. For thirty-one years he had represented his state. He had been on two Cabinets, was head of the Armed Services Committee, and had more back-room power than any living legislator. He was consulted on major issues by Democrat and Republican alike. Nobody, not even the President, would risk scorning Damerest.

The man with him was virtually nondescript: medium tall, medium heavy, blond, crew-cut hair, dark-gray suit, no distinguishing features. He held a zip-open briefcase under one arm.

"Ya needn't worry. We took the private elevator. No one saw us come up," the senator said.

"What the hell are you doing here?" Caldwell asked.

"I was a hop and a skip away. Somebody heard you'd surfaced and called me."

"No, I mean what're you doing in Boston?"

"Been up here for the last two days. On the q.t., been stayin' with friends. We've been worried about you."

"You said that. And who's 'we'? And who are you?" He looked at the nondescript man.

"This is Ralph Simpson. Federal marshal."

"How d'ya do, sir," Simpson said.

Caldwell nodded to him.

"He's got the subpoena," Damerest went on.

"What subpoena?"

"You've been subpoenaed to go in for questioning. No charges, yet. If they come, it'll be the Fed. Violation of the government banking statutes. What I'm tellin' ya, laddie, it can be avoided."

"Really?"

"All your friends are behind you, Johnny. I've talked to the boys on the banking committee and to the federal judge here. I think the way this can be handled, the judge will recommend that the entire matter be investigated by the House committee. The whole thing will blow over. Ya just need to bite the bullet for now." The old man smiled, but his flinty eyes narrowed.

"I don't think so," Caldwell said.

"Oh? And why not?"

"I don't intend to be a whipping boy."

" 'Whipping boy' is it!"

"That's the way it feels."

Damerest stood with his hands thrust deep in his pants pockets, his shoulders hunched up under his ears, leaning slightly toward Caldwell, as if about to make a point to the Ways and Means Committee. "Shit, son, you just got on the wrong side of the old farts on Wall Street. We can unruffle their feathers."

"The hell with 'em. They been down on First Common since my grandfather ran the show."

"I know, son. Your father and I were classmates together. He footed the bill for my first campaign. I couldn't of raised scratch feed without him."

Caldwell had heard the stories many times since he was a kid. "The bastards were after him, now they're after me. Besides, I didn't always agree with Dad, you know that. I won't put up with any heat right now. None of us can afford it."

The old senator smiled, that warm, grandfather smile that hid the heart of a vulture. Caldwell had watched him smile his way out of more than one tight spot. Now the old bastard was using it on him. "Easy," the senator said quietly. "They got your balls in the doorjamb for the moment."

"Bullshit. Why did it happen?"

"It got by me."

"Nothing gets by you, Lyle. Nothing this big."

"What can I say." The old man took out a red bandanna and wiped his forehead. "Good God, it's hot in here. You always keep it like this?"

"The housekeepers do that," Caldwell said. He slid open one of the glass partitions and a gust of cold air shook the drapes.

"Ah, better," the senator said. "Look, just take a peek at the papers Mr. Simpson brought along. It will be handled very quietly. You two can just go down to the Federal Building and . . ."

Simpson walked over to the antique secretary, opened his briefcase and reached inside.

"And how about you, Lyle?" Caldwell said.

"Hardly appropriate, me goin' along with ya. I can do a lot more, stayin' in the background."

Simpson had both hands in the zip-open briefcase. He unscrewed the cap of a small bottle and tipped its contents into a large ball of cotton he held in his other hand.

Damerest said, "I talked to Tessie. She seems to be handling it all very well."

Simpson took his hands out of the briefcase. The cotton ball was in one hand. He was directly behind Caldwell, who said, "She's used to character assassination. They did everything but burn her father at the stake."

Simpson stepped close to Caldwell, the hand with the cotton ball behind his back. The senator moved up close to Caldwell.

"I was very reassurin'," he said.

He moved suddenly, wrapping his arms around Caldwell, pinning the banker's arms to his sides and squeezing him sharply. Air rushed out of Caldwell's nose and mouth.

"What in hell—" Caldwell gasped, but he never finished the sentence. Simpson jammed the cotton against Caldwell's nose. As he gasped, the acrid odor of chloroform flooded through his head and dulled his brain. He began to thrash, to hold his breath.

The senator clutched him again, harder. Caldwell's breath gushed out. He gasped again. His brain was paralyzed. Damerest could feel him growing limp. He squeezed him again. Caldwell's eyes bulged and stared over the cotton swab, like those of a terrified animal. Then they went crazy, crossing, uncrossing, finally rolling up under the lids. As Caldwell sagged, Simpson grabbed him around the waist, twisted him sideways and dragged him through the open door to the balcony.

The show was three minutes old when the hot-line phone began flashing. Chuck Graves, the unflappable anchor man, was in the middle of the opening news segment. Eliza picked it up.

"This is Sid down in the news room. We got a hot flash—Jonathan Caldwell just took a Brodie off the First Common Bank building. He's all over Market Street . . . We got the Live Action truck on the way . . . that's all I know for now." The line went dead.

Liza sat like a statue with the phone frozen in her hand. She cradled the receiver quietly for a moment, then she slipped away from the set and ran out to the hallway, grabbed the hotline phone on the wall and dialed the editing room.

"Is Eddie still there? It's Eliza, tell him it's important . . . Eddie, listen to me—Caldwell just jumped off the bank building . . . I know, I know . . . Is it on the chain? Can you get it back long enough to drop those two thirty-second segments back in? . . . Don't worry, I'll take full responsibility . . . Eddie, you're a love . . ." She hung up and returned to the set.

They finished two more segments and were into sports before the news room called back and confirmed that it was definitely Caldwell. She gave it to Graves, who made that announcement at the end of the sports segment but he had little else to go with.

Perfect. She had all she needed.

In the booth, the assistant director was counting out of the sports slot. "Okay . . . ready Max . . . and three, two, one . . . and roll tape and kill camera three, kill Wally's mike . . . and camera three on Liza. Jeez, look at her—she'd look great in a garbage bag . . ."

"She's got the best ass in Boston," Tubby said wistfully.

"I'm talking about her face, Tubby— Thirty seconds, get in a bit tighter on Jackson . . . camera one on the weather map . . . lookin' good— You can't even *see* her ass, she's sitting down."

"You can sure see it when she stands up," Tubby said.

Liza was still scribbling notes to herself, changes she would make from the crib sheet she had already rewritten twice, part of it after she had turned the story in to be typed for the monitor. Her adrenaline was roaring. The AD's voice crackled in her ear: "Ready three on Liza and let me have a voice check on Liza . . ."

"Hi, my hair is green and my eyes are—"

"Good, and we have a one-minute cutaway and then back to you, Liza, and you have five minutes before the editorial. We're running about two seconds ahead right now . . . lookin' good . . . and okay, camera three . . . and four, three, two, one . . . you're on, Liza . . . and ready Liza's tape . . ."

She looked straight into the camera, leaning forward just slightly. "Good evening, this is Eliza Gunn with Hotline Report. At five-fifty-eight today, two minutes before we went on the air, Jonathan Caldwell, president and chairman of the board of the nation's second most powerful banking institution, fell or jumped to his death from the thirty-second floor of the bank his father started sixty years ago. At three o'clock this afternoon, two hours before his death plunge, I interviewed Jonathan Caldwell in a garage in Boston's North End, talking with him about the scandal that has brought his bank close to failure, and has brought disgrace to one of this country's most powerful business and political families . . ."

In the control room, the monitor girl said, "Man, she's nowhere near the script. She's really straying."

Tubby got restless. "Buck, tell the floor director to give her four, three and two minute time cues. If she goes over we'll lose the editorial and the Old Man'll chew my ass off."

"He'd die of old age before he could finish," Buck said and speared his finger into the floor director's mike button.

"Very funny," Tubby said. He walked to the control board and pressed the loudspeaker button: "Liza, cut your close in half . . . you went almost twenty seconds over on the intro."

Buck's voice came on again as Caldwell's interview rolled on the monitors: "Okay, we're coming up on thirty seconds on the tape. Remember, keep it short, Liza, we're very tight . . . And coming up on end of tape . . . four, three, two, one. What the hell, the tape's running long—"

"Cut it," Tubby cried.

"I can't cut it now, he's right in the middle of talking about— Wait a minute, here we go: Ready three . . . and ready . . ."

"Goddammit, god*damn*," Tubby bellowed. "We're already forty seconds over! I told her five minutes. Four for the tape and a thirty-second live shot going in and coming out. Pull the plug on her. Get her off there."

"I can't do that, she's right in the middle of her closeout," the AD said.

"I don't believe her," Tubby boomed.

"Kill the editorial?" the AD asked.

Tubby scratched his head frantically.

"Kill the goddamn editorial. I don't fucking believe her!"

"It's a good shot, Tubby."

"I don't give a doodly fuck if she's breaking World War III, I gave her five goddamn minutes and look at her . . . she's acting like she's doing a thirty-fuckin'-minute sitcom, fer Chrissakes."

"She's closing out now," the AD said. He shoved a button. "Chuck, we're right on it, so get out fast. And there she goes . . . now, four, three, two, and out . . . and take three, Chuck's mike . . ."

In the studio, Graves gave his usual confident smile. "And that's the news," he said. "Charles Graves, see you at eleven."

The AD flipped switches and sagged in his chair. "That's a wrap," he sighed into the mike.

"Goddammit!" Tubby Slocum bellowed. "I told her five minutes. Did you see the floor director give her a minute and then thirty seconds? She went right on. A minute and twenty-two seconds over. Goddammit!" He stormed out of the control room.

Liza gathered up her things and winked at Graves. "Nice," she said.

Graves smiled. He had been a newsman for twelve years and he knew a good news break when he saw one.

Tubby was waiting for her when she came out of the studio. He waddled along beside her as she took giant steps down the hall toward her office.

"Dammit," the fat man snapped, "I told you five minutes. I *stretched* to give you five minutes. Five . . . not six plus." His face was the color of a boiled lobster. "From now on when I tell ya—"

She stopped and Tubby had to catch himself to keep from running over her.

"Tubby?"

"Yeah?"

"Was it a good shot?"

"What's that got to—"

"Was it good or not?"

"That ain't the point. The point is, I'm the producer of this goddamn show. I can't have the talent running all over me—"

"Tubby?"

"What, fer Chrissakes?"

"Was it a good shot?"

"So it was a good shot. You know it was a good shot."

"Gave you a good show, didn't it?"

"Lizzie . . ."

"It's Eliza . . . E-liza. Bye."

She blew him a kiss and went into her office, kicking the door shut behind her.

"Ah, damn," Tubby said forlornly. As he turned toward the studio, he yelled back at her door, "Being a producer around here is like trying to direct a Broadway show full of deaf-mutes."

The phone was ringing when she entered the office. She dropped her clipboard and notes on the desk, took a deep breath, stared at the phone and lit a cigarette.

Well, shit, she thought, I can't avoid it.

She snatched up the phone. "Gunn here," she snapped.

"Very nice," the voice said. Howe's voice was a deep, quiet, paternal rumble. He never raised it and he rarely showed anger. He didn't have to.

"Look, Mr. Howe, I'm really sorry. I didn't mean to be rude . . ."

"My dear, I have been a newsman all my life. I didn't inherit this business, I started it. Myself. I know a good news story when I see one. Although I must say I am deeply sympathetic toward Johnny Caldwell. He was a good friend. That's not why I called, however. I have an assignment I'd like you to consider."

She tried to remain calm. Charles Gordon Howe, calling *her.* "An assignment?"

"Not in your regular line."

"You mean it will take me away from the show?"

"Yes."

"For how long?"

"That really depends a lot on you. Are you free right now? I'll have my car bring you over."

"Look, Mr. Howe, I've been doing investigative reporting for almost three years and I've got a good reputation. To leave the show now . . ." She let the sentence hang.

"Mmmm." The deep rumble. Seconds of silence. She was getting uncomfortable.

"I've been watching you very closely . . . May I call you Liza?"

"It's E-liza, but everybody does."

"All right, Eliza. I think you may be the best television reporter I've got. That's why I want to discuss this with you. Of course, there's a bonus in this—"

"It's not the money," she said quickly. "Well, I mean, of course money is important. It's just that, people forget you fast. Three months and they won't know who I am. How long will this take?"

"I'm not sure," Howe said. "What do you know about Francis O'Hara?"

"Frank O'Hara? The reporter?"

"The same."

"Uh . . . well, I know he was nominated for a Pulitzer Prize and passed over. He was in intelligence for several years before he became a reporter. Uh . . . he wrote that great series on the CIA for the Washington *Post* a couple of years ago—"

"Not bad," Howe interrupted.

"I didn't know it was a quiz," she said.

Howe chuckled. "Ray Pauley told me you were a feisty one," he said.

"What about O'Hara?" she asked.

"Let's settle the question of the bonus. What do you want?"

"I don't know the job."

"Let's say . . . You'll be off the air for two months. What do you feel is an equitable agreement for two months of air time?"

"I want a shot at New·York . . . or Washington."

"You think you're ready for New York—or Washington?"

"I know it."

"Pauley doesn't want to lose you."

"You asked me, Mr. Howe. Don't you think I'm ready?"

"Okay, we can talk about it."

Eliza swallowed hard. Just like that, a shot at New York. But what did she have to do for it? "So . . . what about Frank O'Hara?"

"I want you to find him and deliver a message for me."

"Find him?" She laughed. "Is he lost?"

"Precisely, Eliza. He's been on the run. The CIA's been trying to kill him for almost a year now."

4

KINUGASA-YAMA IS A GENTLY SLOPING MOUNTAIN on the northern edge of the vast Park of the Shoguns in Kyoto. Along its peak are rows of delicate pine trees, and when the wind is from the west and the pines sway before it, the mountain has the appearance of a lion with a great shaggy mane crouched beside the park as if to protect this, the most venerable place in Japan.

A half mile to the south of the mountain is Tofuku-ji, the tallest and most sacred Shinto shrine in the country. It towers five stories, each story with a roof curved delicately toward heaven, each rooftop representing an element—earth, wind, fire, water and air—and a spire, whose nine rings carved into its shaft represent the nine rings of heaven.

It has been said that the rock garden which lies between Tofuku-ji the Ryoan-ji temple nearby is the most perfect stone garden in existence and is exactly the same today as it was in the fifteenth century, when it was designed by Shinto priests.

The place was deserted except for an old man who was stooped over a long-handled rake, carefully cleaning and resetting each pebble in the stone garden. He did not look up as Eliza hurried past.

A light spring rain had fallen earlier in the morning, but it had stopped and now a chilly west wind ruffled the mane of Kinugasa-yama. She hurried through the park, afraid to take even a minute to enjoy its beauty. Kimura had promised to meet her at eleven-thirty, and it was now twenty-five after. She was keyed-up, for the first time since her plane had landed at Honeda Airport a week before.

She had been on the scent for seven weeks now. Her time was running out. She had called, written or traveled halfway around the world in these past seven weeks, had tracked O'Hara to the Caribbean, to Mexico, as far south as Buenaventura, Colombia, and east to Recife, Brazil. He had doubled back to Maracaibo, then returned to the States. She had followed a cold trail west to Seattle, from there to Vancouver and then back south again to San Francisco.

His trail was thin, devious and maddening. He had changed names half a dozen times; in South America it had been Solenza; in Canada, Carnet; on the West Coast, Barret. She had used the Howe empire's contacts with the customs bureau, the passport office and half a dozen major airlines. Twice she had lost the scent, only to pick it up elsewhere. She tracked down old friends, newspaper buddies, retired intelligence agents, even an old girl friend or two.

It was like talking about a ghost. His friends were mutely loyal. His enemies seemed to have given up the trail. But Gunn could be ferocious in her persistence. It had paid off with bits and pieces of information. As the trail lengthened, cross-crossed, disappeared and reappeared, her dossier on him grew fatter. And yet, after seven weeks, she felt she knew little more than what was on paper.

Basics. Period.

She had memorized every line, waiting for some incidental bit of information that might intersect what she already knew and provide a valuable clue.

Francis Xavier O'Hara: Born San Diego, December 21, 1944. Father: vice admiral in U.S. Navy who had two destroyers blown out from under him by kamikaze at Okinawa. Stationed briefly at San Diego in early 1944. Mother: Ph.D. in languages and history, Cambridge. Died when O'Hara was fourteen. Father commanding officer, U.S. Naval Station, Osaka, Japan, for five years until retirement; remained in Japan after retiring until his death in 1968. O'Hara graduate of American high school, Osaka, 1963; University of Tokyo (majors: languages and history), 1967; graduate degree, Oriental philosophy, 1968. Trained in kendo, tai chi, karate and Shinto discipline. Hobbies: scuba diving, karate, kendo, chess, cross-sticks, and dogs, particularly akitas, probably because they are native to Japan. Nickname: called Kazuo, by Japanese friends. Enlisted U.S. Navy as ensign, 1968; assigned naval intelligence and reassigned to the CIA, 1970; specialty: counterespionage, also involved in covert actions. Resigned 1975. Free-lance writer specializing in investigative reporting, 1976 until 1978. Went underground soon after publishing series for the Washington *Post* on CIA illegal covert operations in Africa, Asia and the Caribbean.

There were some personal references—from teachers, former shipmates, fellow agents, friends, two women he had lived with briefly at different times. There was also hat size, 7; shoe size, 10; weight, 162; height, 5'10"; hair, sandy; eyes, green. No scars. The usual things that pop up in a computer analysis.

Basics.

Yet the more she learned, the more determined she was to find him.

Then the break came. It was the dog that did it.

She had interviewed some old friends of O'Hara's in San Francisco, Don Smith, a managing editor of the San Francisco *Chronicle,* and his wife, Rose, who was with the ballet company. They were cordial, but had not seen or heard from O'Hara in a couple of years. They were much more excited about their new puppy. A gift from a friend. It was an akita.

Her instincts hummed. She checked the American Kennel Club. She was interested in acquiring an akita. Could they tell her the breeder of the Smiths' dog?

Yes, but it would take a few days.

Then she got word from the kennel club. The dog had been bred in

Kyoto. The sire's name was Kazuo. The name plucked a nerve. She went back to her notes. Kazuo was O'Hara's Japanese nickname. The owner of the dog was listed as Akira Kimura. Kyoto was almost a suburb of Osaka, where O'Hara had spent most of his youth.

She had catnapped her way across the Pacific, trying desperately to scan a Fodor's guide to Japan and an English/Japanese dictionary. She had been tired when she left San Francisco and by the time she landed in Tokyo, ten hours later, she was exhausted; wracked with jet lag, sick of bad food, weary from lack of sleep and piqued with frustration.

What the hell was she doing there? In a strange land she knew nothing about, staying in a *ryokan*, a traditional Japanese hotel, rather than a big American spread. Thousands of miles from home. Alone. And chasing a ghost.

Terrific, Gunn, way to go. Little wonder O'Hara had eluded a dozen or more money-hungry assassins. He was as elusive as a dream. A bad dream at that.

If O'Hara was alive, and at this point she really wasn't too sure about that, he had to be here. She felt it. It was the only place left in the world where he might find sanctuary.

She made the first of nine phone calls to Kimura on a Tuesday. Kimura was a Japanese professor who had taught philosophy and martial arts at the American School. It took several phone calls to learn that he was now a Shinto master and that he lived in Kyoto. There was a phone number where she could leave a message. But, she was told, Kimura-san was strange, sometimes he did not return phone calls.

When he finally called back on Thursday morning, she said, "I am interested in acquiring an akita. Some friends have a puppy they got from you. The Smiths in San Francisco?"

He was abrupt. "I have no friends in San Francisco. It is a mistake."

"They got the dog from you, according to the kennel club."

There was a long pause, and then: "Miss Gunn, you are not interested in a dog."

She was flustered by his honesty. Then she decided to be honest too. "Please—*dozo*—I am a journalist with an American television station. I am trying to find Frank O'Hara. We are peers, O'Hara and I."

"O'Hara-san has many peers, but his friends are fewer than the months of the year," the voice on the other end of the line said. It was a soft voice, almost a whisper—his English perfect, his diction impeccable—and yet she felt intimidated by it.

"I have good news for him. Please see me, talk to me?"

"I have heard the same story before. There is one difference, however. You are a woman. They have never sent a woman before."

"Please, just talk to me. If you don't believe me, you've only lost an hour or so of your time."

"I have not said I even know his whereabouts. I was one of his teachers in high school. That was . . ." He hesitated a moment, trying to remember.

". . . seventeen years ago," she said. "He graduated the summer of 1963."

"*Hai.* And I am over seventy. I doubt that I can be of help."

"*Dozo,* Kimura-san. I am desperate. Just have tea with me. I will convince you I'm sincere."

"You have a *denwa* in your room?"

"*Hai.*"

"And the number?"

"Uh . . . it's 82-12-571."

"I will call you back. *Konnichi wa.*" The line went dead.

"Well, damn," she said and hung up. She went to the window and slid the panel back and watched a young gardener, his hair tressed in a *tenugui* headband, raking the sand garden outside her room, picking up every leaf and twig until the beige island surrounded by moss was spotless. He worked soundlessly and seemingly without effort. She stared back at the phone. Her shoulders ached and she felt like going down to the *ofuro* to take a bath, but she was afraid she would miss his call. Eliza had overcome her modesty in the public bath very early in the trip. Now she found that the hot waters not only were rejuvenating but cleared her mind and helped her think.

A half-hour passed, and nothing. She fluffed up the *futon* quilt and lay down, but her mind was much too busy for napping.

When the phone finally did ring, she snatched it up before the second bell. "Yes . . . this is Eliza Gunn."

"Miss Gunn, this is Dr. Kimura. I will meet you but the time will be short. And it must be today. Can you leave now?"

"Yes. Right this minute."

"The train station is ten minutes west of the Hishitomi Ryokan. You may take the local train from the *eki* on the San'in Main Line and get off at the Hanazano station. From there it is only a few blocks to the Tofuku-ji temple. I will meet you at the hall of the Ashikaga shoguns next to the temple. It is now nine forty-five. Eleven-thirty should give you ample time."

"Thank you," she said sincerely. "*Arigato . . . arigato* very much."

"You have nothing to thank me for yet, Gunn-san. *Sayonara.*"

"*Sayonara,* Dr. Kimura."

The gardener, who had worked his way to the shrubs outside Eliza's room, turned abruptly and left the courtyard. He went down the hall and knocked on a door. A big man with a beard opened it. "What's happening, Sammi?" he asked.

The gardener went in. "She's leaving now," Sammi said, changing into his black jogging suit and sneakers.

"Good," the big man said. "I'll give her a few more minutes." Sammi worked quickly but he was not worried about losing her. He knew where she was going. When she left the hotel he was in a pachinko parlor nearby. He watched her go by and waited several more minutes before leaving. He was more interested in the man who was following her.

II

During the twenty-minute ride from Osaka, Eliza leafed idly through one of her travel books, but she had the attention span of an amoeba. Was Kimura leading her on? Or was she coming close to the end of almost two months of hard work? The Japanese countryside flashed by, a dizzying patchwork of lush green farms separated by mini-forests. She knew very little about Kyoto, except that it had been the capital of Japan during the rule of the shoguns, which lasted for a thousand years, and that many Westerners believed it to be the most beautiful city in the world. But she paid little attention to its beauty as she rushed through the giant arched *torii* at the park entrance. She could see Tofuku-ji, rising above the other pagodas, and she ran toward it. Statues of shogun warriors crouched in the shadows of the curved eaves of the temples and lurked under cedar and pine trees. The grounds and stone gardens were immaculately manicured and every building, every tree and pond and garden, seemed perfectly placed and in tune with nature. The rain clouds had passed, now, and soft sunlight bathed the heart of the park.

When she reached the garden of the Tofuku-ji, the grounds were deserted and quiet. A breeze rattled gently through the cedar and fir trees. Somewhere, from inside one of the buildings, she heard the soft ping of wind bells. A fish jumped in one of the ponds. Then it was silent again.

The hall of the shoguns was a small, dark, forbidding hall near the main temple, a startling and strange place, out of context with the peaceful aura of the rest of the park. It was as if they were there to guard the integrity of the place, two long rows of wooden statues, the Ashikaga shoguns, sixteen of them, seated facing one another, their fierce glass eyes aglow in the dim light. She walked timidly into the place, squinting her eyes to get accustomed to the dark, peering nervously from one row to the other as she walked down the highly polished wooden floor, her heels clacking hollowly until she finally rose on her tiptoes and hurried to the other end of the room. She was relieved when she got outside. She stood under the curved pagoda roofs of the Tofuku-ji, wondering whether it would be sacrilegious to smoke.

Behind her, inside the darkened hallway of warriors, there was movement. A man stepped from behind one of the statues, his mean eyes glowing almost as fiercely as the agates in the faces of the statues. He moved closer, then stopped finally and waited, as still as the statutes that protected him. A man was approaching her from the other side of the stone garden. He stepped farther back into the shadows.

He was an ancient Japanese man, erect and proud, his delicate beard and wispy hair the color of snow, his skin almost transparent with age, as if cellophane had been wrapped around his fragile bones to keep them together. He wore a traditional kimono of dark-blue silk, *zori* sandals, a wide, flat thatched hat that looked like a platter, and he was carrying an umbrella, which he used as a cane. He came to her silently, as if his footsteps left no mark behind them. He stopped in front of her. He was taller than she had imagined he would be and he stood for a moment looking down at her.

"Well, Gunn-san, you do not appear very dangerous."

"Me? Dangerous?" She laughed. "I just ran through that museum of statues over there like a four-year-old running in the dark."

She knew Japanese businessmen were sticklers about exchanging business cards and she offered him hers. Kimura looked at it for a moment and put it away in the folds of his kimono. "I am sorry, I do not have a card," he said. He gazed down at her through fading brown eyes, and added, "You are certainly prettier than the others who have come looking for Kazuo."

"Believe me, I am Eliza Gunn and I work for WCGH in Boston and I have come because I am a friend of O'Hara's."

"Ah? And how long have you known O'Hara-san?"

She chewed the corner of her lip. "Well, I really don't know O'Hara. Personally, I mean. I know a lot about him, though. I have a message for him, a letter from Charles Gordon Howe. He is one of the most respected men in journalism."

"I know of Howe. It is rumored he is honest."

"Thanks for that, anyway."

"It proves nothing."

"If he will just meet me, I can tell him whom to call to verify the letter."

"I have not said I know the whereabouts of O'Hara, your friend."

"Okay, so I exaggerated. But if you did know how to get in touch with him, you could tell him it's important to see me, right?"

They walked along the bank of one of the many ponds in the park. The chill wind blew across the water, forming mist that swirled among the mossy rocks at its edge.

"Even if I knew where O'Hara-san was, I would use caution in repeating anything to him," Kimura said. "When a blind man leads a blind man, they are both in danger of falling in the river."

"Supposing I told you the sanction has been lifted. That he's no longer in danger."

The old man made no sign of surprise. He said, "In the Shinto philosophy there is a saying: 'The man who faces a chasm in front and behind must sit and wait.' To take a false step in a time of danger is to invite disaster."

"But I'm telling you, the danger is gone."

"It will take much proof. The one they call Fuyu-san, the Winter Man, has the heart of a weasel and the tongue of a crow. I would trust a cobra first."

"But that's the point. The Winter Man has been neutralized. He's impotent now. It's Mr. Howe who is making the assurance."

"An improvement."

"So I have to convince you first, is that it?"

"Since I am to be the parrot, you must first teach the parrot to talk."

Eliza stopped and stared up at the old man for several seconds. "I think I got that one," she said. "But I'm not real sure. I'll tell you the truth, I'm having a little trouble with your epigrams. Can't you just say what you mean straight out?"

Kimura laughed and then nodded. "My own grandson once asked me the same question. The difficulty lies in trying to interpret the symbolism of our words into the definitiveness of yours. Is 'definitiveness' a good word?"

"Sounds okay to me," she said. "I'm still not sure I get the point."

Kimura stopped. His eyes were warmer, but still wary. "The wise man speaks his truth in symbols. It is your choice to interpret what he says." He looked back at her. "What is truth to me is not necessarily truth to you."

The sun slipped behind a cloud and the wind grew colder. She rubbed her hands together and shook a chill off her shoulders.

"Are you cold?" he asked her.

"A little."

"Come. The Shokin-tei is nearby. Many believe it is the loveliest tearoom in Japan."

He led her away from the main temple, across the manicured lawns and over a short footbridge to a one-story building with a thatched roof and vermilion walls. Inside, the place was spotless, its lacquered floors covered with tatamis. They left their shoes at the door and sat cross-legged on *zabuton* cushions beside a low table. The room was a model of stark beauty. Its sliding glass doors were open and facing the park, and the only decoration was a *tokonama* just big enough for a scroll painting and a bowl of flowers. The room was cool but comfortable. A waitress appeared and took their order. There was no one else in the teahouse.

"So, you know a lot about O'Hara, eh?" he said.

"I've studied nothing else for almost two months," she said, and recited the litany.

"I do not mean to offend you, Gunn-san, but you do not *know* O'Hara, you know *about* O'Hara. To catch a wolf, you must understand a wolf."

"There you go again."

The waitress padded back with their tea and left as silently. Eliza waited until she was gone before continuing the conversation. "His friends won't talk about him and his enemies don't know anything to talk about," she said.

"That is good to know."

"Then how can I learn anything about him?"

"You know he came here as a youth. You do not know that he was very difficult at first. What we call *chiisai*. It would mean in America 'small knives.' One who is of the street gangs. The first year was very difficult. But I was persistent and we became friends and after that, Kazuo was like an empty bucket waiting to be filled."

"And you filled the bucket."

"I merely provided the water. He filled the bucket."

"You were his teacher."

"One of them. I showed him the way. He learned very quickly. He became a master of tai chi and then went on to *higaru,* which is a very difficult form of mental discipline and protective movement. I have seen him stand in the position of the bird, on one leg, for six hours without moving or blinking an eye. He reached the ultimate degree of *higaru,* which is known as *higaru-dashi.* It is difficult to translate precisely. I think you would call it . . . the Dance of the Vipers. And I have seen him achieve the no-mind state in a few seconds by simply listening to the sound of the wind."

"The no-mind state?"

"It is a Zen exercise, a form of meditation that cleanses the mind and frees one of all thought. It is achieved by concentrating on a distinct sound. A bell, perhaps, or a self-spoken mantra. For some, the process can take hours. O'Hara-san can achieve no-mind in seconds by concentrating on any sound, even the fiddling of a cricket. When he achieves that being, he can memorize entire pages of a book by simply staring at them. They become paintings in his mind."

"We call it a photographic memory."

"Excuse me . . . *dozo* . . . a photographic memory is a gift of birth. The no-mind must be learned. O'Hara does not merely learn, he becomes a master. And still the bucket is not full."

"He sounds like some kind of mystic."

"He is simply a man of honor who has learned that the wise man seeks everything within himself. The ignorant man takes everything from others."

"I call that instinct."

Kimura thought about that for a few moments and said, finally, "An oversimplification."

"This is very frustrating," she said. "After all this time, too. What I bring is good news."

"Or the cleverest trap of all."

"Believe me, I'm not very clever, and a trapper I definitely am not."

"Let me explain it another way. You see that stone garden over there. It was designed by Buddhists over four hundred years ago. Everything in it has meaning, the way the stones are arranged, the way they are raked, the placement of the big rocks, what we call stone boats. Only a small part of them is showing, the rest is below the ground, so we can only imagine what is there. I want to believe what I see and hear, but I must not ignore what is imagined."

Eliza's shoulders sagged. "All right," she said, "suppose I show you the documents. That should prove he's a free man."

"But you say these papers are only for the eyes of Kazuo."

"I came to deliver a message to O'Hara," she said. "If I must show you the letters first, then that's what I'll do."

"That would appear logical."

He sipped his tea and delicately placed the cup back on the saucer. "This must be a very powerful man, this one with the message for O'Hara."

"That he is."

He finished his tea and dabbed his lips, and, very abruptly, he stood up. "You will be at your *ryokan* later today?"

"Yes, yes!"

"I must think about this, Gunn-san. You have a quality I admire. You are naïve. It will help in the thinking. *Sayonara.*" He bowed and turned and left the tearoom.

"Well, what am I supposed to do," she called after him, "just sit and wait?"

He waved his umbrella at her without turning. "A disease can be cured," he called out. "Fate is incurable."

"Oh hell," she said, "just what's that one supposed to mean?"

But he was gone.

The day had turned warm and pleasant and, with the Kimura ordeal behind her, she strolled back to the *eki,* stopping along the way for a snack, ordering a bowl of *soba,* a kind of buckwheat noodle popular all over Japan, managing her chopsticks like an expert. Now, as she opened the door to her room, she felt for the first time that maybe, just maybe, she would find the elusive O'Hara.

She knew something was wrong before she went in, so she entered the room cautiously. It was as if someone were there with her. But she could see the entire room from the door. The closet doors were open, as was the door to the lavatory.

She checked outside. A gardener was weeding the lawn in the rectangle formed by the one-story inn. *"Shitsurei shimasu,"* she said.

He looked up and smiled. He was young, and very good-looking, a strange combination of the East and West, with his *tenugui* headband and his Adidas sneakers. She got her Berlitz translation book, and very carefully pronouncing each word, asked him if he spoke English: *"Eigo o hanashimasu ka?"*

He shook his head.

"Aw, forget it," she said and went back inside.

She decided it was a delayed reaction to all the excitement. Just a little paranoia, and why not. It had been one crazy day. She needed to go down to the *ofuro* and relax in a hot bath. Then she saw the suitcase lying on the bed.

It wasn't there when you left, Gunn, old girl.

The maid, perhaps?

Then why is it open?

She went over and lifted the top very gingerly. The O'Hara file lay on top, very neat, but not where she had left it. And on top of it, a slip of paper. The message said:

Give this to the taximan, he will take you to the proper place. Leave at 7:30. It will take 30 minutes. Go to the pier at the rear of the ground floor. Red Dragon Fireworks. 8 p.m.

The address was spelled out in calligraphy.
Swell.

III

Kimura walked slowly through the park, past the topaz gardens and the Zen pools, which were marvelously lush and green, even this early in the spring, and headed toward the city. A priest from the Tenryu-ji temple on Mount Hiei scurried by, taking the path down through a stand of tall Japanese cypress trees, setting off on a lonely vigil, the Walk of a Thousand Days, one which the Zen Buddhists believe would grant him special powers. A thousand days of austerities which the Buddhists believed would reveal to them the secret powers of Zen.

Kimura remembered his vigils well. Three times he had done the Walk of a Thousand Days, and even now he could remember those lonely times vividly. The last was just after his wife had died. He was fifty-five at the time and had walked almost a thousand miles in the three years he was gone, begging at doorways for his meals, as is the custom. The mystical journey had eased the hurt of her death.

He remembered her constantly, and the things he loved most in the world still reminded him of her: their grandchildren; the great temple of Kinkaku-ji, where they had met, and which had since been burned to the ground by a mad Buddhist monk; the giant weeping cherry tree in Maruyama Park under which he had asked her to be his wife; and the gold-and-silver Lotus Sutra scroll, which contains the fundamental text of the Tendai, the definitive teachings of Buddha, and where he had spent three days in meditation before becoming a Master of the *higaru-dashi.*

This park was full of sweet memories, and as he walked through the giant *torii* and left it, he dedicated his happy thoughts to the gods.

He walked past the sprawling International Hotel and the American Culture Center to the Gion district, two miles away. This was the old world, the world he loved. The alleys were narrow and spotlessly clean and bordered by high bamboo fences, the shops were true to the architecture of the sixteenth and seventeenth centuries. Here, among the people he knew best in the world, the Kyoto dialect had not yet been bastardized, and there was harmony in the symmetry of the houses and among the people who lived in them.

He did not go straight home. He turned instead and walked down a bamboo-walled alley to a house that sat back from the rest of the homes on the street. It was a handsome structure, two hundred years old and perfectly preserved, its handmade latticework oiled and shiny.

The owner of the house was known as Mama Momo, Mother Peach, because her complexion was still smooth, unwrinkled and unblemished despite the storms of sixty-odd years. Kimura had known Mama Momo since the year after his wife died; she was an old friend, and an understanding one. He came to the house twice a week, and each time he brought her 5,112 yen, which is $22.54, in a rice paper bag that was hand-painted by an artist in one of his kendo classes. And each time she would wait until he went to the back before she opened the bag and counted the money.

He walked down the hall to the rear of the house and entered a room which was decorated with chrysanthemums, and with sprigs of plum and cherry blossoms. The house was built in a rectangle with its rooms facing a stone garden in the courtyard. Kimura sat on a tatami, stared at the single stone boat near its center and waited.

How much of Eliza's story was true, he wondered, and how much was hidden from view? Was she what she seemed? Kimura's instincts told him to trust her, but looking at the stone boat, he was forced to consider the possibility that she, too, had come to kill O'Hara.

His thoughts were interrupted by a young girl, no more than twenty, who entered the room with a tray of oils and knelt beside him. She bowed and then smiled at him and ran her fingertips down his cellophane cheeks. Kimura took her other hand in both of his and smiled back.

"Ah," he said, in the dialect of Kyoto, "Miei, my favorite."

She giggled and answered in the same dialect, "We are all your favorites, Tokenrui-san." She knelt behind him and slipped off her kimono. Her voice was a bird's, soft and melodic, and she began to caress his chest and shoulders.

There was a knock on the door. Kimura sighed and leaned back on his arms. The girl put the kimono back on.

"Who is it?" he asked.

"It's me."

"*Dozo.*"

A big man slid the paneled door open, left his shoes beside the door and entered the room. He was a shade over six feet tall, Caucasian, with a great shock of black hair, a full beard and slate-gray eyes. He bowed to Tokenrui-san and sat cross-legged in front of him. Miei slipped behind the old man and began massaging his shoulders.

The big man, too, spoke in the dialect of old Kyoto. "Sorry to disturb you," he said.

"I have plenty of time."

"You met the girl?"

"Yes."

"And?"

"I found her refreshingly exuberant and naïve for a Westerner."

"In what way?"

"A certain desperation to get the message to you. But death was not in the desperation. There was . . . innocence? I played some games with her. Reciting abstractions as if they were written in the Tendai. By now she probably thinks everyone in Japan over fifty speaks like a bad American movie."

"But you trust her?"

"Ah, an interesting question. Let us say I am willing to convey her message to you. I am not sure I am willing to advise you to listen."

"I read the correspondence in her room. There are two letters. One from the Winter Man lifting the sanction. The other from Howe, verifying its validity. There is also a document from a man named Falmouth in which he swears under oath that the Winter Man offered him twenty thousand dollars to carry it out."

"So, it would seem her story is true."

"There's a catch," O'Hara said.

"Ah?"

"She's got a shadow."

"Anybody known to us?"

"No. In fact, judging from his manner, I would say he is not even of the Game. He acts more like an American gangster."

"What else?"

"He is large, with a bullethead and little pig ears. They are so small, they're almost a deformity."

"And this man, Little Ears, he followed her?" Kimura asked.

"He watched your meeting from the hall of the Ashikaga shoguns. Sammi stayed with him the entire time."

"Hmm. If it is a trap, does it not seem likely she would have told him where she was going so he could go ahead?"

"Yes," O'Hara said. "Unless they are even more clever than we imagine."

Kimura looked back at the stone boat in the garden for a few moments and nodded. "That is an option," he agreed. "Have you arranged to meet her later?"

"Yes, at the old place in Amagasaki."

"And you will be there ahead of them?"

"Right. Unless she gives him the address first."

"You will know if they are partners. She will tell him where the meeting place is and he will go ahead. If he stays behind her, get between them and force him to make a desperate move. If he does, you will know."

"One other thing. I have checked out her papers. She is what she says she is."

"By tonight you will know. This is the first time I have had any feeling about those who have been sent here. I like the young woman. I hope she is what she appears."

"Either Sammi or I will call you after it's over."

"I will be waiting."

The big man got up and went to the door. He looked back at Kimura and Miei and chuckled. "You certainly have a way with the young ladies. What's your secret?"

"I tell them if they make love to an old man, the gods will add many years to their life."

"And . . ."

"And they believe me."

IV

They drove south on the Kobe highway, around the sweeping curve of the bay until, looking back over her shoulder, on what was an uncommonly clear night, she could see the lights of the big industrial plants and shipyards of Osaka harbor.

The trip along the waterfront into a rowdy little village between Osaka and Kobe, its streets teeming with sailors and workers in hard-hats, took less than half an hour. They were in what appeared to be the red-light district. The driver, an elderly man who muttered a lot to himself, guided the Honda through the heavy pedestrian traffic, entered a narrow, winding street, ablaze with neon calligraphy, pachinko parlors and strip joints, and then turned into an even narrower alley.

The driver stopped in front of a tattoo parlor, twenty or so feet from the main street. He turned to her. "Missu sure about numba?" he asked. "Thisu no prace you go." He checked the piece of paper and shook his head. "Thisee bad place all over."

"How much?" she asked. *"Ikura desu ka?"*

He told her the fare and continued shaking his head as she counted it out. "No good bah, no good bah," he repeated several times."

"Yeah," she said. "It's getting to be the story of my life. I've been in every no good bah between here and Rio de Janeiro. *Arigato,* old buddy."

"Wanna me wait?" he asked.

She brightened. There was a sense of security in knowing somebody in the country was looking out for her.

"Hai. Domo arigato," she said. "I'll just check." She got out and went into the tattoo parlor. The operator was naked from the waist up. He was a short man with an enormous belly and his head was shaved, except for a tuft at the back, which was tied in a pony tail. The man he was working on was covered with tattoos. Hardly an inch of skin on his torso and arms had escaped the needle.

"Uh, anybody speak English?" Eliza asked timidly.

The tattooist stared at her without expression, grunted and went back to work. The needle hummed and the customer jumped as it touched his back.

"Speak Engrish a riddle bit," the tattooed man said.

"I'm looking for the Red Dragon Fireworks office," she said. "It's supposed to be here, in this building."

"Fiewooks?"

"Fireworks. Firecrackers. You know, boom, boom." She made a giant imaginary mushroom with her arms.

"Ah." He nodded and smiled and pointed toward the floor.

"Downstairs? Uh . . . *shita ni?"* she asked.

He nodded again. "Crosed up."

"Crosed up?"

He pantomimed closing a door and locking it.

"Oh, closed up. For the night? Uh . . . *nasai?"*

The tattooed man shook his head. "Alee time."

"Forever? For good?"

"Hai."

Great, Gunn. Down an alley in the middle of Shit City, Japan, and the store's closed. Any other bright ideas?

"*Domo arigato,*" she said, with a tiny bow.

"*Do itashimashite,*" he answered.

She went back outside and walked to the doorway beside the tattoo parlor. There was a red sign beside the door with gold letters, but it was in calligraphy. A light gleamed feebly inside. She tried the door. It was open. She cracked it a few inches and stuck her face up to the opening.

"Hello? Whoever you are? Are you there?"

She pushed it open a little more and went in. There was a small anteroom followed by a flight of stairs. Nobody had used this building for a very long time; refuse littered the anteroom and the steps. She walked to the head of the steps and yelled down: "Hello! Anybody there?"

Still nothing. Another weak lamp glimmered on the end of a chord hanging from the ceiling at the foot of the staircase.

Well, the note said to go down to the pier on the first floor. Let's do it, Gunn.

She started down the stairs.

Across the street, the man with the little ears stepped from a doorway. He had watched her get out and enter the tattoo shop. Now the cab driver was watching the building she had entered. He would be a nuisance. Little Ears strolled across the alley and approached the taxi from the driver's rear. As he got to the window, the driver turned and looked up at him. Little Ears struck him with his right hand, a short, straight blow with the fingertips, just below the ear. The cab driver's head jerked against the headrest, and his mouth fell open. A moment later, he crumpled in the seat.

Little Ears approached the building cautiously. The window in the front door was haloed with dust. He made a small circle with his hand and looked in. The Gunn woman was at the foot of the steps. She turned into a hallway and went out of view. Little Ears quietly entered the building.

The place was scary. Eliza found herself in a long grim narrow hallway. At the far end she could see a door hanging awkwardly from its hinges, and beyond it, the bay. A foghorn bleated far off in the darkness someplace and was answered by another, from even farther away.

She walked about halfway down the hall and stopped. There were sounds all around her: water slapping at pilings; the creaking of old wood; and somewhere in front of her in the darkness, a rat, squealing and skittering across the floor. Squinting down into the darkness, she said to herself, You're not walking down there, Gunn. There is no way you are going one step farther.

"Hello?"

Nothing.

I'm not going another inch. I don't think this is funny at all.

A door opened at the far end of the corridor and yellow light flickered on the floor. She walked a little closer. The sounds surrounded her now. The stairs behind her, creaking with age; the dock, groaning with the tide.

She was nearly at the doorway when a hand grabbed her from behind. It squeezed her mouth shut. She felt cold metal against her throat. She tried to scream, but it was impossible. Breath, foul with garlic, was hot against her cheek.

"Easy, lady," a voice said in her ear. "We're gonna do us a little fishing."

She jerked her head up sharply and the hand slipped away from her mouth and she bit it. Hard. And kept biting until she tasted blood in her mouth. The man screamed and she whirled away from him. Another grabbed her in the darkness and spun her into the room. She was caught in a kaleidoscope of movement, images and voices: a new voice in her ear saying, "Don't worry, you are okay"; a table in the middle of the room with a candle, set in a pool of its own wax, burning at one corner; another man standing between her and the candlelight; a towering, frightening silhouette in a thick fur jacket; black shaggy hair; a black full beard. And those eyes, peering from the dark, shapeless face; cold gray eyes looking right through her; the big man charging past her, swinging through the doorway in a crouch.

Little Ears was backed against the wall, his bleeding hand in his mouth, his face bunched up with anger. He hadn't expected the big man. As he turned, the big man's foot swept in a wide arc and shattered Little Ears' wrist bone. The gun, a police special, spun out of his hand, flew across the hallway and stuck in the plaster wall, muzzle first, its stock and chamber protruding out into the hall.

Little Ears swung his hands up in a classic karate position and leaped toward the pistol, but before he could complete the move, his attacker twisted sideways and lashed out with his left leg. He missed, but the move distracted Little Ears and the big man whirled and caught him deep in the gut with the heel of his other foot. Breath whooshed out of Little Ears like air from a punctured balloon. His face turned red with pain and he jackknifed forward, clutching his stomach. The big man twisted him around with one hand and slammed him in the middle of the back with the palm of the other.

Little Ears flew across the hallway, almost tiptoeing, trying vainly to regain his footing. His arm smashed through the cracked pane of the door, hanging at the entrance to the dock, was caught there for a moment and then the door tore loose and he sprawled headlong onto the dock in a shower of broken glass and curse words. The old dock creaked under his weight. He rolled fast, got his feet under him and jumped into a crouch, but the big man in the fur jacket was all over him. He grabbed Little Ear's wrist, twisted hard, stepped in close and flipped him in a tight loop.

Little Ears kept moving, rolling out of the loop, trying to get back into the hallway. He snapped his wrist and a switchblade slid from his sleeve into his hand. The blade hissed from the handle, glittering in reflected light. Before Little Ears could turn, the big man leaped into the doorway and slashed his elbow into Little Ears' jaw. The blow knocked him back onto the dock. He hit the antiquated dock railing, which cracked under his weight. He staggered away from it and took a hard swipe with the knife. Its blade swished an inch from the big man's face. The big man stepped in fast, getting inside his reach, but Little Ears slashed back and the knife sliced through the big man's jacket and ripped into his shoulder.

The big man did not utter a sound. He feinted with a chop, stepped back as Little Ears made another swipe, then moved in and threw a body block across him, grabbing his wrist and twisting. Little Ears shrieked and fell to his knees. The knife clattered to the floor.

The big man spun him around, wrapped his wounded arm around Little Ears' neck, ground his fist into his throat and held the point of the knife against his jugular. He pressed a knuckle from his fist into Little Ears' carotid.

"Calm down," the big man said. "it would be real embarrassing to get your throat cut with your own knife."

Little Ears grunted something and tried to twist away.

The knuckles dug in deeper. Little Ears growled with pain. The big man said, "Listen to me, pal, if you're after O'Hara, you missed the party."

Little Ears stopped struggling. He moved his head away from the knife. "Aaargh . . . larder . . . furmilpuf . . ." he said.

The big man let up the pressure with the knuckle a little. "What was that?" he asked.

"Somebody's already pushed him over?" Little Ears asked in a husky voice.

"No, the Winter Man called off the sanction. The Game's over."

Little Ears snapped "Bullshit!" and tried to pull away. The knuckle dug in harder. In a moment Little Ears began to go limp. The big man loosened up again. Little Ears was not convinced. He glared at the girl. Then he said, "That lying Winter Man told me this was my stunt. Exclusive, he said."

The big man drove the knuckle into the artery again. His shoulder was killing him, but he kept the pressure on, neutralizing Little Ears.

"If you don't calm down, you're going to have a sore throat for the rest of your life," the big man said and turned to Eliza. "You got the letter from Dobbs?"

Her eyes were as wide as dollar pancakes. She nodded vigorously.

"Well, get it up before this jackass dies on me."

She dug in her bag, thrashing around among clinking mirror, lipstick, comb, brush, hairpins, pens, paper, and finally produced the letter. But Little Ears wasn't interested. He jammed his elbow into the big man's ribs and twisted, and the big man let him go, kicked him hard in the kneecap and threw a hard punch straight to Little Ears' temple. The man hit the railing and it shattered. He soared off the dock, head over heels, and hit the water six feet below, spread-eagled.

The big man leaned back against the wall and sighed. "I hope you can swim," he said, looking down at Little Ears, who was floundering in the frigid black water.

Little Ears struggled to the dock and dragged himself up on it. He collapsed on his hands and knees.

The big man grabbed a fistful of his collar and pulled him up, and dragged him into the room. He held the letter in front of Little Ears' face. "Can you read?"

Little Ears tried to focus his eyes. He was beginning to shiver. He spat water on the floor.

"Read it!"

Little Ears waited until his eyes could focus, and he read the letter. "Son of a bitch," he said. He read it again, shaking his head in disbelief.

"You almost got yourself burned for nothing," the big man said. His shoulder was throbbing.

Little Ears rubbed the spot on his neck. It was already beginning to bruise. His voice was a tortured whisper. "I don't believe this," he said, shaking his head. "I fucking don't believe this. You know what I got in this job? I started following her in San Francisco, for Chrissakes. I must be close to six grand out of pocket. And that don't count the time. Three, four weeks. I must be out, dammit, close to ten grand."

"Send the Winter Man a bill."

"I'll send him a bill, I'll go back and castrate the son of a bitch."

"Good, you'll need this." The big man pressed the release button on the knife and shoved the blade against the wall. It slid back into the handle. He tossed it to Little Ears. "At least you got your knife back," he said.

"Jesus, I don't believe any of this," Little Ears said, still shaking his head, and he dragged his wet, shivering body from the room, pulled his .38 out of the wall and limped up the stairs, the gun hanging forgotten in his hand as he went out the door, still rubbing his throat.

The big man turned to Eliza. "Hey," he said, "you looked pretty good in there, for a midget."

Eliza's eyes were still the size of dollar pancakes, and the questions came tumbling as they returned to the street. "Are you okay? Who was that? Is he just going to walk away from it like that? Isn't he mad or something? You almost broke his neck. You threatened to cut his throat. He tried to kill you. What the hell's going on, anyway? Won't he come looking for you later?"

"He's a headhunter," the big man said. "First thing they learn, never let emotion get in the way of business. If he starts feeling instead of thinking, he'll end face-up smiling at the moon."

She shuddered, for the full impact of what had just happened had begun to sink in. The man with the Little Ears had tried to kill them.

"Kazuo?"

The voice came from behind her, a quiet voice, yet forged with authority. Turning, she found herself face to face with a young Japanese man. He was a head shorter than the big man, wide through the shoulders with no waist to speak of. He wore a black turtleneck sweater, black pants, black soft-soled shoes, and his long black hair tumbled over the sweater at his neck. His brown eyes burned with anxiety.

She froze for a moment, until the big man spoke and she realized he was a friend.

"Are you okay, pal?" he said to the big man.

"Bastard took a piece out of my arm. Was there anybody else?"

"No, he was operating alone," the Japanese said. And then he smiled and raised his eyebrows. "Maybe I should have backed you up. It did not occur to me that he might be a match for you. He did not look that tough."

"A match for me! Bullshit. He was a cheap street fighter. He got lucky. Oh, by the way, Eliza Gunn, this is Sammi. He followed you while I followed the cheap shot with no ears. It's known as a double-up."

She had stopped listening. Instead she was concentrating on the big man's eyes.

"One of your eyes changed color," she said to the big man.

"What?"

"That eye. That green eye on the right. It used to be gray."

He turned away from her and Sammi peered intently at the big man.

"The gods have indeed played a trick," Sammi said with mock seriousness. "They have changed the color of your right eye."

"Let's get me to Dr. Saiwai," the big man said. "I need a little repairwork."

But Eliza would not be distracted. She started to laugh. She laughed very hard. "Contact lenses," she said. "You were wearing contact lenses. The cowboy boots must add an inch or so to your height. The contact lenses change the color of your eyes. The beard and everything . . . *Kazuo* . . . hell, you're O'Hara!"

V

The doctor's house was on the outskirts of Kyoto, a dim, black one-story outline against the gray silhouette of Mount Hiei, which soared up behind it, less than two miles away. O'Hara and Sammi were gone less than fifteen minutes. When they came out, O'Hara had his hand stuffed in his pocket.

"No big thing," he told her. "Twelve stitches, but the cut isn't very deep. That bastard ruined my jacket."

"Tana will fix it. Nobody will even know," said Sammi.

"Who's Tana?" Eliza asked.

"Friend of the family," said O'Hara.

They drove back to Osaka, parked the car and walked to the *nomiya,* the sake bar, across from her hotel. It was a delicate place, dark and quiet, and after leaving their shoes near the door, they found a small booth near the back.

"I will call Tokenrui-san and tell him it went well. He'll be worried," Sammi said and left the stall.

"Is that Mr. Kimura?" Eliza asked.

O'Hara nodded. He was looking at her hard with his green eyes, then he suddenly smiled for the first time and she began to feel warm. She took off her coat.

"You got quite a bite there, pal," he said.

"We can thank my dentist in Nebraska for that."

"Nebraska, hunh?"

"Yep. Webster Groves high school, then the University of Missouri, then Boston, via Chicago. That's the story of my life. Not much to it. Nothing like yours. Does this kind of thing happen often?"

"Only when I get mixed up with television reporters that bite."

She smiled at him across the table. "Cute," she said.

She had one hell of a smile. If ever a smile could be called ear-to-ear, it was that one.

"What does that word mean?" she asked.

"What, 'cute'?"

"No, silly. Token . . . whatever."

"Tokenrui-san?"

"Right."

"Literally, *token* means 'swords.' But in this case it's interpreted to mean 'the Master.' "

"Do you really think of him as your Master?"

"Not the way you mean. In the aesthetic sense."

"You mean like a teacher?"

"That's part of it. He is *the* Master of *higaru-dashi,* which is kind of a . . . combination advanced karate, Shinto and Zen. It's difficult to describe in English. The words are misleading. Anyway, Kimura makes the final choice on everyone who enters the seventh level of the *higaru-dashi.* What's known as the Plane of the Beyond."

"It sounds way beyond me."

"Only because you take the words literally. In Japan, nothing is obvious."

"He tells me you can stand on one foot for six hours without blinking an eye. Is that what you call the Plane of the Beyond?"

"No," he said and smiled again, "it's what I call painful."

The waitress appeared. *"Osake o ippai onegai shimasu,"* O'Hara said, and she nodded and left. "I ordered us sake," he explained to Eliza. "I think we can all use it."

"You seem very much at ease here in Japan."

"It's my home."

"That mean you've given up on the States?"

He made a vague gesture, which he did not bother to explain.

"And these people helped you just because they're your friends?"

"Is there a better reason?"

"But it was dangerous."

"I was in trouble. A year on the dodge is a long time. Besides, the Winter Man tried to dishonor me. That was unspeakable to Kimura. And to Sammi. Here, a person's honor is sacred. To steal it is like stealing your soul. It's a despicable act."

The waitress and Sammi both returned at the same time. They raised their warm cups in a mutual toast and sipped the hot rice liquor.

"Tell me more about Kimura . . . Tokenrui-san? Does Kimura still teach? I mean, he seems so old. How old is he?"

"Sammi?"

Sammi said, *"Nana-ju-ni."*

"Seventy-two," O'Hara said.

"And he's still active?"

"He would never have taken that cut, tonight, you can bet on that. I'll hear about it, too, all right, letting that dipshit get his blade into me."

"You were not prepared. Your head was with the fleas," Sammi said. "Your first two moves were an inch too wide."

"Yeah. I knew that when I felt his knife in my shoulder."

"And Kimura is faster than you?" Eliza asked.

"It is not the speed, it is the mind," Sammi said.

"Tokenrui-san can catch a hummingbird in flight," said O'Hara. "The move is so fast, you don't see it, you just feel the wind, from his arm moving. That wind is called *okinshiwa,* and it has different meanings to different people. To you, the wind could mean confusion; to me, because I am his friend, it can mean security. To his enemies, it can mean danger."

"And then he opens his hand," Sammi said, holding his arm out and unfolding his fist, "and the bird sits there and waits for him to blow on its tail and make it fly away."

"That's the mystic part of it," said O'Hara. "When I understand that, I will feel that I have achieved the Plane of the Beyond."

"It's all very difficult . . ."

"That's because it requires a different kind of thinking than you're accustomed to. Kimura changed my life . . . no, he saved my life. If it weren't for him, I'd probably be a headhunting punk like Little Ears."

"Doesn't it seem strange," she said, "just a few years ago we were all at war. Was he involved in that?"

"Involved?" Sammi laughed. "I suppose you could say that."

O'Hara said, "He hand-picked the officers—and this is the top staff of the Imperial Army we're talking about—who were to enter the seventh level of *higaru-dashi*. He only selected twelve. They were with him for three years before they returned to duty—in 1942. Every one of them was a key man in the Japanese war machine."

She sat quietly for a minute, letting it sink in.

O'Hara said, "You might say he prepared them to kick the shit out of us."

And he and Sammi laughed, and then she laughed too. "And you feel the same way about him, right?" she said to Sammi.

"It's not quite the same," O'Hara said. "Tokenrui-san is Sammi's grandfather."

Neat, Eliza. Next time, take your shoe off before you put your foot in your mouth.

"I'm sorry," she said, "that was dumb, bringing up the war."

"It's no secret," Sammi said, and went on talking fast and running his sentences together. "Anyway, it's a natural question but many people wouldn't ask, he will like it that you were honest enough to find out. There is one other thing. *Higaru* is never used for aggression, it is used to defend. When my grandfather taught these men, it was because he was led to believe that Japan might be attacked."

"He had good feelings about you," O'Hara said, changing the subject. "Now, me—I thought you and that *pistolero* were working a double. Some kind of elaborate sting."

"Well, thanks a lot. I come halfway around the world, get insulted, shoved around, almost killed, just to bring you these letters, and you think I could be—what did you call it, 'working a double'?—really . . . with that dumb ass. If you're in the seventh plane, or whatever you call it, you ought to be able to judge character a little better. Besides, what was all that melodrama back there about, anyway? If all you want is peace and quiet, why didn't you just walk up to him and tell him it was all off?"

"Much too logical."

"Yeah," Sammi said. "This way he knows we were serious."

"Like hitting a mule with a two-by-four to get its attention."

"Also he needs something to show for all those bucks he wasted."

"In any case," O'Hara said, "we had to make sure about you."

"You mean I was just bait!"

O'Hara thought about that for a moment or two and nodded. "That's about it," he said.

"We knew you weren't teamed up after the drive down from Osaka,"

Sammi said. "I boxed him in on the highway. He lost you for a minute or two and he panicked."

"So . . . ?"

"So, if you two had been doubled up," O'Hara said, "you would have told him where we were meeting. And he would have gone in ahead. And he would have set me up."

"How do you know?"

"It's in the spy manual. Chapter two."

"Very clever. Devious but clever."

I wonder if he really can stand in one spot without moving for six hours. And without blinking those eyes. Those green, green eyes.

He's talking, Gunn, pay attention.

". . . Shinto way. The universe is ruled by letting things take their course. It cannot be changed by interfering."

Now, what was that all about.

"I'm sorry, I missed that," she said.

"It means fate is tough to beat, pal."

"Please, don't call me pal. I knew a dog once named Pal. A real ugly bulldog."

"Okay, Gunn. What's it all about? Who got the Winter Man off my ass? And what does Howe want out of all this?"

"I don't know. Mr. Howe will have to tell you that."

He was looking at her across the table. His eyes were even more penetrating, more alive, than with the gray contacts. He stared at her left eye and suddenly a ridiculous memory popped into her head. She tried to ignore it, but it persisted, whispering in her ear, an old wives' tale from high school.

When a man stares into your left eye, he can see your pussy.

Oh, for God's sake, really!

When a man stares into your left eye, he— He's talking to me and I can't hear a word he's saying. All I can hear is that stupid voice whispering in my ear. When a man stares . . .

"Excuse me," she said. "My mind wandered. I'm afraid I didn't hear what you said."

And O'Hara was thinking, She's flashing that smile, that big smile. They ought to declare that smile a national resource.

Easy there, big boy, you've seen big smiles before.

Yeah, but not like that one . . . and not any time in the past year.

"I said, what do you mean, Mr. Howe will explain it," he said finally.

Eliza put the letter from Howe in front of O'Hara. "I've read it already," O'Hara said. "I read it when I broke into your room this afternoon."

"Oh, that's right. Well, then you know. Mr. Howe wants to see you. I don't know why. I don't know why he was so determined to find you and get you out of trouble with this Winter Man. All I know, he wants to talk to you about an assignment. He says nobody else can do it but you. And he's pressed for time."

"Presumptuous son of a bitch."

"Hey, I found you. I delivered the message. If you want to tell him to get stuffed, that's your business. If you decide to go, I have a thousand dollars in cash and a plane ticket to Boston for you. First class."

"You're carrying a thousand dollars in cash?"

"Not where you can get your hands on it."

He's staring again. He's looking straight into my . . . no . . . into my left eye.

O'Hara was listening to the wind chimes overhead, tickled by a breeze from the door. His eyes went blank, then his mind went blank, and in the no-mind state where he had retreated, her face was etched into the white wall. The large gleaming brown eyes, the shock of black hair, the broad you're-dead-buddy smile. Now it was a face he would never forget.

". . . earth to O'Hara," she was saying.

"Yeah . . ."

"Are you interested?"

"Uh . . . interested?"

"In Mr. Howe's offer."

"I wish you'd stop calling him *Mr.* Howe. Sounds like you're talking about God."

"He's old. He's like Tokenrui-san. He deserves it."

"Fine. Then call him Howe-san."

"Will you get serious? What's your decision?"

"I have no idea."

"Well, when do you think the muses are going to get in touch?"

"I'll tell you in the morning."

"Oh."

"I need to do some thinking."

"I can understand that. Who'd want to go back to the land of the living when you can stay here in the garden spot of Japan and raise puppy dogs."

O'Hara leaned across the table, very close to her face, and said softly, "He who knows others is wise; he who knows himself is enlightened."

"How about 'Step on a crack, break your mother's back.' Don't tell me *you're* going to start doing that now."

He liked her arrogance, the way she said whatever the hell was on her mind. But he also felt let down. A part of his life was coming to an end. He knew it. Fate had brought the girl there and fate would lure him back with her.

"No," he said, "I'm going to take you across the street to your hotel and then I'm going home and get some rest."

"The arm hurts, doesn't it?"

"It's beginning to burn a little. The pain will be gone by morning."

"And you'll call me?"

"I'll call you."

"I'll get the car, Kazuo," Sammi said, and he bowed to Eliza. "You come back, okay. We'll teach you the Tao. The Way. Next time."

They put their shoes on and paid the bill and O'Hara walked her across the street to her hotel and O'Hara's shoulder was hurting and he felt rotten, and standing there, he suddenly felt very tired.

"Oyasuminasai," he said and kissed her on the cheek, and started back across the street, and she said, "There's a flight tomorrow afternoon at three," and without turning, he said, "Well, you better make your reservation. It's liable to fill up. *Sayonara."*

He got in the car and they drove off and left Eliza standing in the doorway of the hotel. A kiss on the cheek, she thought. Well, shit. But she'd get another crack at him. He would come to Boston, she was sure of it. And next time he would not have his shoulder as an excuse.

5

O'HARA SAID NOTHING during the drive back to Kyoto from Osaka, nor did Sammi encourage any conversation. He knew Kazuo was deep in thought. The house of Tokenrui-san was on the curve of a street in the old section of Kyoto. It was built in 1782 and had changed very little since then. The cypress bark on its sloping roof had been replaced many times through the years, as had the waist-high bamboo fence encircling it. But the cypress columns around its railed veranda were originals, as were the delicate screens in the main room, one depicting the return of a warrior to his home, and another, by Isono Kado, a famous artist of the seventeenth century, of a hawk perched on a pine-tree branch. The paintings had been rescued from one of the royal houses during the great fire, which had destroyed more than half the temples and homes of Kyoto in 1788.

For years the house was inhabited variously by students, monks and Heian priests, and it fell into disrepair. Then, in 1950, Kimura's son-in-law, Tasaguyi, had acquired it and restored it as a wedding gift and dowry to Kenaka, Kimura's only child. But now Tasaguyi and Kenaka were gone, and he lived there with his two grandchildren, Samushi and Tana.

The house was close to the street and was built like a half-moon, its inside curve facing a lush flower garden built around the fish pond which was fed by a stream that gurgled constantly under a corner of the veranda of the main house. The carp and goldfish, some of them more than four feet long, had been there so long, Kimura had forgotten how old they were.

At the far side of the garden, facing the back of the main house, was a workshop that had been built ten years after the main house. It was this small dwelling, with its large main room and small tub room, that had been O'Hara's home during the two years he trained for his initiation into the *shichi,* the inner council, of the *higaru-dashi,* as well as his sanctuary during the long months of his recent exile.

The sweet smell of wisteria seemed to be everywhere as they entered the main gate and walked around the corner of the house toward the garden. And there was always a silence there, as if God had turned off the sounds of the world. He said good night to Sammi, thanked him and went around to the back to his place of peace, a sanctuary where he had retreated to consider his plight and make the decisions which had kept him alive during the long ordeal of the Winter Man.

From a group of trees near the doorway of the house, there were sounds; a twig cracking, a leaf falling, followed by a low, friendly "ruff."

"Hi, kids," O'Hara said to the big male akita dog, Kazuo-dan, and his mate, whom O'Hara had named Konsato, which means "concert," because when she was a puppy she bayed constantly: at the moon, the stars, the sun, the blossoms and anything else she could raise her head and howl at. The male, a large silver-gray dog, its tail curved up over its hindquarters, stepped out of the shadows to greet him. He was a regal animal, his bloodlines tracing back to a sire that was once guard dog to an emperor, and he carried himself with restrained élan. The female was more frivolous. She hopped about, licking O'Hara's hands and nibbling Kazuo's neck, which the male treated with a kind of annoyed tolerance.

He could sense Tana's presence before he saw or heard her. There was a lacquered vase of white chrysanthemums in the *tokonama* which faced the door as he entered. She had prepared a snack of *makizushi*, tiny rolls of vinegared rice wrapped in thin seaweed and stuffed with asparagus tips and fish or seafood, and placed it on a low table near the sliding rosewood doors that led to the garden. His silk nightshirt was laid out beside hers near the *futon* on his bed.

Once inside, he could hear her singing softly, somewhere in the back of the house.

It was going to be difficult, telling her. He turned into the lavatory which was off a short hallway that led from the door to the main room. He slid the door shut and got out a straight razor and a mug of shaving soap and after, lathering his face, he shaved off his beard. As he shaved, his eyes kept drifting to the mirror and the reflection of the photograph of the Hichitani Chemical plant behind him.

It was a grim, dark, foreboding picture, showing the plant as a gray mass with tall stacks, lurking under an ominous tumor of polluted clouds. In the foreground, the polluted sky was reflected on the shiny ridges of the waves of the bay. The photograph was one of hundreds shot by the American photographer W. Eugene Smith, as part of an essay on the tragedy of Hichitani.

The plant was located on the shores of a nameless bay a few kilometers south of Minamata on southern Kyushu. Hichitani had been, for fifty years, the patron of more than seven hundred workers in this isolated village, and its only industry. There was no private enterprise in the village, except for the fishermen who lived there, and most of their boats were financed by the company. Hichitani provided the townspeople of Minamata with jobs, housing and a company store where they could buy food and clothing. Many of the men and women, whose grandparents had worked in the factory, had never been more than a hundred kilometers from the town where they were born. Its very isolation perpetuated the tragedy. Minamata was the culture for an epidemic of horror than spanned half a century.

The Hichitani corporation produced anodized aluminum—from raw materials to finished product. The effluent from its smelting plant was carried through long pipes and dumped into the ocean on the far side of a peninsula that protected the bay from the open sea. The prevailing tides, however, carried the sea water around the peninsula and back into the bay.

One of the chemicals in the raw effluent was mercury, an almost infinitesimal amount of mercury. But when mixed with water and catalyzed by other chemicals in the waste, the mercury produced mercuric oxide, a deadly poison. The years passed and with each day, microscopic pearls of death drifted in with the tide and settled on the plant life and on the floor of the bay. The bay was a fisherman's paradise, and the fish, the main food source for the village, fed on the plant life and ingested the deadly pearls from the water.

Decades passed. The mercuric oxide slowly infested the bay and its environment. Its effect on the people was gradual, developing over two generations. Then, in 1947, the plant doubled its capacity.

The first big fish kill occurred the following year, a year before the birth of the Matzashi child. Hundreds of tuna, sea bass and mackerel had drifted onto the beach of the bay. It was blamed on the red tide, and the incident was never reported to the press, but a few days after it happened, a group of engineers arrived from the main office in Ube, to study the fish kill. Hichitani later said their findings were inconclusive.

In 1949, the first deformed child was born and the effects of thirty years of pollution began to show. Nobody was too concerned about the Matzashi baby. After all, it was rumored, the husband and wife were directly related. But two months later a child was born with no eyes, and then another with shriveled, wasted legs, and another whose head was three times the normal size. Fourteen deformed children were born that year and five employees of the plant died of dysentery.

The scientists returned. Very quietly. On the team that was sent down the second time was Tasaguyi, a brilliant young chemical engineer. He moved to Minamata with Kenaka, his bride of less than a year, and set up an in-depth study of waste handling at the plant. Kenaka taught school. During the next three years, dozens of horribly deformed children were produced among the workers and townspeople who lived along the bay and fished its waters. Several of the older workers went blind, others died of a painful, debilitating kind of dysentery that killed or crippled its victims. The place seemed cursed, which indeed it was.

The first of the Tasaguyi children, Sashumi, was born in 1952. He was a normal but frail child who was constantly ill. Tana, the daughter born the following year, was deaf at birth. Ironically, it was Tasaguyi who detected the presence of mercuric oxide in the fish, the water and the plant life of the bay, but it was too late to help his daughter.

He sent the children back to Kyoto to live with their grandfather, and still believing the company would take drastic steps to save the village, and to prevent a panic, he quietly presented his findings to the board of Hichitani. The company announced it would build a new waste-treatment facility at the factory and a new water-treatment plant for the town, but still did not reveal to the people of Minamata the danger that lay at their doorstep. By then, there were hundreds of deformed children in the town, and dysentery was almost endemic.

Tasaguyi resigned, formed a citizens' group in the village and announced his findings to the press. A national scandal resulted. But a few months after beginning his crusade, Tasaguyi began suffering telltale cramps and diarrhea. He kept up the fight. The cramps got worse. He began losing weight. Then he awoke one night desperately ill, and died in agony eight hours later. Kenaka was determined to continue his fight, but she, too, was already terminally afflicted with mercury poisoning. Kimura brought his beloved daughter back to Kyoto, where, for the last two months of her life, she was raving mad. He refused to commit her to an institution and instead kept her locked in the workhouse, where he tended to her until she died.

The workhouse had been empty from then until O'Hara came to live there for the last two years of his training as a *shichi.* But the photograph remained on the wall as a perpetual reminder of the horror of Minamata and its devastating effect on this one family.

He finished shaving and went back down the hall toward the main room. O'Hara loved this house. It had been his only real home. It was here he had lived for two years while he trained for the Ritual of the *Shichi.* He had kept an apartment merely as a base during his years in the service, but he was rarely there. And for the past year he had hidden in this ancient house, communed with its ghosts, reaffirmed his mental and physical commitment to *higaru-dashi* and his emotional commitment to Kimura, Sammi and, most of all, to Tana.

The main room was startlingly simple, yet strangely warm and inviting. The only electrical device was a lamp over the tatami on which O'Hara slept. There was a low table with a mat beside it, several candle lanterns and a bookshelf. Nothing else.

Except the flowers. Each day Tana decorated the room with flowers. Red and white and purple and pink, every color one can imagine. It was the flowers that gave the place its warmth and life.

O'Hara walked across the room and popped one of the snacks in his mouth, savoring the shrimp she had mixed with the vinegar rice in the *makizushi.* He could hear Tana in the small room that contained the great redwood tub, preparing his bath. She was singing softly to herself, a birdlike voice that was always slightly off-key. He changed into the knee-length black silk nightshirt and sat cross-legged on the mat.

Tana dipped her arm into the steaming water until it covered her wrist. It was very hot, but Kazuo liked it very hot. She guessed he had been gone for perhaps three hours, but there were no clocks in the house and O'Hara did not own a watch. There was a small fear in her stomach, a gnawing anxiety. Something was going to take him away, to draw him back to the ways of the West. She sensed the danger.

When O'Hara first came to live there, during the preparation for the ritual vows of the *shichi,* Tana was a child. Shy, withdrawn, wary at first of the fair *gaijin,* the foreign devil whom her grandfather had seemed to adopt, she was drawn to him gradually by the same strength and mysticism that attracted her grandfather and brother. He was unlike the other *shichi* candidates she had known. He laughed readily and made jokes on himself. He was gentle and was rarely moved to anger. And, best of all, he learned sign language so they could talk. In the evenings, after the mental and physical strain of the long days of the *shichi* preparation, he would sit near the fish pond, and with fingers wiggling, he would tell her ghost stories from America.

Samushi, whom O'Hara nicknamed Sammy, changing the *y* to an *i* so it would look Japanese, had also resented O'Hara at first. It seemed, to Sammi, an insult that Tokenrui-san, his own grandfather, would assign his grandson to the fair-haired Kazuo for training into the *higaru-dashi.* But the young novitiate soon learned that it was an act of love, for O'Hara was not only classically disciplined, he was an excellent teacher. It was O'Hara who discovered that Sammi had remarkable reflexes and who devised a series of moves to best use his speed. It was also O'Hara who devised the grueling exercises that built up Sammi physically so he could deal with the rigors of *higaru-dashi,* exercises that were so painful that in the early days of the training, Sammi would often work the last two or three hours of the day with tears streaming down his face.

There was, of course, no quitting. To do so would have been to dishonor not only himself and Tokenrui-san but his sister and O'Hara as well. Besides, O'Hara, himself preparing for the mystical journey into the seventh level, conducted a personal daily ritual which was almost crippling in its demands. Sammi's resentment faded, to be replaced first by respect, and then by love. By the time O'Hara became a *shichi* and Sammi was inducted into the *higaru-dashi,* they were as brothers.

When O'Hara left to fulfill his obligation to his father, it was a painful experience for all of them, but it was agony for Tana. She hurt deep inside, the kind of hurt that could not be cried away or beat away or screamed away. It tormented her, and the ache in her chest and her throat stayed with her. She was only fourteen, yet she knew the depth of her feeling was very different from the feeling of deep friendship, the almost family bond, that had grown between O'Hara and her grandfather and brother.

Tana was in love with O'Hara, yet years passed and she told no one, not even Kimura. So for the next seven years, as she grew into a stunning woman, wise but uncomfortably aloof, she thought about Kazuo every single day. She wanted to forget about him, tried to forget about him, but it was futile. The young men of Kyoto courted her and were rejected. Finally she told Tokenrui-san of her plight.

"One cannot try to forget, for the trying itself keeps the memory alive," Kimura told her.

She went to the temples and asked the gods to rid her of her obsession for Kazuo.

And what did the gods do?

They sent him back to her.

Sometimes it was difficult to understand the message of the Tao. So she accepted their gift without understanding it.

She was twenty-two years old when O'Hara came back. At first he still seemed to think of her as a child. Her aloofness vanished. And one night as he started to tell her about some interesting incident from his days in intelligence, she interrupted him and, with her hands, she said, "Tell me a love story instead."

O'Hara did not need the wisdom of the Tao to figure that one out.

But now the dream was threatened. There was no answer in the Tao. Her fate was no longer in her own hands.

She stood in the doorway to the living room and dried her arm. She still did not see or sense him in the room. O'Hara leaned back on his arms and looked across the candlelit room at her. She was shorter than her brother, and very slender. Her skin was flawless and the color of sand. Her black hair hung almost to her waist. Her brown eyes seemed misty under hooded lids, as they always were in candlelight. Her breasts poked at the short nightgown that hung by thin straps from her shoulders.

She was delicious.

He watched her for several minutes and then moved so she would see him. His presence there startled her, for she usually sensed him before she saw him.

She looked at his smooth face, at his green eyes.

She spelled out the words with her fingers, moving them in a gentle, constant flow that reminded O'Hara of a dancer's hands.

"No beard."

"No."

Her hand swept across her eyes.

"No eyes."

"No."

"Then it went well?"

"Yes."

"Now you are safe."

"Yes."

"Does this make you happy?"

"Yes. No man should feel like a hunted animal."

"Or woman."

He bowed sightly. "Or woman."

She looked away from his face, down at his feet and there were tears in her eyes. Her hands moved very slowly: "Your bath is ready."

She turned and went back into the tub room. He followed her in and turned her around, facing him. "Has something changed? Is it not our bath?"

And he kissed her very lightly on the lips, caressing her neck with his fingertips, and moved his hands down her smooth skin and out over her shoulders and slipped the silk gown free and it dropped at her feet and he slipped his arms out of the sleeves of his shirt and quickly pulled it over his head, breaking their kiss for only a second.

He moved closer to her until the tips of her nipples were touching him. And she moved closer, felt him growing hard against her and his hands slipped around her and he very lightly began stroking her back and she began to move her body under his fingers and he got harder and she moved back slightly and began to caress his thighs and his stomach and his memory tumbled back in time to the night she first came to him: dressed in her mother's red-and-white silk kimono, she had entered his dark room, lit the single candle near his bed, and kneeling beside him, had told him with those wonderously poetic hands that she loved him.

She had closed his eyes with her fingertips and then traced every muscle in his body with a touch like feathers, humming in that gloriously soft and delightfully off-key voice, and then she had retraced his body with her lips until finally she took him in her mouth without touching him with her fingers, and the memory aroused him even more and he began to rub her buttocks, moving her very subtly closer to him and she rose on her toes and he felt her hair crush against him and he bent his knees and let his penis slide against her and she arched her back slightly so her clitoris was against him and for several minutes they stood together, moving slowly to the rhythm of her humming and then he bent his knees a little more and he felt himself enter her and her wet muscles closed around him and she wrapped first one leg, then the other around his waist and he slid his hand down between their stomachs and found the trigger of her senses and felt it harden as he stroked her, and the humming became a sigh and the sigh became a tiny cry in her throat and she stiffened and she stopped breathing for several seconds and then she thrust herself down on him and cried out and she began to shudder and the response of her passion was so overwhelming that all his senses suddenly seemed to rush out of him and he felt a spasm, and then another, and another, another, another, and he exploded, and his knees began to tremble but he held her close and stayed inside her and slowly went up the steps and got in the tub and the hot water swirled around them and she cried out again and this time her response seemed to renew him and he felt himself growing longer again, growing deep inside her and she moved up and down, sliding him against her and she felt herself building again, she felt almost electrified, lost in time and space, and the waves began again, building, building.

When it was over, he tried to tell her that he had to go back, had to leave her. But she closed her eyes, for she knew this time the hurts would be harder and the memories would be realities, and this time perhaps the gods would not send him back to her. So she closed her eyes, and that way he could not talk to her. But she spoke to him, a phrase she had practiced many times with Sammi, and although she still was not pleased with the way she said it, it was time.

"I ruv you, O'Haya," she said, and with her eyes still closed, she laid her wet fingertips against his lips.

6

IT WAS A STRANGE SIGHT. No, O'Hara thought, it was beyond strange, it was bizarre.

O'Hara stood on the deck of the 120-foot yacht as it muttered in the sea a couple of hundred yards offshore. He was wearing blue jeans, a white raw silk shirt and a fur jacket, its collar turned up against the cold off-shore breeze. The heavy field glasses through which he was studying the deserted beach had been offered to him by the first mate, a lean, immaculate ex-Navy commander in his mid-forties named Carmody.

As O'Hara's eyes swept the desolate Cape Cod shoreline, a couple emerged from a gorge in the bleak, soaring dunes speckled with sea grass that stood sentinel along the beach. The woman, tall and erect, was wearing a tweed jacket over her shoulders, her brown hair tossed by the heavy wind that sent mist from the roiling surf swirling past them.

The man beside her was built like a wrestler from the waist up, his biceps bulging, his shoulders and chest enormous, muscles lumped around a neck as thick as a telephone pole. His head was as bald as the beach except for tufts of white hair that caressed his ears. In jarring contrast to his torso, from the waist down he was a wasted human being. His legs were atrophied into spindles, mere twigs, and he walked in a laborious, shifting gait, swinging one leg in front of the other while supporting himself by two bright-red ski poles.

The man wore dark-blue swimming trunks and an open yellow windbreaker that flapped in the chilly morning air. No shoes. He shuffled painfully past long shadows, cast in the white sand by a sun which had risen only an hour or so earlier, while the woman, ignoring his deformity, kept pace beside him. She stayed with him until he walked into the surf, then she stopped and waited. He waddled into the sea until the water sloshed at his knees; then, balancing himself unsteadily, he tossed the ski poles back toward her, pulled off the jacket and threw it over his shoulder and fell forward into the ocean and began swimming. His powerful arms pulled him through the big breakers and out beyond into clear water and he swam hard, without letting up until he was fifty feet or so from the Jacob's ladder of the yacht. He looked up at the deck through piercing black eyes that glimmered under heavy brows, and treading water with his powerful arms, yelled, "Ahoy there, would that be Lieutenant O'Hara?"

"Aye, sir," O'Hara yelled back.

"Good show. Charles Gordon Howe here. It's a pleasure, sir."

"Thank you. The pleasure's mine. It's a beautiful boat."

"How's the shoulder?"

"Fine. Just a little stiff."

Howe spoke in a strong Boston accent laced with Irish, clipping his words off short, his *o*'s becoming *ah*'s.

"Good enough. Care to join me, sir? What's the water running there, Mr. Carmody?"

"Fifty-eight degrees, sir. Fourteen and a half Celsius."

"Uh . . . thanks, anyway," O'Hara said. "I think I'll wait until the shoulder's feeling a little better."

"And the water's a little warmer, eh?" Howe laughed, a big, barracks-room laugh. "My beach cottage is right up there on the hill. I move out here every May and stay until September. I'm thirty minutes by helicopter from downtown Boston. Start off every morning with a dip."

Howe took half a dozen hard strokes to the dock and hoisted himself up to a sitting position, his wasted legs dangling in the cold sea, then reached up to the Jacob's ladder, his massive arms bulging, and pulled himself, arm over arm, up the ladder by its railing. The mate, Carmody, was waiting for him with an electric wheelchair and a heavy pea jacket. As he reached the top Howe twisted his entire torso and dropped into the chair. He toweled off, slipped on the jacket and draped a wool blanket over his legs. "Welcome aboard, sir," he said and held his hand out to O'Hara. It was like shaking hands with a trash masher.

The steward, a young man with a pasty complexion, wearing blue bellbottoms and a white starched jacket with a blue dolphin embroidered over one pocket, asked O'Hara, "How do you like your coffee, sir?"

"Black, please, brandy on the bottom."

"Aye aye, sir. The usual, Captain?" he asked Howe.

"Strong tea with a touch of vodka. Takes the edge off, y'know. Breakfast in fifteen minutes, please, Mr. Lomax." Then to O'Hara: "Scrod and scrambled eggs, I believe scrod's a favorite of yours, right, Lieutenant?"

"Yes, thanks. And I prefer simply O'Hara, if you don't mind. I've been out of the Navy almost six years now."

"You earned the rank, by God, sir. Be proud of it."

"I resigned the commission, Mr. Howe."

"But you left honorably, Lieutenant. I'm a strong believer in titles, sir. Aboard this craft, we honor rank."

The steward returned with the drinks.

"This should do until we've had a chance to shower and dress. We can do our talking over breakfast, Lieutenant."

A brass christening plate beside the hatch that led to the main salon identified the yacht as:

THE BLACK HAWK
Catalina Is., Calif.
Launched: October 9, 1921
Owner: Edward L. Doheny

The robber baron Edward Doheny? O'Hara wondered.

Of course, stupid, what other Edward Doheny could afford a tub like this?

A crew of eighteen. Stateroom space for forty. And it could sleep about sixty "in a pinch," whatever the hell Howe might consider "a pinch" to be.

The dining room, like the rest of the ship, had the look of a museum piece, its brass portholes and lanterns gleaming like golden Inca treasure, the solid mahogany paneling oiled and black with age, the floors daring to be scruffed. The silverware, like everything else aboard, was elegant, old and defied appraisal. The walls were covered with photographs in thin brass frames of Howe with almost everybody imaginable except God. Most of them, which appeared to have been taken in the thirties and forties, showed a much younger, trimmer Howe.

"I always enjoy reading your stuff, Lieutenant. A very natural style. Not too formal."

"I write it the way I'd say it. An editor told me that once, and damned if he wasn't right."

"Good advice. Who was the editor?"

"Ben Bradlee."

"Oh . . . Well, have a seat, sir."

Howe took a letter from his jacket and leaned it against the water glass in front of his plate.

Ah, he likes drama, O'Hara thought. The letter is obviously part of the script. A little mystery with the scrod.

"I must admit," O'Hara said, "I know you only by reputation. Were you in the Navy?"

"Measured and fitted and one foot in the door," Howe said. "A week before reporting for duty, some reckless son of a bitch shot me in the spine. A hunting trip down in Georgia. Told me I'd never stand again. The hell with doctors. Three things I have no use for, Lieutenant: doctors, cowards and crooked politicians. And nothing I respect more than a damn good reporter. It's an honor to have you aboard, sir."

He toasted O'Hara with his coffee mug and took a sip, staring across the brim with his relentless black eyes. O'Hara nodded, raised his mug and stared back. "I assume," he said finally, "that you didn't bring me halfway around the world just to have breakfast with you."

"A proper assumption. I've heard you're quick to get to the point."

"Oh?"

"I've also heard that you're tough, that you're naïve, that you're relentless, that you're a pussycat, that you can be difficult, that you're a dream to work with, that you're honest to the bone, and that you're a miserable, lyin', no-good son of a bitch."

O'Hara laughed. "Well, either you've talked to a lot of folks or one poor slob who can't make up his mind."

It was Howe's turn to laugh. "Also that you have a sense of humor. Three things that are real, sir: God, human folly and laughter. The first two are beyond our comprehension, so we must do the best we can about the third."

"I thought John Kennedy said that."

Howe leaned across the table and winked. "I gave Johnny the line."

Breakfast came, and when the steward had returned to the galley, Howe said, "You know a gentleman name of Anthony Virgil Falmouth?"

O'Hara laughed. "I didn't know his middle name was Virgil. There's a certain irony to that."

"How so?"

"Well, Virgil was a poet. Tony Falmouth is an assassin. Somehow they just don't equate."

"An assassin, you say?"

"One of the best."

"You know that for a fact?"

Pause. O'Hara stared at Howe across the table, and finally said, "Yep."

"I see. And d'you trust him?"

"Falmouth? Why?"

"Believe me, I have good reason, Lieutenant. I appreciate the fact you might have some previous loyalties . . ."

O'Hara glanced at the letter and then looked down at his plate, moving things about, absently, with his fork. "There are no loyalties in Falmouth's business," he said finally. "I suppose I trust Tony as much as anyone in the Game."

"The Game?"

"The intelligence game."

"You think of it as a game, then?"

"It's what they call it. The Game. When you're in it, it's the Game. And he's up to his ass in it. He's a British agent. M.I.6, Her Majesty's Secret Service."

"Not anymore," Howe said.

He reached out and handed the letter, somewhat grandly, to O'Hara.

"Good," O'Hara said, "I was wondering when we were getting around to this."

It was addressed to Charles Gordon Howe, Esq., WCGH, Channel 6, Boston, Mass. And in the lower right-hand corner, below the address: "For his eyes only." The back had been sealed with blue candle wax. There was no stamp.

"Falmouth always did have a flair for the dramatic," O'Hara said.

Howe leaned across the table, his black eyes twinkling, and chuckled. "Did anyone ever call him Foulmouth? I can't help thinking of the reference every time I hear the name."

O'Hara continued to examine the letter. He said, without looking up, "I don't think anyone's ever said it out loud. It might be a bit reckless, insulting one of the most efficient killing machines on two legs."

"Oh?" Howe leaned back, and after a moment he added, "Sounds like we're talking about Billy the Kid."

"Tony Falmouth makes Billy the Kid look like Little Lord Fauntleroy."

"Oh?" Another pause. "And yet you'd trust him?"

"I'd trust him as much as any in the Game, which is a long way from saying 'I trust him.' Trust is a negligible word in the Game. They buy it, sell it, trade it, negotiate it."

"And yet Falmouth gave me what I needed to get this Winter Man off your back," Howe said.

"He wants something."

"You think that's the only reason?"

"I know it. Look, Tony saved my ass once. No reason for it. Except he earned himself some Green Stamps."

"And now he's redeeming them, that it?"

"Well, it probably seemed like a good idea to him at the time. If it happened again—say, tomorrow—he might take a slow boat to Bombay and send me a goodbye telegram when he got there."

"Cynical, sir. Downright cynical."

"Absolutely," O'Hara said. "The Game is a world of its own, the dirtiest of all possible worlds. Everything is a lie. Your proficiency depends on how well you lie. They may call it misdirection or put some other bureaucratic handle on it, but lying is what it's all about. In the Game, an honest man is a dead man."

"And that's why you got out?"

"Let's just say my string was getting short. Don't get me wrong, Mr. Howe, I've still got friends out there. They just aren't the kind of folks you'd want to, y'know, sit around the fire toasting marshmallows with."

"How so, sir?"

"Let's just say their values are different."

"I still don't understand."

"Well, I once asked Tony what he wanted out of life, and you know what he said? He looked at me and said, and he was dead serious, he said, 'Happiness is a confirmed kill.' A Rhodes scholar!"

"But doesn't somebody have to do it?"

"Why? After a while it becomes self-serving. If I had my way, they'd ban intelligence the way they want to ban the bomb."

Howe stared at the ceiling. "I suppose. But then we'd have all these spies running around with nothing to do."

"It's not my problem anymore."

"And yet you were in the Game, as you call it, for five, six years?"

"I was snookered. I wasn't a career man. Dobbs liked my style and arranged for me to get assigned to the Company. Then after I gave 'em four good years, the bastard tried to have me killed, which is something else we need to talk about, how you got the Winter Man off my ass."

"The letter, sir. Read the letter."

21 January

Dear Mr. Howe:

I take pen in hand knowing full well that in all probability this letter will be promptly disposed of as the ramblings of one who is either deranged or has spent too many nights alone with a bottle. I assure you, sir, I am in full command of all my facilities, and drink is not one of my vices.

My reasons for addressing this to you are quite simple. You are noted for your aggressive news policy; and you have a passion to be first.

First of all, allow me to introduce myself. My name is Anthony Virgil Falmouth. I retired six months ago, with Queen's Honors, from Her Majesty's Secret Service, after twenty-one years' service. You may verify this by contacting Sir James Townsend, M.I.6, 6 Chancery Lane, London. Telephone: 962-0000, extension 12.

For obvious reasons, I shall ask that you not discuss the contents of this letter with Sir James.

Because of my position, I have become privy during the past few years, but most particularly in the last few months, to the details of a story that is monstrous in concept and terrifying in potential. Its implications reach into the highest political offices of the world. Properly documented, this information would make the Watergate conspiracy seem like mere schoolboy pranks and, in comparison, even the assassination of President Kennedy will pale.

Mere knowledge of this story has put my life in jeopardy. I am on the run, possibly for the rest of my life. Here are my terms:

First, my price for this information is $250,000, to be paid only after your agent is satisfied that the information is true and worth the price.

Second, there is only one person I feel qualified to represent both you and me in this matter. His name is Frank O'Hara. O'Hara is disarmingly honest, he is a former member of the intelligence community, he is a recognized and respected news reporter, and he has known me for more than five years. For these reasons, I feel he is uniquely qualified not only to judge my veracity but to properly appraise the information.

I have not seen, talked to, or communicated in any way with O'Hara for more than a year.

There is an additional problem with respect to O'Hara. I am sure you will recall his series of articles two years ago, exposing a network of illegal covert actions conducted by the CIA in Africa and the Middle East. The stories resulted in the embarrassment, humiliation and demotion of O'Hara's former CIA section chief, Ralph Dobbs, a.k.a. the Winter Man. As a result, Dobbs sanctioned the assassination of O'Hara and offered a fee to several professionals to carry out the job.

I know, I was one of them. I refused the sanction.

O'Hara has been on the dodge ever since. To my knowledge, nobody has turned him up yet.

You will find, attached hereto, a notarized statement concerning Dobbs's offer to me. Since this is a personal vendetta, and in no way officially concerns the CIA, you might threaten to publish the facts. This will neutralize Dobbs and force him to lift the sanction.

If you can find O'Hara and he is interested in the assignment, tell him to contact the Magician. If I have heard nothing by April 1, I will assume you are not interested.

Yours very truly,
Anthony V. Falmouth

The affidavit was attached by paper clip to the letter. O'Hara turned it over, checked out the envelope.

"How was it delivered? There's no stamp on it."

"One of my correspondents was in Jamaica. It was in his box when he came in from dinner one evening."

O'Hara reread the letter and the affidavit, then put them on the table in front of Howe. He finished his coffee.

"Well?" said Howe.

"Well what?"

"Well, what do you think?"

"I'll tell you what I don't think. I don't think I'm going to assume responsibility for your two hundred and fifty thou, or anybody else's."

"We can get to that. What about the letter?"

O'Hara shrugged. "A toss-up. Falmouth's either on to something or he's trying a fast sting and he figures he can suck me into it with him or floss me. Either way, I don't like it."

Having finished his breakfast, Howe carefully put down his knife and fork and pushed his plate a few inches away with a finger. He leaned toward O'Hara and said, almost in a whisper, "What do you think it could be?"

"Hooked ya, hunh?"

"Enough to bring you in."

"And you put it to Dobbs, eh?"

"Just as Falmouth suggested. We had lunch in my jet, flyin' around over Washington. Dobbs fell apart very quickly. About the time the salad was served."

"Well, I owe one to Tony for that. And to you."

"I wouldn't forget the young lady."

"Gunn? Yeah, she looked pretty good in there."

"I have a feeling about this, Lieutenant. My instincts're buzzing. Have been ever since I got the damn letter."

"You must be on every mail-order list in the world."

"Really, sir. You do me an injustice. Give me credit for something. I've been in the news business since I was twelve, setting type for my grandfather's weekly up in Maine."

"I didn't mean to insult you. It's just that I know the territory."

"It's an adventure, by God. If I were twenty years younger and had two good legs under me, I'd be off with you."

"I told you, I won't be responsible for your money, or anybody else's, for that matter. Besides, it's not an adventure, it's madness. The whole damn Game is mad and the Players are all a bunch of fucking lunatics."

"Makes for a great story," Howe cried exuberantly.

"You may be as nutty as they are," O'Hara said.

"It's my money, Lieutenant. So it's my problem, right? Thus far, Falmouth has been on target. You said so yourself—if you could trust anyone, it would be him."

"One helluva big 'if.' "

"What the hell, it's a write-off, anyway. And I'll meet your price. Name it."

"I told you I don't want in."

"A thousand a week, with a guarantee of one year."

"I said no."

O'Hara got up and walked to one of the portholes and stared out at the ocean. The sky was darkening and thunderheads were rumbling down from Provincetown. He felt thunderheads roiling inside him, too.

They're gonna get me into this, he thought, and the very idea made him angry and it was difficult to explain his feeling to Howe, this overwhelming sense of anger that was growing inside him. He knew the scenario before it was recited, knew the characters, the locations, could even recite a lot of the dialogue. It was not just the pervading sense of dishonor; not the excesses of a Game in which people kill, maim and steal with impunity, a blood sport in which the score was kept in head counts, not numbers. No, O'Hara's anger sprang from acceptance. He was angry because he was accepted by the Players in this community of hyenas. He was part of it, like it or not. His escape had failed and subconsciously he was angry at Howe for reminding him of the fact. So when he blew up, it came so suddenly and without warning that Howe was stunned by the outburst.

"I said no, goddammit. NO!" O'Hara slammed his fist on the solid oak table with such fury that the ice in the glasses rattled.

"Lieutenant, you're a journalist. Whatever you fear ain't gonna be solved by raising dogs in Japan. Or, for that matter, by turning down a chance any self-respecting reporter would commit murder to get." Howe took a sip of his vodka-laced tea and said, grinning, "Fifteen hundred. Plus expenses. That's seventy-eight thousand for the year. And a hundred-thousand-dollar bonus when you turn in the story."

"You sure make fast judgments there, Mr. Howe. And here we just met."

Howe picked up the letter and looked it over again. "I was sure about you before I sent Gunn after you. This isn't the Game, Lieutenant. I trust you."

"I'm not even sure I have the news judgment. What the hell story is worth a quarter of a million dollars?"

"Well, if Deep Throat had come to me with Watergate and offered me the story for half a million dollars, I would have taken it like that." He snapped his fingers. "That give you an idea?"

O'Hara turned and leaned against the bulkhead. Outside, the first drops of rain began to pelt the deck.

"Well, shit," O'Hara said.

Howe's eyebrows arched. "Uh . . . does that mean you're interested?"

"I owe you one, for getting me off the hook with Dobbs."

"Not on your life. I did that on my own, no obligation."

But not Tony. He knew Falmouth. He had neutralized the Winter Man, and for that, O'Hara owed him. And even though Howe denied it, he felt an obligation there, too.

"*Shikata ga nai,*" he said.

"Pardon?"

"An old Japanese expression," O'Hara said.

"And what does it mean?"

"Freely translated, 'fucked if you do, fucked if you don't.' "

"Well, now, sir, I don't mean to . . ."

But O'Hara wasn't listening. He had made the decision. "Six days," he said half aloud. "The first of April is six days away."

"You can get anywhere in the world in six days," Howe said quietly.

O'Hara paused for a few more moments.

"Okay, Mr. Howe. I'll make a deal with you. I'll go find Falmouth and see what he's got. But even if his info is worth the two hundred and fifty grand, I still want the option to walk away from it, let somebody else do the dirty work."

Howe's black eyes twinkled again. He held out the vise. "Done. Here's my hand." And they shook. Then he said, "Son, you're too good a reporter to walk away from any yarn worth a quarter of a million dollars."

"Not if it's gonna put me back in the middle of Shit City again."

"You're a reporter, lad, not a goddamn spy."

"Call it what you will, I'll be dealing with Tony and the Magician and that puts me back in the Game, like it or not."

"You know how to find this Magician?"

O'Hara smiled. "I can find the Magician."

"And is he also an agent?"

"The Magician?" O'Hara laughed. "Oh yeah. He's the last of the red hot spies."

7

THE GREEN-BLUE CARIBBEAN GLEAMED below him like a jewel nestled in the hand of God. The Lear jet banked gracefully in the cloudless sky and soared down toward the island of St. Lucifer. Coral reefs swept beneath the plane, shimmering deep in the clear sea, like bunches of tiny boutonnieres. Ahead of them, St. Lucifer squatted in the blazing sun, a tiny island dominated by a single mountain peak cloaked in bright-green foliage. The main town, Bonne Terre, lay before them, its five-thousand-foot runway beckoning from the edge of town, like a long, bony finger.

From ten thousand feet it had still looked like the paradise he remembered, a fertile and unspoiled refuge hidden away between Guadeloupe and Martinique. Although still a French dependency, the island had its own governor and a police force of six. But as the plane whistled down to its landing, O'Hara saw the grim signs of encroaching civilization.

Two years before, when O'Hara had last been to St. Lucifer, there was one hotel, which attracted erstwhile journalists, fishermen, expatriates, drunks and mercenaries, who preferred to call themselves soldiers of fortune. Even travel agents had ignored the island, finding it much too dull to recommend to anyone. So it had also become the perfect crossroads for peripatetic intelligence agents assigned to the Caribbean sector, most of them culled from the dregs of their respective agencies: alcoholics, misfits, over-the-hill operatives and men on the verge of mental breakdown, sent to this sunny Siberia, where they spent most of their time spying on one another. When something big came up, the first team was usually sent in. But routine intelligence business was left to the misfits.

Two years had changed St. Lucifer. The commercial lepers had finally discovered it, and the blight was evident from the air as they swept onto the runway. Hilton and Sheraton had invaded its lazy beaches, and condominiums had begun to spring up along the jungled coast, a harbinger of the Styrofoam and Naugahyde invasion that was imminent. O'Hara could see a golf course stretching out beside the once virgin west beach, and swimming pools glittered like vinyl puddles among the fancy homes on the outskirts of town. Even the main road, which twisted, like an eel, the hundred or so miles around the perimeter of the island, had been paved.

O'Hara could guess the rest: the gaming tables, with their semiliterate mobster overlords accompanied by sleek, overdressed, overjeweled, classless broads. St. Lucifer had become just another tacky, tasteless colony for the fat and ugly *nouveaux riches* and the ephemeral jet-setters. So much for paradise lost.

O'Hara was thinking about the Magician as the plane was taxiing on the runway. What was it Howe had asked—did he know the Magician?

O'Hara smiled to himself. Oh yes, he knew the Magician, all right, the one the French called *le Sorcier.* And oh, what a yarn he could write about him. But the Magician's unique success lay in the fact that nobody ever talked or wrote about him.

Nobody.

The has-been spy community protected his integrity because they needed him. The Magician was their encyclopedia, a listening post for all.

Fate had chosen to throw the Magician, the Game and the Caribbean into the same pot, and in so doing, had created a marvelously catastrophic brew; a concoction of sheer madness. The Magician's macabre sense of humor manifested that madness, while the Caribbean became a bizarre capsule of the insanity of the entire intelligence community. The Magician, a man with no training, no backround in the Game, and no particular interest in it, was to become the master Monopolist of Caribbean intelligence; the owner of Boardwalk and Park Place with hotels; King Shit of the territory.

What were his objectives?

None. He had achieved this unique position for the sheer hell of it. It was his hobby. Michael Rothschild, alias Six Fingers, alias the Magician, alias *le Sorcier,* was wonderfully eccentric.

The Magician had been delighted to hear from O'Hara, delighted his old pal was still alive.

"Sailor! So you fucked the goddamn Winter Man, after all," the Magician had cried out when O'Hara finally reached him via one of the most archaic and unreliable telephone systems in the world. As they spoke, static crackled along the line, like popcorn popping.

"Poor help," O'Hara said.

"Come on down!" the Magician cried enthusiastically.

"I'm looking for Falmouth."

"I got all the details."

"I'm running out of time."

"Don't worry. It's cool. I'll put you with Tony."

"Can't we talk on the phone?"

"Yeah. But you're gonna end up here, anyway. So . . . come on down. It's right on the way."

"Okay, pal, warm up the ice cubes."

Howe had supplied the Lear. And now, as it taxied toward the shack they called a depot, O'Hara's adrenaline was pumping furiously. Falmouth was somewhere nearby, and for the first time since he had accepted the assignment, he was eager to find out what was up his sleeve.

II

The man was absolutely unmemorable. He was neither tall nor short, fat nor thin, handsome nor ugly. He had no scars or noticeable defects. His accent was basically bland, he could have been from Portland, Oregon, or Dallas, Texas, there was no way of telling. He wore gray: a gray suit, a gray-and-wine tie, a gray-striped shirt. In short, there was nothing in his carriage, demeanor or dress that would either attract attention or make an impression on anyone.

The office was on the twenty-second floor of a sterile glass-and-chromium New Orleans skyscraper that had all the warmth and pizzazz of a fly swatter. He checked his watch as he got off the elevator.

Two minutes early. Perfect.

He entered the office of Sunset Oil International.

"My name is Duffield," he told the secretary. He did not offer a card.

"Oh yes, Mr. Duffield, you're to go right in," she said. "Mr. Ollinger is expecting you. Do you care for coffee or something cool to drink?"

"No, thank you."

She ushered him into the office. Ollinger was a man in his early forties, with the baby-skin face and soft hands of the easy life. His soft brown eyes stared bleakly from behind lightly tinted, gold-rimmed spectacles. He was tall and erect and in good physical shape, clean-shaven with short-cropped blond hair, and he was in his shirt sleeves. The city stretched out behind him, a panaroma framed by floor-to-ceiling windows. His walnut desk was a study in Spartan organization: "in" boxes and "out" boxes and not a sheet of paper out of place. On the credenza behind him was a single photograph of a woman and two children, and beside it a small brass plaque with "Thank you for not smoking" printed on it. There was not one other personal effect in the room. It was as if Ollinger had just moved in and had not unpacked yet. His manner was cordial but distant. Some might have thought him intimidating, but to Duffield, he was just another executive with a problem.

"Thanks for getting up here so fast," Ollinger said after the introductions.

"You indicated there is some urgency to the matter."

"You might say that," Ollinger replied with a touch of sarcasm. He sighed, and straightening his arms, placed both hands on his desk, palms down. "Before we start," he said, "I would like it understood that this conversation never happened."

Duffield smiled. "Of course," he said. Ollinger was new at this, and uncomfortable in a situation that was totally out of his control.

"Good," Ollinger said, with a sense of relief. He opened the desk drawer and took out a yellow legal pad with notes scrawled all over the top page. "I hope I can decipher all this," he said. "I was scribbling notes as fast as I could."

"Why not just tell me the basic problem," Duffield said.

"The basic problem is that one of our people has been kidnapped by terrorists in Venezuela," Ollinger said, still studying his notes and not looking up.

"I see."

"Actually, he's a consultant attached to our office in Caracas. It was a mistake. They meant to take the manager of the plant and got the wrong man."

"You know that for sure?"

Ollinger nodded. "Our manager's name is Domignon. He was going to take Lavander on a tour of the facilities but something came up at the last minute. He let Lavander use his car and driver and it was raining, so he loaned Lavander his slicker. They jumped the car less than a mile from the main gate."

"Lavander's the one got lifted, then?"

"Yes."

"Is he the oil consultant?"

Ollinger nodded. "Yes. You know him?"

"Only by reputation. When did this happen?"

"Eight-twenty this morning."

"Have you heard from the bastards?"

"Yes."

"What do they want?"

"Two million dollars."

"What's the time frame?"

"I beg your pardon?"

"How much time do you have?"

"Forty-eight hours." He looked at his watch. "Make that forty-five."

"So we have until approximately eight-thirty the day after tomorrow. Are they aware of their error?"

"They don't care. It's put up or shut up."

"How badly do you want him back?"

"Well, I . . . uh, we have to treat him as if—"

"Mr. Ollinger, is he worth two million dollars to your company?"

Ollinger seemed shocked by Duffield's candor. "There's a man's life at stake here."

"Yes, yes, but that's not what I asked you. Is the man worth two million dollars to Sunset?"

The weight of events seemed to press down on Ollinger. His shoulders sagged and he looked at his hands. "I don't know anybody that is," he said forlornly.

"Is this political?"

"Political?"

"You know, do they want anything else? Do they have prisoners they want released? Is there a union problem in the plant? Are these people revolutionary types? Do they want to nationalize your operation? Is it political?"

"No. All . . . all they want's two million dollars."

"Or what?"

"Or they'll kill him, take another hostage and raise the ante to four million."

"Typical. Do you know these people? Is it a group? A solo with a few hired hands? Some employee with a hard-on?"

"They call themselves the . . . uh, Raf . . ." He looked at his notes.

"Rafsaludi?" Duffield filled in.

"That's it. You know them?"

"We've dealt with them once or twice before. It's a loose-knit, terror-for-profit group trained by Qaddafi's people in Libya. They're not politically motivated."

"So it has something to do with oil, then . . ."

"Not necessarily. They prey on big American companies. Our last experience with them involved a soft-drink company in Argentina. The Rafsaludi is motived by greed, not social reform. That's a help."

"A help?"

"Well, there's an attitude of fanaticism among political revolutionaries. Tends to make them a bit unpredictable. A greedy terrorist is always easier to deal with."

"Oh," Ollinger said. It was obvious that he was uneasy dealing with the problem. "Can it be done without, you know, a lot of—uh, unnecessary, uh . . ."

"You're new at this," Duffield said. It was not a question.

"Yes. I was in the legal department until they made me veepee in charge of international operations two months ago."

"You'd better get used to this kind of thing," Duffield said. "These are cretins. Unless the situation is dealt with harshly, it will happen again."

Ollinger rubbed his forehead. He was growing more uncomfortable by the minute.

"I assume you want the man back," Duffield said briskly, changing the subject.

Ollinger looked at him with arched eyebrows. "Of course," he said.

"Mr. Ollinger, let's be candid. Of course you want this Lavander back. What I mean is, you want him back, but you don't want to pay two million dollars for him, right?"

"That's why I called you. Derek Frazer recommended—"

"Yes, yes, I talked to Derek. My point is, this man is only a consultant, he's not a salaried executive with the company."

"We have to think of him as an employee," Ollinger said. "If word got out that we let terrorists kill a contract consultant . . ." He let the sentence trail off.

"Yes, it would be regarded as a moral responsibility."

"You don't have to remind us . . ."

"Excuse me," Duffield said quietly, "that wasn't meant to sound like a moral judgment. I am merely trying to get a proper fix on the situation."

Ollinger cleared his throat and then nodded. "Yes, uh . . . your analysis is quite correct. If possible, we'd like to do this without any media coverage. Lavander himself is a bit reclusive. Very private. I doubt that he would talk about it—that is, if we can get him out and—"

"It's not an 'if' situation. We'll bring him in, if that's what you want."

"We can't afford to lose him."

"So, I repeat, you want him back, but you don't want to spend two million dollars doing it. Is that a proper appraisal of the situation?"

Ollinger began to fidget. He flexed his shoulders as though he had a stiff neck. Drops of perspiration appeared along his hairline. The armpits of his shirt were black with sweat. Finally he said, "Yes, that's accurate. Also, we'd like to, uh, think it won't . . . you know, happen again."

"Perfectly understandable. How many people know about this?"

"No more than seven or eight. The executives at the plant, the driver of the car, who was released after they grabbed Lavander, and the head of plant security."

"No Venezuelan cops?"

"No."

"State department? CIA, FBI . . ."

"No, none of that."

"Excellent. Well, Mr. Ollinger, I'd like to suggest you leave this matter in our hands. Inform Señor Domignon that he'll be getting a call sometime within the next hour. I'll need some basic information, names of executives, phone numbers, location of plant . . . uh, we may need to slip some equipment into the country without having to deal with customs. But, basically, all you need to do is call Domignon and tell him I'll be in touch. Then you can forget about it."

Ollinger smiled hesitantly. "That's wonderful, really. Now, about the price . . ."

"The price will be three hundred thousand dollars. I'll need it in cash before I leave. My briefcase is empty, you can put the money in there."

Ollinger seemed shocked. "Three hundred thousand!"

Duffield smiled. "Look at it this way, Mr. Ollinger: you're investing three hundred thousand and saving one million seven. If there should be a repeat of the situation, we'll handle it at no additional cost. Oh, and by the way, if the operation should fail for any reason, your money will be cheerfully refunded."

"Quill."

"Duffield here."

"What's the situation?"

"First of all, this Ollinger is a wimp. New on the job and very unhappy he has to handle this. Doesn't want to get his hands dirty. Actually, he was so relieved when I told him to forget it and let us handle the thing, I thought he was going to jump across the desk and kiss me."

"Any danger he may violate security?"

"No, he's quite aware of the need for silence."

"What are the details?"

"The Rafsaludi grabbed a consultant named Lavander in Caracas by mistake; they were after the manager, a man named Domignon. They want two mil by the day after tomorrow, eight-thirty A.M., or they snuff the hostage, grab another and raise the ante to four mil."

"Fairly routine for them."

"Yes, very little imagination. The hook is that they lifted the wrong man. But it's just a wrinkle, nothing that would affect the overall operation."

"Media? Police?"

"No, so far it's clean. A few executives and the driver of the car Lavander was taken from."

"Excellent. State department isn't involved, or CIA?"

"No, it's under wraps. We have the contract and I've handled the funds in the usual manner. Three hundred thousand less my commission."

"Excellent, I'll take it from here. As usual, you did an excellent job, Mr. Duffield. At the beep tone, please feed Master all names and contacts and any other information we'll need."

"Thanks very much."

"Thank you for moving so quickly. Good day, sir."

"So long."

"This is Master Control."

"Clearance for selection."

"One moment, please." A few seconds later a recorded voice came on the line. "Clearance. Your ID?"

"Quill. Z-1."

"Programming Z-1. Voice check."

"Four score and seven years ago . . ."

"Voice check cleared. Your number?"

"730-037-370."

"Your program?"

"Selection."

"Programming selection." There was another pause and then: "This is Selection."

"Antiterrorism."

"Programmed."

"Assassination."

"Programmed."

"Kidnapping."

"Programmed."

"Language, Spanish."

"Programmed."

"Venezuela."

"Programmed."

"Route and intersect."

"Routing . . . intersection . . . we have twelve candidates."

"File and reselect."

"Filed and reprogrammed."

"Availability."

"Programmed."

"Route and intersect."

"Routing . . . intersection . . . we have nine candidates."

"File and reselect."

"Filed and reprogrammed."

"Team operation."

"Programmed."

"Previous team."

"Programmed."

"Assassination, nonpolitical."

"Programmed."

"Caracas."

"Programmed."

"Tracking."

"Programmed."

"Route and intersect."

"Routing . . . intersection . . . we have one candidate."

"Name."

"Hinge."

"Subfile and reselect."

"Subfiled and reprogrammed."

"Delete tracking."

"Tracking deleted."

"Route and intersect."

"Routing . . . intersection . . . we have four candidates."

"Names."

"Falmouth, Gazinsky, Hinge, Kimoto."

"File and hold."

"Filed . . . holding."

A long pause, then Quill said, "Delete Kimoto."

"Kimoto deleted."

"Hold."

"Holding."

Another pause. Then: "Readout . . . Falmouth, team ops, A-level."

"Falmouth, Tony . . . prefers solo ops . . . two previous team ops . . . maximum team size: three . . . commander: one ops . . . command effectiveness rating: A-plus . . . overall effectiveness rating: A-plus, A-plus."

"Delete readout."

"Readout deleted."

"Readout . . . Gazinsky, team ops, A-level."

"Gazinsky, Rado . . . four previous teams ops . . . commander: one ops . . . command effectiveness rating: C . . . overall effectiveness rating: C, A-minus, B, B-plus."

"File overall effectiveness rating and delete."

"Information deleted . . . holding."

"Readout . . . Hinge, team ops, A-level."

"Hinge, Raymond . . . four previous team ops . . . commander: two ops . . . command effectiveness rating: A, B-plus . . . overall effectiveness rating: A, B-plus, A, B-plus."

"Intersect overall effectiveness rating and score."

"Intersection . . . scoring: Falmouth, A-plus . . . Hinge, A-minus . . . Gazinsky, B."

Falmouth and Hinge were obviously the best men for the job.

As was his custom, Falmouth placed a long-distance call to a 404 area code at eleven o'clock. The telephone was in a small efficiency apartment on the Buford Highway in Atlanta. The apartment contained a small desk, a chair and a telephone with a Code-A-Phone 1400 answering machine. Falmouth paid the rent by the year. Since the phone was used only to collect incoming calls, the bill was fixed and was paid each month by money order. It answered on the first ring and the recorded voice said: "Hello, this is the University Magazine Service. At the tone, please leave your name, number and the time you called. Thank you." A beep followed.

Falmouth held a small yellow plastic beeper to the mouthpiece of the phone and pressed the button on the side. A series of musical tones emitted from the beeper. Falmouth could hear the tape in the answering machine rewinding.

"Shit," he said to himself.

The first call was transmitted.

"This is Quill, eleven-ten, Thursday, 730-037-370. Urgent."

The second call was almost the same:

"Quill, eleven fifty-five, Thursday, 730-037-370. Red urgent. One hour."

Deciphered, that meant Quill had a hot one and needed to make contact with Falmouth within an hour. Falmouth looked at his watch. It was twelve-ten. He had forty-five minutes to get back to Quill.

He had to make a decision fast. Time was running out. Howe had three days left to deliver O'Hara. But if Falmouth failed to call Quill, it could blow his whole plan. His back was against the wall. He decided to make the call.

He dialed the number.

"Yes?" the voice answered.

"Reporting."

"Clearance?"

"Spettro."

"Classification?"

"T-1."

"Voice check."

"Jack be nimble, Jack be—"

"ID number?"

"730-037-370."

"Cleared for routing. Contact?"

"Quill."

"Routing."

He was on hold for only a few seconds when the cultured voice answered.

"Quill."

"Falmouth."

"Is your phone clean?"

"Yes, it's a pay phone."

"Excellent. Glad you got back to me. I have something for you. It's a bit dirty, but the price is good."

"Yes?"

"A consultant has been lifted by the Rafsaludi from Sunset Oil in

Caracas. They want two million by day after tomorrow. The subject is Avery Lavander. We want to bring him in whole."

"Have you a play in mind?"

"Yes. A variation on the Algerian switch."

"That would require a preliminary face-to-face confrontation."

"We've had a bit of a break in that respect. The plant manager has arranged a meeting between the Rafsaludi and a company rep tomorrow at two. They're being quite audacious about this, but they're also a bit stupid. It gives us plenty of time to get in there and set up."

"Hmmm."

"Are you familiar with the play?"

"Yes. It requires a team."

"Affirmative. But only two men. I understand you prefer to operate solo, but you happen to be . . ."

Quill's voice seemed to fade away. Falmouth was already considering his options. It would be the worst kind of tactic to turn down a red urgent assignment at this point. But a chill coursed through his body into his stomach. He felt as if he had swallowed an ice cube. The timing could not be worse. And a team play into the bargain. He had made his reputation as a solo. Working alone was something he had learned a long time ago . . .

On the outskirts of Newtonabbey, six or seven miles northeast of Belfast, the grim rowhouses seem to stretch for miles, as if reflected in mirrors. They crowd the cobblestone streets, these dismal clones, caked a monochrome gray by decades of industrial dust that has long since disguised whatever colors the houses once were. One of Tony Falmouth's earliest memories was that his house and all the houses in this drab infinity seemed constantly to be peeling. The grit-caked paint hung in flakes from window sills and porch railings and door frames, like dead skin peeling from a burned body. In his youthful nightmares, the rains would come and the flakes became soggy and the houses began to melt and soon the gutters of the claustrophobic streets were flooded with a thick gray mass of putty, and Tony ran along the sidewalk trying to find his own house in that molten river of gray slime. Then he woke up.

By the time he was ten, Tony Falmouth had already begun to deal with his identity crisis. He had his Uncle Jerry to thank for that. Uncle Jerry was another persistent memory from his youth, although a much more pleasant one. Uncle Jerry, the wiry, hard-talking little Cheshire Cat of a man, always smiling, always humming some nondescript tune; a man so ugly he was beautiful, with a large warty nose and hands so big he could conceal a pint in his fist.

Jerry Devlin, his mother's brother, listened to his dreams and his fears and talked to him. Nobody else did. His father, Emmett, crushed under the weight of family and job and assigned by fate to the worst kind of drab anonymity, had very little to say to anyone. Every night he sat with his pint or two of ale, staring out the window, down through the endless parade of slums, to a place where he could just barely see the ocean between the houses. One night, when Tony was nine, his father got up from the chair and followed his gaze, out the door, down the cobblestone street, and off into the fog and never came home.

The crisis precipitated by the desertion of Emmett Falmouth was resolved by Uncle Jerry and Uncle Martin. Tony was very bright, so it was decided he would stay in school and Jerry and Marty would keep food on the table and make the rent and keep an eye on the kid.

But there was always the weight. He had watched it bend his father until he looked like a hunchback. And now he watched the weight bow his mother, watched the wrinkles spread across her face like ripples on water, watched the color fade from her hair and the life fade from her eyes until one morning she could no longer get out of bed. It took her a month, lying there choking on her own phlegm, to die.

When Father Donleavy came to the house, Tony made a confession. He told the priest he hated his father. Father Donleavy suggested a round of Our Fathers and Hail Marys and told him time would ease the pain. He went to live with Marty, and it was another two years before Tony realized Father Donleavy was full of shit. Time and Hail Marys did not get rid of the anger. Instead, it grew inside him, like a snake coiled in his stomach.

Jerry always came at night. He was always armed. And the only time he spoke with bitterness about anything was when he talked about the British. Marty was different. He was apolitical. He had good friends among the British in Ulster. There was no fight in him and he and Jerry never discussed the Troubles. Nobody ever told Tony his Uncle Jerry was an IRA gunman, after a while he just knew it.

Once, when Tony was twelve, a military payroll was robbed and there was a great deal of shooting and several men on both sides were killed. That night, Jerry came to the house and they sat at the table in the kitchen with the curtains drawn and Jerry took out a package wrapped in yellow oilskin.

"Hide this fer me, will ye now," Jerry said. And Tony climbed out the window of his second-floor room and hid the package in a vent in the roof. Two weeks later Jerry took Tony out to the fields twenty miles from Newtonabbey and he opened up the package. It was a brand-new Webley .38-caliber pistol.

"A grand weapon," Jerry said. "And 'tis toime ye learn to use it. Do it like yer p'intin' yer finger. Keep both eyes open. Imagine yer shootin' at the bloody Black and Tans."

Tony took the gun and held it and put his finger on the trigger and it felt good in his hand and he could feel the energy from it charging through his body. He held the gun out at arm's length and sighted down along the barrel and the gun seemed to be an extension of his arm and his anger flooded down into his finger and he squeezed the trigger.

Boom!

The gun kicked up high and the power of the weapon made him dizzy with excitement and after that he practiced whenever he could, watching the bottles and rocks explode as he squeezed off the shots. Only it wasn't Black and Tans he imagined shooting, it was his father.

" 'Tis one thing to know how to use a weapon," Jerry said. "Just remember, plannin' is most important. Plannin' is everything. Always know how to get into and how to get out of a fix. And don't trust nobody. When ye can, work on yer own. Dead heroes ain't no good to nobody."

When they were finished, he would hide the gun back in the rooftop vent. Occasionally Jerry would come in the night and get the yellow oilskin wrapper. And then he would return it a day or two later. Then one day they came to the house and told Marty that Jerry was dead, informed on by one of his own, and tracked down and killed by a new British colonel in Newtonabbey.

Nobody came to get the gun. A month or two went by, and Tony realized it was his now.

Tony played soccer in the street near the school which also happened to be across the way from the British patrol station. The colonel, whose name was Floodwell, was a stiff and proper man with waxed mustaches and suspicious eyes. Planning, that was important. And doing it alone. Twice a week at exactly six o'clock the colonel left the patrol station and walked three blocks to a narrow little street without a name that sat on The Bluffs. The street was a dead end and beyond the barrier, the land dropped away fifty or sixty feet to the street below. There were houses built into the side of The Bluffs whose basements were on the lower level. The colonel walked down the dead-end street and, using his own key, entered a house near the dead end and there he had a drink of Scotch and dinner and made love to the young woman who had rooms in the house.

Tony planned his first execution all winter long, following the colonel, watching him from the darkness across the street. He found an abandoned house and used it as a short cut home from school each night. He memorized the house, knew every step, sat for long periods of time, listening to the rats cavorting in the darkness, making his plans.

Between the vacant house and his own house, there was a small sentry house squatted on the corner and when there was trouble, the troopers stationed there pulled the barbed-wire barriers across the road. Tony had youth on his side. At fourteen, he was still small for his age. When he went home, he went down through the vacant house and out the basement door and crossed the street and walked close to the houses on the other side, staying in the shadows until he was almost to the sentry box. At first he would startle the two troopers at the check point, but they soon got to know him.

On a Monday in early spring, he loaded the Webley, and folded it back in its oilskin wrapper. He got a potato from the pantry and bored a hole about three-quarters of an inch in diameter through the center of it and put the gun and the potato in the bottom of his canvas knapsack, covering them with books and his lunch. After school, he played soccer in the street near the patrol station. The knapsack lay on the sidewalk in full view of everybody for two hours. By five-thirty it was too dark to play any longer. He said goodbye to his friends and went straight to the deserted house on the nameless street. He got out the oilskin wrapper and unfolded it and held the Webley in his hand and felt its energy, like electricity, sizzling up his arm. He took out the potato. It was a trick Jerry had taught him.

"It's good for one shot," Jerry had said. "Makes a .38 sound like a popgun. Whoever ya hit'll die with potato all over his mug." And he had laughed. Tony twisted it on the end of the barrel. He waited in the dark with the rats. He felt no fear, only exhilaration.

The colonel entered the nameless street whistling a tune, his swagger stick under his arm. He walked with a marching step, jaunty and arrogant, his chin held up high. Tony stepped out of the doorway and stayed close to the house. He started to walk toward the colonel.

He was ten feet away when the colonel saw him. "Hey!" he said. "You gave me a start there, boy. Step out here, let me have a look at you."

Tony looked up at the colonel, but suddenly he wasn't looking at the colonel's thin lips or his long, arrogant nose or his glittering, cold eyes. He was looking, instead, at the face of his father. He stepped out of the dark, held the gun at arm's length and squeezed the trigger.

The potato muffled the shot.

It went *pumf.*

And the potato disintegrated and the bullet ripped into the colonel's head just above his left eye and tore the side of his skull away. Bits of potato splattered against his shocked face. The force of the shot twisted him half around and he staggered sideways, his feet skittering under him, but he did not fall. He kept his balance and turned back toward Tony. The side of his face was a soggy mess. His eye was blown from its socket. Geysers of blood flooded down his jacket. His one good eye stared with disbelief at Tony. He took an unsteady step and fell to his knees.

A window opened down the alley.

"Whos'at? What's goin' on?" a voice called out.

Tony ducked into the shadows and stared back up the nameless street. A door opened near the end of the street, a shaft of yellow light cut through the darkness.

Tony turned back toward the empty house and then his heart froze. Something grabbed his ankle. He turned, and the colonel had one hand around his ankle and his good eye was glaring up at the youth with hate, and his other hand was clawing at his holster. Blood splashed on Tony's pants leg. The colonel tried to say something, to scream, but all that came out was a bloody gurgle.

Tony tried to pull away. He dragged the colonel a few feet toward the vacant house, but the officer had Tony's leg in a death grip. He started to release the pistol from its holster. Tony held the pistol an inch from the man's forehead and fired again. Floodwell's forehead exploded. Bits of skull and blood peppered Tony's face. The colonel rolled over and lay on his back gagging, then a rattle started deep in his throat.

Tony bolted into the doorway of the house, wrapped the gun in its oilcloth packet and stuffed the gun down under his books. He took out his handkerchief and wiped his bloody face as he ran back to the basement steps. He heard footsteps on the street above and he kept running and wiping the blood off his face. When he reached the back door he stopped. He stuffed the kerchief down with the gun and stepped cautiously into the dark street. It was empty. He walked quickly to other side, where the shadows were deeper and started toward the sentry post. He could see the two troopers inside the small blockhouse in the middle of the road. The street was open. The barbed-wire gate was pulled back on the sidewalk. The two troopers seemed to be working on the radio. He could hear its static as he drew closer.

There was only blood on one of his pants legs. That was a help.

He stayed in the shadows, walking very slowly, his eyes on the two Tans standing near the check booth.

"I'm tellin' ya, Striker, it was shots," one of them said, "at least the second one was."

"Awr, ya hear shots in yer sleep, Finch," the one called Striker said.

Tony walked toward the two troopers who were silhouetted by the lights in the booth. In the future, he thought walking in the darkness toward them, he would try to think of everything that could go wrong. He would have more than one plan.

Tony reached the barbed-wire gate that had been pulled back on the sidewalk. The two troopers had not seen him, they were busy trying to tune in their radio, but all they were getting was static.

He held his leg against the barbed-wire fence and pushed until he felt one of the steel knots dig through his pants and into his leg. He pulled up and the barb tore deep into his flesh. He screamed.

The trooper called Striker flashed his torch in Tony's face.

"Help me, please! I've hurt m'self," he called out.

"Jesus Christ!" Striker cried and rushed over to Tony.

"You got yerse'f a bad cut there, son," he said, watching blood pumping through Tony's torn pants. "Dintcha see that wire?"

"I was in a hurry. Played soccer too long, y'know. I'm really in for it now. Late for dinner and me pants is ruined. My uncle'll take the strap to me for sure."

" 'Ere, Finch, get out the kit. Our soccer champ, 'ere, has got hisself wounded on our wire."

Finch was hitting the radio with his fist, trying to clear the static. "Wonder what th' hell's goin' on up 'ere?" he said. He looked at Tony's leg. "Christ, son, you really tore yourself up, now, dintcha. Hold still a minute, I got some iodine and a bandage in the first aid. Din' 'at sound like gunshots to you, Striker?"

"I was fuckin' with the radio, Finch, I really din't hear it," he said. "Hang on, son, this'll have a bite t'it." He bathed the ragged tear in Tony's foot with iodine and bandaged it.

The phone in the booth rang and Finch picked it up. "Whas'at . . . whas'at? Jesus, is he a goner? No, there ain't been a living soul down 'ere for half an hour . . . just a school kid we know, cut his leg on the wire . . . Rightch'are. We'll close her off now, but it's been quiet as a bleedin' church mouse down 'ere." He hung up. "You ain't gonna believe this, Striker. Somebody just blew the colonel's head off. Not two blocks from 'ere, up on Th' Bluff. We got to close up th' street. I told jez I 'eard shots."

Tony squinched up his face and forced out some tears. "Owww," he moaned.

"How far do ya live?" Finch asked.

"Just two roads down, on Mulflower."

"Kin ya walk on 'at?"

"I think so." He tried it. The cut burned but he could stand on it. "I can make it okay. Thank ye, for yer help."

"Watch yer step, lad. Ther's trouble afoot t'night. Get off the street 's fast as yer can."

"Yes, sir," and he limped off into the darkness as Striker and Finch began to move the barbed-wire gate across the road.

By the time Tony was eighteen and had finished high school and had won himself a scholarship to Oxford, he had learned his profession well. To carry the pistol to England would have been foolhardy. Besides, Falmouth wasn't angry anymore. When he killed Floodwell, all Tony could remember was that getting even felt good, but as time went on, getting even became less and less important. Revenge turned to exhilaration. Now the simple act of killing made him feel good, the same way that a forward feels good when he makes a goal. It was what he did and he did it without remorse or feeling and he did it very well indeed. And he did it alone.

The day before he left, he rode his bike out to Land's End and threw the Webley as far out into the ocean as he could. It had served its purpose. In four years, Tony had killed nine people. Two had been British, the rest were informers. Only one of them was a woman.

At Oxford, Falmouth had made quite a record for himself, and for reasons known only to himself, after completing his Rhodes studies, Falmouth joined the British Secret Service. There was no record anywhere of Falmouth's early "training," and M.I.6 was glad to get him. He never went back to Ireland.

". . . with a first-class man."

Falmouth snapped back to reality.

"Excuse me," he said, "there was some static on the line. Could you repeat that?"

"Sorry. I see this as a two-man operation. You happen to be very well qualified for the play and I've teamed you up with a first-rate chap."

"Who?"

"His name is Hinge. He's younger but he's been in the Game for several years. He's quite good, really. I consider him one of our best.

He's been in on four team operations to date and acquitted himself admirably."

"I see."

"I'm sorry, in my haste I only did an A-level check on you. Have you ever been involved in the switch play?"

"Rome. Four months ago. But it was a little different. It was the Red Brigades and we had to lift five people out."

"Of course, now I remember. A very good show, I might add."

"Thank you. It's still a very risky play."

"But most effective when it works."

"Agreed."

"Do you know Caracas?"

"I've been there, but I don't know the city that well. I know a driver there who's as good as they come."

"Excellent."

"What are we dealing with, some revolutionary gang?"

"There's no politics in this. Just a bunch of local gangsters trained by the Rafsaludi, trying to shake down the company, although we have no fix on just how tough these customers are."

"Well, the Rafsaludi can get very nasty."

"Quite. It's a bonus job. Seventy-five thousand."

Falmouth whistled silently to himself. He was already planning ahead.

"It will have to be done fast. Perhaps even by tomorrow night. Certainly no later than the next day. The risk increases by the hour."

"Yes, I know. Let's see, today is Monday . . . you should have Lavander out no later than Wednesday eve."

"All right," Falmouth said. "I'm in. I assume the operation is mine."

"Yes, you'll be in command. Hinge is already cleared. Is Miami convenient?"

"Fine."

"There's a flight on Pan Am at ten-ten P.M. from Miami International. It arrives at thirty-three minutes after midnight. Hinge will not be there until eight A.M. He's coming in through Mexico."

"Weapons?"

"Everything you need will be down there. Your contract is Rafael Domignon. The number is 53-34-631. There will be a packet at the airport for you, as usual."

"Good. How do I know Hinge?"

"Photo ID and the Camel ploy."

"Fine. I'll report when it's over unless we have a problem."

"Excellent, sir, excellent. I'm delighted you're handling this."

"Thanks. Later."

"Goodbye."

Goddamn! What a rotten break. What a rotten, fucking break. But if this Hinge had the stuff, Falmouth could be back in the Bahamas by late Wednesday. If O'Hara shows, he thought, he'll wait.

The packet was delivered by messenger at the Pan Am ticket counter fifty-five minutes before flight time. Falmouth took it to the men's room, entered a stall and sat on the toilet, studying its contents. It contained a round-trip ticket to Caracas and a passport, license and two credit cards under the name Eric Sloan, five thousand dollars in cash and unsigned traveler's checks, a three-by-five color photograph of Hinge, what appeared to be a slightly fuzzy Polaroid shot of Lavander, a list of all executives at the plant in Caracas, confirmed and prepaid hotel reservations at the Tamanaco Hotel, the best hotel in the city, and a filter-tip Camel cigarette wrapped in aluminum foil. He marked the filter tip with a pen and put the cigarette in his package of Gitanes. He studied the photo of Hinge for several minutes, started to burn it, then changed his mind and slipped it into a compartment of his passport wallet. He signed the traveler's checks and put them, with the cash, in his passport wallet, along with the receipt for the hotel. He studied the photograph of Lavander, a gangly, unkempt man with a gray complexion and thin, straggly hair, for several minutes, and when he knew the face, he burned the photograph and flushed the remains.

He left the rest room and went to the airline counter to check in.

Hinge arrived at ten the next morning. The drive up from the airport to Caracas was hot and uncomfortable, with the air still humid from the rains the day before, and storm clouds threatening to deluge the city again at any moment. To make matters worse, the cab was not air-conditioned. Warm, moist wind blew through the open windows, and Hinge was wind-whipped and sweaty. The traffic, as usual, was wicked and pollution burned his nose and throat.

"Pit-fuckin'-city," Hinge said, only half under his breath. It wasn't his first trip to the capital of Venezuela. He knew it well. The city fills a narrow nine-mile-long valley between Mount Avila, a sixty-five-hundred-foot forested mountain, to its north, and the foothills of the Cord Del Maria mountains to the south. Beyond the Cord Del Maria, going farther south, there is not much of anything but jungle and more jungle, and eventually Brazil. The Del Maria foothills had always struck Hinge as *un poco loco,* a little crazy. Schizoid would probably be closer to it. On the western slopes are some of the worst slums in the world, the *ranchitos,* thousands of red huts and adobe shacks that huddle together in squalor, while to the east are the haunts of the rich and the powerful, speckled with costly homes, swimming pools and private clubs, the Beverly Hills of Caracas.

Between them is the sprawling downtown section of, as Hinge would have it, "pit-fuckin'-city"; made rich by oil, grown up far too fast for its own good, and which, despite its towering glass-and-steel skyscrapers, still suffered the same ills as most boomtowns. It was overbuilt, overpopulated, polluted, had a terrible phone system, water shortages, lousy garbage collections, the worst traffic jams in the world and its ugliest whores.

At night it glitters like Tiffany's window.

Hinge wiped sweat from his forehead and tried to ignore the discomfort.

What the hell, he could be in Johannesburg.

Pit-fuckin'-city, squared.

Instead, he thought about the job. Out there somewhere, among the three million people, in the nightmare of downtown or among the squalid *ranchitos,* was poor old Lavander, like a sinner at a prayer meetin', prayin' to be saved. Well, Hinge thought, if me and ol' Spettro can't spring him, he can't be sprung.

So they were staying at the fanciest digs in town. Thank Quill for that. Everything first cabin. Hinge registered and took the key, refusing to allow the bellman to carry his black parachute-silk traveling bag. The room was on the fourth floor.

Good. Hinge didn't like to be up too high. He had once been in a hotel fire in Bangkok, and his fear of hotel fires was paranoid. The elevator whisked him to the fourth floor. The room was large and opulent with a beautiful view of the *teleférico,* a Swiss-type cable car that carried patrons up one side of Mount Avila and down the other to the Caribbean Sea, twelve miles to the north.

He put his duffel-type bag on the bed and opened it, taking out fresh underwear, a shirt, socks and a pair of khaki pants. Anxiety hummed along his nerves. He was already tuning up for the assignment, but he was even more excited knowing that his partner for this job was in the next room. After ten years in the business, he was finally going to meet il Spettro—the Phantom—according to legend the most skilled assassin in the business and a man who could kill you with a dirty look.

At the same time that Hinge was driving toward his hotel in Caracas, O'Hara was pulling up in front of the flamboyant old hotel on St. Lucifer.

Le Grand Gustavsen Hotel sat on the side of a foothill overlooking the main city, Bonne Terre, which had a population of five thousand, to the azure Caribbean beyond. Towering palm trees lined the coral road that led up to its main entrance. Nothing here had changed since O'Hara's last visit to the island. Driving up to the entrance, O'Hara always felt as if he were lost in time. The sprawling four-story, virginal-white Victorian hotel was perhaps the most elegant old gingerbread castle in the world, its latticework a masterpiece of curlicues and filigrees and spindles and arches. Broad porches surrounded the second and third floors of the ancient old hostelry, and the building was framed by tall ferns and palm trees. The main floor of the hotel was actually on the second floor. The bottom floor, once a basement and wine cellar, had been turned into a kind of mini-international bazaar. Hidden discreetly behind French doors were gift shops from England and Spain and the Orient. A famous French *couturier* had a small showroom there. And the newsstand boasted periodicals and newspapers from almost every country in the world, including Russia. A fountain bubbled quietly at the front of the hotel, with a winding *escalier* on either side, leading to the first floor and the main entrance.

The hotel had been built as an investment in 1892 by Olaf Gustavsen, a Norwegian shipbuilder. Three pestering wives and nine children later, old Gus had forsaken it all and retreated to his island castle, where he had married a beautiful local who had borne him a son and died in the doing. Gus welcomed expatriates, soldiers of fortune, itinerate journalists, down-and-out writers, tired-out old spies on the last leg to retirement, and anyone else with a good story to tell. He had, through the years, begrudgingly added plumbing, running water and electricity. His son, Little Gus, who spent most of his time fishing, kept up the tradition of tawdry elegance, never succumbing either to air-conditioning or telephones in the rooms. Messages were accepted by anyone who happened to answer the phone on the desk, and might or might not be delivered. Outwardly, nothing had changed since 1892 except for an occasional coat of white paint. The only modern touch was a small red neon sign near the driveway, which read:

LE GRAND GUSTAVSEN HOTEL
Presents
Six Fingers Rothschild
The Magician of the Keyboard
Appearing nightly

The Magician must have blackmailed the old buzzard to get that put up.

The doorman was a giant of a black man who wore a white short-sleeved shirt and black bellbottoms.

"*Bonjour, monsieur,*" he said, and took O'Hara's suitcase.

"*Bonjour,*" O'Hara said. "*Merci.*"

The place was as colorful as ever. As he was paying the cab driver, two men approached. They were stubby little black men, each with a straw hat cocked jauntily over one eye and each holding a fighting cock in hand. Behind them, an amateur fire eater popped a flaming torch in and out of his mouth.

"*Excusez-moi, monsieur, s'il vous plaît,*" said one of the cockfighters, doffing his hat and smiling broadly enough to show a gold tooth at the side of his mouth, "*Parlez-vous français? Habla Usted español?* Speak Englis?"

"*Je suis américain,*" O'Hara said.

"Ah, monsieur! You have the privilege to meet the greatest *coq* in the islands. This fellow once pecked a tiger to death."

The rooster had seen much better times. Its cone was chewed and ragged, and it only had one leg.

"*Merde!*" his companion exclaimed. "A blind old *grand'mère* hen bit off his leg." He held his cock high in one hand. "This guy once killed an eagle in flight."

"Ha! Such lies! Monsieur, ten dollair *américain* and we will settle this thing right now," said the man with the one-legged chicken.

"Some other time," O'Hara yelled back, following the doorman up the stairs to the main lobby.

The two locals were undaunted.

"*Je m'appelle Toledo. Donnez-moi de vos nouvelles!*" the man with the one-legged bird yelled to him.—I am Toledo. Let me hear from you! And they all laughed.

Double French doors led to the hotel's enormous main room, which served as its lobby, bar, waiting room, restaurant and registry. Sitting just inside the doors was a large hulk of a desk, littered with letters, bills, telegrams, messages, and an antiquated French telephone. The hotel's old-fashioned registration book lay open on one corner. The oak bar, smoothly polished by time, was to the left. Its twenty-foot-long zinc top had once decorated the main room of a famous Parisian brasserie until old Gustavsen had won it from the owner in a game of baccarat and shipped it to the island at great expense. A Montana rancher who had been a regular customer of the hotel for years had presented the old man with a brass plaque when the zinc top arrived. It was mounted at one end of the bar and read: "Won fair and square in a game of chance between old man Gustavsen and Gérard Turin, Paris, December 4, 1924."

To the right of the desk was the restaurant, nothing more than several tables with wicker chairs, but the food was prepared by a young native who had been taught his skill by the previous chef, the great Gazerin. The food alone was worth a trip to the island.

The room itself was a collection of oddities, things left behind or donated or bartered across the bar for drinks: an airplane propeller over the bar, hurricane lanterns of every size and shape, an enormous anchor that had lain in the same spot in one corner of the room for thirty-four years, a wine cooler that Hemingway supposedly gave to old Gustavsen, an Australian bush hat, a blow gun and several darts which, according to legend, had been left there by a pygmy in a seersucker suit. There were several autographed photographs of prize fighters and wrestlers and musicians, hanging awry on the walls, and a good-sized tarpon over the upright piano. The room was dark and comfortably cool, stirred by ceiling fans.

"Tiens, voilà le Marin! Bonjour, bonjour, mon ami," someone yelled from the bar, and O'Hara peered through the darkness to see Justice Jolicoeur approaching him.

Justice Jolicoeur stopped a few feet from O'Hara and posed for a moment, as though he were studying a painting.

"Alors!" he said. "You have not changed by so much as an eyelash. Obviously you weathered your exile well."

He was a wiry little man, and every inch, every ounce, was pure dandy. He wore a white-linen three-piece suit, a thin fire-engine-red tie and a blood-red carnation in his lapel. His boots were of black English leather and his cane was polished enamel with a hand-carved golden swan's head grip. His curly black hair was slicked back tight against his skull, and when he spoke, his polished and cultured *patois* was superbly refined Creole, although for effect he sometimes lapsed into French, which he spoke like a scholar. Jolicoeur was a Haitian who had left the country with the *Tontons,* Papa Doc's vicious secret police, hard on his heels. What he had done to earn the wrath of the dictator was a mystery. Joli, as he liked to be called, never discussed the past. But it was rumored that he had arrived in St. Lucifer with two hundred one-hundred-dollar gold sovereigns in his hollow cane, and immediately conned Gus Junior into a retainer as the hotel's official ambassador of good will. It was worth it to Gus to have Joli around. He gave the place a touch of class.

"Quite," said O'Hara. "And you, you've never looked more prosperous, Joli. Are you keeping busy?"

"You would not believe it. Thanks to the new hotels I have hardly a moment to myself. *Merci, merci, Messieurs* Hilton, Sheraton and you, too, Master Host." He blew them a kiss. "We have had to add a third voodoo show each night, just to satisfy the tourist demand."

"Voodoo? There isn't any voodoo on this island."

"There is now, *Marin.* So far I have imported eighteen families from Port-au-Prince. They make more in tips in one night than they did in a year in Haiti."

"I see you're still working the rooster scam at the door."

"*Oui.* And did you see the fire eater? He adds flavor to the *coq* fights."

"That's almost a bad pun, Joli."

"Monsieur?"

"Forget it. You know, you really oughta get that one guy a new chicken. That one-legged rooster doesn't even look good enough to eat."

"Hey, that's one mean bird, Sailor. Think about it—would you not be mean if you were that ugly and had to hop around on one leg to keep from getting your brains pecked out? *Certainement* he is the world's champion one-legged fighting *coq.*"

"I must tell you, Joli, among the many resourceful people I've known in my life, you are the most resourceful of all. You are the king of all con men."

Joli beamed. His brown eyes twinkled with gratitude. "Ah, O'Hara, you are a true *cavalier.*" And he bowed with a flourish.

"Now, where's *le Sorcier?*" O'Hara demanded.

"He is waiting for you. *Venez avec moi.*"

Jolicoeur led him back past the bar and down a short hall. He rapped ferociously on the door with the cane.

The muffled voice behind the door bellowed, "Jesus Christ, Jolicoeur, come in, don't tear my goddamn door down."

Joli stepped in first and, with a flourish, said, "I am pleased to announce the arrival of *le Marin,* the Sailor, returned from exile."

"Hot shit," Rothschild said.

And the man they called *le Sorcier* jumped up and wrapped his arms around O'Hara. "Joli," he said, "go to the bar and bring back the best bottle of Napoleon brandy we have and a couple of glasses."

"Do we say 'Please'?" Joli said, offended.

"S'il vous-fucking-plaît," Rothschild said.

"Just two glasses?"

"Okay, Joli, three glasses."

"Tout de suite," the little man said and rushed off.

"Jeez, Sailor, you look better than the last time I saw you. It musta been good for you, bein' on the dodge."

Time and the islands had tempered his accent, but it was still definitely Lower East Side Manhattan. He was a slender man, about as tall as O'Hara, deeply tanned, with high cheekbones and a hard, definite jaw. He had the wondrous expression in his eyes and mouth of one constantly about to laugh, which indeed he was. It was the way he looked at life. Life to Rothschild was a joke waiting for the punchline, and he gazed, through stoned eyes, at the world as a madhouse, filled with frantic, scrambling, driven inmates.

An unruly-looking joint was tucked, unlit and forgotten, in the corner of his mouth, and the sweet smell of marijuana hung lightly in the air.

"How about a hit? This is home-grown shit from right up there behind us on the mountain."

"I'm on a tight timetable, Michael. I don't have time right now to get whacked out on your smoke."

"Suit yourself, Sailor. Grab a seat."

The Magician rummaged through his tattered white jeans and then the pockets of his faded blue workshirt, trying to find a light. He was wearing white gloves. Rothschild always wore white gloves. He was not embarrassed by the fact that he was missing the two small fingers on each hand—that's not why he wore gloves. He wore them because people seemed less concerned with his deformity and more concerned with the quality of his piano playing when they could not see where the missing digits had been.

The room was a small office, miserably cluttered, with a rolltop desk, an ancient and decrepit desk chair with a peeling leather seat and two rusty bridge chairs for guests. Junk was jammed in every cubbyhole and opening in the desk. He finally found a book of matches among the debris and lit the roach. He took a deep drag and sighed with relief.

"What are you doing in Gus's office?" O'Hara asked.

"Well, it's a long story. But to make it short, Gus Junior is dead."

O'Hara was genuinely sorrowed. "Well," he said, "there goes one of the greats."

"A true believer," said Rothschild. "What happened, the old boy went out fishing by himself one day, didn't come back. We found him the next day, floating just off the South Spike. Heart attack. Musta been fighting a big one. The pole was still in the cup and he had strapped himself in the fighting chair. Whatever it was, he killed himself trying to land it. The fish was gone, hook was bent out straight."

"I can't think of a better way for the old man to go," O'Hara said.

"Anyway, the old bastard left me the place, all his money, everything! I couldn't believe it, Sailor. I mean, he left it all to me!"

"A helluva responsibility, pal."

"Yeah. I already got some heat about the air-conditioning. I tell everybody, hey, it's in old Gus's will. I can't change a thing. It's a sacred trust."

Joli returned with the brandy and poured three snifters almost to the brim.

"*Merci bien,*" O'Hara said.

"*Ce n'est rien,*" said the little man, and raising his glass, offered a toast: "*À votre santé!*"

"To payday!" O'Hara echoed in English.

"Goddamn, we gave old Gus a send-off would have made the czar happy," Rothschild said. "In his will he says he wants a Viking funeral, like in *Beau Geste,* remember, with Gary Cooper, when they burned the fort with Brian Donlevy at his feet?"

"Before my time," O'Hara said.

"Mine, too, but I've seen it a dozen times on TV. Anyway, that's the way old Gus wanted to go, so I send Christophe downtown, grab one of these runty little dogs always yapping in the street, and I rent a half-dozen fishing boats and we fill 'em with stock from the bar and we wrestled the piano on Duprey's big charter boat and took everybody in the hotel out beyond the South Spike and we laid the dog at his feet and I burned that goddamn fishing boat. I mean Gus, the dog, the boat, every-fuckin'-thing. And I played the damn piano and everybody got drunker than Chinese-fuckin'-New Year. It was beautiful. I'm sure Gus was cryin', wherever he was. Everybody else was.

"A thirty-thousand-dollar Chris-Craft, Sailor, and we burned that fucker right to the water line. Well, why the hell not? I'm still running down numbered accounts on every island in the fuckin' Caribbean. So far I've turned up more than three hundred thousand bucks, and I ain't even been to Switzerland yet." The Magician leaned over and winked. "God knows what the hell's in that account, over there." He leaned back and took another sip of brandy. "So, anyway, you're lookin' at the owner of the damn place. If you're not nice to me, I'll lose your reservation."

"It's all gonna change, Michael. The chains have discovered St. Lucy."

"Yes," said Joli. "Bonjour paradise."

"Hell, they never come here. The tourists, I mean. That's Joli's job, discouraging visitors. But just before the new hotels opened up, these three guys show up one day. I mean, Sailor, these guys look like they eat nails for breakfast, leaning across the desk there and telling me how we are—*we are,* right!—gonna convert the lobby and bar and restaurant into a casino and they're gonna run it for me and I'm gonna get all of ten percent. Ten-fuckin'-percent, can you beat that? So I looks this one bent-nose asshole in the eye and says—shit, O'Hara, you'da been proud of me—I says, 'No dice.' Just like that. The guy with the bent beak kinda rears back, looks at the other two jokers, they look back at me and they flash those this-looks-like-a-smile-but-actually-it-means-we're-gonna-cut-your-heart-out grins and Bent Nose says, 'No dice?' Incredulously. And I says, 'You heard it, chubby, no dice. D-i-c-e'—spelled it out, kinda rubbing their noses in it. It got tense for a minute, okay, I can tell you it did get tense. Then I tore it. I says, 'This place is a CIA front. You wanna start a gang war with the Feds, start shootin'. But no gambling. Period. Everybody got it? And *bon*-fuckin'-*soir* to all of ya.'"

"And?"

"They look at each other, they look at me, they tip their hats, and kinda tiptoe out. That's a year and a half ago. No problems since. Tell you what, Sailor, why don't ya quit, come down here, be my partner. I need somebody to help me run this place. I'm a lousy businessman. What saves my ass is, so is everybody else on this crazy knoll."

"*Oui,* he needs help," said Joli.

"If I went into business with you, we'd be broke in a week. I have to take off my shoes to count to eleven. Let's talk about Falmouth. Okay?"

"You been here ten minutes, ten lousy minutes and you want to get to business already."

"I don't have much time left."

"Christ, you haven't even met Isidore yet."

"Who's Isidore?"

"Ah! Who is Isadore indeed!" Joli said.

"Izzy is my new partner. He lives right over there through that door."

"Michael . . ."

"*Un moment,* my friend," he said and took out his keys and unlocked the door.

Isidore?

Actually, Rothschild had achieved his unique position in the intelligence community by accident. He just happened to be in the right place at the right time: an unimpressive little piano bar called Señor Collada's in Montego Bay, Jamaica. A CIA agent named Jerome Oscarfield was the unwitting catalyst of the gambit.

Oscarfield needed a drop. And there was happy old Six Fingers, the Magician of the Keyboard, plinking out tunes night after night, month after month. The perfect drop. One night Oscarfield slipped Rothschild a small envelope, well sealed.

"Are you a patriot?" Oscarfield asked in a whisper.

"American or world?" asked Rothschild.

"American!" Oscarfield responded, a bit alarmed.

"Just joking," said Rothschild. "I'm red, white and blue, all the way through."

Oscarfield was obviously relieved.

"Now listen carefully. A man who'll call himself Bolo will introduce himself. He'll ask you to play 'Moon Over Miami,' that's how you'll know it's really Bolo."

"I don't do requests," Rothschild said.

"You don't have to play the song," Oscarfield said, his patience wearing a bit thin. "It's like a code, so you'll know it's really him. Just pick a discreet moment and give him the envelope."

"Somebody else could ask me to play 'Moon Over Miami.' It's very popular. I'll tell you a song nobody ever asks for—"

"The song doesn't make any difference," Oscarfield said, cutting Rothschild off, his voice beginning to rise. "You don't have to play the song. It's the combination. He'll say, 'Good evening, my name is Bolo, will you please play "Moon Over Miami." ' You can tell him to go fly a kite, for all I care, just give him the goddamn envelope. There's two hundred bucks in it for you."

"Ah!" said Rothschild. "For two bills I'll be glad to play 'Moon Over Miami.' "

Oscarfield lowered his voice again. He smiled with difficulty. "You don't have to play the song. Tell him you don't know it. Forget the fucking song. Just remember Bolo and 'Moon Over Miami.' That's all you have to do."

"Done," Rothschild said. "What's this Bolo look like?"

"I—uh, I don't *know* what he . . . uh, looks like. I've never . . . uh, met . . . Look, what he looks like doesn't matter."

Oscarfield stared at Rothschild for quite a while. It was a bad idea, he was beginning to think. But he decided to try again. "Let me try once more," he said. "This man named Bolo will come to you and ask you to play 'Moon Over Miami.' When he does, give him this envelope. It's like a code, you see? Who cares what he looks like? I don't care if he looks like King Kong as long as he gives you the code. Okay?"

"We're in business," Rothschild said, sticking out his hand.

"Don't do that," Oscarfield said. "People will see us. Put your hand down. Here, take this."

"What's that?"

"It's the two hundred dollars."

"A deal is a deal," Rothschild said, and as Oscarfield started out of Señor Collada's, he played a few chords of "Moon Over Miami."

Actually Rothschild was simply toying with Oscarfield. Everybody from the pastry chef to the doorman knew Oscarfield's dodge. At first Rothschild didn't really take him seriously. Then, one evening, Bolo showed up. It had to be him. He was the size of a Mack truck and wore dark glasses in the middle of the night and he changed tables three times during one set.

That's him. Got to be, thought Rothschild. Playing musical chairs like that. Nervous as a preacher at a nudist camp. But if this was some kind of undercover job, why would they pick somebody the size of Mount Rushmore?

The answer, he eventually learned, was that the obvious frequently eluded them.

The minute he announced the break, Bolo was on his feet and beside him. He stuck out a hand as big as the piano top.

"I'm Bolo," he said.

"Good," said the Magician.

"Do you know 'Moon Over Miami'?"

"I don't play requests."

Bolo was taken completely aback. He was not programmed for jokes.

"Do you know 'Moon Over Miami'?" he repeated.

"Does it go like this?" Rothschild asked, and began whistling a few bars of "Stars Fell on Alabama."

Bolo looked around the place without moving his head.

"I don't know how it goes," he said. "Goddammit, where's the fuckin' envelope?"

Realizing the big man had no sense of humor, absolutely none, Rothschild slipped him the envelope.

"You're off the wall, y'know that," Bolo growled under his breath and lumbered out of the place.

Rothschild figured that was the end of that. But two weeks later Oscarfield appeared again. "That was nice, the way you handled that," he confided. "Really put old Bolo to the test. I heard about it." He slipped Rothschild another two bills.

Four hundred dollars for not playing "Moon Over Miami." Rothschild was impressed. After that, Oscarfield used him frequently as a drop. He never saw Bolo again. Pretty soon another agent decided to use Rothschild as his Caribbean drop, then another. Then there was Haversham, a British operator with M.I.6. Then an Israeli named Silverblatt. And a Frenchman named . . .

Within five years Rothschild was the postman for the entire Caribbean intelligence community. He became adept at steaming open envelopes. Then he got into cryptology. It became a hobby. Breaking codes. Keeping files. Cross-references. Before long, Rothschild was quite aware that most of the spies in the islands spent most of their time spying on one another. Sometimes members of one agency even spied on other members of the same outfit. Sometimes they didn't even know they were both members of the same agency. The madness of it all appealed to Rothschild's love of the perverse. He began to feel a sense of power. Occasionally he would change the messages slightly, just to see what would happen. In one such instance he almost started a revolution in Guatemala. It was marvelous. It gave the Magician an entirely new outlook on life.

So when he moved to St. Lucifer to become pianist in residence at the Great Gustavsen, the epicenter of the Caribbean undercover network just naturally shifted to St. Lucifer. Rothschild became so important that once, when he went to the States for a three-week vacation, the entire intelligence community was thrown out of whack. At one time there were eighteen operatives, representing every major country in the world, staying at the Great Gustavsen, waiting for *le Sorcier* to return.

By the time he acquired Isidore he was knocking down almost five thousand a month in retainers, from the CIA, the KGB, the Sûreté, M.I.6, and every other outfit in the network.

Isidore opened up whole new vistas. With Isidore his power became even greater.

"*Voilà!* May I present Izzy," Rothschild said as he opened the door to Isidore's room.

Isidore's room was a walk-in closet.

Isidore was an Apple II mini-computer.

O'Hara stared at it in mute appreciation. It was beautiful and very compact. It had a keyboard with a telephone cradle attached to it, and it had its own monitor screen and its own high-speed Kube printer. The main box, Izzy's brain, was about a foot square, with three gates in the front and a large square ready light. A cassette recorder was attached to the telephone modem on the heyboard. The telephone was also equipped with a speakerphone.

Into it, Rothschild had fed mountains of information. But he also made the computer available to agents on a confidential basis, always leaving the room so they could tap out their identification and open up the files of their home-base computers. A video camera built into the wall and aimed at the screen enabled him to collect all of the various codes and machine language necessary to tap into the main computers of most of the major intelligence agencies. By using phone taps, he had also recorded the agents making access calls to their computer centers, and by combining these information banks with his own computer, he had both visual and verbal contact with them.

It was a marvelous hobby.

And it made the Magician one of the most dangerous people in the world.

Having explained his wonderful toy, Rothschild sat down and spread his hands. "How about that?" he said proudly.

"You mean you can plug into the base computers for the CIA, the KGB, like that?" O'Hara asked.

"Mostly on a level-two basis, but in some cases I can even tap their top-secret files."

"Where did you get this thing?"

"Miami. Anybody can buy them. It's learning to use them that's the secret. Let me show you how it works." He slid a picture on the wall to one side, revealing a large wall safe. He spun the dials and opened the safe. It was filled with cassette tapes and floppy disks and video-tapes. He took out a cassette deck and three disks.

He put a disk in each of the gates, and the cassette in the small tape recorder. "These disks store information," he explained. "The first one has the program on it. That's what makes all this work. The cassette has the phone access information on it. Once I get the computer on the line, all I need is the proper access code and I can get a visual print-out on the screen."

He picked up the phone and dialed a number.

"I hope the phones are working today," he said. "I'm calling the access line at Langley."

"The CIA computer?"

"Yeah."

Joli nudged O'Hara. "He spends so much time in here, that is why he needs help to run the business," he whispered.

Rothschild punched the speaker phone buttons. O'Hara could hear the phone ringing. The connection broke and a voice said, "This is Langley Base One. Your identification, please."

Rothschild put the phone in the cradle attached to the keyboard of the computer and pressed the "Play" button on the tape deck. A recorded voice said: "This is Oscarfield, C-One clearance, two-level."

Rothschild pressed the "Pause" button on the tape deck.

The voice said: "Voice ID complete. Access, please."

Rothschild pressed the "Play" button again: "Two-level, file access."

The voice answered: "Tracking, two-level, file access." There was a pause and then: "Proceed."

He pressed the "Play" button again. Oscarfield's taped voice said: "Modem readout, two-level."

Pop! The monitor screen was filled with questions and blank spaces. Rothschild filled them in:

> Access identification: <u>OFLD</u>
> Agent sector: <u>FIELD</u>
> Agent access: <u>L-2</u>
> Agent clarity: <u>B-532</u>
> Subject name: <u>O'HARA, FRANCIS</u>
> Subject agency: <u>PRIVATE</u>
> Was subject formerly attchd? Yes <u>x</u> No
> Previous afltn: <u>CIA</u>
> File level: <u>BASE</u>
> Photos: <u>YES</u>
> Other info: <u>NO</u>
> Accessing file . . .

The light on the side of the computer began to blink. After two or three seconds it stopped and a message appeared on the screen:

Press code key to continue . . .

Rothschild pressed two-three-five and the screen cleared for an instant and then O'Hara's file flashed on-screen.

"I'll be damned," O'Hara said.

"It is truly magic," said Joli. "The whole world speaks to him on this machine."

Rothschild pressed a key and the small white cursor moved rapidly down the screen. He stopped at a listing for "Current assignment":

Subject is on special assmnt. Deep storage.
No contact anticipated for several months.

"The Winter Man really covered his ass, Sailor. As far as your current report goes, you're a fuckin' mole somewhere for the CIA. That way he doesn't have to account for you for maybe a year, until the file is reviewed. So a couple of months from now he'll send down a report that your assignment fell through, then he'll report that you've retired. As far as your file goes, nobody will ever know you were on the run for a year, dodging his fuckin' goons."

Rothschild typed in "ACCESS,PHOTO,SUBJECT,CURRENT" and the letters appeared across the bottom of the monitor screen. He punched the return button on the keyboard and a computerized photo of O'Hara appeared on the screen. He was in a navy uniform.

"Hell, that picture was taken when I was in the Navy!" O'Hara said.

"You look like a child," said Joli.

"It gets weird sometimes," said the Magician.

"How did you get onto this thing, Michael?"

"Would you believe I read about it in the New York *Times*? At first I thought it was just an expensive toy. Then I started realizing the potential. Man, I can tap into the *Times,* the Washington *Post,* United Press. You name it, I got it."

"Look, I think Izzy's just great. Right now I've got other things on my mind."

"If you're worried about missing Falmouth—I mean, if that's what's got you edgy, forget it. Falmouth told me to give you the letter whenever you showed up. He said if the situation changed, he'd call me and I was to burn the envelope. So far he hasn't called. If he does, I'll tell him you're on your way."

"What letter?"

Rothschild reached into a slot in the rolltop desk and pulled out a business-size envelope and gave it to O'Hara.

"You're going to a travel agency in Fort Lauderdale," Rothschild said casually. "The agent there, a dame named Jackowitz, has your plans."

O'Hara looked up at Rothschild. "You read my mail," he said with indignation.

Rothschild slumped and stared contritely at the floor. "Force of habit," he said. "I know it's awful. Forgive me."

"He does it all the time, everybody's mail," Joli said.

The envelope contained a ticket to Fort Lauderdale and a slip of paper with "See Carole Jackowitz, Anders Travel Agency," and the address and phone number of the agency written on it.

"Doesn't waste words, does he," Rothschild said.

"What kind of merry-go-round is this? Why not send me straight to Lauderdale, why here?"

"I guess because he trusts me. This Jackowitz woman is a travel agent. He needed me as a go-between in case something went wrong."

"Something went wrong with what?"

"Whatever you two are up to. He didn't tell me a thing, Sailor, just that the sanction had been lifted on you and he was expecting to meet up with you and it was very hush-hush, not something to gossip about. That's all I know." He leaned over toward O'Hara with eyebrows arched quizzically and whispered, "Want to tell me about it?"

"*Oui,*" said Joli, "We have been trying to guess what it is for weeks."

"Not yet," O'Hara said.

"Shit. My curiosity's been eating me alive for three goddamn months and you say 'Not yet.' "

"I don't have anything to tell you."

"Well, you can be out of here at seven tonight and be in Miami by ten. Or you can wait until tomorrow morning and we'll demolish this bottle of brandy and catch up on the past two years."

"I vote for the bottle," Joli said, offering another round.

"Michael, I've been from Japan to Boston to here in less than three days. My tail is dragging. I've got jet lag. But the suspense is driving me berserk and I'm gonna stay berserk until I find out what's going on with Falmouth and I won't know doodly-shit until I catch up with him. So, Joli, pour us some more brandy and make damn sure my jet's on the way to Lauderdale tonight . . . with me on it."

8

WHEN HINGE ARRIVED at his hotel room, he took a shower and styled his hair with a blower, then he stood, naked, in front of the mirror. His body was hard and tight, sinews standing out like fishing lines along his biceps. He looked at his scars and smiled. Women loved them, loved to trace their fingers along the rigid tissue on his legs and arms and down his left side. He could have written a book with just the lies he had told about those scars. He returned to the bedroom and got dressed. Then he reached into the suitcase and took out a wide, rawhide belt with a large gold buckle on it and held it in his hand for several seconds as though weighing it. The buckle was engraved, its letters aglitter with small diamonds:

UNITED STATES RODEO ASSOCIATION
1963 National Champion
Cheyenne, Wyoming, January 6, 1964

He had come a long way from Del Rio, Texas.

Bucking horses in west Texas in the fresh snow, it didn't hurt quite so goddamn bad when you went off, even though underneath the clean white blanket, the ground was like a brick. The soft fresh powder, early in the mornings when the horse's breath was a thick wide cloud mixed with his own, cushioned the fall, so he wasn't afraid of the crazy ponies with their long winter hair and wild eyes because it didn't hurt like it hurt in the summer, when the drought had baked the earth in the corral until it cracked and the dust made the horses sneeze and they were mad with the heat anyway and they started fighting the minute they heard the saddle leather creaking, oh, God, he hated the summers.

"Show some guts, boy, I'll take th' fuckin strap t' yuh."

"Yes, Pap."

"Git back on that goddamn rogue pony and straighten his ass out or I'll take an inch a hide off'n yer butt."

"Yes, Pap."

"Mount up, goddammit, don't be hangin' around that fuckin' water bucket."

"Yes, Pap."

"Dontcha call me Pap, goddammit, ya bust that fuckin' pony's balls, git him on his knees, then I'm your goddamn Pap. We ain't havin' no fuckin' fairies in this family."

Tall, raw-boned, Texas kid, drawl-voiced and leather-handed, his old man's venal temper and a two-inch fuse, on the rodeo circuit while he washile he was still in high school, and by the time he was twenty-one and old enough to order his own beer in the endless saloons from Wichita to Cheyenne to Phoenix to El Paso, he had big, swollen knuckles from dusting off all the smart-ass bastards that made fun of his name ("Hinkie Hinkle"), and he had the trophies and the belt buckles, and he had hunted with the best of them, brown bear and eight-point buck and jaguar, and he also had more than a dozen broken bones and the miseries and it hurt to get up in the morning and he was living on eggs and bacon and uppers and downers and painkillers and washing it all down with Coors beer.

Twenty-two years old and peaking out.

At the Armed Forces rodeo he got drunk and missed his ride and a honey-voiced lady sergeant from recruiting fucked his brains out all night and all morning and had him signed and on his way to boot camp before his hangover was gone.

Nam,

seven months later,

human game,

fuck breaking horses and shooting longhorn buck.

In eight weeks in 1967 he kills twenty-seven Buddhaheads. Mot Sog, the Army's special assassination squad, for which all records will be destroyed after the war, taps him. One night near the DMZ, using an infrared scope mounted on a Mannlicher single-action CD 13, from more than a quarter mile away, he picks off a Cong agent, sneaking across the lines, so unbelievable a shot that a couple of guys from the Corps of Engineers measure the distance with a transit, just for the record. Nineteen hundred and twenty-seven feet, the longest kill shot in Army history.

After that, it was a honky tonk shooting gallery, like knocking over ducks, bam, bam, bam.

Back in Texas, he went up for hire. In Rhodesia, where he earned three hundred dollars a day plus per diem, he took a postgraduate course in interrogation, and became an expert in the deadly art of persuasion, hanging captured blacks out of a helicopter at five hundred feet by the ankles until they talked, and letting them go if they didn't. When he came home after two years, Pap never cussed at him again, even when he changed his name to Hinge. Pap was afraid to.

He decided the belt buckle was too ostentatious. By now, Spettro probably knew everything there was to know about Ray Hinge. He put on a more conservative belt, checked himself out in the mirror, and walking as straight as a sergeant in the Queen's Guard, he opened his side of the door to the adjoining room and knocked. A moment later Falmouth opened the door from his side.

Hinge was surprised at how tall Spettro was. He was almost dapper in appearance, deeply tanned, with snow-white hair at his temples, and dressed in a three-piece raw-silk navy-blue suit with a tie striped with wine and gray.

Hinge was exactly as Falmouth had expected, raw-boned and hard-looking, with small, agate eyes and leathery hands, and coarse, dishwater-blond hair.

You better be good, Tony thought. For this deal, I need the best there is.

Hinge knew the scenario by heart and recited it with ease. A good actor, that was a help. "Excuse me," he said in a lazy Texas drawl, "I thought this was some kind of closet."

"No problem."

"Say, yuh wouldn't have a spare cigarette, would yuh? I just ran out."

"Sure."

Falmouth handed him the Camel and lit it. Hinge took a deep puff and as heat from the glowing tip was drawn up through the tobacco, the word "Spettro" appeared on the side of the cigarette. Hinge smiled and held out his hand.

"Hinge," he said. "And it's a goddamn pleasure, man."

"Thank you, Mr. Hinge. Call me Spettro."

"Yes, suh."

Falmouth held the door open and Hinge entered his room. There was a briefcase on the bed.

"I just left the lads from the plant," Falmouth said. "We've got one big break. This Rafsaludi bunch has agreed to a meeting this afternoon to discuss payment of the ransom. They think a company man is coming in. There were four of them in the group that pinched Lavander, according to Gómez, the chauffeur who was driving Lavander when he was grabbed."

"Th' Rafsaludi, they let this heah Gómez go, hunh?"

Falmouth nodded.

"Kinda dumb of them, wasn't it," Hinge said.

"It's inconsistent with the rest of their behavior."

"Yuh think he's one of 'em?"

Not a bad start, Hinge. "Without going into a lot of detail, the whole snatch reeks of a setup," Falmouth agreed. "Yes, I think it was an inside job. The chauffeur and, my guess is, four others. I think he made a Freudian slip when he said there were four kidnappers, but you've got to remember, all this information is secondhand. I haven't seen Gómez and he has no idea I'm here."

"What's with the chauffeur?" Hinge asked.

"All he knows is that a company man is flying in from the States, supposedly to handle the transaction. The bloody son of a bitch has volunteered to drive him to the meeting this afternoon."

"We gonna let 'im?"

"Sure. If we say no, he may get curious. Best to keep him under hand; we may need him if this thing goes strange."

He walked over to the bed and opened the brief case. It was fitted with a tray that held a machine gun in a fixed position. The trigger was rigged to the handle. The gun was no more than eighteen inches long, with a metal-frame stock and a flash suppressor and silencer on the barrel. The gunsight was cone-shaped and almost as long as the barrel itself. There was a switch on the side. The clip was longer than the gun itself, but was curved back under the stock, obviously to keep the gun compact. There were two more clips in the tray as well as two pistols and a small metal box. Falmouth detached the trigger mechanism and took the tray out of the briefcase.

"Have you used this weapon before?"

"I never seen one quite like it."

"It's an Ungine. Brand-new. Totally silenced and flash-suppressed. You can't hear it five feet away and you can't see it at night. Effectively, it fires a thousand rounds a minute. The clips hold a hundred rounds each, forty-five caliber. That's six seconds of continuous fire per clip. All you have to do is tap the trigger and you get an eight- to ten-round burst, or you can set it to fire single shot."

Hinge whistled. His eyes were wide with anticipation as Falmouth handed him the machine gun. Hinge looked at it as a jeweler might look at a twenty-carat diamond, turning it over, hefting it to feel the weight.

"Seven pounds," Falmouth said.

"How about range?"

"Four hundred meters."

"Fantastic."

"The laser scope is adjusted to fire the weapon automatically by temperature. It's set for ninety-eight-point-six. All you have to do is swing the weapon around. Whenever the beam hits a human being, pow. The trigger will override the laser, so it can be used either way. There are two switches in the handle of the briefcase. One turns the laser on, the other is the trigger."

"Neat."

Falmouth took out the small box and opened it. Inside were a dart gun that looked like a cigar, four darts, a small bottle of clear liquid, an electrical device about an inch long that looked like a tiny buss fuse, two buttons and two FM tuners, neither of which was any larger than a calling card.

"Lookee here," Hinge said, taking out the cigar. "I usually make these myself. Never saw a store-bought one before."

"This is probably more accurate than the homemade variety," Falmouth said. He took the cigar, fitted one of the darts into the end, and then turned toward the lamp on the far side of the room. He blew sharply into the cigar-shaped gun, and the dart whistled across the room and imbedded itself in the lampshade.

"It's very clean up to seven or eight feet," he said, and then added, "with a little practice."

"What're we usin'?" Hinge asked, pointing to the bottle.

"Sodium dinitrate."

"Good stuff."

"If you hit an artery or blood vessel, it will knock the subject out in about five seconds. Hit a nerve, and paralysis is almost immediate."

"I go for the throat. Right here," Hinge said, tapping a spot near his Adam's apple. "Yuh got a good chance of catching this nerve here. Yuh miss, the jugular's right next to it. I like to go for the nerve. Five seconds can be a long fuckin' time if the subject's hip."

"I agree."

"So, how d'we play it?"

"If my information is correct, you've been the inside man on two switch operations."

"Yes, suh."

"I figger you work the inside, I'll be the shadow."

"Sounds like a winner," Hinge said. And then, smiling, he added, "I'm really lookin' forward to this, man. Workin' with you, I mean. Like teamin' up with Wyatt Earp, fer Chrissakes." And he laughed.

"I'm quite flattered," Falmouth said. Hinge's attitude of hero-worship made him uneasy. It seemed unprofessional to Falmouth, although Hinge probably knew his business. Hell, Quill wouldn't have sent Hinge if he wasn't first-class. Relax, Falmouth.

"A few more things," Falmouth went on. "Your car is a Buick wagon. It's bugged and equipped with a radio transmitter. We can read the signal up to a mile away. They're supposed to call at two and give us directions. You're to come alone in the company car, although they've agreed to let Gómez drive."

"I'll just bet they did."

"The Rafsaludi will meet you at their destination. My thinking is, they'll jump the car somewhere along the way and snatch you, the same way they grabbed Lavander. I'll be tracking you from another car with the best wheelman in South America."

"How about me?"

"We'll wire you, too. I've got an anal transmitter. It's a bit uncomfortable but very effective, and they won't find it with a pat-down. Thing is, old man, we'll do our best to avoid losing you."

"How about a mike? I could maybe give yuh some verbal clues."

"A bit too risky, really. We'll be able to monitor everything you say in the Buick. If they snatch you, we'll rely on the transmitters and visuals."

"Fair enough. How about Gómez?"

"Rafael Gómez. Native of Maracaibo. Quiet type. Thirty-one. A bachelor. Plays it with his hat in his hand around the big shots at the refinery, but apparently he's quite the hotshot with the ladies. He's no genius, quit high school after two years, and no physical threat, so I don't see him as one of the ring leaders. He's worked for Sunset Oil for two years. Speaks shaky English."

"That's good enough."

"Splendid. We've got two hours before we leave, old man. Let's run through the operation a time or two. Maybe we can prevent any surprises."

"Yes, Quill here."

"I thought I'd give you an update on Lavander."

"What about Lavander?"

"We've got two of our best men on it. I'm sure they'll bring him in."

"That's not what I mean. How much does he know?"

"A lot."

"Does he know about Midas?"

"Yes. He analyzed the sample and studied the entire location."

"Was that smart?"

"Lavander is known to be very discreet. He's worked for just about every operation in the world, at one time or another."

"Nevertheless, this kidnapping should serve as a warning. Right now it's very dangerous to have a man outside the organization knowing this much."

"He's very valuable . . ."

"I see. Then I suggest we test him. See just how discreet he is. If he's reliable, we should try to enlist him. If he's not . . ."

"I understand."

"Good. Keep me updated on this, please."

"Of course, sir."

The Algerian switch was an almost foolproof play. Almost, because one could never discount the human factor, and with it, the unexpected. The switch was designed as a logical exercise in fear and was extremely effective against nonpolitical terrorists—the greedy ones, willing to risk their necks for money, but not willing to die for it. They could be scared. Fanatics were different. Fanatics were dangerous and unpredictable. They could freak out without warning. To them, death was martyrdom, and martyrdom was part of the litany. In this case, Falmouth knew the terrorists were money-hungry, period. There was no political motivation behind the kidnapping of Lavander. These guys were not fiery-eyed disciples of anything. Anything, that is, but greed. Everything added up to it.

The switch required professionals, and Falmouth had quickly recognized Hinge as an iceman, a totally amoral and compulsive perfectionist, ideal for the job. He did not like Hinge personally. They had nothing in common other than their profession. Hinge was a typical mercenary. Hinge lived for blood and money, and he had no taste, no class. He ate meat and potatoes with boring regularity, drank beer and sour-mash whiskey, and his reading was confined to *Soldier of Fortune* magazine, the *Business Week* of the mercs, and the occasional books on new weapons, or the current state of the killing art, published by Paladin Press, named after the legendary roving gunfighter and edited, naturally, in Phoenix, where the spirit of the Old West still prevailed. That was how Hinge saw himself, a roving gunslinger, always riding into the sunset looking for some new standard to carry, killing Commies and left-wingers and socialists and anyone else politically to the left of Attila the Hun, because somehow that made it acceptable. Like many of his brethren, he was coarse and unrefined, a killing machine who could not judge a good bottle of wine or a good cigar. In short, he was a boor and a bore. But he was good at his work and that's what they were there for.

Falmouth's driver, a thin little man in his late forties named Angel, had driven a cab in Paris for three years, so he had little trouble negotiating the ass-tightening curves and threading through the traffic on the road from the plant down to Caracas. The receiver for the anal transmitter Hinge was wearing was beeping loud and clear.

Hinge was clever. He kept up a running conversation with Gómez, all of which was picked up by the bug in the Buick and transmitted to the stereo in Falmouth's car, a silver-gray BMW.

"Whaddya call that?" he heard Hinge ask.

"Ees special nursery for strange plants," Gómez answered.

"Strange plants?"

"You know, señor, different . . ."

"Rare plants?"

"Sí. Rare."

A few moments later: "Who's that?"

"Ees a statue of our savior, Simón Bolívar, the greatest hero in all of Venezuela."

"Whatcha call this part of town? It's very pretty."

"El Este. Very expense. Only rich people live here. We will turn down here and drive through part of it."

Keep it up, Falmouth thought, you're doing great. The idea of working as a team was becoming more palatable to him. The fellow was good, no question about that. And Angel was a real pro behind the wheel. Falmouth did not want to get too close. Thus far, Gómez had not seen him and was totally unaware of his existence. It was important to keep it that way. So the BMW followed from a respectable distance as Angel turned into a residential neighborhood of homes that reminded Falmouth a little of Palm Beach and Coral Gables.

Hinge kept talking, his tough Southwestern twang coming in loud and clear.

"This heah's a terrible road," he said. "Why don't they pave it?"

"Ees the shortest way to go. Ees only a mile, about, from here."

"Good."

Angel chuckled. "Bueno. I know where they are."

"Good," Falmouth said. "The signal's fading. Wherever they are, the reception isn't worth a farthing."

"Thees road they are on, eet follows around the mountain, like the snake. Very bad road."

"You know it, then?"

"But of course, señor. Ees the only dirt road around here."

Angel circled up through the foothill subdivision and then turned down a paved street, which suddenly ended. He turned to Falmouth.

"Thees ees the road, señor."

"Let's move with caution. We don't want them to spot us."

"*Sí,* no problem."

Falmouth was bouncing in the back seat of the car as Angel guided it around the potholes and washes in the miserable dirt trail on the edge of the mountain.

Suddenly Gómez's voice came through the loudspeaker, much louder than before. "*Por Dios!*" he cried, trying to act surprised.

"Well, goddamn!" Hinge answered, acting equally surprised. A moment later there was a burst of automatic gunfire from somewhere outside the car.

Hinge said, "Okay, stop. They got an automatic weapon and they wanna make sure we know they got it."

There was an edge to his voice, not of fear, but of anger. Jesus, Falmouth thought, don't lose it now.

"Okay," Falmouth said to Angel, "Slow 'er down. Give the bastards a chance to do their mischief."

"*Sí.*"

Two men with shotguns came toward the car. Gómez got out to meet them, his hands held high over his head. He was putting on a good act. Hinge grabbed the moment.

"This's it, the joy ride's over. Car: dark-blue Pontiac Grand Prix. 1974. Very dirty. Lotsa dents. Two guys with shotguns coming toward us. Another in the bushes with an automatic weapon, one on the hill, spotting. Jesus, it's Jesse James time. These turkeys have bandannas pulled over their faces. Okay, here comes one. *Bonas nokkers.*"

The one who approached the car was short and squat, like a box, with long greasy black hair topped by a brown beret. The bandanna did not hide his beard or his funky left eye, a gray mass floating between narrow eyelids. He pulled the door open, holding the shotgun toward Hinge's chest with one hand. "*Vamos,*" he ordered and motioned Hinge out of the car. "*Pronto!*"

Hinge got out, holding the briefcase close to his chest. Gray-Eye looked at the case and then back at Hinge. "*Habla Usted español?*" he asked.

Hinge shrugged.

"You speak Spaneesh?" Gray-Eye snapped.

"No," Hinge lied.

"Hokay, I speak Englis, *un poco,* leetle beet, *sí.*"

He laughed and reached for the briefcase, but Hinge turned away from him, as if to protect the case. The terrorist snatched it away from him and opened it with one hand. A half-dozen file folders spilled out and were whisked away in the wind. Hinge looked distressed. Gray-Eye's shoulders sagged. "Sorry," he said in mock apology. He threw the case on the ground, and spinning Hinge around, tied his hands behind his back, then quickly frisked him.

You're the one gets it, pal, Hinge thought. You sick-eyed spic pig, you go down first.

"Please, my case." Hinge nodded toward his briefcase. "It was a gift. From my wife. Uh . . . *de mi esposa.* " Gray-Eye looked back at the case and sighed and picked it up.

The other gunman, who was younger and had his long hair tied in a pigtail and wore a gold earring in his right ear and was very jumpy, yelled *"Pronto, pronto!"* at Gray-Eye, then got in the car and pulled up to them. He was heading back, toward Falmouth.

"Oh, goin' back the way we came?" Hinge said, in as loud a voice as he dared.

Gray-Eye pushed Hinge into the car and threw the attaché case on the back floor of the Pontiac. They drove off in a whirl of dust, leaving Gómez standing beside the road with his hands still high in the air.

Falmouth had heard Hinge's last remark above the roar of the get-away car. "Jesus," he said to Angel, "they're coming back this way!"

Angel slammed on the brakes and spun the steering wheel, whipping the car around in a perfect one-hundred-and-eighty-degree spin, dropping into low gear as he did, digging out, as the car completed its half turn, and heading back in the opposite direction. Fast.

"Beautiful," Falmouth said.

Angel drove back to the paved road and took the first turn, U-turned and parked. He was ready for them when they came back.

"Magnífico!" Falmouth said with admiration. He slid down in the seat and took a 9-mm. Luger from its armpit holster and slid it under his thigh. If there was trouble, the Game would be over, anyway. It would be survival time.

The blue Pontiac came down the dirt road a minute later, squealed around the curve and headed away from them, back toward the main road to Caracas. There were three people in the car.

"I give 'em couple blocks, okay?" Angel asked.

"No, there were only two of the *pistoleros* in the car. There should be two more coming right behind them. Let's give them a minute or so. We don't want to get in the middle." The beeper was going crazy beside him on the seat.

Another minute dragged by and then a black '76 Chevy came down the dirt road and followed the first.

"That should be them," Falmouth said. "Let's roll."

Angel eased away from the curb and followed them.

The beeper was singing loud and clear on the seat beside him as they wound back through the El Este section toward the highway into town. The Chevy was in view, moving at exactly the speed limit. They weren't taking any chances.

They were almost to the highway when it happened: a kid roaring suddenly out of a driveway on a motorcycle, seeing the BMW too late and veering to miss it, the bike sliding out from under him and the two skidding crazily in front of Angel, and Angel, slamming on the brakes and swerving at the same time, missing the kid and his Honda by inches, fishtailing for a moment too long and the BMW hitting the curb, teetering for a moment as though it were going to turn over, then righting itself, and as it did, the back right tire exploding like a bomb. Angel wrestled the car to a stop and jumped out. The tire was hanging in shreds from the wheel.

Angel kicked the car. "Shit," he bellowed. "Shit, shit, shit!"

In the back seat, Falmouth listened as the tone on the beeper grew fainter and fainter and finally beeped out. Hinge was on his own now. He was not in any immediate danger, but the whole switch operation depended on Falmouth's snatching one of the terrorists as they left the meeting. Hinge's trip was now a total waste.

"You're right," Falmouth said. "Shit."

Falmouth was sitting on the balcony sipping a gin and tonic and watching the *teleférico* climbing slowly up the side of Mount Avila. He had left the door between the two rooms open and heard Hinge come in, heard a door close and then heard Hinge's toilet flush.

A few moments later the Texan joined him on the balcony. The younger man was obviously surprised and distressed. "What happened?" he asked. "How come you're back?"

"A kid pulled out in front of us on a motorbike. Angel hit a curb and blew a tire."

"Well, Je-sus Kee-rist!" Hinge snapped.

"Easy," Falmouth said. "Get yourself a drink and we'll talk about plan Baker."

The hard-faced Texan went back into the room. He was edgy, but he was not a complainer. Like Falmouth, he was already thinking about their next move. He poured a generous slug of gin over ice cubes and returned to the balcony.

"You mean we got a plan Baker," he said.

"There's always a plan Baker," Falmouth said, still watching the cable car as it reached the peak of the mountain.

"Problem is, we ain't got one of theirs, we ain't got shit," Hinge said. It was not a pointed remark, he was thinking out loud.

"What happened at the meeting?" Falmouth asked quietly.

Hinge sighed. As Spettro had said, there was always the unexpected. Hinge reported in a kind of abbreviated rote, an emotionless summary of the facts.

"Four of 'em, like you figured, plus the driver, Gómez. Four creeps, spent a month or so with Gaddafi's bunch, think they're the fuckin' PLO. Blindfolded when I got in the car. My guess is we went downtown. A lot of traffic noise. Drove for about eight minutes. Parked in what sounded like an indoor garage. Never went outside. Up one flight of stairs, straight ahead forty paces to office. Took off blindfold to talk. The four were back-lighted. Three thousand-watt floodlights behind them. Couldn't see faces clearly. One did the talking. Tough talker, brown beard, left eye is kinda gray. Driver of pickup car wore ponytail and an earring in his . . . uh, right ear. Looked to be about thirty. Office was small. Shades over windows, conference table, six chairs, telephone. Period. Not even an ashtray." He stopped and took a sip of his drink.

"What did they ask you?"

"Did I have the loot? The loot's nice and safe, I tell 'em. Are we ready to deal? I gotta know my man's still alive, I says. They make a phone call. It's this Lavander. English accent. Scared shitless. All he gets out is his name and 'Please help me.' Deal is, we connect again at ten-thirty tonight. I bring the cash, they bring Lavander. Anybody follows me, they terminate the hostage, snatch another one, it's the same ol' ballgame but the price doubles."

"Where do you meet them?"

"Same script as first time. They call with an address. I head into town, they intercept me somewhere along the way. They figure it worked the first time, why not use the same gag again. Stupid *pipiolos.*"

"You did fine, Hinge," Falmouth said. "Sorry things got queered. Couldn't be helped."

"Sure. Sorry I got my ass a little outa joint, there. There's one other thing. The turkey with the weird eye? He's mine, okay?"

"My pleasure."

Hinge smiled. "Okay, so . . . what's plan Baker?"

Falmouth looked up at him and smiled back.

"Gómez," he said, and handed Hinge a sheet of paper with the chauffeur's address on it.

The house was a red hut among many red huts on the western ridge of the mountains that separate Caracas from the rest of Venezuela. Its main room was small and barren. The bed doubled as a sofa. A furniture crate beside it served as an end table. There was a small lamp on the crate but it was turned off. Posters of John Travolta, Rod Stewart, Blondie and Farrah Fawcett covered the walls, and a transistor radio, with the heavy beat of disco music pounding from its small speaker, was on the floor beside the sofa bed. The only other furniture was two wooden chairs near the windows, one of them stacked with dirty laundry. There was also a phone on the floor in one corner. A handmade rug covered part of the linoleum floor, its corners raveled and dirty. Flimsy strips of cotton hung limply over the windows. Beside the lamp on the crate was a small-caliber pistol.

Gómez was getting laid on the sofa bed.

This woman is a noisy one, God, is she noisy, Gómez thought. My neighbors, they will think, I'm killing someone in here. But this tiger, this man-eater, she may kill me.

"*Todavía no, todavía no!*" she cried and he was trembling and he felt like exploding. She wiggled under him, squealing with delight, then screaming, then groaning. Her legs were wrapped around his hips, and each time he thrust into her she tightened them a little more, digging deeper into his back with her fingernails. Sweat dripped from his chin onto her forehead and she giggled and then shoved up hard against him. In the semidark room he could see her face under his, and her eyes were rolled back and crazy.

"*Más, más, más,*" she demanded and he didn't have much more to give and felt himself peaking and his ass getting tighter as he tried to hold back.

He barely heard the door crash open.

For the next few seconds, everything seemed to happen in confused, blurred slow motion:

> two grim figures framed in the doorway
> the girl, opening her mouth to scream
> a faint sound
> *bupbupbupbupbupbupbupbupbupbupbup*
> the woman, her chest erupting into pulp, slamming back against the wall
> the slugs, ripping into her, making more noise than the gun itself

the girl falling on her side, her head dangling limply over the side of
the sofa bed, her sweaty black hair hanging straight down to the
floor

red stains widening across the sheet toward him

turning, finally, reaching for the gun

again that dull sound, almost inaudible

bupbupbupbupbupbupbupbupbupbupbup

the gun and the lamp and the crate vanishing in an explosion of
splinters

falling back on the bed, still gasping for breath, still erect, his eyes
staring in terror at the form beside the bed, pointing a machine gun
at his eye.

It was all over in a few seconds. What in God's name!

In the semidarkness the finger of light from a flashlight led the other
figure into the bathroom, then the kitchen.

"*Qué quiere Usted?*" Gómez cried out finally.

"Shut up," the one with the machine gun snapped. "And speak
English when ye're asked."

He heard the sound of water running into the bathtub. The other one
came back and he recognized his drawling voice.

"Nobody else here. The sucker's really big time. Got himself a
fuckin' bathtub. Running water. Goddamn new phone over there in the
corner. I mean, look at that brand-new phone, I'll bet there ain't been
five calls made on it yet."

Hinge picked up one of the chairs and went back toward the bathroom with it. "Shit, ol' Ray-fi-el, he's dreamin' of bein' a fuckin' millionaire, aintcha there, Ray-fi-el."

Gómez said nothing. He looked at the girl, at the blood gushing from
her butchered chest, like water pouring from an open spigot. He started
to get sick.

"Forget her," the Texan ordered. "You get sick, I'll rub your goddamn nose in it."

Gómez swallowed hard, forcing the sour bile back down.

The new one, who was taller and thinner than the Texan, handed his
gun to Hinge and stuffed a washcloth in Gómez's mouth and tied it in
place.

The Texan picked up the shattered lamp and carried it into the
bathroom.

"Let's go," the tall one said, pulling Gómez off the bed, half dragging
him into the bathroom. They shoved Gómez into the chair and tied his
hands behind his back and tied each of his legs to a leg of the chair.

The Texan, the one Gómez knew as Mr. Lomax, smiled down at him. He leaned the machine gun against the wall and pulled the double-strand wire from the shattered lamp and separated it into two strips. He took out a knife and stripped a foot or so of insulation off both strands of wire. When he was finished he had two long strands of cleared wire, still connected at one end to the plug.

"This oughta give ya a little charge," Hinge said, and giggled as he wrapped one wire around each of Gómez's ankles. The chauffeur's eyes bulged even wider. He twisted violently in the chair.

Hinge turned off the water. He and Falmouth lifted the chair and set it in the bathtub. Gómez looked down. The water was well above his ankles.

Hinge picked up the plug and knelt on the floor near the socket.

"I didn't think you'd have electricity there, Ray-fi-el, I thought we'd have to use gasoline on the bottom of your feet." He giggled again and held the prongs of the plug in front of the socket and popped it in and out, very quickly. Gómez jerked as if someone had just kicked him. His scream was trapped in the gag. He was breathing hard through his nose, shaking his head, back and forth.

"Didn't like that, now did ya, ol' buddy?" Hinge said. "Lemme tell ya what we're gonna do. We're gonna ask you a coupla questions and if we don't like your answers—well, shit, man, I'm just gonna plug you in and we're gonna go have ourselves some dinner someplace and come back after dessert. How does that grab yer ass, Ray-fi-el? Hmm?"

Gómez kept shaking his head.

"The one with the funny eye, uh, *el malo ojo,* where does he live?"

Gómez looked up at Falmouth, who produced a hotel pad and a pen.

"He's gonna untie yer hands, Ray-fi-el, and you just write that sucker's name and address down, *comprende,* motherfucker?"

Gómez shook his head no.

Hinge thrust the plug in the socket. This time he left it in for a full second. Gómez jerked forward against the ropes, then snapped back. His head lolled over the back of the chair. His eyes rolled back in their sockets. Falmouth dipped a cloth in the tub water and wiped off his face. He stuck smelling salts under the nose of Gómez. The chauffeur gradually came around. He was grunting and breathing hard through his nose and spit dribbled from the gag at the corners of his mouth. He looked up at Falmouth and then at Hinge, trying to focus.

"What we want, friend, is names and addresses. The one with the *malo ojo* and the driver of the car that took me, the little shit with the cute little ol' earring? And the other two at the meetin'. And we wanna know where ya took me and where this Lavander fellow ya snatched is. Ya savvy all that, or am I talkin' too fast for ya?"

Gómez stared at him, dull-eyed. He was having trouble breathing.

"It's real easy, man. Ya write those names and addresses down on that piece a paper there, and you're through for the day. Okay? Otherwise, I'm gonna give ya another fuckin' ride."

He held the plug down near the socket and slipped the prongs in just far enough to keep the plug from falling out. Gómez stared down at the plug, hanging half in and half out of the socket. He nodded his head hard and murmured through the gag.

"Well, shit, looka there, that turkey's ready to talk awready. I tell ya, pardner, the ol' bathtub trick never fails. Untie him, there, see can he write plain."

Falmouth untied Gómez's hands and held the pen toward him. The chauffeur took it with a tremoring left hand.

"South paw, hunh," Hinge said. "You shoulda been a baseball player, Ray-fi-el, it's one helluva lot healthier than the game ye're in."

Gómez wrote names and addresses on the tablet.

"Phone numbers, too," Hinge said. "Obviously you boys got yuhselves some new phones like that one in on the floor there, hunh? Just for this little caper."

Gómez wrote the phone numbers below the addresses. His eyes jumped fearfully back to Hinge. He looked like a rabbit staring at a rattlesnake. Hinge took the paper and read the names and addresses.

"How about Lavander. *El prisionero?*"

Gómez shook his head wildly.

"I don't think he knows where they've got Lavander," Falmouth said.

Gómez nodded his head in wild-eyed agreement.

"Hell, he's just a fink they pulled in to drive the fuckin' snatch car," Hinge said. He looked at the list. "Pasco Chiado, Lupo Areno, Billy Zapata and—who's this . . . Chico. Chico what?"

Gómez shrugged his shoulders and shook his head.

"He means this one only has a surname. That's common down here," Falmouth said. "Means this Chico is a bastard. Literally. It's an acceptable condition in Venezuela."

"Which one has the *malo ojo*?" Hinge asked, wiggling a finger in front of his left eye. "Chiado?"

Gómez shook his head.

"Areno?"

And Gómez nodded. Hinge looked at the paper a few more moments. "Wanna let yer pal check out this office?" he said to Falmouth, who took the slip and went into the other room.

"Case ye're lyin'," Hinge said to Gómez. Gómez shook his head again. He shook his head hard.

"But *supposin'*, man?" Hinge said, smiling.

Gómez raised his eyes as if in prayer, still shaking his head.

"How's it goin'?" he called to Falmouth.

"He's calling me right back."

"Four-oh."

The phone rang and Hinge could hear Falmouth talking very low into the phone, heard him hang up.

"You were dead on," Falmouth said, coming back into the bathroom. "It's an old office building in the La Pastora section. The first floor's converted into a garage for the tenants."

"Hell, I didn't think he'd lie, pardner. Not ol' Ray-fi-el. Right, Ray-fi-el?"

Gómez stared back and forth between his two captors. There was abject terror in his eyes.

"One or two more questions—this Chiado, is he married?"

Yes.

"Is that his car?"

No.

"Areno's car?"

Yes.

"So how does Chiado get to the meeting?"

Gómez wrote down the words *"el ómnibus."*

"Sonbitch," Hinge said, "can you believe it. A two-million-dollar heist and this guy Chiado goes to collect the loot in a fuckin' bus."

"Perfect," Falmouth said.

"Four-oh," Hinge said, and he pressed the side of his foot on the plug and shoved it into the socket.

The wire hummed and Gómez thrashed frantically in the chair, his screams muffled by the gag. The chair fell sideways against the wall and the legs slipped out from under it and the chair toppled over backwards in the tub. Bubbles dribbled up from Gómez's nose. His body was seized with spasms. Then he went limp. After a while the bubbles stopped.

Hinge unplugged him. "Doesn't take but a minute," he said. "Let's stuff him and his galfriend in the trunk, let Domignon take care of 'em. That sonbitch hasn't done shit in this deal but sit on his ass and thank God he wasn't the one got snatched."

Psychologically, it was necessary to take another hostage, one who was married and who was one of the leaders. Gómez would not have worked. Besides, he was dead. And Falmouth decided Areno and his pals would probably be glad he was. Fewer people to divide the loot with. So they checked over the list again and the obvious choice was Chiado. He lived close by in the slums of the foothills. And he would be taking the bus to the downtown section, which would leave him wide open.

They drove slowly past the house in a Firebird that Angel had arranged for Falmouth to use. It was, like Gómez's house, little more than a hut hard by the side of a pockmarked street. Hinge focused his compact Leitz binoculars on the windows as they passed the house. Chiado was eating dinner with his family. His wife, a young woman bordering on obesity, was nursing a small child. There were two other children at the table.

"He's there, awright," Hinge drawled. "Chowin' down with a fat wife and three rug-runners."

They drove to the corner, turned and drove six blocks to a main street. Angel was waiting for them.

"Eleven forty-five, right?" Hinge said as he got out.

"Eleven forty-five," Falmouth repeated and drove back to the Chiado house while Angel and Hinge went off into the night to be hijacked again.

Hinge felt exhilarated as they took the blindfold off. It was the same room, squalid and bare except for the negotiating table and the telephone and a .45-caliber pistol lying on the table in front of Areno. Hinge sat in the same chair with the briefcase, handcuffed to one wrist, resting in his lap. Now his blood was racing in anticipation of the next few minutes. He felt no fear. He was never afraid. Rather, he was stimulated by the potential danger of the situation. There had been a tense moment when the Rafsaludi intercepted them and Areno realized that Gómez was not driving the car. Hinge explained that Gómez had not shown up and that he had picked another driver, not wanting to be late. Areno nervously accepted the explanation.

Hinge looked at his watch. It was ten forty-one. He looked around the room. No Lavander. No Chiado, either, of course. "Where's our man?" he asked Areno.

Areno glared at him with his good eye and shrugged. "One of our people ees late," he said.

"That don't answer m'question. Is Lavander with him?"

The leader curled his lips back and showed two rows of ragged yellow teeth. "We decide to feel the weight of your money first, gringo. Hokay? Then maybe you get back thees scarecrow of yours."

The three men laughed.

"The deal was, we trade here. The money for Lavander. That's the deal."

The leader shrugged and held out his hands, palms up. "We change our mind, hokay?"

Another round of laughter.

Hinge smiled. "No Lavander, no dinero, hokay?"

He shifted in his chair. The handcuffs rattled as he moved the briefcase on his lap. It was pointed at Areno, the spokesman.

"Hey, señor, I could cut your arm off with one leetle whack of my machete."

"Reckon ya could, pal."

Areno showed his bad teeth again.

Hinge smiled back. "The case stays with me until I see Lavander, got it?"

The leader was still grinning, but the grin turned nasty. "You talk big, for a leetle man. One needs friends with heem, to talk like that."

"Oh, I got a lot of friends. F'r instance"—he looked at his watch—"one of them is at ol' Chiado's house right now. Why dontcha call him before we do any more talkin'."

The three terrorists looked at one another quizzically. How did the gringo know Chiado's name? What kind of trick was he pulling?

"You better call him," Hinge said, in a voice that had become flatter and harder.

The leader stared at him for several seconds and then picked up the receiver and dialed a number.

"Never know till ya try, right?" Hinge said.

Falmouth sat behind the wheel of the Firebird about a hundred feet from Chiado's house. On the back of the front seat on the passenger side there was a small clear plastic dish, no larger than a tea saucer, with a parabolic mike the size of a fingernail in its center. It was aimed at the open front window of Chiado's house with a thin chord from the mike to the speaker in Falmouth's right ear. The setup could pick up conversations a thousand yards away.

Chiado lay beside Falmouth on the front seat. Around his throat was a thread of C-4 *plastique* no thicker than a nylon fishing line. Imbedded in the back of it was a tiny radio-controlled fuse. Chiado had been dead for more than an hour, ever since Falmouth dropped him in his tracks. Chiado had seen the tall gringo, with the cigar, leaning over the door, locking his car. As Chiado approached him the big man turned to him, pointing to the cigar, and said, in perfect Spanish, *"Deme un fósforo, por favor."* And an instant later Chiado felt something sting his throat and it began to burn and the burning spread like a fire down his neck into his chest and down his arms to his fingers and then the world seemed to spin away from him and the man with the cigar got smaller and smaller. The dart had hit the main nerve in Chiado's throat. Falmouth threw the terrorist in the front seat, pulled down a dark street and garroted him.

Falmouth's ear was deluged with sound. Two crying children, a woman's shrill commands rising above the blaring radio somewhere in another part of the house, another child whimpering in her arms. Then the phone rang and she answered it.

"Que hay! . . . Buenas noches, Areno . . . Qué pasa?"

Falmouth put the car into gear, leaned over and shoved Chiado's body into a sitting position. He drove toward the house, opened the car door, slowed down, and twisting sideways, kicked Chiado out in front of the house. He blew the horn several times as he drove away and saw Chiado's wife, phone in hand, staring through the window at her husband's body. Falmouth pressed the fuse button.

The *plastique* blew Chiado's head off. It bounced, like a soccer ball, across the yard.

The woman shrieked. And kept shrieking, hysterically, into the phone and then suddenly she began to scream, over and over, *"No! No! Pasco, no! Está muerto!"* And she began screaming again.

Falmouth drove, without speeding, six blocks to the first main street, parked the car and went down an alley. He found the rear door of the restaurant, just as Angel had described it, went in through the kitchen and walked casually past the tables and out the front door. Nobody paid any attention to him. The cab was waiting.

"Rico?" Falmouth asked.

"Sí, señor.

"Bueno," he said and got in the cab. *"Lléveme al Hotel Tamanaco, por favor."*

Areno's eyes bulged as he listened to Chiado's wife, screaming hysterically over the phone. He slammed down the receiver.

"Los bastardos lo mataron!" he yelled and grabbed for the pistol on the table. Hinge turned the briefcase toward him and pressed the laser trigger hidden in the handle. The green laser ray swept across the wall and pinpointed itself on Areno's chest. There was a series of faint sounds and the man with the beard was lifted up on his toes and smashed into the corner. His chair clattered against the wall. A dozen

bullet holes appeared in his chest. Blood squirted across the table and against the wall as he fell in a limp pile, like a suit falling off a hanger. He lay there, his good eye crossed, the gray eye staring bizarrely at the ceiling. His mouth popped open and he made a deep, gurgling sound and his left foot jerked violently for several seconds. Then it went limp.

The two others stared in disbelief.

Hinge turned the briefcase in their general direction. A green spot roved the wall.

"Now, lissen here, boys, that little green spot on the wall, that's called a laser. And if it touches one of you *chinches,* the gun just naturally goes off. You *comprende*? Watch."

He put the briefcase under his arm so nothing was touching the handle and slowly swept it down toward Areno's body. The bright-green pinpoint of the laser moved across the wall and down to Areno's forehead.

Bupbupbupbupbupbupbupbupbupbup.

Areno's head seemed to explode from the inside.

"Now do you assholes *comprende*?" Hinge said.

The two terrorists stared at Areno, then at Hinge. They both raised their hands.

"That ain't necessary, *muchachos.* You just listen real good. We want our man back, alive and unharmed. Ya have one hour to drop him off in front of the *teleférico* station on Cota Mil Street." He turned toward Chico, the bastard, and spoke directly to him. "And if he's not there, we're going to kill you, and yer wife, and all yer children, and yer *perros* and *gatos* and *cochinos* and *pollos* and we're going to burn yer house to the fuckin' ground. You *comprende* that, asshole?"

He turned to the next man. "And then we're gonna do the same for you, pal. We're going to kill you, and yer wife and yer children, and yer dogs and cats and pigs and chickens and burn yer house to the fuckin' ground.

"And you're not gonna know when it's comin'. It could be before the sun rises tomorra, or it could be a month from now." Hinge smiled. "Get the point? Y'got an hour. *Una hora.* And don't let it happen again, hokay?"

And he turned and left the room.

At eleven thirty-two, Avery Lavander, scared, unshaven, gaunt-eyed, but in relatively good health, was shoved rudely from a car in front of the cable-car station in the El Centro district.

And two hours later Falmouth, who could not get away from Hinge quickly enough, was on his way back to Miami.

9

O'HARA WALKED DOWN TO THE EDGE of the pier and squatted, Indian fashion, waiting for the sun to rise. The ocean was as docile as a lake. The cruisers, with their outriggers swaying gently in the morning breeze, were silhouetted against the scarlet dawn. The sun had not yet broken the horizon, but its reflection spread across the night sky like a splash of blood.

Somewhere on the other side of the marina, a motor coughed to life, and a sleek speedboat keeled steeply and growled out toward open water.

If isolation was Falmouth's game, he had picked a great place. Walker's Cay, a reclaimed coral reef not much larger than a football field, hardly deserved to be called an island. One of the Abaco chain, it lay a hundred miles or so due east of Palm Beach, the northernmost fishing atoll in the Bahamas.

The fifteen-hundred-foot oyster-shell runway was half the length of the island. The beach was a strip of sand two or three hundred feet long near the runway. The customs inspector, a paunchy ebony-skinned man in red-striped black pants and a starched white shirt, was also chief of police and maître d' of the hotel restaurant. Radiophone service was limited to one hour in the morning and one hour in late afternoon. And from the tiny balconies of the ancient hotel one could see the entire length of the island and all the boats that entered the marina. It would be almost impossible for anyone to gain access to the island without being seen, day or night. But the place had a kind of battered charm, and the food was excellent.

O'Hara had been on Walker's Cay for about eighteen hours when the burly, disheveled fisherman appeared at his door at one-thirty in the morning.

"Cap'n K. at your disposal, sir," the man said, with a smile that revealed several gaps in his teeth. The tart smell of gin drifted in with his words. He offered his card, which looked as if it had been rained on, then left out in the sun to dry, and as O'Hara gave it a cursory glance, Cap'n K. snatched it back, stuffing it in the back pocket of his Levi's. He wore a windbreaker open almost to the waist, revealing a tangle of graying red chest hair, and lace-up Keds, with a small toe peeking through the torn canvas side of the left one. A rude shock of red hair tumbled from under the peaked captain's cap, which had seen much, much better times.

"I'll be picking you up on Pier Two at five-thirty, sir," he said, in a voice cultured in the South Bronx. "And we'll be makin' wake, *toot-sweet.*"

"Oh, really?" O'Hara said. "And just where the hell am I going?"

The grin got bigger, the gaps more prevalent. "Why, it's part of the arrangements made by the travel company," Cap'n K. said around a chuckle. "The best deep-sea fishin' in the world is within sight of this very island."

And with that, Cap'n K. winked and strutted out, a bit rheumatically, and down the hallway, snapping his fingers. "It's the *Miami Belle,*" he said over his shoulder, and began singing a badly off-key version of "Give Peace a Chance."

Ah yes, O'Hara said to himself, welcome to the islands. Twenty-four hours and the nuts were already popping out of the woodwork. "Five-thirty," he had sighed and closed the door.

So here he was, squatting on a pier in the middle of the ocean at five-thirty and the sun not yet up and not even a cup of coffee in sight, just because some boozy old fart had appeared at his door in the middle of the night.

"Over here, sir," a gravelly voice called through the amber light. Cap'n K. loomed above O'Hara, a bulky shadow framed against the flaming sky, on the flying bridge of a sleek, well-kept fifty-foot cabin cruiser. The captain was sipping from a steaming mug.

"I was a shark, I'da bitcher foot off by now. Come aboard and get yourself some java. And ya might throw off the lines on your way."

He turned and pressed a button and the twin five-hundred-horsepower engines under the boat cleared their throats and rumbled to life. O'Hara unhitched the fore and aft lines and jumped aboard. The boat moved beneath him, backed slowly out of its slot and then eased out toward the open sea.

O'Hara went below and checked the cabin. It was empty. So was the galley, which was spotless. A coffee pot steamed on an electric stove.

Nearby were a Braun electric grinder and three bags of coffee beans. O'Hara checked the label on one of them. Tanzanian Kilimanjaro.

He poured himself a cup, went back on deck and sat on the gunwhale, watching Walker's Cay grow smaller as the sun made a spectacular entrance. Gulls swept down over the wake and bitched at him. The engines got serious and the *Miami Belle* picked up speed.

By the time the sun cleared the horizon, Walker's was a mere speck. Small, sandy islands abounded, protected by jagged peaks of coral jutting from the placid sea. Here and there, fishing boats plied the troughs, trolling for big game. Several big sharks, ten-footers or larger, glided close to the boat, looking for a handout. Clumps of coral drifted below them, thirty feet down, yet seeming close enough to touch through the crystal water.

They had been out fifteen or twenty minutes when Cap'n K. altered his course, circling a flat, sandy island. On the west side, away from the fishing traffic, near the mouth of a tiny inlet, a man was hunched under a broad-brimmed straw hat, fishing from the back of a small rowboat.

"Ahoy down there," Cap'n K. barked. "How's th' fishin'?"

Tony Falmouth looked up and smiled. "The bloody bugs've damn near done me in. Thirty minutes, and they've sucked me dry. Here, get this lifeboat hooked up and get me aboard while I've still got some blood left in me."

"Gotcher, *toot-sweet,*" the red-haired master of the *Miami Belle* yelled down. He throttled back and threw a line to Falmouth.

Falmouth looked good, but tense. He seemed taller than O'Hara had remembered and was definitely thinner. A little grayer, too, maybe. But his handsome features were etched by a deep tan and he still had the smile of a rascal. The year and a half had treated him kindly, particularly in a game where a week could sometimes do terrible things to a human being.

The tall man climbed on deck and lit a cigarette. He threw the match underhanded, watching it arc out and vanish, with hardly a sizzle, into the mirrorlike sea.

"Cheers, Sailor," he said, as if they had met yesterday. And O'Hara grinned and stuck out his hand.

"Glad to see you're in one piece, lad," Falmouth said. "For a while there I was a little worried maybe they'd get you." The years had refined everything about him, including his accent, although it was still softly tempered with an Irish lilt.

"I knew you were around somewhere," O'Hara said.

Falmouth raised an eyebrow. "Oh? And how's that?"

"A discussion we had one night over dinner in San Francisco. About coffee."

"Jesus, that must have been four years ago."

"About that."

"And you remember the kind of coffee I like?"

"No, I remember you like to grind your own. Now, the captain there, he looks like it would be fine by him if the coffee were made out of buffalo chips. There's three bags of gourmet coffee and a grinder down in the galley."

"Neat," Falmouth said. " 'A' for the course. Want to put some legs under your java?"

"Brandy?"

"I think we can accommodate you."

Falmouth went below and emerged with a bottle of Courvoisier. He doused both cups liberally.

"Before I forget, thanks for getting me off the hook in Washington," O'Hara said.

"My pleasure, Sailor. Listen here, I was on the cuff to you. Let's not lose our perspective, eh?"

"So, we're starting dead even."

Falmouth hesitated for just an instant. "So to speak," he said.

Cap'n K. secured the lifeboat in its rig on the stern. He wiped his hands on an oily rag. Then he asked, "Anybody want a bagel with their coffee?"

"A bagel?" O'Hara said. "Two days ago I was on Howe's yacht having scrod for breakfast."

"Well, fuck it, then," Cap'n K. said and disappeared down the hatch toward the galley.

"Where did you dig him up?" O'Hara asked.

"Expatriate American," Falmouth said. "Knows these waters better than the fish. Was a lawyer once, big pistol. About ten years ago he got fed up, said the hell with it, took his two boys outta school, bought himself a boat and he's been here ever since. The boys run the business now. They also have an air charter service that works the islands. And a very handy radiophone."

"You thinking of becoming a beach bum, now that you're retired?"

Falmouth looked at him with mild curiosity for a moment and then said, "It's a thought. The bloody rascal not only knows more about these islands than anyone alive, he sees nothing, hears nothing and says nothing."

"What in hell are we doing out here in the middle of nowhere?"

"Nobody can sneak up on you out here."

"Getting a little paranoid, aren't you?"

"There's good reason," he said, without explaining the remark.

O'Hara had never seen him this edgy. But Falmouth changed his mood quickly. "Pour yourself some more mud and try one of Cap's bagels. We'll get under way. Take a little sun, catch a fish or two. I'll tell you a story will turn your toes up."

"Can we set the lines while we're lyin' idle?" Cap'n K. asked, interrupting them as he emerged from below. For the next few minutes there was a flurry of activity. The captain turned the *Miami Belle* out toward the open sea and tied down the wheel. He came back to the stern, dragged a four-foot barracuda out of the bait box and buried a hook the size of a grappling iron deep in its gills. He threw the hook overboard and fed the line out about fifteen feet, then set the rod in a bracket in the gunwales. He pulled up some slack in the line, hooked it over a small pulley and reeled the line out to the point of the outrigger and set it in place with a clothespin.

He repeated the procedure with the other rod, using a tattered fishhead for bait. Then he leaned on the side of the boat. "Just remember," he said, "the big ones, the billfish, they hit twice." He held up two fingers to make his point.

"First time, they use that schnozz on the end of their nose, they use that to stun their meal, they lay back a second or two, whap, they hit again. That time the hook goes in, okay? You'll know it. When they make that first hit, the line'll snap outa the outrigger, the line picks up the slack so the bait don't run away from the fish, then bang, he'll hit it again. Then you haul ass, *toot-sweet,* set that hook in good, or the fucker'll spit it out. Then it's you and him, one on one." He waved disdainfully at the other rod. "The other line's fixed for smaller stuff. They'll hit it and dive deep. Maybe we'll pick up something tasty for dinner."

He went back to the bridge and eased up the throttles. The bait skittered along the surface of the water, fifty or sixty feet behind the boat.

Falmouth settled down in one of the two fighting chairs in the stern. "I figgered we'd mix a little pleasure with business," he said. "Grab a chair and let's chat."

"For the record, Tony, why me? Why pick a guy on the dodge?"

"Well, Sailor, we know each other and you know the territory and you know I'm not a bullshitter. . . . Who else would I pick, Walter-bleedin'-Cronkite? Stickin' it to that bloody Winter Man and bringin'

you in, I felt I owed you that. Once done, you're the best man I know
for the job."

"Job?" O'Hara said.

"It's what you do now, isn't it? Reporting for a living." Falmouth
lit a cigarette and threw the match to the wind.

"How come you turned down the Winter Man's offer?" O'Hara
asked.

"Hell, we're friends. Also I don't like him. It's bastards like that give
the Company a bad name. Besides, Sailor, I wasn't all that sure I could
turn you up. I'm not a tracker. My specialties are planning and execution. And even if I had turned you up, I wasn't that sure I could take
you."

He looked stone-hard at O'Hara for a moment, then laughed.

"Anyway," he said, "what son of a bitch would kill a buddy for a
lousy twenty-fiver, right?"

"Maybe that's why that cheap bastard got such bad help," O'Hara
said.

Falmouth took off his shirt and threw it on top of the catch box. "To
begin with," he said, "I'll have to tell you a little story, for it to make
sense, if there is any sense to it at all, Sailor. It will put the whole thing
in proper perspective. But you won't mind. It's one helluva yarn.

"This was in the fall, eighteen months ago. I had pulled a really shit
job. But for two years, most of them had been. I got to tell you, Sailor,
I was fed up with the Service. Squalid little executions. Agents who'd
turned around. Doubles. Defectors. This one was up in Scotland. M.I.5
—which, as you know, is basically counterespionage—had turned up
a mole in a very sensitive spot in one of our nuclear installations, way
the hell and gone out in nowhere. A place called Tobermory, on the
Island of Mull, over in western Scotland. Colder than a banker's heart
and as dreary as a Russian love story. This chap had been sleeping for
twelve years, moving slowly up the ladder until he was where they
wanted him. I don't remember now what turned him up. Like I said,
it was an edgy situation. He was politically connected, an earl, something like that. Home Office didn't want to go through a messy trial.
So they sent me in.

"My cutout was this pissy little bastard named Coalhelms, who did
everything as inconveniently as possible. He was a typical civil servant.
A really horrid little man. Anyway, there I was, waiting for Coalhelms
to show up with the background on the mark. We were to meet at the
Thieves' Inn, an ale house right on the sea, up over the rocks. Got to

be the loneliest pub in the bloody fucking world. Always foggy and damp so it cuts through you. I was taking a dram and sitting there, letting my eyes get accustomed to the place, for it's all candlelit, and I was looking across the room, kind of not focusing on anything in particular and suddenly I realized I was staring at this giant of a bugger sitting at the bar and he's looking back at me with the coldest pair of eyes you've ever seen in all your life. Yellow-haired he was, and wearing tweeds with one of them country-squire, gnarled-up shillelaghs. And a tweedy cap over one eye. Beard and mustache, curled up and waxed at the corners, like a Highland colonel. He looked the perfect Scottish squire.

"And he was—except when I knew him he had red hair, and when last I saw him he was wearing a navy wet suit and his name was Guy Thornley. I recognized him quickly, even though I hadn't seen him for eight years or more.

"You may have forgotten who Guy Thornley was, although I'll wager the name is familiar to you. Thornley was attached to M.I.5, and his specialty was underwater surveillance and sabotage. But he was a bit of a rogue agent. Did what he wanted. The summer of nineteen sixty-eight, the Russians brought several warships up the Thames for some kind of political shindig and among them was a wireless trawler, an electronic spy ship. It was much too tempting a morsel for Sir Guy to pass up, so he decides to go down and take a peek at her underbelly.

"Nobody ever saw him again. The Thames didn't give him up. There was never another word from him. He vanished.

"The accepted theory is that the Russians had a scuba lock team down there, they wasted Thornley, then took him aboard the trawler and dumped him when they were well out at sea.

"An acceptable and logical theory. I believed it myself until that October night eighteen months ago. Sitting there in the Thieves' Inn, looking at him, I knew there was no mistake on his part that I recognized him, and no mistake on mine that he made me.

"What I did, I went outside and lit up a fag. I figgered whatever he was up to, I might as well give him some room. If I had known what he was up to, I would have got out of there straightaway, although I doubt I would have got far.

"I wasn't two puffs into the butt, he comes sauntering out. There we are, in fog as thick as chocolate syrup, and he says, 'Coalhelms isn't coming, old man.' Just like that.

"'Twas like I stuck my finger in an open socket. The hair on my arms stood up as straight as the Queen's Guard. It was a setup, of course;

the worrisome thing was that I had walked into it eyes open. I was in the drop because I had trusted that office monkey and suddenly there I was, standing there in the fog with the ocean crashing down below us, talking to a bloody ghost. Worse, I knew we weren't alone. Someone else was close by, I could feel him breathing down my neck. I figgered to hear Thornley out, however it played.

"He had seen my K-file, that was obvious, for he knew about Guardio and Trujillo and that take-out in Brazil four years ago. He knew almost every job I'd ever done, Coalhelms had obviously lifted the file for him.

"Top-secret information, right?

"Not on your life. Because it wasn't Thornley on some deep cover job, nothing like that. What happened is, he offered me a bloody job! Guaranteed me a hundred thousand a year. Told me I'd be called in only when needed. I could live anywhere in the world I wanted to, and all the transactions would be cash deposits in any bank of my choosing.

" 'We're nonpolitical,' he says. 'This is strictly business. Our clients are the biggest companies in the world. You might say we're a personal service for world industry. You handle your first assignment, which is a breeze, properly, and you can take early retirement from the Service and live as good as Prince Charlie.'

"I was that stunned, I could hardly talk. And then he tells me some of the other chaps who're in on the Game, counting them off on his fingers, and it was then the scope of this Service, as he called it, came clear to me, for he was talking about the best lads in the business.

"Gazinsky, the KGB man who kidnapped Zhagi Romoloff, right from under the West Germans' noses; Kimoto, the dapper little Japanese saboteur; Charley Simons, probably the best electronics man in the CIA, maybe in the world; Taven Kaminsky, the tough Jew who set up Israel's antiterrorist outfit; Kit Willoughby from Australia; Amanet, the Iranian arsonist from the Savak; a couple of lads from the British antiterrorist group.

"And to top it off, a couple of real beauts: Danilov, the Bulgarian jeweler turned assassin, maybe the most dangerous man in the bunch. Those skilled hands of his developed a pellet no bigger than the head of a pin infused with a single drop of riticin. Do you know about riticin? A drop no bigger than a grain of sugar can kill a horse. The pellet is air-injected, right through clothing.

"And finally, the Frenchman known only as Le Croix, who was in charge of the French torture squad in Algeria for two years, had all pictures of himself destroyed, and got his name because he used to crucify his victims.

"An impressive rogue's gallery of the keenest and most cold-blooded operatives in the world. Not a thimbleful of warm blood in the lot.

"My options were pretty bleedin' thin. Try to take out Thornley, and some shooter lurking behind me in the fog? A dead man's choice.

"Go along with it until I got out of the drop, then turn up Thornley and run for my life? There'd always be a Gazinsky or a Lavanieux or a Danilov behind me, waiting to drop the curtain on me.

"Or listen to his proposition, buy a little time maybe? It wasn't the money. Hell, there wasn't any option. I knew that somewhere in that fog my executioner was waiting for my decision.

"It was join or die. They had made up their minds they wanted me. They left me little damn choice in the matter.

"What's a feller to do—right? And now that I'm in, what're my options? Stay in until I fuck up and either they kill me—or somebody else does. Or run.

"My first job—my initiation, as Thornley called it—paid me twenty-five thousand dollars.

" 'Who's the mark?' I asked.

"And Thornley says, 'Coalhelms.'

"Just like that. I could hardly get my wits together, it's that shocked I was. Finally I says to him, 'Why? Other than he's an insufferable little squeeker.'

" 'You never need to know the why of a thing,' Thornley says. 'If it's to be done, there's a reason for it. But since it's your first time out with us, I'll tell you this much: he's outlived his usefulness. He's proved to be a bad security risk for your people.'

" 'They're your people, too,' I said.

" 'Not anymore,' he says. 'Nor yours, either, after tonight.'

"Actually, Coalhelms was nothing more than a test.

" 'And just who in hell runs this club?' I asked.

"And that was the first time I ever heard of Chameleon."

Bang!

The line on the port side twanged loose from its outrigger and screamed through the reel: *aweee-aweee-aweee-aweee . . .*

It was a game fish, breaching long enough to jump high in the air once, then spitting out the hook. O'Hara used the momentary distraction to try to correlate everything Falmouth was saying.

He ignored the brief fishing drama, concentrating instead on the steady throb of the motors, using the sound as a kind of mantra, slipping briefly into a trancelike form of meditation. Kimura called it *shidasu hakamaru,* "going to the wall."

To O'Hara, it was like being in a bright white room with no seams or doors. Against this glaring white milieu he projected images and words, imbedding them in his memory. He had only a vague visual recollection of Thornley, but there were others he knew:

Gazinsky, the tall Russian with the cadaverous head and eyes like a cat, always a bit of food in his beard; Tosiru Kimoto, the Buddha-like Japanese with his three-piece suits and white-on-white shirts, who had once blown up four Russian missile pads and got out without losing his breath; Amanet, the sleek, black-haired little Savak terrorist, whom he once saw in Algiers, drinking fresh goat's blood as if it were a cocktail.

Then there was the Frenchman, Le Croix. Tall, short, fat, thin? He had no visual impression of the man other than that he had once heard Le Croix had lost an eye in the fighting in Algeria and had exacted a terrible price for it—he had personally executed twenty-two Algerian rebels.

Finally, there was Danilov the Jeweler, whom he had seen only through binoculars, strolling through the Tuileries in Paris. "Remember that face," his partner had told him, "he is one of the most dangerous men in the Game. And watch the umbrella. There's an air-injection needle in the tip, loaded with poison. He can hit you right through your overcoat."

O'Hara remembered Danilov well: short, squat, a face round as a cabbage, pencil-thin mustache, thick glasses accentuating gleaming, beady eyes tucked among thick folds of flesh, his tongue, a snake's tongue, constantly licking nervously at his lips, as though sensing some unsuspecting prey nearby. And the omnipresent black umbrella with its pinhead of death lurking in the tip.

The images would remain, as well as the imagery of Falmouth trapped in a nightmare of his own making, performing a pagan ritual of death as his "initiation."

The concept was terrifying, the Players, themselves, proving the Game far more dangerous than he had imagined.

"Christ, din't I teach ya better'n that?" Cap'n K. barked from the bridge. The big fish had thrown the line and was gone.

The captain throttled back and came to the stern and baited the big hook again. "Ya didn't snag him," he said irritably. "That was a two-hundred-pounder there, Tony. Two-hundred-pounder!"

"We're talking business," Tony said, setting the line and clamping it by clothespin to the outrigger.

"Fishin' and talkin' don't mix," snapped the captain. He returned to the bridge and slammed the throttles forward.

The activity jarred O'Hara back to reality. He waited until Falmouth was back in his chair.

"Did you really burn Coalhelms?" he asked.

Falmouth looked at O'Hara, his gray eyes turning flinty for just a moment, then he nodded. "That I did, Sailor."

"Why?"

"It was just like any other job."

"For twenty-five thousand dollars?"

"That's not the point."

Falmouth's candor shocked O'Hara. "The point! Why didn't you just go to M.I.5, turn Thornley up for the deserter he is?"

Falmouth seemed to collapse in the middle. His shoulders sagged. His face drew in, the creases around his eyes and mouth growing deeper. His voice was haunted, the voice of a man whose sins were parading past him, the bodiless faces of his victims hovering before his eyes.

"Look," he said finally, "I'm tired, okay? I'm pushing fifty. I don't run as fast as once I did. Nor jump as high, nor move as quick. You can't stay tops in the Game much past forty. You forget things. Your eyes start to go. You don't have the stamina you once had. Your reflexes are shot. You start making little mistakes now and again. Not fatal ones, but when it happens, that black angel whispers in your ear just the same."

"Christ, there must've been something you could—"

"You just don't get it, do you, man? You're trying to make a moral issue where there are no morals. Dontcha see, lad, I had no choice. You bet your sweet lovin' ass I did it. And thankful I did now, or I'd be long gone. You don't retire from this bunch. You botch it, try to get out, you're a dead man. What I'm saying, Sailor, you retire in a box and that's the only way. Well, I ain't lookin' to get laid out in McGinty's front room with a hole in me. I've always planned on dying in bed. So forget the moral judgments, hey? We're not here for judging, we're here to pop their balloon. You blow this operation open, and I'm a free man. Otherwise I'm on the dodge for the rest of my life, which is not a thing I have a taste for right now."

There were a few moments of uneasy silence.

"It isn't easy, you know, admitting you're losing your edge, when that's all you've got."

And more silence. Is this really it? O'Hara wondered. Is it that simple? Is Tony too scared to resist some nameless, faceless assassin in the dark? Or is there more to it? Some kind of plot? He examined his own paranoia, but found no answers. Falmouth's self-entrapment made as much sense as anything else so far in his chilling yarn.

He changed the subject. "What's the objective of all this and who the hell's Chameleon?"

Falmouth leaned back, closed his eyes and let the sun bake his face. The pain of admitting that he was growing too old for the Game faded slowly from his handsome features. "The objective is greed."

"What companies are involved?"

"The biggest in the world. Our enemies are their competition. If the enemy's got somethin your client wants, steal it. If you can't steal it, kill the ones who're doing the work.

"Blow up their laboratories. Burn 'em out. Slow them down. Drive 'em out of business. Steal their secrets. Our clients? Hell, you name it. United Telephone, Continental Motor Company, Sunset Oil, the Boston Common Bank and Trust, Global Steel . . ."

He waved his hands to indicate the futility of listing them all.

Talk, O'Hara thought. So far Falmouth had given him very little but talk. Nothing could be proven. "All I'm hearing is talk," he said.

"All right, how about Guardio, the South American strong man. Did you hear about his assassination while you were on the dodge?"

"They do have newspapers in Japan, Tony," O'Hara said, managing a smile.

"The whole coup was set up by Chameleon."

"You said this was nonpolitical."

"Absolutely nonpolitical, old man. Strictly business. American Electric paid the bill. Guardio was planning to nationalize the power companies, and A.E. had fifty million invested down there. Thornley went in four months ahead and began plotting with the generalissimos. I went in a month before the coup, took me that long to work up the kill. I took out Guardio while he was in church. The generals closed all the doors, trapping the family and loyalists inside. There was a force of four hundred mercenaries just over the border, maybe thirty miles away. Guardio wasn't cold yet when they hit the park across from the church in choppers. Backup for the army. I was back in New York having dinner at the Four Seasons that night. The mop-up took four days and the price tag was two million dollars."

"They have their own army?"

"A brigade of British Highlanders, under contract to the British Army with agreement that they can take leave anytime, as long as the country isn't under some kind of military alert. They can be put in the field, fully equipped, in less than thirty days."

"We can't prove any of this," O'Hara said.

He got up and leaned over the stern, watching the motors churning up the wake. There were too many holes and not enough details. He needed more names, possible defectors. Anyone who would talk to him. He focused on the sound of the engines, going to the wall again. But it didn't work. Something stronger than details was pulling at him. This had the makings of a great story and now his reporter's instincts were humming. He felt the excitement of a scoop nibbling deep in his stomach. But he needed more than Falmouth. He needed to cross-check before he started doling out Howe's money.

"How about Thornley?" he asked. "If I can turn him up, it would be a good starting place."

"I haven't seen him since the Guardio business."

"Any defectors? Anybody else ever run?"

Falmouth hesitated. He gave himself some thinking time by lighting another Gitane.

"Well?" said O'Hara.

"Do we have a deal?" Falmouth said.

"Not yet. I couldn't begin to put a story together with what you've told me. I need names to go with faces, and faces to go with jobs. And I want to know who it is that's on the run."

"I never said anyone was."

"You can't be the first one to want out of this madness."

"The world is mad!" said Falmouth. "You were in the Game for five bloody years, O'Hara, didn't you learn anything from it? With greed comes money and with money comes power, and that's what it's all about."

"Not the world I want to live in."

"Right, Sailor. So here's your opportunity to change it. Do you doubt I'm risking my life telling you all this?"

O'Hara considered an answer but Falmouth pressed on, "Just remember, where there's a need, there's always something or someone to fill it."

"And that someone is Chameleon?"

"Chameleon's just the beginning."

"It'll do for starters. Who is he?"

"Ah, who is he indeed? A faceless figure. A wisp of air, never seen by the Players, or none that I've met. Chameleon's all I know, and that from some of the other boys I've worked with. But he's the head of it, I've heard that often enough to know it's the truth."

"You don't know where the headquarters is? Where this Chameleon operates from?"

"No. I can tell you all I know about him in about thirty seconds. He's Oriental and he's been around awhile. That's why you're a natural for this one, old man. You know Japan as well as you know your left hand, and you know the Players, so you can understand the significance of what I'm saying."

"How do you know he's an Oriental?"

"From Thornley. From others I heard he was the most dangerous one in the bunch. It was Chameleon burned Colin Bradley."

"Bradley's dead?"

"Aye. Popped up in the East River with a bullet in his brain. Somebody wanted Chameleon taken out and Bradley thought he was up to the job. Got his bloody head blown off. That's what you get for thinking."

"Who wanted him out?"

"I don't know the answer to that, but I would guess it was one of the enemy."

"You make it sound like war, Tony."

"And that it is. But not a cold war, Sailor," and he leaned over and said in a rasping stage whisper, "a bloody *dollar* war."

"How does this Chameleon conduct business, how does he run this crazy show you're talking about, if nobody has contact with him?"

"Through Master."

"Master?"

"A computer. Everything is done by computer. The only human contact I have on the top side is a man named Quill."

"He's your cutout?"

"Yes."

"Quill?"

"Yes, Quill."

O'Hara shook his head. "Sounds like you've been reading too much Dickens," he said.

"Well, that's his name, dammit. Quill. Never met him and the only way to reach him is through Master."

"And Master's the computer?"

"Right. To get into it, you have to go through a series of checks. Voice prints. Number intersects. Variable code names, like that. The operation's so simple it's terrifying. A job comes in. Quill programs Master, determines the best man for the job and makes contact. Everything is taken care of. Tickets, money, contacts, hotel reservations, cars. Even weapons, if there's something special you might need. The pay is deposited in the account of your choice before you get your bags packed. It works as smooth as sand running through an hour glass."

"What about the man himself—what's his background?"

"Never seen him. Wouldn't know 'im if he came up out of the water there and spit in my eye."

"You've been at this for eighteen months, you've never *seen* any of the top Players?"

"And maybe never will. It isn't necessary."

"How about some of the operations?"

As the sun swept overhead, boring relentlessly down on them, Falmouth detailed the Guardio operation and then went on, describing the accidental murder of Marza and the destruction of the Aquila car, how he set up the bomb in the computerized dash, where he stayed, trains and planes he took.

"The Aquila job was so clean they're still trying to figure out what went wrong. It's delayed work on the car for months. They still haven't recovered from the shock of Marza's death."

"I want a deposition from you with all those details."

Falmouth thought for a moment. "When the money's paid," he agreed.

O'Hara pondered that for a moment and then nodded. "That seems fair enough," he said. "There's got to be a pattern to all of this, something that ties it all together."

"I tell you, Sailor, stop looking for some kind of logical order to it."

But O'Hara's mind was trained to consider both the logical and illogical possibilities of any situation. There has to be some common thread, some ultimate goal in this madness, he thought, but Falmouth laughed at him when he said so.

"It's the Game for fun and profit, plain and simple. There's a fortune being made. What do you think the Marza play cost? My end was a hundred and fifty thousand. They probably charged the client half a million."

O'Hara was still unconvinced. To him, there had to be an overall objective to the Master operation other than "fun and games." Perhaps only Chameleon knew what it was.

"You try to figger some kinda conspiracy in it, you'll have a Chinese puzzle on your hands," Falmouth insisted. "Sometimes the jobs make no sense at all." He recounted Hinge's tale of killing a man in Hawaii to retrieve the negatives of a dozen photographs, then destroying the film he had just killed to acquire.

"And who is this Hinge?" O'Hara asked.

"Bloody cowboy. Kills without thinking or hesitation. Men or women, no matter. He can do the trick with gun or knife, he can do it with darts or with rope. Hell, he could probably spit us both to fucking death."

"Nobody can kill you, Tony."

"I used to think so, until I worked with this new lad two days ago in Caracas."

"What the hell were you doing in Caracas the day before yesterday?"

"I got an assignment. I didn't know whether you were going to make it or not. I couldn't turn them down without showing my hand."

"Who's this young hotshot, a merc?"

"Was, before this."

"They're a dime a dozen, Tony."

"Not this one. There aren't a dozen like him. Made a kill from nineteen hundred feet in Vietnam. And he was using a bloody *night* scope!"

"What was this job you two did?"

"Chap named Lavander got lifted by some local *muchachos*. We had to bring him in. But it's what's happened since that may give you the hook you're looking for."

"And how's that?"

Falmouth leaned over, his eyes gleaming, and smiled. "I'll tell you that when we have a deal," he said.

O'Hara was watching movement twenty or so yards beyond the lines that skittered along the surface of the sea. He was still uncomfortable about turning over two hundred and fifty thousand dollars to Tony Falmouth, but if Falmouth had additional information for him, it could change his mind.

"I think I'll go back to Japan," O'Hara said. "Live a nice, simple life. No computers running private intelligence agencies or ghosts running computers. It's all too complicated. I didn't want to take this job in the first place."

The fin of a big fish sliced the surface for a moment and went under again.

"You can't back off now," Falmouth said.

"The hell I can't."

"You do and I'm a dead man."

"Just do a few more jobs and then run," said O'Hara.

"I'm already on the dodge. I agreed last night I'd do another job, but I didn't return Quill's call to get the details. You don't accept a job, then disappear, not without creating a certain level of anxiety in the heart of Mr. Quill. By now he's figuring either I've run or something happened to me. Whatever, he's assigned someone else to the job, and that's where I can help you."

"And how's that?" said O'Hara.

Falmouth's gray eyes were twinkling, his lips playing with a smile. "Because I know the mark," he said. "I know where he's going to be hit. I know when. And I know the assassin."

And after he let that sink in, he added, "And I'll give you the runner as a bonus."

A runner. Someone else on the dodge. Now, that had possibilities. The bonus is what turned O'Hara. If someone other than Tony was dodging Chameleon and he could turn up the runner, he could verify Falmouth's story.

The fin split the surface of the ocean again, this time about ten yards to the lee side of the line.

"I'll make a deal with you," said O'Hara. "If you give me that information, I'll pay you half. If I score and the information is clean, I'll deposit the other half anywhere you say or meet you and give you the rest."

"Goddamn, we're playin rough, aren't we, Sailor."

"It isn't my money."

Falmouth nodded very slightly and then stuck out his hand. "Done," he said, and they shook.

"Let's hear it," said O'Hara.

"Listen here, Sailor, I can't lie to you, tell you I understand everything that goes on here, okay? But I can tell you this . . . there's always a reason for them doing what they do. I'm not back from Caracas ten hours than I pick up an urgent from Quill. So I contact him. Now, understand—Hinge and I put our *cojones* on the line to spring this Lavander fella, right? So here it is, not two days later, and Quill tells me he's got a fast job. He says it'll all be over in four or five days. I'm to meet a cutout in the Caribbean area somewhere and stand by for a possible hit. The cutout will make the decision. And who's the bloody subject? *Lavander.*"

O'Hara was genuinely surprised. "Lavander!" he exclaimed.

"Lavander. See what I mean? Can you make any sense outa that?"

"Hell, they're your pals, Tony, you make a guess."

"I thought a lot about it. Logically? It's got to be that he's become a security risk to someone."

"Why?"

"He knows too much. About *some*thing, I don't know what. He's worked as a consultant for a lot of big companies all over the world.

So he knows a lot about a lot of people. He knows a lot of company secrets."

"You think they'd kill this man just because he's a security risk to some corporation?"

"Absolutely."

"Why the cutout, why not just send you in to waste the poor bastard?"

"Guessing again, I'd say the cutout's gonna give him a very subtle third degree. If he gives the wrong answers, *au revoir, Monsieur Lavander.*"

"You say you know the place."

"Not exactly. But I do know he's leaving Honduras very soon on a Caribbean cruise, courtesy of Sunset Oil, a little bonus for his trials and tribulations. I also know he's traveling under the name J. M. Teach. And last night Quill told me the job would be over in four or five days. Shouldn't be hard to track down a steamer leaving Honduras sometime in the next day or so and find out her first port o' call."

"Why's he traveling under an assumed name?"

"Because he's weird. I told you, he's an eccentric. I saw him for just a moment or two after he was released. There he was, eyes like a couple of wells, looked like he hadn't slept in two days, and the first thing he asks is, 'Did you check me out of the hotel while I was gone?' I mean, he was genuinely concerned about it. A true nut."

There was a flash of sunlight on fin in the wake of the *Miami Belle;* the big line snapped from the outrigger, then the line jarred again and the reel began to sing as it fed out.

"Christ, we got a big one," Falmouth cried. "It's all yours, Sailor!"

O'Hara moved the rod quickly from its sheath on the rail to the cup between his legs and Falmouth tightened his safety belt as O'Hara began the fight.

The fish, a blue marlin, was enormous.

"Three hundred pounds!" Falmouth guessed. "She could be a record, lad."

The fight lasted the better part of two hours. By the time it was over, O'Hara's arms were leaden, his hands blistered. Cap'n K. maneuvered the boat perfectly, using its big engines to tire the fish as O'Hara reeled the fighting marlin closer to the stern.

"Ya got 'im!" the captain yelled down. "Get 'im close enough to the stern so we can knock the fucker out. It's gonna take all three of us to get him aboard."

The fish sounded one last time, leaping high from the water, his tail thrashing angrily. Then he dove deep. O'Hara kept the pressure on. The marlin's beaked head appeared a few feet from the stern. The fight was gone out of him.

"You did fine there, Sailor. What a beauty! Well," Falmouth said, "too bad"—and he bent over and pulled an old, rusty machete free of the rail where it was sticking out, and he reared back and the blade whistled past O'Hara's head and hit the stern with a *chock.* The line was cut. The marlin speared the surface one last time, snapped its head and plunged into the wake of the boat. It was gone.

The captain screamed, "What in hell are ye doin'? That was a god-damn three-hundred-pound marlin, yuh crazy bastard!" Cap'n K. continued to rave from the bridge, screaming obscenities at the wind, the gulls, the sea, at everything.

Falmouth looked down at the stunned O'Hara, who had sagged back in the fighting chair and was shaking the pain from his arms. "Wouldn't do, would it now, us coming into Freeport with a record marlin on board. There'd be pictures and God knows what all, right? That's all the papers have to write about there."

O'Hara nodded very slowly. "Tony," he said, "I'm beginning to believe you. Now, who's going after Lavander?"

Falmouth leaned over and smiled proudly. "Why, Hinge, of course. He knows Lavander. Besides, it's got to be Hinge. If they think I'm running, they'll send Gazinsky or Lavanieux after me."

"Why not Danilov?"

"Because, Sailor, he's the runner."

10

"MR. HOWE, PLEASE."

"Mr. Charles Gordon Howe?" the secretary asked.

"That's right."

"I'm sorry, Mr. Howe is in conference and can't be disturbed."

"Tell him O'Hara's on the phone."

"I have explicit instructions not to disturb him," the secretary said sternly.

"Just tell him it's me, I'm sure he'll take this call."

There was a momentary pause, then an annoyed: "Just a moment, please."

He was on hold for hardly a breath before he heard Howe's crusty, laced-with-Irish brogue. "Where are you, Lieutenant?"

"Down in the islands, but that's not important. I need to do a little traveling. Is your Lear jet still available?"

"Where d'you want it and when?" Howe asked immediately. There was excitement in his voice.

"As soon as possible. Fort Lauderdale airport."

"Can I assume we have a story, then?"

"I'll need a couple more days before I can commit for sure."

"You're a cautious one, I'll say that."

"It's your money, Mr. Howe."

"Fair enough. I assume you've met this Falmouth feller already."

"Yes."

There was silence on the line as if Howe were waiting for O'Hara to go on. Finally the publisher said, "Well?"

"I'm not ready to talk about it just yet. I can tell you I've paid him a hundred and twenty-five. He gets the rest if his information is good."

"I assume from what you've just said that you feel you're on to something."

"I wouldn't have parted company with all that money if I didn't think he had something. Putting it all together may be a problem."

"I have the best libel lawyers in the business, Lieutenant. I want to be accurate, not cautious."

"I'll keep that in mind. Usually it's the other way around—the publisher tells me to be cautious."

Howe chuckled. "My feelin' about you, Lieutenant, is that if we have anything, it will be big."

"Thanks."

A pause.

"Are you in any danger, Lieutenant?"

O'Hara thought for a few seconds, then said, "There's an element of risk. We're dealing with some pretty mean characters here."

"You know them, then?"

"Personally or by reputation. Right now, all I got's conjecture. Talking about it further could be counterproductive and increase the risk."

"I don't think I need t' tell you to be careful."

"Not at all."

"Good. As I said from the start, lad, I trust you. But I'll admit, my curiosity is about to short-circuit. Besides, I got a bit of a surprise for you."

"What is it?"

Howe chuckled. "You'll find out soon enough."

"I don't like surprises, Mr. Howe."

"Oh, I think you'll like this one."

O'Hara dropped the subject—Howe was probably going to send a couple of live lobsters down in the plane. "I'll be back in touch in about three days," he said. "By then I'll be able to tell you whether I flushed your hundred and twenty-five."

"I'll have the Lear at Fort Lauderdale in four hours. If you need anything else, have any trouble, call me anytime. I may not be able to get war declared, but I can damn sure come close to it and will if it's necessary."

"Thanks. I'll be in touch."

Getting through to the Magician was not as simple. The lines were tied up when he first called. He made the second call from Fort Lauderdale, after Cap'n K.'s air charter dropped him off. The line exploded with static and when the connection was finally completed, the operator sounded as if she were talking from somewhere near the center of the earth.

"Le Grand Gustavsen Hôtel, s'il vous plaît," O'Hara shouted.

"Hôtel?" she said.

"Oui. Le Grand Gustavsen."

"Pardonnez-moi—did you say Heelton?"

"Gustavsen!" O'Hara yelled, wondering how she could have mistaken Grand Gustavsen for Hilton.

"Ah, oui, Goostafsen. Un moment, s'il vous plaît."

More static, more noise, before someone finally answered. It was a gruff voice; obviously a guest passing by the desk had picked up the receiver.

"Yeah?"

"Is the Magician there?" O'Hara said.

"The who?"

"The Magician. Rothschild. The man who owns the hotel."

"You mean the piano player?"

"Right."

"I don't know."

"Just give me someone connected with the hotel, please."

There was a loud clatter on the other end, as though the man who had answered had thrown the phone across the room.

A few moments later Jolicoeur answered. *"Allô. Que desirez-vous? May I be of service?"*

"Joli? It's O'Hara."

"Ah, François! Comment ça va?"

"I'm doing okay, Joli. *Où est le Sorcier?"*

"At the market."

"J'arrive ce soir. Voulez-vous me donner la pièce avec la salle de bain?"

"Volontiers! Quelle heure?"

"Don't know yet. *Très tard. Vers deux heures, peut-être."*

"Bon! Où êtes-vous?"

"Florida. I'm waiting for the plane now. Tell him I'll need his help."

"Excellent! We will put clean sheets on your bed."

"Damn generous there, Joli."

"Pour vous, mon ami, le mieux. We have a job, then?"

"We may. Listen, when Mike gets back, tell him I want a readout on four names. Can you hear me clearly?"

"Oui."

"Very good. You have a pen?"

"Oui. Shoot."

"Anthony Falmouth, spelling F-a-l-m-o-u-t-h. Formerly with M.I.6. Hinge. H-i-n-g-e, no first name available. A mercenary. Gregori Danilov. D-a-n-i-l-o-v. Bulgarian secret service. Avery Lavander. L-a-v-a-n-d-e-r. British subject. An oil consultant. Oh, there is one other. All I have is a cover name . . . Chameleon, like the lizard. Check all sources on that one. That ought to keep you busy until I get there."

Jolicoeur repeated the names to O'Hara.

"Perfect. See you later, pal."

"À bientôt, François! We will be ready when you get here."

"Anders Travel, Carole Jackowitz speaking."

Her voice was a touch of Bronx mixed with Brooklyn, tempered by Manhattan chic.

"Hi, Ms. Jackowitz. My name's O'Hara—remember me?"

"Oh, sure. The gentleman with a one-way ticket to Walker's Cay, right? Was it a suicide trip? *Nobody* takes a one-way trip to Walker's Cay. It isn't much bigger than my backyard."

"I swam back."

"I see. And . . . uh, where would you like to swim back from this time?"

"Honduras."

"Um hm. Anyplace in particular or do you want to trust my judgment?"

"Actually I'm interested in a cruise boat."

She laughed. "No one-ways on a cruise ship. What's its name?"

"I don't know."

There was a long pause. "You don't know the name of the ship you want to catch in Honduras?"

"Right. But I'm sure it will be leaving sometime in the next day or two."

Another pause and a chuckle. "I'm checking," she said musically. There was another pause, and then: "I'll be damned. Oh, excuse me, I didn't mean to swear, but a cruise ship did leave Port Cortez this morning. Hmm, the *Gulf Star.* King Line. Well, there are better lines I could recommend—"

"Where does it go first?"

"First port o' call is . . . Montego Bay, Jamaica. Three days. Let's see, today's Tuesday . . . it'll be in early Friday morning. Want to pick it up there?"

"I don't want to pick it up at all, I want to send twelve dozen roses to one of its passengers."

"I knew there was a catch to this. Sorry, we're not a messenger service."

"No romance in your soul, hunh?"

"Only if the roses are going to me, dahling."

"You've been a great help. Sometime when I'm in Pompano Beach I'll call. Maybe we can have lunch."

"If you're sending twelve dozen roses to *any*body, we can skip the lunch thing and start right off with dinner."

"Bye, Carole."

"By, Mr.—uh . . ."

"O'Hara."

"Gotcha."

The King Steamship Line had a special operator to take messages for its passengers. O'Hara got him and said, "This goes to Mr. J. M. Teach. He's boarding the *Gulf Star* in Port Cortez, Honduras."

"Go ahead."

" 'J.M. . . . colon . . . Have additional information on the Master plan.

Period. Do not leave ship in Montego Bay until I contact you. Period.'
Sign it . . . 'Quill.' "

O'Hara half slept on the Lear as it streaked southward out over the
ocean but was wide awake when they landed in St. Lucifer. He was
beginning to feel a little like a yo-yo. Japan to Boston to St. Lucifer to
Fort Lauderdale to the Bahamas to Fort Lauderdale, all in three days,
and now, at one-thirty in the morning, he was back in St. Lucy. A cab
was waiting for him at the airport, which was closed for the night. Even
customs was locked up. But what would anyone smuggle into St. Lucy,
anyway, day or night?

He heard the Mag, playing a furious version of "C-Jam Blues" as he
climbed the stairs to the main floor. The big room was almost empty.
A young couple nuzzled each other at a table, and there were a few
hangers-on at the bar. Jolicoeur was one of them and he excused himself
as soon as he saw O'Hara. The Mag was oblivious, his six fingers
rambling across the keyboard.

"*Bon soir, mon ami,* good to see you! We have interesting news."

When the Magician saw him, he finished the tune he was playing,
closed the piano and put a stand-up sign on its top that said: "Closed.
Don't mess with the piano. Violators will be shot at sunrise." He
ambled across the room, a cigarette hanging at the corner of his mouth.
"That was quick," he said, giving the weary reporter a bear hug.

O'Hara looked at him through bleary eyes. "Lead me to my digs, I
don't think I can stand up much longer."

As they walked down the hall, Rothschild told him they had run all
the names through the computer and had print-outs on three of them
—Lavander, Falmouth and Danilov. There was nothing on Hinge so
far, and checking out Chameleon had turned up dozens of references
to zoological and biological booklets, articles from nature-study magazines, even several encyclopedias.

"What're you so interested in chameleons for?"

"Told Joli, it's a cover. Try the CIA, military or naval intelligence,
like that. Also you might run Colin Bradley, CIA, through that infernal
machine of yours. Chameleon supposedly burned Bradley last Christmas."

"What is going on?" the Mag asked.

"Later . . ."

O'Hara entered the room, conveniently located across from
the Mag's suite, dropped his suitcase and said, "Wake me around
noon."

"We been getting these reports together ever since you called," the Magician said. "Aren't you even gonna read them?"

"Can't," he mumbled. "Too much jet lag. Fishing. Sun. I'm a wreck," and peeling his clothes off, he collapsed in bed.

"Call me for lunch," he said and immediately fell into a deep sleep.

The knocking on his door was insistent.

"Go away," he groaned.

The knocking continued.

"Do not disturb. Go away."

More knocking.

"*À demain! À bientôt! Au revoir!*" he yelled.

It did not help. The knocking became more intense.

"Shit!"

That didn't help either.

He stumbled out of bed and opened the door a crack, peering around the edge.

He stared at Lizzie Gunn for several moments, squinting his eyes. "Oh my God," he said.

She held a steaming cup of coffee in her hand. "Coffee?" she said brightly.

"I don't believe it," he said finally.

"Found you again," she said. Her smile was so bright it hurt his eyes.

"What time is it?" he asked.

"Eight A.M."

"Eight A.M.!"

"Right. Eight A.M."

"Unbelievable."

"Don't you want your coffee?"

"Not unless you want to see a grown man throw up."

"May I come in?"

"Is there any way to stop you?"

"Nope."

"Let me get back in bed. I'm naked."

"I don't mind, I had three brothers."

"Well, I'm not one of them." He staggered back to bed and pulled the sheet over his head.

"Not very hospitable," she said.

"I may die of terminal jet lag. Or lack of sleep. They're both waiting for me . . . in long black robes, just outside the door, there." He spoke from under the sheet.

She sat down in a chair and poised the coffee on her knee. He looked back at her from under the sheet. "You're not going to go away, are you?"

"Uh uh."

"Were you obnoxious as a child?"

She shook her head, still smiling.

"Had to wait until you grew up, hunh." He retreated back under the sheet.

"Mr. Jolicoeur said you'd be this way."

"How the hell d'you know Jolicoeur?"

"He was in the lobby, if that's what they call it, when I got in." She took a sip of the coffee. "He kissed my hand."

"He kisses everybody's hand. It's one of the things he does, he kisses hands."

"Well, nobody's ever kissed my hand before."

"Why don't you go back down to the lobby. I'm sure he'll be glad to kiss your hand all day long."

She continued to sip her coffee. He sat up suddenly. "How the hell did you find me? How the hell did you get here this fast?"

"The pilot had to file a flight plan in Boston and another one in Fort Lauderdale."

"That's all it took, hunh?"

"Well . . . I used to date him too."

"The pilot?"

"Uh huh."

O'Hara shook his head. "I should of stayed in Japan," he said, half aloud. He stared at her through lumpy eyes. "Does Howe know you're down here?"

She nodded. "Yep."

"You're the surprise Howe was talking about."

"Howe told you I was coming?"

"Not in so many words. He sent you to follow me, right?"

"Well, not exactly . . ."

"Well, exactly what did he do?"

"He finally agreed that a little competition never hurt anybody."

"That makes a lot of sense, Gunn, assigning one of his reporters to scoop another one."

"I thought we could work together. After all, you're print, and I'm video. There's no real competition. This way Howe gets it both ways. He really gets his money's worth."

"Always thinking, aren't you?"

"I try."

"How much do you know so far?"

"Well, he let me read that letter from—uh . . ."

"Falmouth."

"Right. I might as well have been reading ancient Greek."

"See what I mean."

"I can learn."

"This is not a game for neophytes. These—"

"Neophyte, my ass! I've been a reporter—"

"I'm not talking about reporting. I'm talking about the Game, about dealing with some of the most dangerous people in the wor—"

"And I'm a woman, right?"

"Will you let me finish? It hasn't got anything to do with sex. I know these characters, know how they operate. I've worked with—or against —most of them. You don't know the territory. You make one slip, they'll drop you like they swat a fly."

"Don't worry about me, O'Hara, I've dealt with the Mafia."

"Compared with the bunch I'm talking about, kid stuff."

"Kid stuff indeed!"

"Kid stuff nevertheless. You're good, I'll give you that, but—

"Thanks a lot."

"Stop interrupting me."

"Stop patronizing me."

"Patronizing you, my ass."

"You're patronizing me."

"I said you were good. You're very, very good, okay?"

"That's patronizing."

"Ah, shit." He buried himself under the sheets again.

"I can help, O'Hara. Trust me."

"Good doesn't matter if you're dead."

"I told you, you can't scare me."

"I'm not trying to scare you, I'm trying to convince you this is an assassin's game."

"And it takes one to know one, right?"

"I'm not an assassin, never was. But I know the people. I know the mentality. I can cope."

"I've been coping ever since I was thirteen years old."

"With *them*! I can cope with *them*!"

"I found you in Japan and I found you here. Let's not just pass that to the end of the table."

A pause. O'Hara tried again. "Let's try it from another angle. *If* there is a story and *if* I decide to pursue it and *if* we can get enough leads to even give it a shot, *if* all these ifs work out, it's still going to be a very . . . hairy game."

She smiled at him. "You can't lose me, O'Hara." Her brown eyes flashed with anticipation. "I know it's got to be really big. I mean, Mr. Howe didn't send me hiking all over the world looking for you for nothing. And you're not down here bopping around in Howe's Lear jet for laughs. C'mon, O'Hara, I can help. Just try me."

"Wake me again at ten," he said. "I'll sleep on it."

She sighed and put the coffee cup on the dresser and left. As soon as she was out of the room, O'Hara got up wearily. After he shaved and showered he stood for nearly an hour in a corner of the room, slowly performing a series of body movements known as the Butterfly, ridding his body of aches and stiffness. Then he sat quietly and meditated for twenty minutes.

When he had finished his morning ritual, he felt alive again and ready for the day.

Five minutes later she was back, this time with the Magician and Joli.

"What a remarkable recovery," she said. "An hour ago you acted like you were dying."

"An hour ago I was. Okay, let's see what we've got, and then I'll fill you in on what's happening."

"First of all," said the Magician, "I didn't turn up anything on this Hinge character."

"Military intelligence?"

"Blank. So far he seems to have kept himself off all the books."

"Okay. Next?"

"Falmouth. Here's a print-out on everything I turned up. I cross-checked CIA with M.I.6. Very interesting."

To O'Hara, however, there was very little information that was new. A few details he did not know, but mainly it confirmed that Falmouth had retired. There was nothing beyond that. Both the CIA and M.I.6 seemed to close the book on their ex-agents when they retired.

The Danilov dossier, however, turned up several items: that Danilov was suspected of not six or seven but twelve assassinations, including two in the United States; that he had developed the riticin pellet and the weapon with which he injected it into his victims; that he had worked on several occasions for the KGB, no big surprise there. The big surprise was that for two years and until eighteen months ago, Danilov had been operating in the Caribbean area, developing Russian contacts in Haiti, where he was well known. He had retired a year and a half ago and had been seen on two or three occasions by other agents in both Port-au-Prince and Cap-Haïtien.

Had he been working in Haiti for Master? If so, doing what? Joli could help there. He still knew every acre of the country and kept up with its political and social gossip.

The report on Avery Lavander was more complete than he had expected. The Magician had culled it from several sources, among them three different wire services, two American magazine chains, several newspapers, *Paris-Match,* the *International Herald Tribune,* and even an obscure British news magazine that had published the only profile ever written on the man. It was largely made up of innuendo and gossip culled from interviews with other people, among them his former wife, Margaret, who had endured twelve childless, sexless years with him before running off with a trombonist in the London Symphony and who had got even with Lavander by telling everything she knew about him. As usual, Lavander had refused to talk to the man who had written it.

O'Hara put together a mental picture of Lavander, a true eccentric who operated in his own private world, refusing to see reporters and avoiding photographers; who demanded, and got, astronomical consultation fees, which were deposited, in gold, in banks of his designation, all over the world; who kept a small book listing, in code, all his deposits, where and when they were made and who paid him, apparently the only record he did keep. Such was his reputation that before Lavander would grant an interview to a potential client, he required a deposit of ten thousand dollars in Krugerrands, yet he was pitifully frugal, preferring to stay in dismal hotels and taking his meals in the most mundane restaurants.

Despite his weird appearance, bizarre behavior and maddeningly irascible nature, most of the major oil companies, at one time or another, seemed to have availed themselves of Lavander's services, for he appeared to be a man devoted to a single purpose, and that purpose was oil. The various reports confirmed that he had little interest in food, women, books, music. In fact, he had little interest in anything but oil.

Oil was his life, every form of it: oil in the ground, oil in wells, oil in pipelines, oil in the stock market, oil in tankers, refineries, trucks, pumps, cars, cosmetics, pharmaceuticals. Oil in big business. Oil in every conceivable form. He was, in fact, the world's most knowledgeable human being on the subject. And because he was apolitical, an industrial mercenary who served no flag or master but himself, working only as a contract consultant, he moved comfortably within the international oil community, with contacts in OPEC, in Latin America, Canada, Southeast Asia and among the African oil producers. He knew how much oil was being shipped, who was getting it, what it cost and how much remained in reserve. He could predict shortages and price changes, and he knew how to find it and where to find it and the best way to get it to market.

Falmouth was right. Lavander could be a considerable security risk to a lot of companies. The question was, Which one had put out a contract on him and why?

So far, the Magician had turned up nothing on Chameleon.

O'Hara digested the information, memorizing all the details he felt worthwhile. Then he put the reports aside and said, "Nice going, Mag."

"Does it help?"

"Immensely, only I'm not sure just how for the moment."

"Can you fill us in?" Eliza asked.

"All right, but not until all three of you promise the information will not be shared with anyone . . . *any*one, okay, Gunn?"

"Yes, of course."

"Swear to it. Swear you will not reveal any information on this story until it's a wrap."

"I swear it."

"Okay. Here's the story so far . . ." and he told them in detail about his meeting with Falmouth, about Quill and Master and Thornley, about the Marza job, the murder on Maui, and the coup in South America.

"Right now we have three leads. The first is Lavander, who's slated to be grilled by a cutout and executed by Hinge if he gives the wrong answers—"

"What's a cutout?" Eliza asked.

"The man between an agent and his contact in the home office. A go-between. Usually he carries information back and forth. Sometimes he has the power to issue an assignment, as in this case."

"Do we know the cutout?" the Mag asked.

"No, but we do know the assassin. Hinge." O'Hara took a Polaroid photo from his wallet and passed it around. "That's Hinge. Falmouth gave me the picture. He used it to visually ID Hinge on the job in Caracas. Lavander's using the name J. M. Teach on this trip. Our best shot is to try to get to Lavander before he leaves the boat."

"Do we know *where* he's going to be?" Eliza asked.

"This is a calculated guess, but I think he's arriving in Montego Bay, Jamaica, Friday, early in the morning. I . . . took a wild flyer. I sent him a message telling him not to leave the boat and signed it 'Quill.' "

"What if he doesn't know who Quill is?" said the Magician.

"Well, he can't run. It won't be delivered until after the boat leaves Honduras. Then there's no place for him to go."

"How about Hinge?" Eliza asked.

"He could come in just about any way, but considering the time element I think we can assume he'll fly in."

"We can cover the airport at Montego Bay," the Magician suggested. "It isn't that big."

"All we have to do is watch customs," said Eliza.

"But of course!" cried Joli. "There is only one customs room. Everyone enters the terminal through the same door."

"I'll cover the airport," Eliza said. "Even if he's cautious, he wouldn't expect a woman to follow him."

"Why not?" said O'Hara.

"Too macho . . . at least from what you've told us about him. He wouldn't like to admit a woman might be in the same game he's in."

"Maybe. But I also told you he's a professional. He doesn't take chances. And he kills by instinct—and in more ways than you can even imagine, Lizzie."

"Don't start that."

"What?" the Magician asked.

"That Lizzie shit. My name's Eliza."

O'Hara looked at her and smiled. His eyes made contact with hers and they defied her to look away. Well, she thought, it's about time. The first sign of any response to me since I got here.

And O'Hara thought, She's going to get us in trouble. She's big trouble, I can tell by that look in those eyes and the set in her jaw.

The Magician was just the opposite, he could play it like James Bond or Laurel and Hardy, depending on conditions. And Joli would have other things to do.

"Okay. I don't know Lavander except by description, and Montego Bay isn't that small. He gets loose and we're in trouble. Suppose Mike and I take the boat and try to get to him before he gets on the street. E-liza, you cover the airport. If Hinge shows, give him plenty of rope —you get too close and he makes you—notices you, that is—he'll kill you. Remember, this guy likes guns better than people. If you're lucky, you may stay with him until he lights someplace."

"Then what do I do?" she asked.

O'Hara thought for a minute. "We'll keep it simple. Use the hotel drop. Where will we be staying?" he asked the Magician.

"Half Moon Bay Club. We'll get three cottages. You can get in and out without ever going near the lobby."

"Good. We'll use the switchboard. If you make Hinge and you stay with him until he stops someplace, call the desk and leave a message for us to meet you there."

"There's two of us," the Magician said. "We can check every five, ten minutes."

"And what about me?" Joli asked indignantly.

"Joli, we've only got two leads to Chameleon. One of them is Lavander, the other is Danilov. Danilov's on the dodge, and if he knows Haiti as well as it appears he does, he could be hiding there."

"That's a long shot there, Francis," said the Magician.

"I wouldn't know where else to begin looking. He's running. It would seem logical he might go over to Haiti. If he is the Russians' key man there, it seems likely that he knows the place better than any of them. He also has friends there. Joli, do you think you could hide a cabbage-faced Bulgarian assassin in Haiti?"

"Monsieur, I could hide a bright-yellow elephant with green polka dots in Haiti."

"Good, see what you can dig up on him. Anything at all."

"Ah, it has always been one of my fantasies, to play the role of Inspector Maigret. If this Danilov has ever put a foot in Haiti, I will know about it, *vite!*"

11

BY NINE O'CLOCK THE KING LINE PIER in Montego Bay was a madhouse. Local merchants had arrived at dawn to set up their stalls and makeshift shops, turning the pier into a noisy but colorful flea market. The big cruise ship was tied down, its anchor was dropped and its gangplank was swung into place. The passengers, in their white suits and cotton dresses, trudged eagerly down to the marketplace, to haggle over straw baskets and hats, postcards, coffee beans, wooden sculpture and toys. The din was heightened by a calypso band beating on steel drums in the middle of the square.

O'Hara and the Magician were waiting at the bottom of the gang-plank when the first passengers came down, looking for the man they knew only by the meagerest description. He was small, thin and eccentric, that was about all they knew. Several times they had approached men who vaguely fit the description.

"Are you Mr. Teach?"

The answer was always a shake of the head or a hurried "No."

In ten minutes the first rush of passengers had left the boat, and the gangplank was empty. The steward drifted away from the top of the landing bridge to attend to other duties. O'Hara and the Magician boarded the boat. With the rush of activity, nobody paid any attention to them. They were both dressed in sports clothes and could easily have been mistaken for passengers. The purser was standing nearby with a checkoff list in hand. O'Hara decided to take a chance.

"Excuse me," he said, feigning anxiety, "I seem to have missed Mr. Teach. We were going ashore together and now I've forgotten his cabin number."

The purser looked at him with a frown but before he could ask any questions, O'Hara looked at his watch. "I'm sure he said to meet him here. Is there any other way to leave the ship?"

"No, sir," the purser said, checking over the passenger list. "Mr. Teach is on A deck. Cabin One-one-six."

"Of course! Thanks," O'Hara said and rushed away before the purser could ask any more questions.

The Mag waited at the foot of the gangplank while O'Hara went in search of Cabin 116. He found it with little trouble, but Lavander did not answer his knock.

"Mr. Teach," O'Hara called, "it's the steward. I have a message for you."

Still no answer.

Several passengers nodded "Good morning" as they drifted by on their way into town. When the corridor was empty, O'Hara took out a penknife, slipped the blade through the crack in the door and pressed the latch back as he turned the handle. The latch popped. O'Hara swung it open very slowly until he could see the entire cabin.

Empty.

He checked the head. Empty too. He closed the door, bolted it and began to search the room.

The cabin was small but tastefully decorated, the bed a mess and the porthole open. The sounds of pandemonium from the dock drifted into the room as O'Hara quickly searched it.

Lavander obviously traveled light and paid little attention to clothes.

There were two suits and a pair of slacks hanging in the closet. His fingers traced pockets and lining. Nothing there. One of the suits looked as if it had never been pressed, the other had a coffee stain on the lapel. There was one tie, hanging lopsided on a wire hanger, an atrocious, multicolored flowered tie that still had the knot in it. The suitcase was empty. A few undergarments and shirts were in the dresser drawers, nothing else. There was one book on the night table beside the bed, a scholarly-looking volume entitled *The Kingdom of Oil.* O'Hara flipped through it casually. Small type and a lot of it.

He checked the cabinet in the head, Lavander's travel kit, the pockets of a bathrobe hanging behind the door. Nothing.

The entire search didn't take five minutes.

He looked around again, checked under the mattress, and was finally satisfied that there was nothing else in the cabin.

As he reached for the doorknob, there was a knock on the door. O'Hara froze. He moved back a few steps. Knuckles tapped on the oak door again.

"Señor, it is the maid."

"Un momento."

"Sí. I weel be back," she said and moved on down the corridor.

O'Hara unbolted the door and checked the hallway. The maid was in the cabin next door. He locked the door behind him and went up on the upper deck. It was empty. So were the dining room, the bar, the game room, the salon. The pool area was attended by a lifeguard who was asleep in a deck chair. Nobody cared, because nobody was there, either.

He went back and tapped on the door again. Still no answer.

The Magician was sitting on a crate sipping a piña colada when O'Hara went ashore. "Well?" he asked.

O'Hara led him down through the flea market. "He's gone," he said. "My message must have backfired. He's probably running scared. I checked the upper decks, dining rooms, everyplace."

"Maybe they're gonna meet on the boat," the Magician said.

"I doubt it. If the cutout meets him on the boat, they'll have to kill him on board. Much safer luring him out in the open. No, he's out here, somewhere."

"He could be meeting with the cutout right now, all we know."

"A definite possibility." O'Hara looked at his watch again. Eleven o'clock. "Hell, he could be dead by now."

They stopped on the far side of the marketplace and looked around. Somewhere out there, Avery Lavander had an appointment with death.

Their only chance to save him was if Eliza spotted Hinge when he arrived. That, of course, was assuming he was not there already, in which case Lavander was most definitely a dead man.

The Montego Bay airport terminal was a large two-story building. Its main waiting room encompassed most of the first floor, with a half-dozen airline counters lining the wall facing the entrance. Customs inspection was carried out in a small room on the east end of the building and was cursory at best. The restaurant was on the second floor, directly over customs.

Eliza had been in the airport since six-thirty that morning and it was now close to noon. Three planes had arrived so far. She was sure Hinge had not come through the gate yet. She checked her list. Five more planes were due before sundown: two from the States, one of which stopped in Puerto Rico and was at the gate now; one from Mexico; an Air France jet from Paris via Port-au-Prince; and a small island connector from Kingston. She found a seat in the waiting room near the door and settled down with a flight schedule. She had rented a car and bribed a porter to let her park it near the front door.

Another planeload of tourists streamed from customs and hurried past, yelling for taxis. Hinge was not among them. She hardly glanced at the tall hawk-faced man with shiny black hair as he went by carrying an attaché case. He was Derek Frazer, vice president of AMRAN, a new oil consortium out of Houston, and he had an appointment in less than eight hours with Lavander.

The day dragged on. After each plane arrived, she called the hotel, leaving the same basic message. Her last had been: "EAL 610 from Miami has arrived. Your luggage is not on it. The next plane arrives at six-five."

Then she went upstairs to the restaurant and took up her dreary vigil at the window overlooking the runway. The next plane was not due for two hours.

O'Hara and the Magician had spent the morning perusing the town of Montego Bay, hoping to luck into Lavander. Finally they settled in at a small bar across from the pier, where they had been sitting for hours, watching the gangplank, hoping Lavander would return. Or perhaps leave. O'Hara realized he could easily have missed him when he searched the boat. Lavander could still be aboard, but it was a slim chance. In fact, it was wishful thinking.

O'Hara knew by early afternoon that he had overplayed his hand.

What had seemed like a good idea, a way to keep Lavander from leaving the cruise ship, had turned into a disaster. Perhaps Lavander was afraid of Quill. And there was also the distinct possibility that he did not know who Quill was, in which case the message could have spooked the eccentric consultant right into Hinge's arms. It was one of the things he hated about the Game. There was no margin for error when dealing with people like Hinge. In the Game, death was the penalty for a bad call. He brooded about it until the Magician dismissed the ploy with a wave of his hand.

"Stop agonizin'," he said. "It could have been a good idea."

"That helps a lot," the reporter said drearily.

"He's a weirdo, Sailor. You can't tell which way a weirdo's gonna jump. Hell, you took a shot and fucked up. Don't let it get to you."

"I could have cost Lavander his life."

"Ah shit, *que será* is what I say. It was a long shot, anyway."

As the day wore on without a sign of the eccentric consultant, they became more and more convinced that it was too late, that somewhere on the island Lavander's body was waiting to be discovered.

Normally, Lavander would have stayed on board until just before the meeting with the AMRAN executive, but the message he had received made him uncomfortable. Who knew he was traveling under the name "Teach"? And who in God's name was this *Quill*?

It had bothered him for two days, so he left the ship by way of the cargo hatch as soon as it docked. Now he would have to kill the entire day waiting for the meeting.

AMRAN wanted to discuss a matter of *bénéfice réciproque,* and that intrigued him. Even if the talk turned out to be a bust, he was sure he would learn something, for even gossip sometimes provided him with invaluable information, bits and pieces here and there which, when fitted together, added to his remarkable knowledge of the oil business.

Lavander's appointment was not until eight o'clock, so he moved from restaurant to teashop to bar to newspaper vendor, trying to keep busy. Lavander was not a man long on patience, and his annoyance turned to irritation and then to anger as the day grew hotter and the streets more crowded and he was reduced to fighting his way through the rush of street hucksters, who offered everything from caged crickets to expensive watches, and kids who trotted beside him, whispering, *"Ginja, ginja.* I got you best price for best smoke in Jamaica."

"Get on, you little urchins, I'll report you to the police," Lavander snapped and one of the kids made a face at him and ran off into the crowd.

Lavander was an easy fellow to make fun of. He was almost a visual joke: a wizened, dour little man, thin and unkempt, with bulging eyes, a gray, unhealthy pallor, pouty cheeks and straw-colored hair, which seemed to sprout, helter-skelter, like alfalfa, from his oversized head. His white suit seemed permanently unpressed, one of his coat pockets was hanging half out, his bow tie was on crooked, and his shoes had never seen a bootblack's brush.

Lavander never walked, he scurried, constantly looking around, like a rodent foraging the dark corners of a warehouse. His eccentricity was compounded by a wildly neurotic paranoia. He imagined reporters lurking everywhere, waiting to pounce and demand interviews. That not one newsman had approached him for several years was inconsequential. He frequently switched airline reservations at the last moment, sometimes to a totally different country, then doubled back, taking laboriously involved routes to places where there were direct flights, and changing hotels two or three times. It was his only recreation, this madness for privacy, as if his almost religious overview of the oil business had crowded rationality out of his mind. Since the horror of his kidnapping, Lavander had become even more suspicious, more paranoid.

And so he scampered around the city, sitting in parks, reading several American and European newspapers, killing time, unwittingly waiting for destiny to catch up with him.

The plane was twenty minutes late arriving, but Hinge still had over an hour until the meeting between Frazer and Lavander. Plenty of time to check out Trelawney Square and the pastry shop where they were to meet. He had memorized Frazer's picture and then burned it in the plane's lavatory.

Hinge felt comfortable moving through customs. They checked his bag with a piece of white chalk and moved him on through.

He immediately noticed the girl sitting on a bench in the waiting room, studying an airline timetable. There was no mistaking her reaction when she saw him. Recognition? Interest? Perhaps she had mistaken him for someone else.

Was she following him? But why? Why would a woman be waiting for him in the Montego Bay air terminal?

He went to a phone booth and searched his pockets for a coin. She had moved to another bench closer to the door. He could see her reflected in the glass panel behind the telephone.

He stood in front of the dial when he made the call, then casually turned sideways in the booth. She was in a phone booth on the opposite side of the terminal.

It could be paranoia. She seemed to be laughing while she was talking. It didn't hurt to be overly cautious. He would keep an eye on her.

He asked the restaurant operator for Mr. David Jackson. Derek Frazer answered very quickly.

Hinge said, "Is this Mr. Jackson?"

Frazer said, "Which Mr. Jackson do you want?"

"Avery Jackson."

"Is this Mr. Garrett from Texas?" Frazer asked.

"Yes."

"When did you move?"

"Fourteen months ago."

"Very good. Any problems?"

"Smooth as velvet."

"The car is taken care of. They're holding the keys for you at the rental counter. The package is in the trunk."

"Thanks. It's the Nelson Pastry Shoppe on Trelawney Square. Eight o'clock, right?"

"That's correct."

"What time do you leave?"

"I'll be going straight to the airport from the square."

"I'll call the drop when I've delivered the package."

"Thank you."

The girl was gone when he finished. He looked around the terminal, then entered the rental office and got the keys. The car was a red two-door Datsun coupe. He opened the trunk. There was a small canvas bag in back of the spare. He closed the trunk, got in the car and drove off.

A blue Datsun pulled out and started following him. He watched for the lights after turning on the main road to town. It was still behind him. He slowed down and the blue car drew closer. When it was less than half a block behind him, he turned off the main road, coursing around a park. The blue car stayed with him.

It had to be the girl.

But why?

Hinge did not have time to get involved. He needed to do something fast. He floored the accelerator and turned into the next street on his right. The Datsun surged under him as he took the next turn, then another. Then he flicked off his lights and whipped into a palm-lined driveway.

He killed the engine and waited for her.

O'Hara had been looking at the *Gulf Star* for several minutes without speaking. It was almost seven o'clock and Lavander had yet to show his face.

"I better check the hotel again, see if Hinge was on that last plane," the Magician said.

O'Hara continued to stare at the ship. Finally, as the Magician stood up to go to the phone, he said, "I'm going back on board."

"Why?"

"Remember I told you how frantic Lavander was about his hotel room after he was released in Caracas?"

"So?"

"Why should he care? The company was paying his expenses. What was so important about the room?"

"Maybe he was worried about his baggage."

"I've seen his baggage. Believe me, it has nothing to do with his baggage. I mean, Tony said it was the first thing out of his mouth."

"So?"

"So I think he hid something in the room and he was worried about getting it back."

"Money?"

"Could be. I doubt it. He's got money stashed all over the world."

"So what d'ya think, Sailor?"

"According to your information on Lavander, he keeps personal records in a book. Maybe the book's too big to carry around. So, he hides it."

"You've searched his room."

"Maybe I missed something. I got this worm in my stomach that keeps telling me I missed something."

"What if Hinge has shown up at the airport?"

"I won't be gone long. You call the hotel; I'll be back in ten minutes."

He had no problem getting aboard. The corridor was empty. Most of the passengers were still living it up in town. He popped the lock and cautiously entered the cabin again.

The maid had cleaned the small room. O'Hara closed the porthole and pulled the curtains and turned on the lamp. He sat down on the bed and slowly looked around the room. He checked the closet again and the suitcase. He checked the lavatory again. He lifted the mattress and checked under it and then felt the mattress carefully, then replaced it.

He sat back on the bed again.

He stared at the dresser. He got up and took out the drawers, one at a time, starting with the top drawer. The fourth drawer down stuck as he pulled it out. He took out the fifth drawer, lay down on the floor, struck fire to his lighter and held it in under the drawer. There was a black letter-sized notebook taped to the bottom.

O'Hara pulled it free and sat on the floor, leafing through page after page of figures and code words. Not one page in the book made any sense.

He replaced the drawers, stuffed the book into the back of his pants, shut off the lights and left.

The Magician was waiting in front of the bar. "He arrived on the six-ten from Miami," the musician said excitedly. "It was twenty minutes late. She called and left a message about five minutes before I called."

"Then Lavander's still alive."

"C'mon," the Magician said. "I've already squared the bill. Let's get back to the hotel so we can catch her next call in person."

Eliza drove slowly through the dark. She had circled back to the little park after losing Hinge and now she was near tears. Had he seen her? Or did she just lose him? Either way, she had lost their ace in the hole.

She kept circling, hoping to blunder upon Hinge. After ten minutes of fruitless driving she gave up. She started looking for a telephone. The dark streets led her back to the waterfront. She passed a noisy club, and a block ahead, saw a phone booth on the opposite side of the street.

She stopped, rooted through her cluttered shoulder bag, found a dime, dropped the car keys in her bag and ran across the street to the phone booth.

It took forever for the operator to answer.

"Cottage Sixteen, please," she said.

"Thank you."

It rang several times but there was no answer. She jiggled the hook and got the operator back. "I want to leave another message, please."

"Go ahead."

Headlights turned into the darkened street two blocks away, but her back was turned to them.

"For Sixteen. The message is: 'Have lost the luggage. I am coming back to the hotel.'"

"You are having a terrible time with your baggage," the operator said. "Perhaps our manager can be of some assistance."

The car was moving slowly down the street toward her.

"Uh, I think the airline has taken—"

She turned and saw the car, less than a block away. The red Datsun. Hinge's leathery face loomed behind the wheel.

"—care of it. Thanks very much. Bye."

She hung up but it was too late to get back across the street. He was almost there. He was so close she could see those cold reptilian eyes staring at her through the open window.

She took off her shoes and ran. She ran faster than she had ever run in her life. She could have made the Olympics, she ran so fast. She ran away from the street, through the darkness, down a long narrow alleyway, toward the beach.

Hinge stopped and jumped out of his car.

Eliza ran along the beach until her breath was gone and her legs ached and finally she fell on her hands and knees in the sand. She turned quickly and looked back expecting to see Hinge. But the beach stretched behind her, gray in the moonlight and empty.

She looked all around.

Nothing.

Overhead, ominous clouds were beginning to chase the moon and lightning glittered near the horizon.

Great. Now it's going to start raining.

She sat for a few moments to catch her breath, then walked up to the line of trees that ran adjacent to the water's edge, and using them for protection, started cautiously back toward her car.

But Hinge had opted not to go after the girl. There was no time for that. He watched her run frantically into the darkness and he thought, Who is she? What in hell is her problem? Is there something about this I don't know? Or is she just some flake?

He stopped beside her car and looked inside. In the glove compartment he found the rental agreement.

Eliza Gunn. Staying at the Half Moon Bay Club, cottage 16.

He put the contract back and slammed the glove compartment shut.

Smiling, he returned to his car and drove off. He had other things to do. There would be time to handle the girl when he was finished with Lavander.

When Eliza reached the street, it was empty. No sign of the red Datsun. She hesitated for several minutes, hiding in the darkness of the shrubs and trees near the road, building up her nerve before she ran across the street and jumped in the car.

She felt lucky as she started the car and drove back to the hotel. She had not talked to either O'Hara or the Magician all day. Perhaps, she thought, they had intercepted Lavander and everything was all right.

12

IT WAS DARK WHEN LAVANDER STROLLED into Trelawney Square but it might have been the middle of the day. The shops were all open and there was a carnival atmosphere about the place.

He found himself opposite the pastry shop and stepped into a gift shop. Walking to the back, he picked over some things while watching the square. Then he went through the back door and walked around the block, staying in the shadows, and appraised the street.

Derek Frazer, the man who had been described to him over the phone, was sitting near the window of the Nelson Pastry Shoppe. Lavander concentrated on him for a while. Frazer had the kind of sharp features some women consider handsome. Lavander knew the type. A typical corporate flunkie dressed by Brooks Brothers, with an innocuous title, vice president in charge of something or other, some catchall term to cover a variety of sins.

Frazer was sipping his coffee and reading the wretched Kingston *Journal.*

Well, that wouldn't take him long. Lavander chuckled to himself. He was sure nobody was following him.

Lavander was right: Hinge did not have to follow him. All Hinge had to do was watch Frazer. It was an old but effective trick, shopping the contact instead of the mark, one that would never have occurred to an amateur like Lavander.

Frazer had spotted the consultant the minute Lavander entered the square, watching him benignly from over the top of the newspaper as the little man played out his odd melodrama. Frazer assumed that the assassin was also watching.

Lavander finally crossed the street and entered the pastry shop. Frazer looked up, smiled, raised a finger and his eyebrows, and stood as Lavander walked to the table, offering his hand. He almost crushed several of Lavander's fingers. He's taken the executive-handshake course, I see, Lavander said to himself.

"Hi, I'm Derek Frazer."

How jaunty, the little man thought. "Lavander, here."

"Well, this is quite an honor, quite an honor indeed. It isn't every day one meets a living legend."

His voice, cultured early in some executive-training program to be flat, authoritative and intimidating, was oddly patronizing toward Lavander. The Britisher found both Frazer's attitude and his looks manufactured and offensive.

Lavander shrugged. "Yes, there aren't that many of us about."

Frazer thought, An egomaniac. An absolute, flying, whacked-out egomaniac.

"What would you like?" Frazer asked, motioning to the waitress.

"Strong tea and something sweet. A napoleon, I think." The waitress nodded and left.

Frazer smiled and rubbed his palms together. "Well, sir, we . . . uh, first of all, we are indebted to you for taking . . . time out of your vacation to talk with us."

"You use the collective pronoun, Mr. Frazer. Is someone joining us?"

Frazer smiled indulgently. "Of course, I'm speaking for my company. I'm sure you know us. AMRAN. Kind of the . . . uh, the new kids on the block, see what I mean?"

No doubt about it, Lavander thought, I don't like this Frazer chap at all. They've sent a shill to do a man's job, and that offends me more than anything. But business was business, so Lavander would hear what he had to say. "Yes, yes, I know all about AMRAN," he said impatiently.

"And I assume the deposit to your bank was verified."

"I'm here, am I not?"

"Quite! Well, then, at least we don't need to be concerned about credentials for my company. That saves us some time, see what I mean?"

"I have plenty of time," Lavander said nonchalantly. The waitress brought his pastry and tea. When she left, Lavander looked across the table at Frazer, his bulging eyes twinkling in anticipation of the conversation. "Now, what is it you want?" he asked.

"We're new, as I said. We don't pretend to know all the answers, but we know you know a lot of them. We're interested in a consulting situation."

"You have serious problems already," said Lavander, sipping his tea noisily.

"I beg your pardon?"

"Among AMRAN's less fortunate decisions was the inclusion of the Hensell Oil Company in your consortium, sir. You have acquired a bankrupt partner." He raised his eyebrows and leaned toward Frazer. "Hmmm?"

"We . . . uh, I assume this conversation is confidential."

"Really!"

"Sorry," Frazer said quickly. "Point is, sir, we need their outlets. They're in thirty-seven states. Twelve pumpers, see what I mean?"

"Actually forty-two states, under three different corporate names. You could have waited another three months and had Hensell for ten cents on the dollar." Lavander waved his hand disdainfully, like a king dismissing a pauper.

"It was cheaper than making a giant investment, particularly at a time when things are a bit—"

"You haven't studied your figures. You have yourself a problem company as an equal partner at a time when the market is unstable."

"We'd have lost them. Somebody else would have snapped them up."

"Not as an equal partner. Subsidiary, perhaps."

Frazer leaned back. "There's also the matter of oil properties, specifically Hensell's holdings."

"What have you allocated for development?"

Frazer hesitated. He seemed to be considering whether to answer the question or not.

Lavander laughed. "Would you like me to tell you, hmmm?"

"Three hundred million," Frazer said in almost a whisper.

"Another questionable move. Over half of those holdings are in the Montana Strip. The field is erratic, sir. I know it well. Over a million acres and there are no patterns. You'll drill a dozen dry holes for every strike, and the yield is going to be low in the bargain. I would guess no more than . . . twenty to twenty-two barrels a day per well." He shook his head. "You'd be better off spending the development money in Alaska or the North Sea."

"Too crowded," Frazer said. "Our other companies have resources—"

Lavander cut him off again. "Of course, your other four companies are healthy. American Petroleum will be showing a five hundred and fifty percent profit increase over last year. Sunset Oil will be up at least four hundred percent. Very nice. Very nice that the Americans are such sheep. They'll pay through the nose for a while. Question is, how long will they put up with it?"

"Long enough to pay the fattest dividends in history," Frazer said.

"And if the Middle East cuts you off?"

"I . . . uh, we don't anticipate that for some time."

"It will happen. Suddenly and soon."

"Well, we'll cross that bridge—"

"Fact is, you have very safe reserves. I know it and you know it. All the oil companies do. Stored away somewhere. Let's be bloody honest, shall we? Your company is sitting on at least—what . . . five billion gallons proven reserves?"

"That's confidential information, Mr. Lavander . . ."

"It was announced by your company in an annual report not two months ago. Confidential indeed! I suggest we be honest. Actually it's closer to fifteen billion, hmm?"

Frazer was genuinely surprised at Lavander's wealth of knowledge.

"Look, old chap," Lavander said, "I don't care, y'know, what you tell the poor fools in Congress or the people on the streets of America. But please don't race me off, hmm? Actually you're really sitting on fifty to sixty billion gallons in undeclared reserves, right? All oil companies have far more oil in reserve than they admit. How else could you all fix prices, eh?"

"Everyone does it," Frazer said.

"Of course, of course, but the numbers! Dear me, the numbers! Provoking a shortage when you have a surplus. Sooner or later someone is going to blow the lid off the whole ugly business."

"We're hardly in a position to take the lead in a general house cleaning."

Lavander gazed at the colorful city square. "When it happens," he mused, "people will go to jail, politicians will be ruined, it could go as high as the Cabinet, y'know. It will make your Watergate and Abscam scandals seem as innocent as a day at Disneyland."

"That won't happen."

"The American people were humiliated by Watergate and Abscam," said Lavander. "They'll be infuriated when they find out just how badly the oil companies are exploiting them. I'm suggesting you use some common sense. There's plenty of money to be made. You don't have to break the law."

"If that does happen," said Frazer, "the ax'll fall on all the others before it falls on us. We're new."

"The weak ones always go first. Law of nature. You're new, you have problems. The investigators will sharpen their teeth on you new chaps. The hyenas will eat you first, then the big competitors will become very repentant, they'll say, 'Oh, excuse us, we miscalculated,' the politicians in their pocket will say, 'Naughty, naughty,' fine them a couple of hundred thousand dollars, excuse them for the good of the economy. What good will that do your AMRAN? They'll already have ruined you."

"A dismal viewpoint, I must say."

"Realistic. The script is already written."

"Let's hope you're wrong this time."

"I have a reputation, Frazer. I've never associated, in any way, with anything unsavory. I can help AMRAN, but only if you agree to listen to me and accept my advice. The price is a thousand dollars a day. Thirty days payable in advance. If we go beyond that, you pay another thirty days in advance. And I reserve the right to step out anytime I feel your decisions might place me in jeopardy. That's my standard deal, take it or leave it."

"Well, of course I'll run this by management and—"

"This is Friday, Frazer. I will expect your answer by Monday. Say five P.M.? You can send me a message aboard the *Gulf Star.*"

"That's a bit short, what with—"

Lavander's face clouded up. He was becoming impatient. He cut Frazer off. "Right now Hensell's U.S. output is about twenty thousand barrels a day. The company's reserves are down to—I'm guessing, of course—sixty million forty-two-gallon barrels. One of the reasons Hensell was going under, they were buying sixty percent of their crude from the Middle East. At *premium.* Hmmm?"

Frazer stared across the table at Lavander. His neck was turning pink under the ears.

Lavander pressed on. "Point is, Mr. Frazer, your AMRAN was sold a bill of goods by Hensell's people. You bought a pig"—he stopped and laughed—"without looking in the poke."

You insufferable bastard, Frazer thought. But he kept his temper. His job was to keep his temper.

"What's going to happen, old chap, is that AMRAN is going to have to dip into its oil capital, so to speak. Tap the reserves of the other members of the consortium, to reduce Hensell's Middle East commitments. And then, sir, you are on dangerous ground, having to explain oil reserves you supposedly don't have. The Mafia has the same problem trying to wash its money. You're going to have to wash your oil." He chuckled again, then added, "Enough free advice for one day."

Anger burned deep in Frazer's stomach, but he had to keep playing the game. "So what would you suggest?"

"I suggest you retain me to keep you out of the soup and to clean up this mess."

Frazer stared at him across the top of his coffee cup. "That's why we're here," he said slowly, after a several-second pause.

Lavander raised his eyebrows. He looked down into his teacup. "I see—hmm . . . I see a message and the message says, 'Frazer doesn't have the authority to make a commitment.' Am I correct?"

"My job is simply to open up negotiations. We know by your reputation that you can help us. The question is, Can we afford you?"

"A grain of salt in the ocean. Of course you can afford me. I can help you. The ball is in your court. Let me know." He started to get up.

Frazer said, "Uh, perhaps we have a little something extra in the kitty."

"Ahh?"

Frazer took out a pint jar from his briefcase and set it on the table. It contained sand, sand as white as sugar but streaked with a black compound. Frazer picked it up and shook it, then looked at Lavander and smiled. He held the jar toward Lavander and said, "I've heard you can look at a core sample and taste it and tell within two city blocks what part of the world it came from and how rich the strike might be."

Lavander could not conceal his curiosity. But he did not touch the jar. "When we have concluded our business, Frazer."

He's a crazy old coot, all right, Frazer thought. Crazy-smart. He's playing games. Corporate one-upmanship.

Frazer was more interested in results. "I am authorized to retain you for a minimum of sixty days," he said. "We will have sixty thousand, in gold, in whatever account you desire, Monday morning, when the banks open." He smiled and jiggled the jar again. "Care to see our hole card?"

Lavander looked at the jar, his brown eyes aglitter. But he still made no move to take it. He was caught in an inner struggle between commerce and curiosity. "I'll be traveling for the next two weeks or so," he said. "Will that be a problem?"

"Not at all, sir. We'd like you in Houston by the first of the month."

"Then it's acceptable," he said. "Uh . . . may I?"

"Of course," Frazer said. He's taking the bait, he told himself. We will soon know.

Lavander took the jar and held it up as if it were a rare diamond. He spread a paper napkin on the table and smoothed it out with his hands. Then he opened the jar, shook several grams of the sand onto the napkin and recorked the jar. He held up the napkin between his hands, making a trough of it, and shook the sand around, watching it carefully. He put the napkin back on the table, took out a jeweler's glass, and separating the grains with the handle of a spoon, stared intently at them through the loupe. He dipped his tongue into the sand, tasting it as a wine steward might sample a vintage bottle.

Frazer watched him with interest. Gone for the moment were the egocentricities and the sarcasm, replaced by a pro at work. Lavander scooped up some of the sand and let it run through his fingers, back onto the napkin.

His lips were moving like a palsied old man's: "Semitropical to tropical. Not Africa . . . let's see, let's see . . . the Middle East? No, wrong color. Not coarse enough . . . hmm . . . a little too fine for Mexico. Or California . . . hmm."

He stopped suddenly, peering up at Frazer for a fraction of a second, then, just as quickly, looking back.

He's on to it, Frazer thought. Now let's see what he does next.

Lavander made a funnel of the napkin, poured the sand back into the jar and handed it to Frazer. "I'd like some more tea," he said. As Frazer turned to summon the waitress, Lavander folded the napkin, with two or three grams of sand in it, and slipped it into his pocket. Frazer acted as if he hadn't noticed; instead he said, "Well, let's see how good you are!"

Lavander seemed wary. "Central Pacific," he said, "someplace north of New Zealand. Perhaps somewhere along the Tonga Trench."

"I've just agreed to pay you sixty thousand dollars as a retainer for two months' work, sir," said Frazer. "And the first thing you do is try to bullshit me."

"I beg your pardon!"

Now it was Frazer who took the offensive. "You know that core sample didn't come from anywhere near New Zealand."

"Then why ask?"

"It's supposed to be your forte."

"Testing me?"

"Why not? All I know is your reputation. And I knew that before I got here. How about the quality of that strain?"

"You know the quality, Frazer."

Frazer nodded very slowly.

"I'm dealing in approximations now. Guesses," said Lavander. "To be accurate, I'd need some time in the lab."

"We have all that," Frazer said. "I just want you to know we had good reason to make the deal with Hensell."

"This is from the Hensell properties?" Lavander said with surprise.

"It wasn't in the package as part of their oil property, Hensell acquired the tracts for other reasons. Our engineers more or less blundered into it, testing core samples for something else."

"I see."

"We feel we're on to something, see what I mean? Nobody else is even aware there could be oil in this area."

Lavander had lost control of the meeting, temporarily. Now was the time to get the ball back. "You're wrong," he said flatly, and let the remark hang there for effect.

"Wrong?"

"Where is this field, roughly," Lavander said quietly, almost whispering.

Frazer leaned over the table. "North of Micronesia, roughly."

Lavander's ego was wavering, his need to put Frazer in his place and control the meeting becoming obsessive. "There is a strike . . . uh, northwest of there. Very high quality, just like yours."

"Impossible."

"I'm telling you a fact," Lavander said, bristling at the thought that his word should be questioned.

"We've had photographic aerial surveillance, very high resolution, and the entire area for three thousand miles has been scanned by satellite. Nothing between us and Japan."

"And I'm telling you, there's a strike . . . not some core sample—a strike!"

"Where?"

"Between you and . . . Japan. Could even be part of the same strata."

So there it is, Frazer thought—he actually said it. His ego's bigger than his discretion, a fatal personality flaw.

"Look," Frazer said, "you've convinced me. I'm off for Mexico tonight to meet my wife. I'll take care of your business Monday morning and see you in Houston on the first. Our offices, nine A.M.?"

"Excellent, I like an early start," Lavander agreed, and then, "Oh! The check!"

"On me," Frazer insisted and summoned the waitress.

Lavander said goodbye and scurried from the shop. After Frazer had paid the check, he picked up his newspaper and walked outside, tore it in half and dropped it in a waste container.

Hinge had had less than an hour to plan the elimination of Lavander. He had left Eliza's car and had driven his own Datsun to a dark side street just off the square, where he parked and got the small bag from the trunk. Inside were a cigar-type blowgun, a hypodermic needle, a small vial of mercury and a double-edged knife in an arm sheath. The knife blade was eight inches long and sharpened on both edges.

Beautiful.

Simple tools for a simple job. In all probability he would not need the dart gun.

No guns. Carrying a gun in Jamaica could be inviting trouble. Besides, this job did not call for bullets.

He strapped the sheathed knife to his left forearm. Then he loaded three drops of mercury in the syringe opening, inserted the needle in the cigar blowgun and put it in his shirt pocket.

Fast and neat, he thought. Nothing complicated. Hit and run. Lavander would be an easy mark. Now to find the spot.

His information on the mark was skimpy and of little value, but he did know that normally Lavander preferred walking to taking cabs, particularly over short distances.

Hinge hurriedly measured the distance from the square to the pier, by walking the obvious route first and heading away from the square and down the main street four blocks and then west another two. He arrived at the pier in seven minutes. During the next forty minutes he tracked back to the square, figuring the various combinations Lavander might choose if he tried a short cut. There were few paths he could take. The toughest for Hinge would be if he stuck to the main street. It was fairly well lit and there was a lot of traffic. The others had led him down long narrow side streets through the warehouse district.

By the time Lavander had arrived at the pastry shop, Hinge was waiting across the square. He watched the mini-drama unfold in the shop. He had the advantage on Lavander. Lavander had to cross the square on the way back to the ship, and Hinge, who was between Lavander and the ship, had a good head start when Lavander left.

Hinge first concentrated on Frazer, saw him leave the shop and tear his newspaper in half, throwing it in a litter barrel. With this simple move, Frazer had approved the death of Lavander. Now Hinge began stalking his prey.

Lavander stopped a local and asked for directions. Hinge watched the man, first indicating a route down the main drag, arcing his hand off to the left, then pointing straight down through the warehouses.

Lavander decided to take the short cut.

Hinge was elated. He hurried down the main street two blocks and cut west to the end of one of the long passages. And he waited.

Lavander was sweating by the time he reached Talisman Way, a narrow, cobblestone alley barely broad enough for two people to pass comfortably, stucco warehouse walls rising on either side, cutting off what light there was. But Lavander could see the lights from the pier at the other end. He started down. Thunder mumbled overhead and a streak of lightning lit the passage for a second.

He was perhaps halfway down the tunnel-like walk when a man appeared at the other end and started toward him. Lavander felt momentary panic. But in the dim light at the end of the street, he saw that the man was dressed in a suit and was white, so he assumed he was a tourist. Nevertheless, he quickened his pace. The man coming toward him was whistling.

As they drew closer together the man stopped whistling and said good-naturedly, "Hey, pal, how about a little *ginja*? Best in Jamaica."

Lavander, his face burning with indignation, turned angrily, looking up at the man. "I'm not interested in your damn—"

He never finished the sentence. As he started it he was aware of a blur of movement, a sudden burning sensation in his neck, and his voice seemed to fade and the man was smiling at him, he could see the hard edges of his face, lit from the pier lights spilling into the street, and the man was holding something in front of Lavander's eyes and Lavander seemed to have trouble focusing, then saw what it was, a stiletto, its thin blade soiled by a splash of blood, and then it was gone and he felt something tug his suit jacket and then the back pocket of his pants and the man was wiggling something else in front of his face and it was Lavander's wallet, and Lavander felt as though he were in a dream and he could not feel his feet and he was floating and then he tasted salt and the burning sensation in his throat turned to fire. He looked down, saw a bubbling, crimson stain down the front of his white suit, then saw more crimson splashing down, and he realized it was his own blood and he opened his mouth to scream but his windpipe was filled with blood and he grabbed at it and a finger slipped into the slit in his throat.

The ground began to blur, to spin away from him.

He could see his feet, moving one in front of the other, but there was no feeling in them.

Something hit his knees and it was a few moments before he realized he had fallen.

Lavander began to crawl toward the lights, trying to scream, to attract attention, but there wasn't anybody to hear him and then he felt the edge of the building and he crawled out onto the pavement and looked up and saw the face of a woman and she opened her mouth and seemed to be screaming, only he could hear nothing. He tried to speak, but his teeth started to chatter and for a moment his body was racked with spasms and then his back arched and he fell face down into King Street and died.

At the airport Frazer checked in and confirmed his reservation. Then he walked across the terminal and stood near the public phones. He had been there ten minutes when the first phone in the line rang. He picked it up immediately.

"This is Mr. Jackson," he said.

"Avery Jackson?"

"Yes, that's right."

The cold flat voice on the other end said, "The package has been delivered."

"Any problems?" Frazer asked.

"Nothing I can't take care of."

"Thanks very much."

Frazer hung up, smiling with satisfaction as he left the booth. Ten minutes later his plane was announced. He bought a copy of *Paris-Match* and an Italian edition of *Playboy* in the newsstand and then boarded his plane.

Hinge hung up the phone and went back to his car. A rumble of thunder rolled slowly across the sky, and dark clouds drifted past the face of a full moon. Lightning shimmered among them and he felt the first tentative drops of rain. He ignored them. He was a few hundred yards from the entrance to the Half Moon Bay Club. He drove down to the palm-lined entrance and parked the car in the shadows, and hunching his shoulders against the raindrops that began pelting him, he hurried down to the beach. He stayed well back from the ocean as he studied the layout of the sprawling beachfront hotel, actually scurrying away from one small ripple of a wave.

The beach swung in a wide crescent from the squat two-story hotel at one end to the far side, where a stone breakwater separated its beach from that of the Holiday Inn. The registration desk was attached to the main building but was in the open, under a roof of shingles covered with palm fronds. Adjacent to it was an open-air bar and restaurant over-looking the bay. People were moving under the shingled awnings to escape the rain while a calypso band, accustomed to sudden storms, continued playing in the restaurant, its steely music echoing out across the bay.

The cottages began just beyond the restaurant, stretching around to the breakwater. They were built fifty or sixty feet from the water's edge, one-story stucco units, most of them dark. He counted them. Eighteen in all. Lights gleamed from the last three in the line. Despite the impending storm, the sea was placid, slapping lazily at the shore.

It started raining harder as he followed the beach to cottage 16.

13

O'HARA AND THE MAGICIAN ARRIVED at Eliza's cottage two minutes after she did. She stammered as she described her encounter with Hinge, the terror still in her eyes.

"You're lucky," O'Hara said. "He probably didn't have time to chase you." He shook his head. "We acted like a bunch of amateurs this time around."

"I'm the amateur," Eliza said. "If—"

"Nobody's t'blame," said the Magician.

"Yeah," said O'Hara, "we fumbled in the clutch. Best thing we can do is move on."

The bright spring colors of the cottage, the yellow-and-green-print slipcovers, the vase with cut flowers on the dresser and fresh fruit on the night tables did not help their mood. They sat glumly mulling over their options.

"Maybe we should call the police, at least they could put out an APB on Lavander and Hinge," Eliza suggested.

"This isn't the Bronx," O'Hara said. "I doubt they have ten cops on this end of the island."

"What a mess," Eliza said, genuinely concerned over Lavander's welfare, or lack thereof.

The Magician scratched an unshaven chin. "Well," he said, "you think this is bad, how'd you like to be caught in the middle of a fight between six truck drivers and fourteen midgets in the Soperton, Georgia, Waffle House at one o'clock in the morning?"

"What!" Eliza said, and started to giggle.

"This is about ten years ago. I was down on my uppers and playing calliope for a little half-assed circus, and it went broke in Texarkana and there we were, stranded in the middle of nowhere. So I got the fourteen midgets together and formed this basketball team. I thought it would be a real novelty, them riding on each other's shoulders to make baskets, running between the opponent's legs, stuff like that. Only it turned out to be a one-line joke, funny for about half the first quarter, after that the audience started throwing their popcorn boxes at us. We were stuck in Dalton-fuckin'-Georgia, with all our games canceled, so broke we were rubbing buffalo nickels together hoping they'd mate.

"Dismal.

"And then, damned if I didn't find out these little suckers could sing! Man, they could belt it out like angels. Fourteen-part harmony. So we changed our name from Mike Rothschild's Little Big Men to Jesus Rothschild and the Gospel Midgets, and lo, everybody loved us. We were doing state fairs, charity gigs, revival meetings. The black people loved us. Kids loved us. Red dirt farmers would come with their families and fruit jars and get drunk and get religion. Sweet Jesus, we were saving souls and making money. Hallelujah, what a summer!"

"Magician, what in hell are you talking about?" O'Hara asked.

"There's a point, stick with me. One night we pull into Soperton, Georgia, which is about as big as a flea's ass, and it's maybe one o'clock in the morning and we pass this Waffle House, which is open, so we all pile in for coffee. There's maybe half a dozen or so truck drivers in there raising hell and one thing leads to another and it's getting a little nasty what with the midget jokes and shit, so Herman Heartfinder, who was kind of the spokesman for the little guys—he also had a very bad temper—he says for them to go easy on the midget jokes. This one driver says to Herman, 'Hey, shortie, if your pecker was twice as big as your mouth, you'd still have to jack off with two fingers,' and Herman stands straight up, all three-foot-six of him, and lets fly with one of those old-fashioned glass sugar dispensers, the ones that weigh about two tons. Splat, right across the side of the head. All of a sudden, it's John Wayne time. Truck drivers and midgets, all kickin' the shit out of each other and, incidentally, wasting the Soperton, Georgia, Waffle House while they're at it.

"Right then I figured Soperton, Georgia, was no place to be if you're a six-fingered Jewish piano player hustling fourteen midgets who are at that moment inciting a riot. So I just walked away from it, down to the Trailways bus station, where I stood around for about an hour, listening to the police cars and ambulance, until the bus came and I headed south and got off when we ran out of road in Key West."

He stopped and smiled rather grandly and added, "And *that's* the point."

"What's the point?" Eliza asked.

"The point is, this is no place for us to be right now."

"Amen," said O'Hara.

"But Lavander could still be alive. If the police had a description of Lavander and Hinge . . ."

"They wouldn't do doodly-shit," said the Magician.

"Lavander's had it," O'Hara said. "By now Hinge is probably on his way back to Tucson or wherever he's from, and all we've got is Lavander's little black book of gibberish."

Outside, Hinge huddled close to the cottage to escape the driving rain. He was grateful for the storm, since it provided excellent sound cover. The raindrops, battering palm leaves and ferns, sounded like drums accompanied by the timpani of thunder. He had moved as close to the window as possible, standing just outside its orbit of light but close enough to hear their conversation through the open window.

My God, he thought, they know my name and they know about Lavander! And what's this about Lavander's book?

Who the hell are these people, anyway?

It made no difference. Hinge decided very quickly that he had to kill all three of them. The question was when and how. He concluded that each of them had a cottage, accounting for the lights in the last three cottages. He would wait until they were each in their rooms and take them one at a time.

Piece a cake.

He continued his eavesdropping.

"I think the book's going to give up something," said the Magician. "All we gotta do is break Lavander's code."

"*All,*" Eliza said.

"He carries the book with him. Obviously he makes entries in it all the time, so he must have memorized his own code. And if he memorized it, I can break it. And if I can't, Izzie certainly can." He got up to leave. "What time did the pilot say he'd meet us at the airport?"

"Five-thirty," O'Hara said.

"I'll wake everybody up," he said and left, scampering through the rain to his cottage, the last one in the row.

O'Hara hunched deep in one of the yellow-and-green chairs and said, "I'll sleep here in the chair."

"I'll be all right," Eliza said.

"We've already underestimated Hinge once tonight. I'd feel better being here."

Thunder rumbled outside the window and lightning snapped close by.

"Better be careful, O'Hara, I'm liable to get the wrong impression, think you have a heart after all."

"Now, what does that mean?"

"Up until now, you've been a robot."

"A robot!"

"That's right, a robot."

"Well, I don't feel like a robot," he said, looking at her through half-closed eyes.

O'Hara had already dismissed the Lavander affair from his mind. They had botched it. Enough said. Now he concentrated on his competitor across the room, for that was how he still thought of her. Five feet tall, proficient and dangerously naïve.

That was the professional view. Personally, other things about her crowded his mind. She was prettier than he remembered from their brief meeting in Japan, and he had been too startled when she showed up in St. Lucifer to really pay any attention to her. Now he realized what a stunning woman she was. Her tininess simply added to her allure. Shaggy jet-black hair, cut short with curled strands peeking around her neck; wide, almost startled eyes, appearing even more vulnerable because of her size; a wondrously perfect nose and a tentative, pouty mouth that could, in an instant, become the most dazzling smile he had ever seen.

Beautiful, smart and tempting.

Very dangerous.

She was momentarily flustered and avoided contact with his green eyes. She sat on the edge of the bed and looked down at the floor. O'Hara intimidated her and had since before she met him. The biographical material she had read had commended him for many things, including his investigative ability. But it was his apparent mastery of the Japanese philosophy that both fascinated and unsettled her. He moved with oiled grace, which she attributed to his martial-arts training in Japan. She remembered the speed with which he accepted and defeated his attacker in Japan. Unruffled. Even with a stab wound, he was simply unruffled. In fact, he was uncomfortably calm. And now he seemed able to accept the inevitability of Lavander's death without guilt or remorse. And yet, what she read to be something almost mystical might simply be the result of years of armoring. Perhaps O'Hara was so thoroughly shielded that he just *seemed* mystical.

She sighed and said, "I can't get used to the fact that we may have caused Lavander's death."

"No, didn't cause it. We didn't *save* him. There's a big difference."

"But can't we do something? I'd recognize the car. And it was a rental, so he'll have to turn it in and—"

"A good hunter knows when the hunt is over."

"There you go. Mr. Kimura talks like that all the time. 'The smart man doesn't wear wet socks.' How's that?"

"Actually, it would be, 'The wise man does not put on his sock until the sun blesses it.' "

"Oh, bullshit." She paused for a second. "I'd just like to get another look at that creep, anyway. I've never seen a real live assassin before."

"You really have a taste for this, don't you?"

"For what?"

"Chasing the big story. How did you get into this business, anyway? Hell, you've read my K-file, you know everything about me right down to my underwear size. I don't know anything about you."

How did she get into the business? Well, it had started because she was chubby.

When Eliza Gunn was growing up in Nebraska she was plump. Well, perhaps "plump" is being generous. Actually she was somewhere between plump and fat. Chipmunk-cheeks-and-dimpled-legs chubby is what she was.

She lived in Ozone. Once you got a chuckle out of the name, it was all downhill. Dull. Dull. Dull. The only statue in town was of Calvin Coolidge, who once waved at Ozone from the rear of a passing train. So much for Ozone, Nebraska.

Her father owned the local drugstore and was a kind, patient, Christian man. Reserved, the kind that thinks a pat on the head is as good as a hug. Alwyn Gunn died thinking that only perverts read *Playboy* and that Quaāludes were tranquilizers. And that was in 1977.

Her mother died when she was three in a car wreck driving back from a shopping trip to Omaha. The drive was so dull that she fell asleep at the wheel. Alwyn hired a housekeeper, a German widow whose husband had died in a fall off a tractor, and went about business as usual. He never remarried. Too much effort.

Chubby kids are cute. Until they get to be about six. A fat twelve-year-old is not cute. Eliza didn't enter puberty, she stomped into it.

One of the reasons Lizzie Gunn was chubby is that if you lived in Ozone, there was no reason to be skinny. Actually there wasn't much reason to do anything but eat, read books and get pregnant. A lot of Eliza's friends got pregnant. Eliza read books and ate. Among his many virtues, Alwyn Gunn was a lover of books. When she was just beginning to read, Alwyn would bring home half a dozen kids' books to her from the library. By the time she was ten she was into the adult section.

She also realized, at about age ten, that she was different from everyone else. Not because she was chubby/fat, but because she didn't *want* to be like everybody else. She had no desire to be one of the gang. If she couldn't win, she would rather have come in ten minutes after everybody else. Anything to avoid being part of the herd. Fat or thin, the thought of being common repelled her. It was mental, not physical.

She also had a passion to find out. To be the first to know. To have a secret nobody else shared.

The more she read, the more her fantasies blossomed.

No, they exploded.

She rode to Valhalla with Kipling; stormed the gates of Moscow with Tolstoy; conned her way to New Orleans with Twain. She learned class from Shaw, grace from Galsworthy, elegance from Henry James. She was Anna Karenina, Sarah Bernhardt and Holly Golightly. She made up stories in school, told them to her toothbrush in the bathroom, to her dog, her cat, to anyone who would listen. And when old movies started appearing on television, she was Rosalind Russell, James Cagney and Pat O'Brien all wrapped in one, in hot pursuit of the big story. The scoop.

She was editor of the school paper, a job usually relegated to chubby girls who wore glasses, since it was assumed that they were more serious than pretty girls with tits and ass, or to boys, who were too horny to do anything right. She wore her father's old fedora with a press pass in the brim, barked orders and drove everybody crazy. The paper won the Sigma Chi award as the best high school newspaper in the state. She got a personal award for best editorial. It was about the passing of the town's last blacksmith. That was when she was sixteen, her junior year.

And then she became seventeen. That year something happened to Lizzy. She got skinny. Skinny the way girls dream of being skinny.

It happened suddenly. Like a cocoon bursting open, the fat just fell away and suddenly there was Lizzie Gunn, five feet tall, ninety-four pounds, with the best tits and ass in Ozone High School. The Hairbreath Harrys of the school went crazy. Her phone rang constantly, now she *was* cute.

She was also independent, somewhat eccentric, a daydreamer and a loner. Slimmed down, she had boundless energy.

Ozone to Missouri U. to Lincoln to Chicago to Boston. Life had been upbeat ever since. After Ozone, nothing would ever be dull again. Dull dissolved into the six o'clock nightly news and a constant what she called "twiddle" in her stomach. Her stomach had been in a "twiddle" ever since. And now, sitting with Frank O'Hara chasing a chimera named Chameleon, all her fantasies, daydreams, aspirations, everything! had come true.

She kept the story short. Sunk down in the comfortable chair, he kept looking at her over his kneecaps as though he were sighting a gun. This time she stared back, and when she was finished she went right back to the subject at hand.

"I can't believe a man is probably getting killed at this very moment and we're just sitting here helplessly."

O'Hara got up and walked to the bed, and taking her hands, guided her to her feet. He put his arms around her and hugged her. It was a friendly hug, meant to restore her sense of security. She was moved by the simple act, and the warmth of his body was reassuring.

"It got too nasty, too fast," he said.

"You were right," she said, "those Mafia guys were kid stuff."

He ran his finger down her cheek and along her jaw.

"M-m-maybe you're right, maybe I'm not cut out for all this." My God, I'm stammering, she thought.

"We did the best we could. Life's a lot easier if you can accept the inevitable." He stroked the soft part of her ear.

"I thought I was so clever, following him that way and then I turned a corner and—"

"We can't brood over it. I made a bad call. The man's a pro. It's what he does. Put it behind you." He lightly stroked her neck with his fingertips.

She moved a little closer. He began to stroke her cheeks with his fingertips, then ran them lightly over her lower lip.

She thought, Does he think he can do this for a minute or two and I'll just fall into bed?

He said, "Close your eyes, Lizzie."

She felt his wet lips slipping back and forth on hers and then his tongue barely touching her lips.

She thought, yep, that's exactly what he thinks.

Her mouth pouted open very slightly and the end of her tongue touched his.

And she thought, He's right.

The storm was getting worse. Lightning etched the clouds and speared the earth. The world lit up for a second, then *pow!*—the power went off and there was utter darkness.

Hinge inched closer to the window.

She slipped away from him for a moment and her lighter flicked. There were five candles in the room and she lit them. The flames wavered in the cool breeze blowing through the windows.

"I'm a candlelight freak," she said in a whisper.

"Some tough cookie," he said, taking her shirt collar in his hands and drawing her lightly to him again.

Her emotions were hardly stable. She was tingling from the excitement of the night—and aroused by it. She found O'Hara irresistible, the pirate who comes swinging out of nowhere, snatches her out of the slave market and carries her away on his ship. It was a fantasy created when she first became aware of her sensuality, one that had persisted through the years. And finally she had met the pirate.

And she was the girl in his fantasy: vulnerable, lovely—but wonderfully experienced.

Hinge moved closer. It was raining harder and the wind was coming up and the garden around the cottage was turning into a mudhole and lightning seemed to be showering to the earth and in its garish light, he watched the man's fingers unbuttoning the girl's blouse. It seemed to take forever. Then the blouse fell open, but the man was between Hinge and the girl. He moved to the next window, saw him silhouetted against the garish flashes of lightning, barely tracing her full breasts with his thumb; taking her blouse off and dropping it on the bed; kissing her throat, her shoulders, the edge of her breast.

Hinge took the cigar from his shirt pocket and put it between his teeth and slipped the knife out of his sleeve. He risked the chance that the lights might suddenly come back on or that he would be seen in a flare of lightning. They were too involved to see anything. The guy ought to thank him. What a way to go. He would dirk the man first and kill the girl with a dart if he did not kill the man with his first thrust.

O'Hara and Eliza were a single moving form in the candlelight, illuminated sporadically by the yellow glare of the storm, fumbling with belts and buttons, finally entwined, hands searching, lips tasting, as he lowered her slowly to the bed.

Fronds slapped one another in the wind, and the pelting rain stung his face. He could see them through the louvered window, dimly on the bed, naked now, lying sideways facing each other.

Eliza felt O'Hara pressing against her, his lips seemed to be all over her body, on her nipples, her stomach. His tongue explored her while she moved her hands over his back, feeling his skin, the deep arch in his back, his hard ass. She pressed slightly and he responded lightly. It was beginning. She could feel it on the back of her neck, under her ears, welling up in her stomach. She forgot where she was, who she was with, everything but the feeling that kept building, the wonderful electric responses to each touch and kiss.

Hinge started around the corner of the cottage. He reached out to try the door.

He did not hear or see the wire loop drop over his head, was not aware of its presence until it bit into his neck.

He reacted immediately and by instinct. First he shoved himself backward toward his assailant. He bunched up his neck, swelling the muscles against the wire. Then he reached back, trying to grab his attacker. Nobody.

He was on the Leash.

The wire jerked him again and he went backwards across the sidewalk into the wet sand, rolling as he hit the ground and twisting so that he came to his knees facing the assassin. He saw only a tall, dim figure holding the garrote wire.

It was an old trick, using the Leash. The wire ran through a small ratchet, which could be tightened by pulling the wire. The killer stayed three or four feet behind the victim, constantly throwing him off balance until the wire suffocated him.

The wire had cut deep. Hinge could feel its harsh edge against his windpipe. He slashed out with the knife and tried to cut the wire. Moving quickly behind him, the assailant jerked him over backwards.

Hinge half rolled, half flipped, and landed on his feet. He jumped at the figure and slashed at him, felt the knife bite into his forearm and tear through flesh. The cigar was still between his teeth but he could not get a clean shot at the tall man's throat.

The assailant jumped back and pulled him over again.

Hinge was losing his strength. His breath came in small gasps as the wire cut deeper. He rolled in the wet sand, grabbed the Leash and pulled the assassin toward him. The tall man lurched forward and landed close to the water's edge on his hands and knees.

The storm-swept beach was lit up for a second by an arc of lightning. Hinge saw the soggy face of his killer, and his eyes bulged.

Spettro!

He stuck his tongue in the end of the cigar and spat the dart straight at Falmouth's face. But the wind and Falmouth's sudden move toward Hinge conspired to ruin his aim. The dart hit Falmouth's jacket in the shoulder. He brushed it away as he collided with Hinge, and the two men went down in the wet sand again.

The surf rolled up over their feet.

Hinge was terrified. He began to growl like a dog, twisting and scrambling away from the water, clawing the sand with the hand that held the knife while he pulled at the deadly collar with the other. Falmouth grabbed his ankles and dragged him into the surf. In the flash of lightning, Falmouth could see the terror in Hinge's eyes. And he could hear the scream of horror trapped in his mangled throat.

He's afraid of water, Falmouth thought. Hinge is afraid of water.

The Texan thrashed frantically as the gentle surf washed over him. Gagging, gasping for air, he reached out blindly for Falmouth, slashing the darkness with his knife.

Falmouth rolled him into deeper water. Hinge could not last much longer. The wire was doing its job. Now, if he held Hinge underwater, it would be all over. Suddenly Falmouth felt a vise on his throat. Hinge's thumb and fingers dug into the flesh. His hand was like iron. Then Falmouth felt the knife pierce his side. The blade burned into his flesh.

For a moment Falmouth thought, He's got me, the bloody cowboy's neck must be almost cut in two and he's still fighting. Even in the water, Hinge was far from beat.

He twisted hard, twirling Hinge with him into still deeper water, holding him under with the Leash. He groped with his other hand, found the knife still sticking in his side, pulled it free and let the tide carry it away. He grabbed Hinge's hand with his own and tried to pry the fingers loose, but it was like trying to pry open a possum trap. Falmouth's lungs burned as he and Hinge tumbled in the sea, then he broke the surface and gulped air. He hauled Hinge to the surface by the wire and stared at the grotesque obscenity that death had made of Hinge's face.

He took Hinge's thumb in his fist and broke it and pried the fingers away from his throat and fell against the rock piling and dragged himself out of the water. And he lay on the rocks in the driving rain, massaging the gash in his side and his bruised throat. A moment later Hinge's body bobbed to the surface, face down, and Falmouth watched it, bumping against the rocks, while he got his wind back.

Inside the cottage, as the storm raged on, O'Hara's mind flashed back and forth, like the lightning, between now and the past, between Jamaica and Japan. But then he felt her, heard her begin a tiny chant to herself, felt the wetness, and felt her hand, searching for him and finding him, and he felt her vibrancy flowing into him and felt her soft skin against him and it was the way she smelled and moved and whispered and touched and kissed. It was the way she cried out and it was her silence. It was the way he felt inside her.

And for a while there was no Japan.

14

"WELL," SAID THE MAGICIAN, "Lavander's dead. I just picked up Kingston radio on the shortwave. They're callin' it a mugging. Throat slit, pockets cut out, like that."

He had been holed up with his computer, Izzy, chipping away at the code in Lavander's book, since their return to St. Lucifer early that morning.

"It's really no big surprise," O'Hara said.

"No, but I'll tell you what is," the Magician said. "Another body drifted into Montego Bay with the tide. White male. No identification yet, but it appears he was strangled."

"Strangled?"

"Yeah, but let's worry about one homicide at a time," said the Magician.

"We blew it in Jamaica. That's the short and the tall of it. The question is, Where do we go from here?"

"Yes, we don't have much to show for our trip," said Eliza. "A dead man and a book we can't read."

"I can break that code," the Magician said confidently. "I been workin' on it all morning, just a matter of time. It's a letter code, I can tell from the sentence structure."

"What's that mean?" Eliza asked.

"What it means is, the code substitutes one letter for another. Okay? Like *a* is given the value *z* or *b* or *g* of whatever the goddamn code calls for. Something simple so Lavander could memorize it. See what I mean? Who the hell can remember twenty-fuckin'-six different letter substitutions, right?"

"Lavander might. He was supposed to be some kind of nutty genius," O'Hara said.

"So how is Izzy going to solve this problem?" Eliza asked.

"It's an anagram, a simple goddamn anagram," said the Magician. "Some words are obvious, like 'the' and 'and' are the three-letter words used most in the language, okay? Then there's repeaters, like certain letters repeat more than others, vowels and double-letter combinations. *T, l, n,* like that."

"It will take forever, trying to decipher all the possible combinations," Eliza said.

"Not with Izzy. First, see, I simplify it for him. Like I pick a sentence, then program Izzy to look for the repeaters. I try the 'the' and 'and' combination of three-letter words, keep narrowing it down. Finally I get three, four words that begin to make some goddamn sense."

"I still don't understand."

"C'mon, I'll show you."

"By the way, has anybody seen Jolicoeur since we got back?" O'Hara asked.

The Magician shrugged. "He's probably putting a shine on some new scam."

Izzy sat humming quietly in his oversized closet. The television monitor was covered with nonsense words. The Magician sat down and studied the screen. "Okay," he said. "Can you follow me on this? First, see, I pick a trial line, something directly outa the book." He pointed to a line on the screen:

Cpl Zbwqn Mfclbngcmwngx Ygnj Xca

"Looks like Aztec," Eliza said.

The Magician ignored her. "Next, I ask Izzy to analyze the line for me." He typed "ANLYZ" on the keyboard. A moment later the computer began printing out information on the monitor screen:

No of words: 5
Longest word: 13 ch

Shortest word: 3 ch
Others:
5 ch: 1
4 ch: 1
Different letters: 15
Capitals: 5
Three-letter words: 2
Repeat frequency:
13:0;   12:0;   11:0;   10:0;
9:0;   8:0;   7:0;   6:0;   5:0;
4:   2—c, n;
3:   1—g;
2:   5—b, l, m, w, x;
1:   7—a, f, j, p, q, y, z
Double-letter combinations: 0
Three-letter words: Cpl, Xca . . .

The machine paused. Another message appeared:

Holding for sub direct . . .

"Okay," said the Magician, "let's save old Izzy a little time here. There are no double-letter combinations, so we'll try the two-and three-letter words, okay? It would also be a fuckin' fluke, this sentence beginning or ending with the word 'and' or the sentence ending with the word 'the,' right? You with me so far? Okay, now it's likely, see, that the sentence might start with 'the.' So let's let Izzy recompute the trial sentence, substituting 'The' for 'Cpl.' "

He typed "SUB THE/CPL" and hit the return key.

The old sentence appeared immediately:

Cpl Zbwqn Mfclbngcmwngx Ygnj Xca

It was followed by the new sentence with the substitutions:

The Zbwqn Mftebngtmwngx Ygnj Xta

"Now let's see what we've got with only the new letters." He typed "LIST SUB ONLY."

The machine displayed the following:

The ----- --te---t----- ---- -t-

"Where do you go from here?" asked O'Hara.

"I'll just put this here in hold. Then I go to the next sentence I picked.

It's trial and error, okay, but Izzy does all the goddamn work, and fast. So what I do, I keep substituting until finally I come up with a word or two makes sense. I'm gonna break this code, Sailor."

"Stay in touch," O'Hara said. "I'd like to keep track of you through the years."

But Eliza was fascinated. She had worked with word-processing machines and had some knowledge of computer language.

"Maybe he can do it," she said optimistically.

The Magician leaned forward, his eyes flashing, his gloved fingers wiggling in front of his face. "And just maybe we'll get lucky, come up with something, a list of his clients, maybe?"

"We need a break," O'Hara said. "Right now we're running on empty."

"Don't be so skeptical," Eliza said. "It's the only shot we've got."

"Not quite, *mam'selle et messieurs*!"

Joli stood in the doorway, his mouth a keyboard of gleaming white teeth. "I told you I could hide a yellow elephant in Haiti. *Au contraire,* they could not hide a flea from me there. I have found the elusive one."

"Danilov?" O'Hara cried.

"Oui. But of course."

"In Haiti?"

The little man nodded rather grandly. "And I suggest you two move quickly."

"Two? I'm not included in this?" Eliza said.

"I am afraid, Eliza, you cannot go on this expedition. Both of us must stay behind this time."

"Why?" she demanded indignantly.

"Me, because I cannot go back to Haiti. You, because this place where Danilov hides is only for men."

"Only for men. Where is he, the Port-au-Prince YMCA?"

"No. He is in a monastery."

"A monastery?" O'Hara said.

"Oui. It is near Cap-Haïtien. La Montagne des Yeux Vides. I have arranged with a friend to meet you at the airport. He will lead you to the place and see to your entry."

"When?" asked the Magician.

"As soon as possible. It would be best to get there before dark. It is now only"—he looked at the gold watch that glittered on his wrist—"twelve-thirty. If you leave by three o'clock, you can be in Cap-Haïtien by four-thirty and at Les Yeux Vides by sundown."

"Here we go again," the Magician said. "Howe's going to think we've gone west with his Lear jet."

"I'll find the pilot," Eliza said. "Hopefully he's not off deep-sea fishing or something." And she raced from the room.

"Joli," O'Hara said, "how did you find Danilov so fast? Chameleon's probably had some of his best operators tracking him for months."

"Because Joli knows everybody in Haiti," the Magician answered. "He may not be able to go back, but he sure can pull a lot of weight over the phone."

"How did you do it, Joli?" O'Hara asked.

The little man beamed with pride. "It could remain my secret, but . . . first, I must admit that I know this Danilov. He was in and out of the hotel here many times for about a year. *Le Sorcier* was much too busy with his computer to pay any attention, but Joli! Hah, I got to know him, not by occupation, of course, he did not talk about that. But he confided that he had been visiting Haiti a lot, so I put him in touch with some of my friends. I knew if he was in Haiti, I could find him, and *voilà,* I did it!"

"A monastery," O'Hara said. "Who would ever think to look for the master assassin of Europe in a monastery!"

"Yeah," the Magician agreed, "and what self-respecting monk would take the bastard in?"

"You will soon find out," Joli said rather haughtily and left the room.

Cap-Haïtien, the quiet city in the Basse Terre—the narrow strip of lowlands at the foot of the mountains of northern Haiti—was forty-five minutes behind them, as was thirty miles of the worst road O'Hara had ever seen. The Magician had taken it in stride, having spent the better part of ten years in the Caribbean. But as the dusty old Chevy growled and groaned up one of the many mountains that ridge the country's northern seacoast, even the piano player began to show signs of nervousness. Black clouds lurked over the stiletto peaks, and rain had already begun to fall on the mountains beyond. The road ended abruptly at a stone wall. Beyond the wall was five hundred feet of nothing. A boy, no more than nine or ten, was waiting with three mules.

"Those are donkeys!" the Magician whispered. "Joli didn't say anything about ridin' a fuckin' donkey."

"Joli didn't say much of anything."

"That fuckin' little chocolate frog. He's got a very perverted sense of humor. This ain't the first time he's tied a can to my tail."

"And we're not there yet," said O'Hara.

Billy, the guide, had said hardly a dozen words since he picked them up at the airport. He was not unfriendly, just uncommunicative. He was a tall man, rib-thin and the color of milk chocolate, with bulging muscles in arms and shoulders, and enormous, knobby hands. His face was long with hard angles and deep cheekbones. The youth with the mules looked enough like him to be his son.

Billy got out and motioned them to follow. He spoke briefly in French to the boy, and the youngster got in the car. Then Billy motioned them to get on the mules.

"We should hurry. It would be best to get there before the storm hits."

"How far is it?" the Magician asked.

"Maybe thirty minutes up the mountain, not far."

The Magician looked sadly at O'Hara.

"Thirty minutes up a mountain on a mule and he says it's 'not far'?"

They clopped uneasily up the side of the cliff on the three mules. The sheer face of the mountain dropped straight down to the path, which was barely five feet wide. Then the mountain dropped away again, into the valley, hundreds of feet below them. Wind howled around the craggy face of the cliffs, carrying the damp promise of rain, and thunder grumbled through the spires above and below them.

"I'm gonna have Joli's ass this time. This time I'm really gonna, y'know, rip a nice chunk of it off and nail it on the wall over my piano."

"Hell, Magician, he found Danilov for us."

"He didn't tell us we were gonna ride fuckin' donkeys up the side of a mountain on a path no wider than a slab of bacon. Some sense of humor. He's like all them goddamn frogs—perverted!"

"He's not a frog, Magician. He's a Haitian."

"He talks frog and he acts frog and he's perverted and that makes him a frog t' me," the Magician yelled.

"And what would you do without him?" O'Hara yelled into the wind.

"Sleep better at night," the Magician yelled back.

The mules were just ornery enough to be scary. Billy led the procession. The Magician, bitching constantly, was in the middle, with O'Hara bringing up the rear. The wind howled at them, cutting through their summer windbreakers. The path became wet and slippery and then the rain started. And then the path got even narrower. Billy broke out a flashlight, sweeping it back and forth, keeping the path in view.

To the west La Citadelle, the mountaintop fortress built by King Christophe in the early nineteenth century, brooded over the northern coast, its high, grim walls capping one of the many jagged mountains around them. It soon vanished in the swirling rain and fading light.

They climbed higher.

The Magician passed the time griping about Joli while O'Hara preoccupied himself by thinking about Lizzie, about how soft and warm she had been in Montego Bay and how eagerly she had jumped at the chance to work with Izzy on the code while they were gone. The lady pulled her weight, no doubt about that. Thinking about her helped pass the time.

Forty-five minutes of hard riding through the storm brought them to the end of the trail, a tiny plateau protected only by a low earthen wall. Wind and rain lashed them. There was a hitching rail for the animals, room for the three mules and the three of them and not much more.

O'Hara looked up. The cliff disappeared up into the fog.

"Now what?" the Magician said woefully. "Do we fly the rest of the way?"

There was a bell attached to the face of the cliff and Billy rang it several times before a voice called down from above.

"*Oui? Qui est là?*

"*C'est moi*—Billy," the guide yelled back.

"*Ah, oui, Billee. Un instant.*" A moment later a thick rope dangled down from the darkness above with a basket attached to it. Above the basket was a loop of rope, like the strap in a subway.

"Who will be first?" Billy asked and he smiled for the first time.

"We're going up the rest of the way in *that*?" the Magician exclaimed with alarm.

"*Oui,*" said Billy.

"I'll go second," the Magician said, hunching his shoulders against the wind and rain. "Or maybe I'll wait here."

"A little nervous?" O'Hara asked.

"Sailor, I'm scared shitless," he said.

"I will go up first," the gangly Haitian said. "So they will know everything is in order." He gave the flashlight to O'Hara and got in the basket, sitting on his knees and holding the rope strap with both hands.

"*Allez-y!*" he called to the man above and a moment later the basket rose into the darkness.

"*Allez,* my ass," the Magician said. "What am I doin' here, anyway?"

"You told me you were bored and wanted to perk your life up. This is called perking things up."

"It's called freezing things off, that's what it's called." He stared grimly up into the darkness, listening to the rope groaning and the slow, steady *click* of the pully above.

Then the pully stopped clicking. A few seconds later Billy yelled down, *"Allez donc!* Come up. It is safe."

"Merci," O'Hara yelled back.

The swing basket dropped out of the darkness. O'Hara helped the Magician into it. The musician clutched the rope handle and clung to the rope. His knuckles were white, his eyes squeezed shut. "Things aren't bad enough, we had to pick the goddamn monsoon season for this gig!" he cried. His voice was lost to the winds as the basket, buffeted about, was hefted into the rain and strobe-lit by the lightning that zigzagged above the mountain.

When the basket was lowered the third time, O'Hara settled into it and whistled through his fingers. He felt himself being drawn slowly up the cliffside. As he neared the top he could hear the steady clinking of the ratchet pulley. The basket was being raised and lowered like a bucket in a well.

When he reached the top, O'Hara was instantly overwhelmed by the eeriness. It was not so much the place as the ambience of the place: the hooded monk, a faceless specter bent over the crank of the basket; the monastery itself, an adobe maze commanding the cramped mountain top like some medieval gaol, its squat, weather-scarred buildings, connected haphazardly by roofed walkways; and underscoring it all, a chilling and constant moaning pierced by an occasional scream that reminded O'Hara of Dante's description of the torments of hell.

Billy and the Magician were huddled in the low arched doorway of what appeared to be the main building.

"I am Frère Clef," the hooded monk said.

"O'Hara. This is Mike Rothschild, and you know Billy."

"Oui. Bonsoir, mon ami."

"Bonsoir," the Haitian replied.

Frère Clef turned back to O'Hara. "You should know that those who have joined our order have taken a vow of silence," he said. "I am the gatekeeper. By tradition, I alone may converse with visitors."

He spoke softly, his accent a hybrid. British, a touch of French, perhaps even a bit of Spanish.

"We understand you are here to see the man with the umbrella and that you are sympathetic with his plight."

"That's correct," O'Hara said.

"Bon. Please follow me."

Billy elected to wait in the grim anteroom while the monk led O'Hara and the Magician along walkways that protected them from the rain. They went down through the catacomb-like monastery, past doors with barred windows, and suddenly O'Hara realized where the wailing was coming from and why, and the name of the place made sense for the first time.

La Montagne des Yeux Vides: the Mountain of the Empty Eyes.

Well-named. Lifeless eyes peered out at them from behind bars, arms reached out to touch them, and with each crack of lightning, a chorus of woe arose from the lips of inmates.

The monastery was an insane asylum, the silent monks its caretakers.

The Magician cast O'Hara an apprehensive look and rolled his eyes heavenward.

Another crack of lightning, another chorus from the damned.

They entered the last of the buildings and went down a short flight of wide stone stairs. Torches flickered in sconces on the bare walls of the grim, winding hallway. The building, chilled by rain and wind, smelled dank and foreboding.

The hooded man stopped at the first cell. "I have told him you are coming," he said. "But his reaction may be . . . a bit startling."

"Frère Clef, is Danilov insane?"

"You didn't know? Oh yes, Brother Umbrella is quite mad. He seeks repentance in his madness." The monk peered through the barred door. "You will find that he . . . what is the word—meanders? He meanders in and out of the real world."

"Are you treating him?" the Magician asked.

"I am afraid those who have been sent to Les Yeux Vides are beyond treatment. Brother Umbrella was brought to us by friends, but he asked to be secluded here."

"He asked to be brought here?" said the Magician.

"Yes. He was suffering extreme paranoia and had become occasionally irrational. He thought everyone was trying to kill him. He even believes his umbrella is deadly."

Believes! O'Hara thought. Obviously the monks of Les Yeux Vides did not not know who Danilov really was. Or care. And they thought his deadly umbrella was harmless.

"How long has he been here?" O'Hara asked.

"Four months. And since coming here, he has slipped further away from reality." He pointed to a bell beside the door. "You may ring the bell when you are finished. Oh, one other thing. He believes this is his home. He does not realize he is one of them. Good luck."

The monk unlocked the door and slid back the large shot-bolt lock.

"Monsieur, you have guests," he said and padded silently back up the stairs.

They entered the room cautiously, remaining near the door, and their eyes were assaulted by flickering candlelight. Candles were everywhere, casting a ghoulish yellow light over Danilov's cell—or cells—for it was actually two cells connected by an arch carved through the stone wall. The main room was a surprise: there was a large oak table, pushed against the wall opposite the arch, covered with papers and notebooks; a large bookcase, choked with books in many languages against another wall; a cot with several down pillows opposite it; a small table beside the cot; a high-backed chair at the desk, and two others shoved haphazardly in corners. The walls were covered with maps, photographs of flowers and wild animals, and a small black-and-white photograph of downtown Sofia, the capital of Bulgaria, which appeared to be a dismal, grim-looking city.

The other room contained a bed, a night table and a large, bulky free-standing closet. Nothing more.

There was a large vase of daisies on the floor near the desk, where Danilov was sitting, pen in hand, bent over a sheaf of papers and writing furiously.

"Un moment, un moment," he said with the wave of a hand. And when he had finished what he was working on, he turned around. His face told the whole story, for here was a man haunted by his own ghosts, driven to insanity by age, conscience and fear; an assassin, urged further into madness by his own bizarre, self-imposed imprisonment; a madman sequestered among madmen, totally oblivious of his predicament. His cabbage-face was drawn and sunken. Self-destruction lurked in eyes that were listless one moment, bright as a diamond the next. His hair, what there was of it, had turned pure-white and clung, in sweat-matted disarray, to his skull. His palsied hands were knotted with arthritis. Beads of perspiration clung to his worn-out face. He was wearing a pair of soiled, hopelessly wrinkled white pants and a white dress shirt, open almost to the waist.

"Parlez-vous français? Habla Usted español? Sprechen Sie Deutsch?"

"English. We speak English."

"Englis," he said, "so you are Englismen, then?" He spoke the language well, although with a guttural accent.

"Americans."

"Americans!" He stared at them suspiciously and then said, in a fevered and annoyed tone, "Yes, yes, what is it? I'm a busy man. Can't you see I'm busy? Eh? Look at this desk, just look at it! Projects,

projects, pro— Never enough hours in the day to get . . . My secretary . . . I haven't seen . . . uh, she's off on holiday. That bitch."

He frantically moved papers around on the desk.

"Danilov?" O'Hara said.

The haunted man peered at him through the flickering candlelight. "I know you," he said. There was panic in his voice. "You're here to kill me." He backed into the corner of his cell-like room, whimpering like a scared puppy, holding his umbrella in front of him, its point gleaming dangerously. O'Hara backed away from the deadly weapon.

"I want to help you," O'Hara said.

"I don't want help. Get away from me. You're one of them."

"One of whom?"

Danilov's mood changed suddenly. "Don't try to— You think I'm a fool? How did you get— All right, all right, where's Security? Security! How did you get— *Security!* They sold me . . . sold me . . . Oh, those bastards . . ." He closed his eyes and beat one fist on his knee.

"Nobody sold you out, Danilov. I promise you, your secret is safe with us. I've been on the dodge myself—for over a year."

Dailov's mood changed again. He giggled and spoke in mock musical tones. "Don't believe you," he said, as if he were singing a song. "You lie. Everyone lies. Did you know that lying is an art?"

He waited for an answer, his eyebrows raised, then went on, "In the KGB they teach lying, like they teach point in ballet. Basic. Basic!" A long pause. "Who are you? I do know you, don't I?"

"We've never met officially. My name's O'Hara."

"O'Hara . . . O'Hara . . . Irish, eh? IRA?"

"American."

"Yesyesyesyoutoldmethatallrightallright," he babbled in frustration. Then, just as quickly, he became almost playful again. "Well, slip the doodle-do, right?" He leaned on the umbrella and danced a jig around it. "The cock-a-doodle-do." He raised his head and crowed like a rooster.

"Mad as a fuckin' hatter," the Magician whispered. "Let's get the hell outa here. This guy's absolutely tutti-fruiti, off-the-wall, bananas, Sailor."

"We didn't come all the way up here to end up with nothing, Magician." O'Hara raised his voice and called out, "Mr. Danilov?"

The little man stopped and peered forlornly over his shoulder at O'Hara.

"We have a similar problem, Mr. Danilov."

The little man stopped his dance and looked at O'Hara quizzically.

"Oh, really? The soil up here . . . terrible, terrible. But . . . I have prevailed, sir." He pointed to the daisies. "Grown in pure rock. This place is a veritable Gibraltar. But . . . I did . . . prevail."

"My problem is not gardening," O'Hara said.

"Oh?"

"My problem is, my own section chief sanctioned me."

Danilov looked at him with suspicion. Then his mind began to shift; there was a glimmer of recognition, perhaps. "Happens all the time," he said. "When you trust someone, that's the one not to trust. I call it my reversal theory, eh? Or is it the other way around?"

"We want to help you, Danilov."

"To do what?"

"Do you know why you're here?"

"Peace. Serenity. I don't want to leave here. I like it here. No suprises anymore. I can't stand surprises. Can't stand . . . wondering. Every day is the same here. Food is the same. People are the same. I have a garden, just outside there. But it's raining. Later, perhaps, we can take a stroll. Perhaps in the morning. Perhaps, perhaps, perhaps, perhaps, perhaps, perhaps . . . Time will tell, eh? Are you a guest here too?"

He skittered close to O'Hara and said in a low voice, "I must warn you, the food is wretched. But the service, ah, the service . . . superb. Absolutely . . . superb. Not a lot of jibber-jabber, and quite prompt. Certainly not . . . not of course, of course not . . . abso*lutely* not the Plaza or the Savoy, but then, the food was never any good in Egypt, either. Do you travel?"

"I'm leaving," the Magician whispered. "I listen to much more of this, I'll be certifiable."

O'Hara ignored him and pressed the point. "Mr. Danilov, do you know who I am?"

Danilov strolled the room again, studying O'Hara's candle-jaundiced face flickering before him. "My friend? My brother? My teacher, my priest, my driver, my enemy? *L'ennemi,* yes. My . . . own . . . executioner."

"Do you know who I am?" O'Hara insisted.

The mad Bulgarian sat down again and pursed his lips. "I was always very good at tests," he said, still pondering, and then he said, "You're the one they call the Sailor."

O'Hara was taken aback. "That's right," he said with surprise.

"And you," he said to the Magician, "are the one with the hotel."

"Be damned," the Magician said.

Danilov turned back to O'Hara. "You ditched it."

"Right again."

"Ditched it. Yes, I remember you. I ditched it too. Not an easy thing to do."

"Why do you think that is?"

"Because they don't want that. It's unsafe. They prefer to give you the long sleep."

"Who is 'they'?"

"The faceless ones, telephone voices, kill this one, kill that one. For what reason? Never mind. Oh, excuse me, *excusez-moi, monsieur.*"

"Who is Chameleon?"

"I know and I don't know."

"What does he look like?"

"Everybody, nobody. He is a chameleon. The chameleon is never what it seems."

"What do you know about Master?"

He became cautious again. His eyes flicked around the room. "It's very dangerous, you know, to underestimate them."

"Underestimate whom? You mean Master?"

"They're philosophical racists. Couldn't do it. Wouldn't do it and now . . . no place left for me but here. It is my . . . rabbit hole."

"Why did you run, Danilov?"

"Too old. Arthritis." He held up his deformed hands. "Senseless. Too many faces. The jolly fat man in the rain . . . you can't retire. No such thing as quitting. When you are no longer useful, they dispose of you. Understand? They shove you down the . . . what do you call it?" —he made a sound like *brrrttt*—" . . . garbage disposal."

"And the only reason Master wants you dead is because you got arthritis?"

Danilov nodded ruefully. "Yes, the unpardonable. To get sick. Tried to keep them from finding out. But eventually there were . . . things I couldn't do anymore."

He dry-washed his hands, over and over. Then he said, "I failed them. No such thing . . . failure."

"How did you fail them?"

"Chameleon."

"What about Chameleon?"

"I missed Chameleon."

"Missed him? Were you trying to kill him?"

"Oh yes."

"Did Quill tell you to kill Chameleon?"

"You must find the ant before you can step on it."

"Did Quill tell you to find Chameleon?"

Danilov nodded slowly. He was staring at one of the candle flames, as though hypnotized.

"And that's the reason?"

He nodded. "Failure. They wanted me to do that job in Hawaii, too, but I was too far away. Couldn't hold that against me."

"What job in Hawaii?"

"The man with the pictures from the *Thoreau.*"

O'Hara looked at the Magician, his eyebrows rising into question marks.

"You mean the oil rig that sank?" the Magician asked.

"Yes. Where we lost Thornby."

"You mean Thornley, the British agent?" said O'Hara.

"Yes, only he changed all that. Buried at sea, I understand. Poetic, don't you think?"

"Did Thornley recruit you into Master?"

"Yes. Paris. Three years ago. My first job was . . . was . . . Simmons. Texas. In Houston. Gave him the old whack with the umbrella. Dead in six hours. Heart attack. They never knew." He smiled and winked.

"Let's get back to the *Thoreau* for a minute. Did they actually sink the *Thoreau*?"

"Yes. With all hands. A hundred and some. Eighty million . . . a hundred million dollars. It was a terrifying feat. All we lost was Thornby, hardly a fair trade, yes? Took out one of the legs with *plastique.*"

"And they wanted you to get pictures of the rig that someone else had taken, is that it?"

"The photographs were of the pumping system. Very revolutionary. But they didn't want to see them, they just wanted them destroyed, and the chap that took them. All the same day. Quaint, eh?"

"What do you mean, the same day?"

"The same day they sank the *Thoreau* was the day they wanted me for the take-out in Hawaii. I suppose they got someone else to do it. I was in London, couldn't get out. Bad weather. Not surprising."

"Danilov, who ordered the take-out on Chameleon?"

"The phone."

"Was it Quill?"

"Yes."

"Quill gave you a sanction on Chameleon?"

"Yes."

"Why?"

"There are no reasons. There are never any reasons."

"Can you guess?"

"He has become a problem."

"Doesn't he run Master?"

He nodded.

"So Quill wants to get rid of Chameleon and take over the whole operation?"

Danilov shrugged. "There are no reasons," he said.

Outside, the storm had subsided. Thunder still rumbled between the mountain peaks.

"Where is Chameleon?"

"I lost him."

"Where did you lose him?"

"Tokyo."

"He lives in Tokyo?"

Danilov shrugged again. "Perhaps."

"So Quill ordered you to seek and destroy Chameleon and you followed him to Tokyo and lost him. Is that when you ran?"

"No. Found him and lost him in Tokyo."

"Where? Where did you lose him?"

"On the street. *Poof!* he was gone."

"How did you get on to him?"

"Too long. One thing and another. Others failed before me."

"Danilov, how many people have you killed for Master?"

"How many?"

"All right, who?"

"Simmons in Houston, Richman in New York, Garcia in Los Angeles, a man in Teheran, another in Greece. And . . . it was cold and rainy . . . always cold and rainy . . . jolly man. Fat. The boat man. This was in . . . in . . ." His memory had clouded over again.

"Did anyone other than Quill ever give you an assignment?"

"Cutout."

"Who?"

He shook his head. "Left a message at hotel. 'Your football tickets are at the box office.' That way I knew to get him at the arena."

"Which one was this?"

"Simmons. I remember now, the one in the rain . . . that was in Japan. Bridges. Name was Bridges. The jolly shipbuilder. Fat man. Got him coming out of a restaurant."

"Anyone else?"

"I . . . don't remember . . ."

"Danilov, how did you recognize Chameleon in Tokyo?"

"I . . . don't remember . . ."

"And you've never met Quill."

"Quill is a voice. Chameleon is a ghost. Midas is lost."

"Midas? Who is Midas?"

"Midas . . ."

"Is it a person? A place?"

"I . . . don't remember . . ."

He looked up very suddenly, sat straight up in the chair with his hands on his knees, the umbrella at his side. "The teacher will now recite Pound. You can recite Pound, can't you? What a strange name —Ezra. What a heavy burden to put on a son."

"Danilov . . ."

And then he fell to his knees and began a bizarre litany: "Nabikov, Ivan, a street in Paris, on his way to work. Gregori, Georg, London, right in front of Parliament . . ." and continued chanting the list of his victims.

"You lost him, Sailor," said the Magician.

"Damn!"

"You got a lot."

"He knows a lot more."

"Not tonight. He's gone back in his rabbit hole."

Danilov looked at them, his alabaster eyes twinkling with madness again. And roaring like a forest beast, he grabbed the umbrella and jumped up and began slashing at the candlesticks.

"He's lost it, man. Let's get the shit outta here."

O'Hara and the Magician backed toward the door as the madman continued to smash out the candles. He charged through the darkness when they reached the door, the deadly umbrella held like a spear before him. They ducked out the door and slammed it shut.

"Wow!" said the Magician, "that was a cl—"

The umbrella came slashing through the window in the door, its tip brushing O'Hara's hair. He fell sideways and slammed the bolt shut.

Danilov began to scream. He screamed as they made their way back through the serpentine passageways to the gate. He was still screaming as they were lowered, one by one, down from the pinnacle of hell.

15

"OKAY, SO YOU BROKE LAVANDER'S CODE," said the Magician. "Let's see what you got."

Rested, showered and attended by fresh fruit and coffee, they hovered over Izzy as the Magician prepared to conjure information from its memory, his fingers poised over the computer's keyboard as though it were a Steinway. He was humming "Body and Soul" as he urged the computer to talk to him.

Eliza explained that she had run several combinations of sentences from the Lavander book through the computer, trying to break the code by trial and error. Then she began thinking about what the Magician had said: if it was not written down, it would have to be simple because nobody could remember twenty-six letter substitutions. Twenty-six. The alphabet. And she remembered from her childhood a sentence that contains every letter of the alphabet: "The quick brown fox jumps over the lazy dog."

Her next step had been to experiment with the alphabet, running it forward and in reverse under the sentence, trying to decipher his alphabetic code. That didn't work.

"So," she said, "I left the sentence on the monitor, and then I started running the alphabet under it, moving one letter to the end of the alphabet each time. In other words, I started with *b* as the first letter, then *c*. I got up to *l* and that was the key."

The Magician said, "So what we got is . . .

"The quick brown fx jmps v lazy dg . . .

"And under that we put the alphabet, starting with *l* instead of *a:*

"lmnopqrstuvwxyzabcdefghijk . . .

"Put em all together and what've yuh got?

"T h e q u i c k b r o w n f x j m p s v l a z y d g . . .
"l mn o p qr s t uv w x yz a b c d e f g h i j k . . .

"And there it is. L equals *t,* *m* equals *h,* and so forth." He turned to Eliza. "Neat."

"Yeah, pretty good, Gunn," O'Hara said. "*L* for Lavander, that's easy to remember too."

"Does that qualify me to work with you big-timers?"

"Well, it's a good start," O'Hara had to admit.

"Thanks a damn bunch," she said.

"So we got a code, where do we go from here?" the Magician said, ignoring their banter.

Eliza had set up a temporary key-definition library in the computer, replacing the letters on the keyboard with the code letters, and had typed almost all of the information from Lavander's notebook into the computer.

"What's the file name?" the Magician asked her.

"LAV/1."

The Magician typed out "LAV/1" and the screen filled with rows of words and figures. Many of the entries were names of banks with lists of deposits under each heading. Most of the remaining entries, however, were names of companies with coded lists of figures under them.

"Christ, here's a bank in Grand Cayman with over a hundred grand in it!" The Magician was genuinely awed.

"So far, there are deposits listed in there for almost a million dollars," Eliza said, "but that's not what's really interesting. He's got production figures, oil-field capacities, refinery operations, everything you can imagine on a dozen or more oil companies, how much they say they pay for crude oil, how much they really pay. It's an encyclopedia of juicy information."

She pointed to two figures on the monitor screen. "Published Reserve Capacity versus Actual Reserve Capacity," she said. "In every entry, the actual reserves are millions of barrels higher than they report. They're lying to the public, O'Hara."

"What's so surprising about that? They kill people, blow up oil rigs, assassinate politicians. What's a little lie to the public mean to them? They have to do something to justify ripping us off."

"That's a bit cynical, isn't it?"

"Realistic," O'Hara said.

"What's all this got to do with Chameleon?" the Magician asked.

"I've said all along, there's got to be a pattern to this. An objective other than just killing for profit. I think we're right in the middle of some kind of international oil scandal."

"Maybe Hinge killed Lavander to get this book and you beat him to it—maybe it's just that simple," Eliza said.

"It's a possibility," said the Magician.

"Yeah, in which case every company in that book has a motive for killing the old boy," Eliza said.

"We need to turn up one bad guy," O'Hara said. "Without at least one client we can name, the story falls flat. What the hell motivates the people who hire Master? Who wanted Lavander assassinated? Why was the *Thoreau* sabotaged? Why was Marza's car blown up? Who was behind the murders of Simmons and the rest of them? Not just generally. Specifically, why were these things done?"

"I could make a coupla good guesses," the Magician said.

"Not worth a doodly-shit," Eliza said. "I see his point."

"And if we can't get it?" said the Magician.

"What we need is Chameleon himself," said O'Hara. "You tried military and naval intelligence, right?"

The Magician nodded.

"How about the OSS?"

"Their files went into the CIA when they reorganized," the Magician said. "I've already checked them."

"How about inactive cases?" O'Hara said. "Maybe they've got him cubbyholed somewhere. Go back to MI. I've turned up more than one sleeper by checking deep."

The magician punched Military Intelligence Files and queried the index.

"Hell," he said, "we got 'Inactive, U.S.,' 'Inactive, Europe,' 'Inactive . . .' Look at all this shit."

"Call up Inactive and run Chameleon through them all."

The Magician started pounding Izzy's keys and kept coming up with the same answer: "No such file." Then, under "Inactive, Japan," they got a strike:

—Chameleon. N/O/I. Head of Japanese training unit for intelligence agents. On list of war criminals, 1945–1950. Believed killed at Hiroshima, 8.6.45. Declared legally dead, 2.12.50.

Period.

"What's N/O/I. mean?" Eliza asked.

" 'No other indentification,' " said O'Hara.

They stared at the entry for a long minute. Finally O'Hara said, "He must've been on the hot list. Took them five years to declare him dead."

The Magician said, "Not much there."

"It seems like it would be a common code name, Chameleon," Eliza said. "Maybe there's more than one."

"Maybe," O'Hara said. "Or maybe he didn't die at Hiroshima."

"He'd have to be, shit, close to seventy. That was more than thirty-five years ago."

"You don't stop functioning when you're seventy," said O'Hara. But he tucked the information in the back of his mind for future use.

"Let's go on to something else," Eliza said. "What other outside sources can Izzy tap?"

"Name it. UPI, the New York *Times,* Washington *Post,* Dow Jones, the *Wall Street Journal,* the CIA, the British Secret Service, la Sûreté . . ."

"Can we feed the names we picked up from Danilov in this thing and scan some of them for information?"

"That's what it's made for, and it's not 'this thing,' Sailor," said the Magician. "Just call it Izzy. Anything this smart should be treated with a little respect."

They settled down to work, scanning the wire services and newspapers to get information on the victims. It was tiring because it was boring, typing in requests, getting "No info available" back. Hours went by. It was amazing how many Simmonses and Richmans popped up, obviously not connected. Then they got a hit.

They had queried United Press International to scan Houston newspaper obits from October 1976 through October 1977 for Merrill Wendell Simmons. According to Danilov, he had killed Simmons three years earlier, which would have been in the spring. But the cutout had left his "football tickets" at the box office, which would indicate Danilov was mistaken on the date. It might have been in the fall.

Danilov was mistaken. It had been three and half years.

The machine spelled out:

—UPI/Ref/Houston Chronicle/11.12.76/p.1C@File:HUCH/76/11/12/NWS./2555-242.

"Let's see who he was," O'Hara said.

The Magician typed out the file number and the obit appeared on the screen.

—Houston, November 12 (UPI)—Millionaire oil tycoon Merrill Wendell ("Corkscrew") Simmons, former SMU quarterback, who parlayed a single oil lease won in a poker game into the sprawling American Petroleum Corporation, died of a massive heart attack at his home in suburban Houston tonight. He was 56 years old.

The business magnate had appeared in excellent health and had attended an SMU homecoming game in the afternoon. He complained of feeling ill while preparing steaks on an outdoor grill in his backyard and collapsed a few moments later. Simmons was rushed to Houston General Hospital, where he was pronounced dead on arrival at 7:25 p.m.

A fairly detailed biography followed.

"Well, that's one confirmed kill for Danilov. Who's next?"

It was their first break and it renewed their energy. They kept seeking information, checking and cross-checking each name and the new leads it created. Slowly, the information began building up.

—Jack "Red" Bridges, President, Bridges Salvage Corp., Tokyo, Japan, died, heart attack, 6.21.77.

—Arnold Richman, Sunset Oil International President, died on business trip to New York, 2.9.77.

—Abraham Garcia, President and Chairman of the Board, Hensell Oil Co., died of a heart attack on a business trip to Los Angeles, 9.18.78.

"That's the four of them. He must have been telling the truth," O'Hara said.

"This Chameleon has a real hard-on for oil companies," the Magician said. "Three oil-company execs have been kayoed, plus the *Thoreau* was sabotaged."

"Let's not forget Lavander," Eliza said, "he was in oil up to his eyebrows. And speaking of that, all of the companies these guys worked for are in this book. Just look, here's Hensell . . . Am Petro . . . Sunset . . ."

O'Hara looked at the decoded entries which Eliza had run off on the printer. On the second line of each of the three entries was the word "AMRAN."

"What's AMRAN?" O'Hara asked.

"I dunno," the Magician said. Eliza just shrugged.

"Can we find out from Izzy here?"

"I'll try Dow Jones."

Half a dozen references popped up immediately.

"Bingo!" cried the Magician. "Now we're cookin', man. Let's scan the profile outline from the *Wall Street Journal.*"

"What's the date?" O'Hara asked.

"November 9."

"Pretty recent. Let's see it."

The outline flashed on the screen:

—AMRAN Ltd. Consortium formed October 28, 1979. Comprised of Intercon Oil Corp., American Petro Ltd., Hensell Oil Products Corp., Sunset Oil Intern'l Inc., The Alamo Oil Company, The Stone Corporation, Bridges Salvage Corp. Objectives: Stronger market position, joint experimental ventures, consolidation of markets, increased financial strength. Chief Executive Officer: Alexander Lee Hooker, Gen of the Army (Ret.); V.P., Operations: Jesse W. Garvey, Gen, U.S. Army (Ret.); V.P., Marketing: (Position vacant since death of Vice President Ralph Greentree, 1.3.80.) Chief Financing Institution: First Boston Common Bank. Home office: Tanabe, Japan.

"I'll be damned. I thought the Hook was dead. I haven't heard anything about him in years," O'Hara said. "And their main base is in Japan."

"Where's Tanabe?" asked Eliza.

"On the east coast of Honshu, about a hundred miles from Kyoto. Desolate goddamn place."

"Chameleon's really got it in for AMRAN," said Eliza. "He's killed most of the executives in the consortium. The *Thoreau* was owned by Sunset Oil. The guy who was killed on Maui had pictures from the *Thoreau.*"

"Anybody wanna take bets on how old Ralphie Greentree died?" said the Magician.

"Just for the hell of it, Magician, check Alamo and see if they've had any recent deaths in the high echelons."

The Magician asked for a profile on Alamo Oil. There it was, four lines down:

—David Fiske Thurman, Chairman of the Board, Alamo Oil Company, killed in single-car wreck, outskirts of Dallas, Texas, 4.8.77.

"Try Ralph Greentree."

—Ralph Greentree, former Executive Vice President of Alamo Oil Company and Marketing V.P. of AMRAN, drowned while vacationing in Honolulu, 1.3.80.

"It's getting better," O'Hara said. "Guess who was on Maui two days before that?"

"Hinge," Eliza said.

"Right. Greentree drowned three days after Hinge killed the man on Maui and lifted the film from the *Thoreau.* Honolulu's a thirty-minute plane ride from Maui."

"What else?"

"Try one more. Try this Stone Corp., see what we can find out." Izzy revealed the following:

—The Stone Corporation. Holding company in the power and energy field. Corporation's widespread holdings are not a matter of public record, but are known to include nuclear power plants in Ga., N.C., Ala., Fla. and national and international oil-refining properties. Temporary Executive Officer, Melvin James, replacing C. L. K. Robertson III, who died in crash of private plane, 6.25.78.

"Jesus," said the Magician, "I'd like to think some of these people actually died in accidents. But I've got serious doubts."

"How about this final entry?" Eliza said. They had overlooked the last paragraph of the outline:

Newest acquisition: merger with Japanese conglomerate, San-San. 5.10.79

"What's this San-San?" Eliza said.

"It's a very powerful company over there," said O'Hara. "But I really don't know much about it.

"I've had it," the Magician said.

He got up and stretched. Eliza slipped behind the keyboard, changed disks and started feeding the last few entries from Lavander's book into Izzy.

"Don't you ever get tired?" the Magician asked in a somewhat annoyed tone.

"It's youth," O'Hara said.

Their energy had carried them for hours and now, suddenly, all three of them seemed to fall apart at once. They decided to take a break and let Izzy print out the remaining entries in Lavander's book.

Eliza, spotting the entry as they were leaving for dinner, said, "O'Hara, better look at this."

There it was, on the print-out, one of the last entries:

—Midas/Io.354,200/109,12/lgr.Ghawar/es.2bb./d.0-112.

The three of them hunched over the printer, staring at the entry for several seconds.

" 'Midas is lost . . .' " O'Hara said.

"What?" said Eliza.

"That's what Danilov said, 'Midas is lost.' Midas isn't a person, it's a company or place. Wonder what all these figures mean. And what is 'Io.'? And 'Ghawar'?"

"I haven't seen another entry like this," Eliza said. "Usually you can tell what the figures mean."

"I'm too tired to figure out what anything means anymore," the Magician said. "I gotta get some shut-eye."

"Okay, let's pack it in. Izzy can run the print-out on all this and we'll take it with us."

"Take it with us where?" asked Eliza.

"Japan."

"Japan!"

"Right. AMRAN's in Japan. Hooker's in Japan. Bridges was in Japan, Chameleon's in Japan, San-San is in Japan. Obviously there's only one place to be, so let's all get some rest. The next stop is Tokyo."

BOOK THREE

*Any event, once it has occurred,
can be made to appear inevitable by any
competent journalist or historian.*

—JOSEPH PULITZER

1

ETCHED IN THE GOLDEN TABLETS on the wall of the ancient Japanese temple of Oka-Ri, it is written: "The seasons change with the days, man's memory changes with the years." An English poet, centuries later, expressed the same thought more succinctly: "In the end, all history is memory and gossip."

There were days when General Hooker would sit alone for hours in the darkness of his office, companioned only by the faulty machine in his chest, gleaning the troubled days of his past to conjure faltered memories. On the blackest of these days he could hear the thunder of cannon and the cry of bugles, but his mind's eye saw only swirls of dust, clouding faded days of glory. Names and faces eluded him like ghosts at sunrise, and the names of places drifted in and out of his tick-tock solitude without streets, spires or parks.

Only Garvey knew and understood Hooker's agony. It was Garvey alone who came to his aid when the old man sometimes cried aloud, calling the names of fallen comrades or forgotten battlefields.

"Did you call, General?" he would say.

And the general would repeat the name, and Garvey, his own memory blemished by time, would make up a face and an incident and a place to go with it, and Hooker, satisfied, would return to his uneasy reverie. He had been writing his memoirs for ten years and had amassed a gigantic manuscript. Editing it, sorting truth as reality from truth as Hooker wished it were, would have taken another decade, and so the manuscript was unpublishable.

There were rare occasions when the dust of yesteryear dissipated for an hour or so and Hooker would have a very clear vision of the past. These experiences were almost orgasmic for the old man. He would sit entranced, watching the moments play out through glazed and age-grayed eyes. And so, among the hundreds of handwritten pages of tainted facts, there was a handful of brilliantly re-created battle scenes and incredibly precise character studies. All the rest was imagination.

Hooker was not a prisoner of his past. Weeks might go by when he attended to business lucidly. But there were those days when he would awaken and tell Garvey, "Colonel, I'm going to work on my memoirs today," and he would disappear into the office and Garvey would cancel appointments, rearrange schedules, make the proper apologies, and carry out most of the business as usual. Two or three times during those days, Garvey would respond when he heard Hooker calling out.

This was just such a day, although Garvey had reminded him of his appointment with O'Hara later in the afternoon. Should he cancel?

"No. That wouldn't be prudent," Hooker said and winked. He was feeling good.

Hooker had been inside the office for a couple of hours when Garvey heard him cry out his most frequent refrain: "Bobby, where are yuh, Bobby?"

Garvey entered the large office.

"You called, General?"

"It's Bobby again. At Bastine."

Garvey remembered that day well. And he remembered the boy just as well.

Bastine. March 9, 1942. On that day Garvey began his three years as a prisoner of war at the notorious Suchi Barracks. Hooker was to escape to glory and eventually return to Bastine to free him. And Bobby vanished forever.

"It's all right, old man," Hooker said exuberantly, "I can recall it quite clearly, thank you . . ."

He had stood that morning on the porch of the glistening white Officers' Club building, pole-straight, his campaign hat and dark glasses covering most of his hawklike face, clean-shaven, showered and dressed in freshly washed and ironed khakis, waiting for the inevitable on what he knew would be the most humiliating day of his life.

He listened to the dull *thump, thump* of the big Japanese guns followed by the sighing 105s as they came in and then the sudden *bam* of the explosions.

The Japanese were twenty miles away and closing the gap fast. The Americans were in rout. For days, what was left of Hooker's command had fought up the slender Bastine Peninsula, leaving dozens of dead for every mile they gave up. But the night before, the Japanese had launched a brutal assault. Now they were besieged, and in an hour or two the last of the food, ammo and morphine would be gone. It was a matter of hours.

All around him the general saw fear, panic, anger. You can't win a war with broomsticks, he thought, and that's about all they had left. Still, his men had held this beleaguered finger of land for three months against staggering odds. Now Japanese shells were falling on the base. A nearby maintenance shed erupted suddenly in a cloud of black dust, disintegrated and showered the area with bits and pieces of wood and tools. Something inside—a lawnmower, gasoline, something—blew up and what was left of the shed burst into bright-orange flames.

Hooker ignored the chaos around him, the screaming shells, the sudden shock of the explosions, fire and falling trees, and stood rereading the message that had just interrupted his coffee:

> You will rendezvous at your headquarters at 0700 hours this date, with two USN PT Boats under command, Captain Alvin Leamon. Be prepared to turn over your command to Colonel Jesse W. Garvey and leave that place immediately. Each boat will accommodate six officers. Take with you those men who can support you on our march to victory.
> Good luck.
> Franklin Delano Roosevelt,
> Commander-in-Chief

The message had been decoded and reconfirmed and he reread it with ambivalent feelings. He was humiliated by defeat. But he knew his rescue meant he was destined eventually to wreak an even more horrible revenge on the Japanese. He had an hour in which to select ten key officers from his battered staff and leave the place that had been his home for so many years. The boy, of course, would go with him. He checked the time. Six-ten. The boy was safe in the bomb shelter with those civilians who, because of age, sex or infirmity, could not fight.

They had moved headquarters into a concrete cannon emplacement near the bay, and it was there he found Garvey, eye-weary and body-sore, unshaven, his clothes in tatters, hunched over a chart of the Bastine Peninsula, dictating orders into a field phone. Their telephone lines had been obliterated weeks before.

Garvey stared at him bleakly. "The Japs've got two destroyers and a cruiser in The Sluice. They're shelling Sackett from the sea, bombing him . . . shit, there must be fifty thousand Japs coming at us on the ground."

"What's your estimate?" Hooker said.

"Three hours, maybe. No more than that. They'll be shelling us from out there in the bay, another hour or so. What the hell's the difference, General? When Sackett and what's left of the Third Battalion get here, there's no place else to go." He waved toward the point of the peninsula, a few hundred yards to the north. "We'll have to swim."

Hooker knew what he was saying. They had been discussing when to surrender for days. Both men were burned out, exhausted far beyond the ability to make keen decisions. And neither of them could face the final one.

"A lot of our boys are using personal pistols and their own shotguns. We're just about out of rifle ammunition."

The situation dictated immediate surrender, but the paper in Hooker's hand changed that. Hooker handed him the order and Garvey read it and handed it back.

"If the message were from anyone else, I'd ignore it," Hooker said. "Now we've got to hold this point until the Navy gets here."

"Good," Garvey said, "at least one of us is getting out of this shit hole. Who do you want?"

"Who's left?"

"The best man we've got is Sackett, but he may be dead by now. If he's not, I doubt that he can fight his way back here. He was in a box surrounded on three sides when I talked to him half an hour ago. He only had a dozen men left at the command post in Capice and he was going to hold it as long as possible."

A heavy shell landed nearby and the thunderous explosion showered dust down from the roof.

"Damn! Why did they wait until now to issue this order."

"The Japs didn't break through at Capice until late last night. Up to now we've been fighting a pretty good holding action, considering we're outnumbered maybe fifty to one on the ground, and we haven't had any air or sea support for over a month."

"I suppose you're right. They realize the issue is in doubt here."

"Doubt! Hell, it's a matter of hours now. Moving you out fast like this, at least we don't have to worry about a security leak."

"I'll round up my people immediately," Hooker said. "Perhaps the Navy will get here early."

"How about the boy?"

"He goes with me, of course."

They sipped coffee and drew up a list of the key officers in the company.

"I'm leaving Irv Kaler with you," Hooker said. "He's a fine field officer but he also has the best command of Japanese on the base. You may need him to interpret for you for the next few . . . months. But I want Sergeant Finney. I'll need a first-rate top kick."

When they finished the list, Hooker called a runner and ordered him to have the men report to the dock. He looked at his watch. Six twenty-five. Another shell hit close on and the earth shivered underfoot.

Hooker stood at the doorway for a moment and then put out his hand.

"I wish you were going with me, Jess," he said.

My God, Garvey said to himself, the old man's got tears in his eyes. Garvey smiled. "You'll come back and get me," he said.

Hooker suddenly embraced the tough little colonel. "You can bet your pension on it, General," he said. His voice was trembling with sorrow and anger as he took his old brigadier's star from his pocket and pinned it on Garvey's collar. "I know how long you've been waiting for this," he said. "Sorry it couldn't have been under better circumstances. I'll be back for you, Jess."

"I'll be waiting."

Hooker marched back to headquarters and walked through the wreckage of the sturdy old teak-paneled building. Papers and files littered floors already covered with shards of glass. Doors hung askew and thin layers of smoke drifted in through broken windows and clung to the ceiling like puffs of dirty cotton.

He stood in the shattered remains of his office for a moment or two, then turned sharply and headed for the pier.

Fifteen miles away, two PT boats roared up The Sluice, staying close to the shore of the main island. Sailors on deck watched the terrifying battle on the peninsula opposite them through binoculars.

"Jesus," one sailor said. "They's fuckin Japs everywhere! It's like watchin' an ant hill."

Captain Leamon was in contact by phone with the commander of the other PT boat, Peter Coakley, a lieutenant from Boston, only out of Annapolis two years. Coakley was a brash red-headed youngster with a John Wayne attitude about the whole stinkin' mess.

"Remember your orders, Lieutenant," Leamon had told Coakley an hour before. "We're to proceed with extreme haste to Bastine. Do not— repeat *do not*—engage the enemy for any reason. Just . . . get by them."

Leamon was watching the three Japanese naval vessels through binoculars. "They aren't ten miles from the Bastine pier," he said.

Coakley was watching too. "They're sittin' ducks, Al," he said. "The cruiser'll be between us and the destroyers. We could pick—"

"Do I have to tell you again, Lieutenant? Our mission is to take VIPs off Bastine."

"Nursemaids, that's what we are," Coakley said bitterly.

"You want to burn in hell, you'll get a chance soon enough. But not today."

"Goddamn taxi service," Coakley growled.

"Lieutenant, you want a court-martial?"

"C'mon . . ."

"We ignore the surface vessels. Is that goddamn clear, Lieutenant?"

"Yes, sir."

"I mean is it *god* damn clear?"

"Yes, sir."

"Then let's roll."

The two destroyers and the cruiser were hardly a mile in front of them, concentrating their fire on the narrow peninsula. The steady *pum* of their big guns grew louder.

"Okay, I'll take the first run. You stay close to the shore, wait'll I'm clear, you run for it."

"Got it," Coakley yelled back and cradled his phone. He turned the slim high-powered boat into shore, throttled back and lay close to the trees. Leamon was moving up The Sluice like hell's bat, the bow sitting high out of the water, the stern settled deep. Blossoms of death burst overhead, showering the sea around them with flak. Shells geysered fore and aft, starboard and port. The sleek torpedo boat streaked up The Sluice and the shelling got heavier. The sky was black with the smoke of antipersonnel bombs. Leamon kept right on going.

"Son of a bitch, he's gonna make it," Coakley yelled. "Okay, buckos, hang on to your balls, here we go." And he edged the boat away from shore out into the narrow isthmus and slammed the throttles forward.

Hooker and his men were watching the sea drama from the pier.

"Here comes the first one," a West Point major named Forester yelled. Hooker stood beside him, his small group of officers huddled around him. Hooker had decided to leave his son in the bomb shelter until the last minute. Now it was time.

"Sergeant Finney."

"Yes, sir."

"Please go to the civilian bunker and bring the boy to me."

"Yes, sir."

Finney was a tough professional soldier. His shirt was buttonless and lay open to his belt and one sleeve was hanging by threads at the shoulder. He handed his BAR to one of the officers, jumped in the general's jeep and took off across the lawn toward the bunker. It was no more than five hundred yards from the pier. He was almost there when the shell exploded directly in his path. The jeep went up on its back wheels, skittered sideways and turned over. Finney vaulted out of the seat, hit the ground and rolled over several times. The jeep slid to a stop a few feet from him and exploded.

"I'll get him," the young baby-faced lieutenant named Grisoglio said and started to run toward the bunker, but Finney got up on his feet, shook his head and ran the rest of the distance.

"Hold your place, Lieutenant," Hooker ordered.

Leamon was guiding the fast little torpedo boat into a narrow channel that had been cleared through the wreckage of sailboats and fishing craft. There was barely room for the sleek torpedo boat to fit through. He talked the long, narrow vessel through the junkyard, gently steering it past the burned-out wrecks.

"Hold the lines, don't tie us down," Leamon yelled to his skeleton crew. "Tell the general to come aboard fast. We don't have any time. Coakley's right behind us."

Hooker turned to his group, picked out six officers and ordered them aboard. He could see Sergeant Finney and the boy leaving the bunker and running toward the pier.

"With the General's permission, we got to clear this pier fast," Leamon yelled.

Hooker nodded curtly and immediately jumped aboard. "Lieutenant Grisoglio, you're senior officer on the second boat. Tell Sergeant Finney to keep an eye on the youngster, please. I'll bring the lad over here with me when we stop for the night."

"Yes, sir," said Grisoglio, who was shot in the leg and was using a tree limb for a crutch. He threw Hooker a sharp salute.

"All right, Captain," Hooker said to Leamon, "move out."

They backed through the wreckage and Leamon spun the wheel and the PT boat turned in the water and headed out toward the bay and open sea.

Hooker watched as the pier grew smaller and finally saw Bobby and Finney with the rest of the officers. Thank God, he thought. He waved, and the eight-year-old youngster stood erect and threw him a sharp salute and Hooker watched until the smoke obliterated the dock and he could no longer see him. Hooker turned his attention to the second boat, now speeding up through The Sluice, adjacent to the destroyer, dodging the shells.

Coakley was running wide open, adjacent to the destroyer when the shell hit. It tore into the side of his craft. It was a hard hit. The boat shuddered, debris erupted from the deck and was wafted away in the wind. One of the crewmen soared head over heels over the side. Seconds later, a sky bomb exploded over the foredecks. The boatswain was hurled against the main cabin, his chest riddled with flak. The master's cabin was ripped open like a paper box. Glass showered to the winds. Coakley was hit with a blast of scorching hot air. Hot metal ripped into his side and shoulder. The wheel was wrenched from his grip and he felt himself tumbling across the deck into the railing. He was stunned for a moment and then he realized he was on his hands and knees, staring at his own blood, dribbling onto the deck. He heard a crewman yelling "Fire!," heard flames fanning in the wind. His boat was burning around him.

Coakley got to his feet and grabbed the wheel. He ignored the pain in his body; it no longer mattered. He whipped the stricken PT boat around and headed straight toward the destroyer. Flames twirled in his wake, and sizzled up the side of boat, but it was still skimming across the water like a zephyr, racing through the smoke and din, straight at the enemy ship.

"Motherfuckers," Coakley screamed. "Motherfuckers, motherfuckers, motherfuckers . . ."

Leamon watched in shock as Coakley's torpedo boat raced straight into the side of the destroyer. There was a moment when everything seemed suspended in time. Then the torpedoes went, then the big ship's ammunition holds went. The destroyer lurched and rolled in the water. An orange ball of fire roiled from the hole in her side, and then they heard another explosion and another and another.

"God, oh God!" Leamon cried out. He turned to the general, who was standing beside him watching the death throes of the warship. "Do we go back, sir, for the rest of your people?"

Hooker looked back at Bastine, but there was nothing to see, just black smoke, endless explosions and flames, billowing up through the black pallor.

"I have my orders," Hooker said. "And so do you."

"Yes, sir," Captain Leamon said and guided his speeding boat away from Bastine.

And now Hooker sat in his study, the tears fresh on his cheeks, and he remembered it was that day, among all the days of his life, that he most wanted to forget.

The box came about four-thirty in the afternoon. It was delivered by a cab driver who had picked it up at the train station where it had been delivered from . . .

Ad infinitum.

It was always the same story. Impossible to trace. Just a plain white box with holes in it, marked *"Namamono"*—"Perishable."

The general was seated in the dark when he entered the office.

"Excuse me, sir?"

"Come in, Jesse. I was just dozing here. Thinking about the old days."

"Bad news, sir."

"What is it?"

"Another present."

"God damn!"

Garvey put the box on Hooker's desk. "Want me to open it for you?"

"I'll do it."

He took the letter opener out of his drawer, snipped the string and flipped off the top.

It came out slowly. They always did, searching the air with their tongues, their eyes moving in different directions. Jesus, were they ugly.

He waited until it had dropped over the side of the box and was strolling across the desk. He nicked it in the side, deep enough to pierce the skin. The chameleon squirmed, its tail lashing behind it. It was a small one, no more than nine or ten inches long. He stuck it again.

The chameleon began to thrash in pain. He jabbed it again and again. Then he put the sharp side of the opener on the chameleon's neck and held it hard against the desk. Its tongue bulged in its mouth, a rolled-up ball of red tissue, trembling in its partly open mouth.

"Is there a message?" Hooker said.

Garvey took out a piece of paper. "It says: 'The fish will eat the fisherman.' "

Hate boiled in Hooker's throat, and with a mighty slash of the letter opener, he decapitated the lizard.

2

THEY HAD FLOWN FROM MIAMI to San Francisco and taken the Great Circle flight over the Pole to Tokyo. Then they collapsed for two days. The pickings were slim. The Magician was going to check out Red Bridges' shipyard and then snoop around, see what he could dig up. Eliza had a lunch date with Ira Yerkes, the Tokyo bureau chief for

Howe News Service, hoping to pick up some background on AMRAN.
O'Hara set out to find an old friend in Japanese army intelligence. As
usual, they would use the hotel telephone as a drop in case of emer-
gency.

She had interviewed Yerkes two years before, while he was back in
Boston on vacation. He was tall and slender, in his late thirties, and
hyper; a darkly handsome man who could hardly sit still long enough
to eat lunch. He hadn't changed a bit. She remembered him as a man
buzzing with energy and mildly flirtatious, but who acted as if he
always had someplace else to go—right that minute, and not necessarily
on business, just anyplace at all. It was his nature, and possibly because
of it, he was one of the best reporters in the Howe chain.

He picked up some sandwiches in an American-style restaurant and
led her to a small park at the edge of the Ginza, near his office building,
spread out the food like a picnic and immediately lay back with his eyes
closed, facing the sun.

"I really need to get some rays. It's been an inside wintuh," he said.
His long New England vowels seemed strangely out of place in Japan.
"So what're you doing in Tokyo, where are your cameras, all that
stuff?"

"That's part of it. I'll probably have to arrange for a camera crew
and truck before I leave."

"No problem. The old man's got the best in Japan. And twice as
much as he needs. You speak the language?"

"Uh-uh."

"That could be a problem. Maybe I'll go with you as interpreter."
He looked up suddenly. "Are you on to something hot?"

"Nah."

"You got a reputation for poppin' outa the box with some crazy shit,
lady."

"Tourist stuff. Maybe a little something on Japanese industry."

"A little something on Japanese industry she says," Yerkes said
around a laugh. "You can't do a little something on Japanese industry.
That's like doing a little something on Uncle Sam. Where do you start?"

"How about oil?"

"There isn't any in Japan. Not enough to do thirty seconds on.
Refining, maybe. Lotsa refining."

"What do you know about AMRAN?"

"Don't tell me you're interested in Hardluck Hooker."

"Why do you call him that?"

"You don't know about Hooker?"

"I know he was a big-shot general in the war. What do you want from me—I wasn't born until 1949."

"So—it's history. He's got a great war record but he steps in shit every time he turns around. He got chased outa the Philippines by the Japs, his son was killed in the war, he got axed out as a presidential candidate, and half a dozen of his partners in AMRAN have dropped dead on him. He's been trying to put this consortium together for years."

"I didn't know about his son."

"It's been soft-pedaled. Excuse me, you're in my sun . . ."

"Sorry."

"That's better. Anyway, the Hook was military governor of one of the southern provinces here during the Occupation. He was very sympathetic to the needs of the country, helped put it back on its feet. Even arranged some loans for some of the local big boys. He doesn't talk about the kid anymore. Bad politics."

"Why does AMRAN have its main offices over here?"

"Why not? Oil is an international business. Also I think the old man likes it here. The Japanese either love him or hate him."

"Hate him?"

"The younger ones think he was a dictator. Maybe he was, but what the hell, he was the conqueror. He could have been a real asshole."

"What do *you* think of him?"

"He's a war hero, right up there with Patton and MacArthur. History'll probably give him about eight out of ten."

"Can I talk to him?"

"If you luck out. I did a piece on him about a year ago. I said he was the most tragic figure in World War II. Some dipshit on the international desk changed it to 'one of the most tragic figures.' Anyway, if you're interested in AMRAN, check the assignments desk in Boston. I filed a ten-page wraparound on that yesterday."

"On what?"

"On their merger with San-San."

"What's San-San?"

"San-San means The Three Sirs, a triad. It grew out of the war. It was a little scandalous. The head knocker, Shichi Tomoro, was one of Japan's industrial giants during the war. MacArthur let him off with a wrist-slapping, then Hooker helped finance their whole gig. Now it's one of the most powerful industrial groups in Japan. Very strong politically, and they got more money than the Rockefellers."

"What kind of industries?"

"Oil refining. Shipbuilding. Electronics."

"Maybe I should talk to Tomoro."

Yerkes raised his chin slightly to get the full benefit of the sun. "You're too late. He packed it in a couple of months ago."

"You mean he's dead?"

"Dead, cremated and scattered to the winds."

"How—"

"He had a wild-boar preserve up on the north end of the island near Aomori. Accidentally shot himself."

Chameleon at work again, she thought. It had to be. It fit the pattern perfectly.

"Ira, ever hear of anyone called Chameleon?"

"That's his name, Chameleon? What does he do—sit around the house and change colors?"

"It's his nom de plume."

"Nope. Why?"

"Just curious."

"Bullshit."

"What do you mean, bullshit?"

"I mean bullshit. C'mon, you just don't casually ask about somebody called Chameleon, for Christ's sake. What is he, some hot new rock singer?"

"Punk rock."

"Oh, forget it. I'm just getting into disco."

They got up to leave and Eliza remembered the "Midas" notation in Lavander's book. "One other thing, Ira, does the word 'Ghawar' mean anything to you?"

He carried their trash to a basket and dropped it in. "The only Ghawar I know is in Saudi Arabia," he said.

"Saudi Arabia?"

"Sure. It's the largest oil field in the world."

The Kancho-uchi, headquarters of the secret service, was in a three-story building in an obscure corner of the government complex. O'Hara was escorted to the third floor by a young woman in a white suit. She was formal to the point of making him uncomfortable. Hadashi was waiting for him at the door of his office.

O'Hara had not seen Bin Hadashi for three years. The Japanese agent had changed little. He was in his early thirties, a tall man for a Japanese, slender, his hair cropped short. He was a cum laude graduate of Princeton.

"Hey, Kazuo, where you been," Hadashi said with a broad smile. "I heard you were on the dodge. Your own man was trying to get you hit, hunh?"

"Something like that."

"Some asshole."

He led O'Hara into a small spotless office. There were no pictures on the walls, and the desk was empty except for the telephone and a can of apple juice.

"He was never anything different," O'Hara agreed.

"And then he called it off."

"Yeah."

"What an asshole. You still writing for a living?"

"Trying. There're easier ways of feeding yourself."

"What you snooping around here for? You want something, right?"

"Just a little information."

"That's the hardest thing to get around this place. You know how we Japanese are. Inscrutable bastards."

"The guy I'm looking for may be the most inscrutable bastard of all. You ever hear of a Japanese agent calling himself Chameleon? This was back during the war."

"Which war, World War II?"

O'Hara nodded and held up two fingers.

"This guy—Chameleon—was a spy, that it?"

"He was head of some kind of special training section for Japanese agents."

"Never heard of him."

"Any old-timers around here who might know something?"

"You think this guy's still alive?"

"A hunch."

"Anybody that dates back that far is either dead or retired."

"Then, how about somebody who's retired? I just want to talk to somebody who remembers him."

Hadashi pinched his nose a couple of times. "You buying lunch?"

"A rich publisher back in the States is buying."

"In that case, I thought of a guy. And he's right here in the building."

"Will he talk to me?"

"He'll talk to anybody who'll listen."

They went down in the elevator to the subbasement and walked through a grim, poorly lit subterranean tunnel to what appeared to be the basement of the adjoining building. Steam pipes hissed angrily overhead.

"They must dislike this guy to put him down here."

"They've probably forgotten he's here."

They entered a large room which was divided by rows of steel shelves stuffed with file folders, books, logs, seemingly endless stacks of paper. The old man sat cross-legged on a tatami. He was sorting through files, using a brush and black ink to log entries in calligraphy on a ledger sheet. There was no desk in the room, just the mat and the old man and a very modern brass gooseneck lamp over his shoulder.

He was ancient, a shrunken memory of a man with wisps of white hair that flowed down almost to his shoulders. He had no eyebrows. He wore thick horn-rimmed glasses. His face was so wrinkled, only a prune could love it.

He finished the character he was drawing and looked up.

"Ah, Hadashi-san, how nice of you to come by." His soft voice sounded like an echo of yesterday.

"It is an honor, Kami-sama. I have brought you a small gift." He handed the man a package of Redman chewing tobacco.

"The spirits will reward you at the proper time. Thank you, my friend."

He immediately opened the package and stuffed a cluster of brown ringlets into his cheek.

"This is my friend O'Hara, although he is known here as Kazuo. He has a question and I think only you can answer it."

"Ah, quite a distinction. You understand I am only a clerk. I have never been more than a clerk. I am the custodian of all this. Records that have been fed to a computer. Our history has been reduced to beeps on film. But these are the true records. I am indexing them."

"How long have you been doing this?" O'Hara asked.

"Oh, I really don't know. Ten years perhaps, and I am only a little way along. It takes a while, you understand, one tends to get interested in the files. I spend a lot of time reading. There's no hurry. When I'm through they'll just make me quit and go home and die."

"How long have you been clerk of the records?"

"Since 1944. I was too old for the service." He paused to draw another character in his ledger. "All the records went through my hands. I have a good memory for small facts."

"Do you remember an agent called Chameleon?"

His eyes widened. He laid down the brush and leaned back, staring at the ceiling. "The Chameleon I am thinking of was a true chameleon. He changed colors constantly, so who can say what his true color was."

"I am talking about the man whose code name was Chameleon."

"So am I. Nobody knows who he was. It is a secret that went with him to the gods."

"He's dead, then?"

"Since 1945. He died at Hiroshima. It was verified by your own intelligence people. It was in the records."

"What do you know about him?"

"Only what was in the records. That he existed and that he died. Nothing more."

"So, the only proof that he is dead is that the Japanese secret service says so."

"Would they lie?"

O'Hara took out a slip of paper. It was the print-out from Izzy of the CIA report on Chameleon:

—Chameleon. N/O/I. Head of special Japanese training unit for intelligence agents. On list of war criminals, 1945–1950. Believed killed at Hiroshima, 8.6.45. Declared legally dead, 2.12.50.

"Perhaps someone wanted to protect him. Why did it take the U.S. Army Intelligence five years to verify his death?"

"That you will have to ask Army Intelligence. But I don't think they were at fault. They would have declared him dead long before that, except for one man."

"Who's that?"

"Your General Hooker. He was passionate in his desire to find Chameleon."

"Do you know why?"

"I would rather not guess."

"How could a man in the military service conceal his identity from so many people?"

"Perhaps that was one of his many colors. Perhaps he was not in the service. It is possible he was a civilian serving the Emperor. There were many like that."

"In which case the people who served under him would certainly know who he is."

"That is of no consequence, Kazuo. The records for that section were destroyed just before the war ended. They were kept with the unit at all times. I never saw them. I saw only the final report, closing an empty file."

"Did the section have a name?"

"Yes—Chameleon. That is all, just Chameleon. They had their own headquarters in the south."

"Where?"

"At Dragon's Nest, a fortress in the mountains."

"And that's all there is to know about Chameleon?"

The old man nodded slowly as he mulled the tobacco in his cheek. "There is nothing more to know. He was a chameleon and he died."

Hadashi looked at O'Hara and shrugged. "Thank you, Kami-sama, you have been a great help."

"It was nothing. Next time ask me something difficult. I have little left to do but show off."

On their way out of the building Hadashi remarked, "It's probably a strange coincidence, but this Dragon's Nest the old man was talking about . . ."

"Yeah?"

"It's in Tanabe. It is now AMRAN's corporate headquarters. And Hooker is head of AMRAN."

3

HE HURRIED THROUGH LUNCH and left Hadashi with a fast "Thank you," anxious to meet Lizzie and the Magician and exchange information. But something else was gnawing at his brain, an insistent thought that had been bothering him ever since they arrived in Tokyo. He was thinking about what Kami-sama had said, feeding it into his memory bank for future reference, and it merely bolstered his ideas.

If chameleon had died at Hiroshima, why had it taken Army Intelligence five years to officially declare him dead?

Taking shortcuts through alleys and side streets, he hurried across the city toward the hotel. He was three blocks from it when he first sensed that he was being followed. He stopped at a street corner and casually looked around but it was hopeless to try to single out anyone in the crowds. He slowed his pace, began zigzagging through more isolated byways, hoping to confirm his paranoia. O'Hara did not like surprises, and the intuition was undeniable. So he altered his course, working in a tightening spiral toward an enclosed alley that connected two of the most crowded boulevards in the Ginza, Showa-dori and Chuo-dori.

The walkway was dark and forbidding, coursing through a building that had been condemned several months earlier. It was rarely traveled because it was dim and the building was unsafe. Only two overhanging lights illuminated the block-long passage. O'Hara entered it and started toward Showa-dori.

In its dying years, before the building had been scheduled for demolition, the passageway had become a seedy shopping mall, its cheap antique shops and trinket parlors now deserted. Some were boarded up, windows had been smashed out of several of them, others were exactly as they had been left when the building was closed. Doors stood open, sale signs still dangled in dusty show windows, trash littered the vacant stores. If he *was* being followed, O'Hara felt sure he'd be able to confirm it here.

Was he simply being followed? Or was he marked?

Walking down the alley, he listened to each step crinkling in the glass underfoot. The sounds of traffic faded away, and then he heard the telltale echo of his own footsteps. One. And a moment later another echo behind him. Two.

The third man was in front of him in one of the deserted stores, betrayed by a rustle of cotton, an errant breath. O'Hara exhaled slowly through his mouth, slowing down his own keen senses, listening, judging distances. The two behind were ten or so yards back. The other, the one in the store, was closer.

They were good, moving swiftly on feet of air. The alleyway was alive with energy. Ions swirled about O'Hara like seaweed in the surf.

Then they surprised him. The man in the store stepped out and stood before him not six feet away, a trim, hard-bodied youth in black, wearing Adidas sneakers, his back pole-straight, legs slightly bent. O'Hara flashed a look back up the alley. The other two were frozen in place, statues of rock framed against the dim light at the mouth of the alley.

These are not street fighters, O'Hara thought. They have too much style. The one in front moved slightly; residual light etched the side of his face. His smile and his bow were as subtle as a memory, but he made the challenge. Traditionalists, thought O'Hara, probably Okinawan. They were working as a triad and he guessed that the man directly behind him, the man in the middle, would be the best, the one in front the fastest and the last man would be the backup, the toughest to take out. He instantly decided on his moves.

It was O'Hara's turn to surprise them. He whirled on the ball of one foot and made three hop steps toward the two men behind him, heard his challenger accept the bait, and then O'Hara stopped and executed three basic *higaru* moves almost as one, focusing his first blow on the lead man's stomach before he even turned. The moves were designed to confuse the man at his back, to make him think O'Hara was attacking the middle man, a fast left to right jag, a thrust forward, and then as the lead man rushed forward, O'Hara executed a perfect *ushiro-geri,* forward and down from the waist until his head almost touched the ground and lashing out with a vicious back kick, straight into the attacker's gut. O'Hara's foot shattered the hard muscles in the lead man's stomach and thrust deep up into his diaphragm. Something inside of the man exploded, his face seemed to crumble and he flipped forward to ease the force of the kick, but it was too late—his reflexes were not working. He landed badly and flopped over on his back in time to take a second kick to the temple. He rolled away, unconscious. The moves were so fast that the other two hardly had time to react. O'Hara dove between them, rolled and landed on his feet and launched himself straight up, shattering the third man's jaw with the top of his head. The surprised assailant soared backward through one of the empty shop windows in a shower of glass.

The man in the middle whirled and kicked, jumped sideways, crouched and struck. O'Hara was waiting. He parried the blow, caught the fighter's wrist and twisted it out and down and thrust a knee into his side. The fighter rolled away from him, got his feet under him and charged again, this time throwing a *uraken*, a back fist strike at the jaw. It was perfectly executed, his fist moving in a rotary movement and arcing past O'Hara's elbow and catching the American on the edge of the jaw. The blow knocked O'Hara sideways into the boarded-up front of another store. He shattered the boards, burst through them and felt a nail tear at the shoulder of his jacket as he fell into a dusty window display of tasteless, gaudy lingerie. He kept rolling, bending his back and flipping back on his feet as the middle man dove after him, pressing the attack. O'Hara met him and then rolled back again, using the attacker's own momentum to throw him farther into the store. Flipping backward and landing on his knees on the middle man's chest, he struck twice, the first a *nukite*, a spear hand thrust straight to the bridge of the nose, the second a crippling chop to the throat. The middle man gasped, tried to throw a *nukite* and missed. O'Hara's third blow should have finished him, but the fighter was tough. He rolled, threw O'Hara off balance, then twirled violently the other way, and O'Hara was thrust off.

The backup man now appeared in the shattered storefront, his face slashed by broken glass, one arm sliced open and bleeding. O'Hara did not retreat. He leaped sideways, deep into the darkness of the store, out of sight of the two remaining men for an instant, then charged the backup man from the darkness, jogging to the right and left and twisting sideways and diving under the man's outstretched arms, coming up with a palm-heel shot that demolished what was left of the man's jaw, knocking him back into the alley. A second later he felt a knife foot shot to his kidney, a blow that sent pain streaking up his spine and cramping his shoulders. It knocked him forward, but again he did the unexpected. He took two quick steps and then thrust backward, twisting as he did and colliding with the middle man, dropping to his knees, grabbed two handfuls of sweater and flipped the man over his head through the shattered window. The middle man landed on top of his backup.

O'Hara ignored the pain in his side and attacked again, this time using his favorite move, one which combined the arcing swing of the side foot blow with the ball of foot, a move requiring total commitment, for he had to literally twist in midair, picking up momentum from the swing of his foot, then turning it so the ball of his foot landed up under the nose. It was a perfect strike and the middle man sighed as he whirled away and collapsed.

But the backup man was still not out. His arms whipped into a defensive position as he stood and then just as quickly he tried his own side kick to O'Hara's ribs and followed with combinations, an elbow shot followed by a two-fingered thrust up under O'Hara's chin that snapped his head back and missed his windpipe by a fraction on an inch. Backup's mistake was overconfidence. As O'Hara's head jerked backward, the backup stepped in and tried a back fist strike.

O'Hara landed flat on his feet, saw the peculiar augering punch coming, moved backward with it, let it glance off his cheek, slashed down with his own arm and locked Backup's elbow under his own. He spun him around, snapped a knee into the man's groin, and as he arched forward, got his other hand under Backup's chin and twisted. The elbow snapped and O'Hara let the arm go, completed the move by swinging Backup in a full circle, letting him loose and hitting him twice with two spear hand punches. Backup dropped in a heap at his feet.

O'Hara turned toward the other two. It was all over. He instantly shook out the aches, massaged the pain from his kidney as he ran out of the passage, leaving the three attackers behind, and continued his journey back to the hotel.

He entered the hotel and found a quiet place near a rock garden in the corner of the lobby. Focusing on the water, he went to the wall and, entranced, began playing back everything he knew so far. The chain was becoming clearer to him. Chameleon, Hooker, Danilov—they were the keys. And one other. Dragon's Nest.

Everything led to Kyoto and beyond, to Tanabe. They were getting close, the attack proved that. He didn't know how long his three assailants had been following him, but it was safe to assume that they knew about Eliza and the Magician. They were all in danger.

It was Eliza who broke his concentration. "What happened to you?"

She was standing over him, looking at the torn jacket, the two bruises that were beginning to appear under his jawline.

"We're shaking them up, whoever 'they' are," O'Hara said. "I just got jumped by three pros a few blocks from here. I don't know how long they've been following me, but the message is perfectly clear. Somebody's nervous."

She was more concerned about O'Hara than about the implied danger to all of them. "Are you all right?"

"I'm fine. I may have a sore throat for a couple of days, but other than that I'll live. Have you heard from the Magician?"

"No, but I have some interesting news," she said and recounted her conversation with Yerkes. "And there's one other thing," she added.

"What's that?"

"You remember the notation in Lavander's book about Midas? It said 'lgr. Ghawar.' Remember that?"

O'Hara nodded.

"O'Hara, Ghawar is the largest oil field in the world. It's in Saudi Arabia. Maybe Midas is an oil field and the 'lgr.' means larger than. Larger than Ghawar."

"Which would make Midas the largest oil field in the world."

"Right!"

"Well, where is it?"

"I don't know the answer to that one."

"You just can't hide the largest oil strike on earth."

"Maybe the Magician's turned something up," she said. "I'll check the message desk."

"Wait," O'Hara said. "When you find the Magician, I just want you both to get out of Tokyo. Get the Howe satellite van and drive down to Kyoto tonight. I'm going on ahead by train."

"Can't we all go together?"

He shook his head. "I've made arrangements to talk to Hooker. The sooner I get there, the better."

She touched the bruises on his throat. "You're sure you're all right?"

"I'm okay. I just want you two out of Tokyo. Besides, the answers aren't here, they're at Dragon's Nest."

She kissed him lightly on the lips. "Look, I'll just check the desk . . ."

"I've got to go," he said, "or I'll miss the train."

"But—"

"I'll make reservations for you at the Royal Hotel. You should be there by morning."

"But—"

"Just check out the van, round up the Magician and do it." He kissed her on the cheek.

"But—"

He was gone.

God, she thought, he's maddening, the most impulsive man I've ever met. She went to the desk and checked both her messages and O'Hara's. There was an urgent message to meet the Magician at a street whose name she could not pronounce. She rushed out to try and stop O'Hara, but he was gone.

"Shit," she said aloud and hailed a cab.

The place was near the waterfront, down a dirty rut road that led across the railroad tracks and past a coal shack. The place was a dump, an overgrown lean-to with a red, white and blue sign that said "Harry T.'s." Rusting metal beer signs pockmarked the place, while behind it the sprawling Bridges shipyard obscured the bay.

The Magician was standing near the door of the place with his hands in his pockets looking forlorn. The sleeve of his suit was torn loose and there was a large rent in his pants.

"My God," said Eliza, "you look like an eighteen-wheeler backed over you.

"Worse," he said.

"Worse?"

"Worse. I got attacked by a bear."

"By a bear?"

"I'll tell ya all about it. Where's the Sailor?"

"He got this hot flash. He went to Kyoto. We're supposed to meet him there tomorrow night."

"Shit. What am I doin' here?" the Magician said to nobody in particular and looked off into space shaking his head. "The last thing I needed was that fuckin' bear, I'll tell you that."

"Magician, what in hell are you talking about?"

"What happened is, I was doin' these waterfront bars down here tryin' ta get a lead on Red Bridges. I mean if there's one, there's fifty bars down here. I was just hopin' to, you know, luck into something. I am, after all, a piano player, not fuckin' Front Page Harry."

"Maybe the next time there'll be something you can do on the piano."

"I can piss on it, if it's anything like the piano in there," he said, jerking his gloved thumb toward Harry T.'s. "Anyway, they's a lot of American sailor types around here, workin' these yards, and everybody is telling me if I want info on Bridges, I need to talk to Kraft American."

"Who?"

"Kraft American."

"Is that somebody's name or what you had for lunch?"

"It's the guy's name, okay? What do I know. So that's how I wound up here."

"Why here?" asked Eliza.

"Because Kraft American owns the joint."

"So? Is that it?"

"No, there's more. I just didn't get to it all yet."

"Why?"

"I had a run-in with this bear in there. Y'know, four legs, lotsa hair, long nose, big teeth, *big* fuckin' teeth."

"What kinda bear?"

"I dunno, a Japanese bear, I guess. He's wearing this little straw hat that says 'Win with Nixon' on the brim."

Eliza started to laugh. "I don't believe a word of this."

"Look, what are we standin' here talkin' about it for? There's a fuckin bear at the fuckin' bar drinkin' a fuckin' beer. Go see for yourself."

"I'm just going to take a look inside," Eliza said.

She took a look. "My god, it is a bear! That's a *big* damn bear, too! I mean, look at that son of a bitch!" Eliza said.

"I wouldn't talk about him like that," said the Magician.

"What the hell is a bear doing drinking beer in a bar?"

"How the hell do I know? Ask the bartender, he used to work for Bridges. He's the one we need to talk to."

"That's Kraft American?"

"That's what I understand."

The bartender, a barrel of a man with a crew cut, a nose that had been broken so many times it wasn't sure which way to point, and arms as thick as a tire tube, was wearing a black T-shirt with "Hot Tricks at Budakan" stenciled across the front in bright-yellow letters. The tattoo on his left arm, an anchor embroidered with roses, had "USS Billfish" bannered across it. A toothpick lingered forgotten in the corner of his mouth.

"Wouldn't it be illegal serving a bear beer? You can't even take a dog in the supermarket back in America," Eliza whispered.

"You can reason with a dog," the Magician said, which made as little sense as the bear at the bar drinking beer.

"Gooda see yuh," the bartender said. "Everybody calls me Kraft American. I own the place. What'll it be?"

"I need something really strong. A piña colada," the Magician said. "And beer for my friend."

"Okay I make that piña colada with Russian rum?" Kraft American asked.

"Russian rum?" the Magician said, somewhat aghast.

"It's all I got till my delivery tomorra."

"Sure," the Magician said with a shrug. "It fits in perfect with everything else."

"Uh . . . what's with the bear there?" Eliza asked.

"Yuh mean the one with the hat?"

"I don't see any other bear in here."

"What can I tell you," Kraft American said apologetically. "He comes with the store, okay? The guy who owns the place before me, he's kind of like a patriotic nut. The bear is just one thing. You haven't gone to the john yet. You sit on the seat, a recording of 'God Bless America' plays. Anyways, the deal is, the guy wants out. He offers me the place. The only catcher is, see, the bear stays. And his rah, rah, rah, America hat stays too. And the flag-wavin' toilet seat, everything."

"Does he have a name?"

"Name's Harry S. Truman."

"Does he often tear a man's clothes off his back?" the Magician asked, still annoyed.

"It was the piano. I woulda warned ya, but I didn't see yuh siddown to play. Only problem we got with Harry S. is that the goddamn bear goes apeshit when he hears flat musical notes. Hurts his ears or sumpin. That piano ain't been tuned since they built the Canal. The only way, see, to calm Harry S. down when he gets outa sorts like that, all yuh gotta do is whistle the 'Star-Spangled Banner.' "

"You ever know a guy name of Red Bridges?" Eliza asked.

"Know him? Shit, yuh can't count the nights I wheeled his ass outa here. Red was in here alla time. He loved Harry S. I mean, they was asshole buddies. Red'd sit there, tell that goddamn bear his troubles, he'd never talk to anybody else. He used to bitch about the dish."

"Dish?" Eliza asked.

"Yeah, enormous thing, maybe as big around as, uh, half a football field. Like that."

"What do you do with it, invite a thousand of your closest friends to dinner?" said the Magician, looking around for a laugh.

Kraft American laughed. "That's a good one," he said. Harry S. belched, then rolled his lips back and smiled at everybody.

"Actually, what it is, it's an underwater environment thing."

"How come it was so big?" Eliza asked.

"Uh, I dunno this fer certain, okay? This is scuttlebutt. But from what I hear, this saucer-type thing could sleep maybe twelve, fifteen people. Had regular apartments in it, like they was gonna live down there. It was designed by that Greek guy, y'know the one does all the underwater shit."

"Nicholas Kaginakas?" Eliza said.

"That's the one. He died too. He was here for a while and then he went back to Greece and one day he dropped dead."

"What did Bridges make before they started building the dish?" Eliza asked.

"He was hot and heavy into the salvage business. Then Red bought about—oh, fifteen, sixteen of those old Liberty ships from World War II. Big, ugly bastards, but they could hold a ton. He worked on them for a while, refitting, putting in tanks."

"What for?"

"Red comes up with the idea that you could gut them, put in storage tanks and use them for oil tankers. He did lotsa business, none of 'em ever came back to complain. They was very unique, y'know, had ballast tanks in them like a submarine."

"Ballast tanks?" said the Magician.

"Yeah. I guess so's they could equalize the way they float, empty and full."

Harry S. picked up his empty mug between his paws and rapped on the bar, and Kraft American went down and drew him another beer.

"What d'ya think?" the Magician whispered to Eliza.

"Didn't Danilov say something about killing a man in Greece?"

The Magician nodded.

Kraft American came back with a piña colada and one draft beer.

"This dish, you know where they took it?" the Magician asked.

"Nope."

"And Red Bridges died before it was finished?"

"Yeah. Old Red was gettin' fed up with the operation. It got bigger than he had planned. See, Red was just a good old pirate, a salvage jockey. He loved lookin' for old wrecks. If he'd made a fortune dredging up some old treasure ship or a war vessel full of relics, that woulda made him happier than a pig in shit—pardon the French, lady. But converting old tubs into tankers and building some underwater flyin' saucer, that wasn't his thing.

That definitely was not his thing. He din't wanna be no big-timer."

"Did he ever find anything when he was salvaging?" the Magician asked.

"Sure. Just before he quit we found an old Jap troopship lyin' in twelve fathoms off the Volcano Islands south of here. She was running from Iwo Jima in '45 and our dive bombers caught up with her. Then he got involved in this big-time shit and he never went back. She's still down there, rusting away."

"Nobody else went back either?"

"Far as I know, Red never reported the find. He was always planning to go back there when he retired."

He stopped and shook his head forlornly, then went on, "He really agonized over selling the yard, though, after thirty-five years. I heard him tellin' Harry S. all about it one night. He got a little soused, was unloadin' on old Harry. Some people he worked with after the war wanted to buy him out. Poor son of a bitch dropped dead before he could make up his mind."

"Before?" said Eliza.

"Yeah. Two nights before he passed away, he's in here with a bag on. He's bitchin' about gettin' in a squeeze with the big boys. But what big boys he didn't say."

"And nobody ever said what happened to the dish?"

"Nope. Hauled it outa here—shit, must be three, four months ago now. Actually I'm glad it's gone. Everything was very hush-hush, the guys'd come in, wouldn't talk shop. That's about the time they started hiring a lotta Jap guys. Hadda pass security tests, the whole shithouse mouse."

Harry S. belched again. "Ye're excused," Kraft American said.

"Who owns the shipyard now?" Eliza asked.

"Uh, some big outfit over here. Can't remember offhand, seems t' me it's down south somewhere."

"AMRAN?" Eliza ventured.

"No, sumpin like—"

"San-San?" said the Magician.

"Yeah, you got it, man. That's it, the San-San Company."

Harry S. grumbled into his beer.

"Whatsa matter, Harry, you got the blues?" Kraft American said. "He gets the blues, y'know, sits there with his face in the glass like some drunk, moaning."

"Maybe he's horny," the Magician suggested.

"I never thoughta that," Kraft American said and moved on down the bar to talk it over with Harry S., who continued to stare bleakly into his glass.

"It's beginning to fit together," Eliza said. "One more thing, Mr. Kraft American, did Red ever mention the word 'Midas' to you?"

"Sure, lotsa times."

"He did?"

"Yeah. That's what they called the dish."

4

IT WAS ALMOST MIDNIGHT when he arrived at the house in Kyoto. He slipped through the gate, but the dogs were with him before he got to the garden. They went crazy. The male, Kazuo, threw back his head and groaned low in the throat, like a shy wolf serenading the moon.

"Quiet," he said in a hushed voice. He knew Kimura would be asleep by now, and there was no light in Sammi's room. He went to the house in back. Tana was asleep, curled in a ball on her tatami, her black pigtail in a twist over her shoulder.

O'Hara was weary from the traveling. It had been three days since he had loosened up. He went down the hall away from Tana's bedroom to the practice hall. It was no larger than a big bedroom and its floor was covered with mats. One wall was mirrored, like in a ballet studio. He looked for the flowers. Tana put fresh flowers in the room for him every day whether he was there or not. The vase was in the corner, filled with yellow carnations, and the longing started.

The room was dark, streaked with light spilling in from outside, but he lit no lights.

He was relieved that Tana was asleep. He needed time to prepare his body, to clear his mind, to erase from it everything but the immediate objective.

Chameleon.

The ghost was nearby. He felt suffocated by its shroud. Everything else was immaterial.

He took off his shirt and sat for ten minutes in the lotus position in the center of the room without moving or blinking his eyes, listening to wind chimes, going to the wall. Then he unwound slowly, like a snake awakening in the sun, and in a series of moves so swift and smooth that he might have been a ballet dancer executing an intricate pas, he ran four stances: *yoko-tobi-geri,* the flying side kick; *neko-ashi-dachi,* the cat stance, for fast movement; *zenkutsu-dachi,* the forward stance, for punching; and *kiba-dachi,* the horse stance, for attacks to the side. And then, just as quickly, he ran four blows: the Tang hand, for chopping; *Taisho,* the classic palm, heel; and *mawashi-zuki,* the roundhouse strike to the collarbone.

He repeated the moves a dozen times, each time increasing his speed.

And then, just as quickly, he slowed the pace down, down, down, and twisting as if in slow motion and in one long move, he returned to the lotus position, where he sat motionless for another ten minutes.

He stood up and shook out his hands. He was ready.

And that is when he saw Tana. She was standing in the doorway, naked, her body streaked with dim light, with her hands at her sides and sleep in her eyes.

"The dogs told me you were here," she said.

He stepped into a shaft of light and held his hands so she could read them. "You were so peaceful I didn't want to awaken you. I forgot about the dogs."

She smiled. "And would you have slept in here so as not to awaken me?"

"Perhaps."

"I can sleep anytime." She came close to him. "You have not come back to stay."

"No. Only to talk to Tokenrui-san."

"He is away until tomorrow at the time of the last meal. But I would like to talk to you, to watch your lips."

He reached out and touched her very lightly on the lips, and she, in turn, touched the end of his fingers with her tongue.

"Sadness is written in your face," she said.

"I am tired."

"It is not tired that I see."

"It is the wrong time to talk about it."

She did not question his judgment. It was his thing to talk about and his right to pick the proper moment. Besides, he was here, even if only for the moment.

"I have missed you, Kazuo. It is hard for me to sleep without the comfort of your arms."

"And I have thought much about you."

She stroked his face with her fingertips. "It is good to touch you again."

Her nipples touched his chest and grew hard. She closed her eyes and said, "I have thought about you until I feel like a bee and am wet with wanting you."

He pressed against her and stroked her back, felt her move tighter against him. Her fingers moved to his pants and unbuckled them. She slid her hand down the front of them, felt him and wrapped her fingers around him and felt him surge at her touch. With her other hand she unzipped his pants and let them drop away. She took his hand with hers and put it between her legs, and guiding his fingers between her lips, began stroking herself with his hand. She licked her other hand and stroked him harder.

He felt her stiffen, rise up on her toes and begin to tremble. Her small screams seemed caught in her throat and then she opened her mouth and they came forth, a rush of cries that sent blood surging through his hard penis.

She guided him to her, felt him slipping into her and she wrapped one leg around his waist and rose and lowered herself on the toes of her other foot.

She enveloped him, sucked him deep into her, squeezed him and then released him, then she did it again. And again. And he too began to tremble. He groaned, only it was more like a growl, and then she wrapped her other leg around him and he grabbed her cheeks and began to rock her hips. Fire burned down his back, under his sac and then roared up through him and burst into her and she bit his lower lip as he cried out.

He dropped slowly to his knees, fell forward on one arm and lowered her to the floor. She lay there and looked up at him and her breath was still coming in short gasps.

"It was so quick it is a memory already," she said. "Come to bed, Kazuo, and you will awaken inside me and we will greet the sun with our cries."

5

THE SHORT JAPANESE WOMAN WALKED briskly down the fenced street to the kendo school. She could hear the sharp, flat reports of the bamboo swords striking each other before she entered the large, brightly lit room.

Inside, it might have been a scene from the seventeenth century. There were twenty students in all, each well protected by thick head-gear and ribbed masks called *men,* hard, bamboo-backed jackets called *do,* by *kotes,* leather gauntlets covering their their hands and wrists, and a padded *tare* shielding stomach and groin.

She walked down the side of the room to a podium in the front and stood silently in the corner, watching the master *sensei,* the teacher, as he seemed to float around the room, watching each of the teams as they dueled, occasionally stepping in to make a point. The *shinai* "swords," made of four bamboo slats laced together at the grip with leather, smacked sharply as the students attempted to score points, striking at the top of the head, the right wrist, the right torso and the throat.

The *sensei* taught by example. When he wished to instruct a student he simply moved in, taking over the role of the opponent. His moves were dazzling. She saw him score three points with what looked like a single move. He bowed to the student and moved on, working his way across the room until he was near her.

He leaned his *shinai* against the wall.

"Excuse me, Okari-san," she said. "I would not interrupt your class, but it is important."

"I understand, Ichida," he said quietly. "I assume things are happen-ing in Tokyo?"

"*Hai.* The one known as Kazuo is much better than we thought."

"So? Kei and his friends did not discourage him, then?"'

"Kei is in the hospital. His jaw is broken. The others were also hurt. He said it was like fighting the wind."

The kendo master said nothing for several seconds. He watched his students at work, and without turning, asked, "And has he made progress, this Kazuo?"

"Perhaps. He first went to the Hall of Records and then to visit a man named Hadashi at the Kancho-uchi. He was at the Kabuki Theater asking questions about make-up and actors who have worked there in the past. And now he is here."

"In Kyoto?"

"Hai. He stays at the home of the Tokenrui. And he has made plans to go to Tanabe later today."

"Interesting."

"He knows the country and our ways. He moves easily."

"He is just like the others. He was once with the CIA. They are all alike. What about the Englishman?"

"He is much more subtle. It is as if they did not know each other."

"And the other two?"

"They were still in Tokyo last night."

"I will deal with them later. Thank you. I am sorry about Kei, but I am sure he will recover. It is comforting to know I can rely on my friends."

The Japanese called Ichida bowed again. "Shall we continue to follow him?" she asked.

"No. But keep the two in Tokyo in view. First I must dispose of the assassin, O'Hara, who poses as a journalist. After that, we will deal with the others."

And with that he turned, and moving with the grace of a dancer, whirled through the students like a dervish, scoring point after point after point until he had challenged them all. And then he stopped and removed his *men* and laughed.

6

O'HARA COULD SEE THE FORTRESS, way up in the cliffs on the side of the mountain, as they drove up the curving road from Tanabe. Its high stone walls seemed to grow out of needle pines and elm trees. Below it sprawled the islet-speckled Iyo-Nada Bay; beyond it, the island of

Shikoku, and beyond that, to the west, Hiroshima. Far below, at the foot of the mountain, the pancake-shaped storage tanks of the Yumishawa Refinery glittered in the early-afternoon sun.

The castle above them had been built in the seventeenth century by the shogun Tukagawa Ieyasu as a warning to all who entertained the idea of invading Japan from the south. General Hooker had used his considerable influence to arrange a long-term lease between the Japanese government and AMRAN, turning Dragon's Nest into the consortium's international headquarters. The view was spectacular. Fishing boats and freighters speckled the blue water of the bay far below, and the drive leading up to the fortress was lined with rose bushes and azaleas. Twenty minutes up the grassy volcano brought the taxi to its main gate.

Getting into the place was not quite as pleasant.

A security guard appeared at a doorway in the massive wooden gate of the twenty-foot stone wall and demanded credentials, letters of introduction, then searched O'Hara. He was Japanese and built like a sumo wrestler. His uniform, a dark-green suit over a black turtleneck sweater, seemed about to explode its seams. The small patch on his right arm said simply: AMRAN SECURITY. He also wore an identification badge over his breast pocket. At first he appeared concerned that O'Hara had no briefcase, but finally he shrugged off his anxiety. His examination complete, he motioned O'Hara to follow him through the small door.

O'Hara had made arrangements for the taxi to wait and he followed the guard into the *dai-dairi,* the inner courtyard. It was half the size of a football field, cobblestoned, and devoid of trees, gardens or any other pleasantries. On the far side of the yard were three one-story structures. O'Hara recognized the classic layout: in the center, the *shishin-den,* the ceremonial hall and main building of the compound; on its right, the *seiryo-den,* "the pure cool hall," usually the shogun's living quarters; and on its left, the *kaisho-den,* or barracks. The buildings had low-sloping tile roofs, curved at the bottom and supported by thick wooden pillars painted bright-red. The classic beauty of the architecture had been perfectly preserved except for two things: enclosed walkways connected the three buildings, and all the doors were sealed except the main door into the *shishin-den.*

There were three satellite dishes located on the roof of the ceremonial hall, and several spotlights on top of the wall. Without seeming obvious, O'Hara studied the exterior as he walked across the courtyard. Several men and women in black smocks worked in the yard, mopping, raking; obviously AMRAN kept the place spit-polished. Then he sensed that someone was watching him and he turned his head casually. There was a man in the shadows under one of the the sloping rooftops, a vague form except for one cruel eye that caught a reflection of sunlight. The man began to move away, but not before O'Hara noticed his other eye, black-patched, with a jagged scar that streaked from his hairline to his jaw. Then he was gone.

Was it just a casual observance or was it a deliberate watch? He had the uncomfortable feeling that perhaps he knew this man, but he couldn't recall where or when they had met. A sense of elusiveness swept over him as they entered the main building. It was like trying to remember a dream. He shrugged and decided to forget it.

The sweeping entry hall had been turned into a reception room. Light came from windows in the eaves of its twenty-foot cantilevered ceiling. The oak beams were buffed and spotless. The walls were covered with ancient delicate paintings on silk screens. But the only object of furniture was a typically American stainless-steel desk. It sat in the middle of the room, and it was bare except for a guest log and a multibutton telephone. Small television cameras high in the beamed ceiling constantly scanned the room. There were also metal and electronic-chip detectors in the base of the walls. Nobody could get into any of the buildings without going through this room, and nobody could get through this room with any kind of metal or electronic device.

The man seated behind the desk wore the green suit and black turtleneck of the security force, with three stripes on his sleeve. He wore his holster Western style, with the muzzle hanging almost to his knee. He was broad-shouldered, thin at the waist, straight as a rifle barrel, hard as a diamond, and his leathery face was heavily tanned. Not an ounce of fat on him, and judging from the expression on his face, it would probably be painful for him to smile. O'Hara knew the type. Probably an ex-career top kick or drill instructor.

He recognized the man beside the guard immediately from history books and old newsreels. He had been gaunt then, wraithlike from three years in a prison camp, his hollow eyes reflecting a glazy kind of joy, his khakis hanging from a bony frame. He was heavier now, almost dapper with white hair and a white waxed mustache, its ends curling toward the ceiling. He snapped a swagger stick against starched khaki trouser and came toward O'Hara with his hand out. General Jesse Garvey, the Martyr of Suchi Barracks.

"Mr. O'Hara?"

"Yes."

"Welcome to Dragon's Nest. I'm General Garvey, exec veepee, and this is Sergeant Travors, Security."

"My pleasure," O'Hara said to Garvey. "I recognized you immediately, sir. It's a real honor."

"Thank you."

"Looks like an Army post," O'Hara said with a smile, looking back at Travors.

"General Hooker runs it like the Army. Force of habit, s'pose."

"I guess so."

"Well, he's waiting. Come along."

As they walked across the big anteroom O'Hara heard muted sounds from behind the walls: electric typewriters, computers beeping, tape recorders rewinding. Somewhere in the enormous old building there was a lot going on.

Garvey ushered him into a room and pulled the door shut behind him. It was suddenly as quiet as a church at midnight.

The room was enormous, probably the audience chamber of the shogun, O'Hara thought, and very dark. No sunlight entered the room. Its windows were sealed with thatched bamboo screens, and the opposite wall had been converted into an enclosed greenhouse. Grow lights cast vague, purple shadows among the plants and ferns while ancient statues of temple dogs and guard lions stood silent sentinel in dim corners. His heels popped on the hardwood floors.

It was hot and humid and smelled vaguely of pipe tobacco.

O'Hara sat down in a large leather chair, part of a group near the entrance to the room. A single light, shaded with a Philippine basket shade, shed a tiny orb of light on the end table next to the chair. There was nothing to read.

He waited. The only sound was the ticking of a clock somewhere in the chamber.

He began to perspire. He figured that the humidity in the room must be close to a hundred percent, and the temperature had to be over eighty.

He attuned himself to the space, listening to every movement: dew dripping off the plants; the tiny feet of an insect scratching across the floor; the faint electric hum of the grow lights; the metronomic melody of the ticking clock.

And there was something else. Slow, shallow breathing. Someone else was in the room with him.

O'Hara began to peruse the darkness through squinted eyes. The sound was coming from a particularly dark corner near the plant house.

A match scratched, a burst of amber light followed by flickering flame. In its wavering light he saw Hooker's historic profile, the hawk-like nose, the granite jaw, the long, classic neck.

"That was very good, sir. Excellent! You were on to me in . . . less than a minute. Incredible concentration."

He plucked the string on the lamp; an obese Buddha, his red-enameled belly glistening in the light, sat cross-legged at its base, staring through inscrutable, painted eyes out into the room.

"I must apologize for that bit of melodrama. My eyes are very sensitive to light."

The old man sat behind an enormous campaign desk, bare except for the Buddha lamp with its ancient fringed shade and pull string, an antique wooden letter box and an appointment book. There were eight high-backed chairs in a row in front of the desk.

"I also apologize for the humidity. I'll be eighty on my next birthday. My blood's gotten a bit thin. If it's less than eighty-two degrees, I get chills. How about a drink? It'll help."

"Tea would be fine."

"Hot or cold?"

"Cold, please."

He pressed a button somewhere under the desk and Travors appeared at the door.

"Iced tea for Mr. O'Hara, Sergeant. I'll have a glass of soda, please."

"Yes, sir." And he was gone.

"Some things never change," Hooker said. "I was in the military for so long, I still think of my assistants in terms of rank rather than title."

"There does seem to be a lot of security people on the premises."

"One can never be too careful," he said somewhat cryptically.

"Actually this is quite a fortress," he went on. "Took 'em five years to build it, 1607 to 1612. It was meant to discourage foreigners from entering Japan after the shogunate shut the country down. I'm sure you noticed the view on your way up. It commands the entire bay and the island of Kyushu."

"It's quite impressive."

"Five years of hard work, and the old boy never came to see it when it was finished." He shook his head. "All that labor. Fact is, Dragon's Nest has never been attacked."

"How come you decided to use it?"

"Sentiment, I suppose. It was my summer HQ when I was military governor after the war. Before that, some special branch of the Japanese secret service was billeted here."

A Japanese woman scurried into the room with their drinks, bowed and left. She was young, in her early twenties, and quite pretty, and she never took her eyes off the floor.

"Well, Mr. O'Hara, here's to your health and good luck on your story. How can I help?"

Age had etched the rigid lines in Hooker's face into deep crevices. His high cheekbones stood out like the pinnacles of a cliff. His skin was almost transparent from age and his eyes glowered from under heavy white brows. He stared keenly at O'Hara through tinted sunglasses as he tapped tobacco into the chalky bowl of his clay pipe.

"I'm doing some background for a story on the oil industry," O'Hara said. "Your consortium interests me because it's new."

"A youngster, so t' speak. Actually, there's a lot of experience in this group." Hooker abruptly changed the subject. "You've come a long way to do your research."

"I was in Japan on other business."

"I see. Do you like the country?"

"I grew up here."

"Oh? What part?"

"Tokyo, then Kyoto."

"Ah, I assume then that we have a love of the country in common."

This is a lot of bull, O'Hara thought. By now the old bird knows chapter and verse on me. Why is he playing games?

O'Hara nodded. "Kyoto is my favorite spot in the world."

"A bit tranquil for an old soldier like myself," Hooker said, leaning back in his chair and gazing at O'Hara over the smoldering bowl.

"You're also the only American petroleum operation based in Japan," O'Hara said, "and that interests me."

"Well, there's nothing mysterious about it. There are a lot of reasons why we located in this particular spot."

O'Hara smiled. "That's one of the reasons I'm here, to find out some of them."

"Good. Fire away."

O'Hara took out a pad and felt-tip pen. He could still hear a clock ticking somewhere but there was no sign of it. The sound seemed to be coming from the general. A watch perhaps.

"You seem concerned about something, sir," Hooker said.

"It's nothing. I keep hearing a clock ticking somewhere."

"Ah. The clock is in here, Mr. O'Hara," he said, tapping his chest. "A noisy but efficient pacemaker. My doctors don't want to go tampering with it now." He laughed. "If it stops ticking, please call my doctor."

O'Hara began with obvious questions about Hooker and his association with AMRAN.

"I was president of Intercon Oil. We first proposed the consortium."

"When did you get involved in the oil business, sir?"

"Oh, fifteen, twenty years ago. When I was a candidate for President. Some of my staunchest supporters were Texans. When I dropped out of the race, I was asked to take over Intercon. The company was in trouble. Lack of strong top management. In two years we had it purring like a freshly tuned jeep."

"Why did you propose a consortium?"

"It gave the companies involved new financial strength. Like any industry, it takes money to make money."

"Do the members of the consortium share information?"

Hooker nodded. "The technology of all the companies is mutually shared, but they operate individually. Their profits are their own. AMRAN is not a profit center, it is more of a . . . service organization."

"Are you still connected with Intercon?"

"Only in an advisory capacity. Most of our time here is spent on AMRAN operations."

"When was the consortium actually formed?"

"We finally got chartered about a year ago. It took quite some time to put this together. You can imagine the problems, trying to bring several major companies under the same umbrella. It took a helluva lot of negotiating to satisfy the needs and demands of each of the corporate structures. I repeat, Mr. O'Hara, each of these companies retains its autonomy."

"Yes. How long did the negotiating take?"

"We started talking about it back in . . . oh, seventy-five, thereabouts."

"Which companies eventually joined?"

"My own, Intercon. Then there was Sunset Oil, Hensell, American Petroleum . . ." A swift recollection, a brief flash from the past, pierced his concentration, uninvited and unexpected, and erased what he was about to say from his mind. "I'm sorry," he said, perturbed, "what . . . uh, was I saying?"

"You were giving me a list of AMRAN members."

"Of course! Let's see, where was I . . ."

He went on, but the memory persisted, forcing him to deal with it. *It was in Sydney,* he thought. *The first box came right after we got set up in Sydney.* He shook the thought off.

"Intercon, American Petroleum, Hensell, Sunset . . ." O'Hara reprised the list for him.

"Of course . . . let's see, there's Bridges Salvage Corporation, The Stone Corporation. Then we have an arrangement with a small Italian motor company."

"Why a shipyard?"

"Oil tankers, old man, oil tankers. Why feed the Greek industry when we can build our own?"

"Self-sufficiency?"

"Something like that."

"And The Stone Corporation?"

"It's a holding company for several power facilities in Florida, Georgia, Alabama, some other Southern states."

"It also owns oil refineries, doesn't it?"

The general put another match to his pipe, using the time to further study O'Hara. We must not underestimate this man, he thought.

"Yes."

"Here in Japan?"

Hooker nodded. "Right down at the foot of the hill. The Yumishawa works. We keep them busy. It is the second largest in the world."

"And you ship oil from other parts of the world to be refined here?"

"Right again. I can arrange a tour for you, if you're interested."

"Perhaps later in the week."

Hooker slowly released a billow of smoke toward the ceiling. "Good," he said, "I think you'll find it educating."

"Is Yumishawa profitable?" O'Hara asked.

Hooker smiled. "We're not a charitable organization; we're in business to make money. Yumishawa had the capacity we needed."

"Is that what brought you back to Japan?"

"AMRAN is an international company. We use several Japanese refineries. Also, I happen . . . uh, to—"

Hooker's eyes seemed to cloud over as he spoke. He looked as though he were daydreaming. "—like living here."

The old man was having difficulty concentrating. Dark memories had begun to intrude and linger in his mind, sharp and persistent memories. He listened intently to O'Hara, trying to crowd them out of his consciousness, but they remained, edging out reality . . .

It was the second—no, it must have been the third chameleon.

He remembered the box, although there was nothing distinctive about it, just a plain white box, and he remembered staring at it for a very long time, listening to the creature moving about inside it as hate welled up inside him.

He had been in Sydney for two months, plotting the island stepping-stone campaigns that would take them closer and closer to Honshu. The house was a white frame Victorian mansion that had once belonged to a governor, a spacious and airy place that had been converted into his campaign headquarters. There were security MP's everywhere.

And yet she had managed to get inside—with the box.

She stood before him in the big room, her face as placid as a lake, that inscrutable countenance revealing nothing. Life had been kind to her. Her skin was clear and smooth, and her almond-shaped eyes alert.

"I remember you as being much prettier," he lied.

"I beg your pardon?" said O'Hara.

"Oh, excu— My mind wandered. Business . . ." His voice trailed off.

"I was asking whether you yourself initiated AMRAN," O'Hara said.

"In a way. It came together almost out of . . . uh, necessity. Several of the companies had lost their . . . executive officers during the negotiations. Each time it happened we virtually had to start over, dealing with new people."

"What happened to these key people?"

"Died. Natural causes mostly. Three died of—no, maybe it was four—heart attacks, and there was an auto accident . . . At any rate, there were a great many delays. Frustrating, y'know, trying to put this together with these sudden changes in management . . ."

He was speaking almost by rote, for his mind kept skipping backwards in time.

In the Philippines, politics had kept her quiet and in her place. Politics and one hundred American dollars a month, a cheap enough price to avoid a scandal that would have ruined his career.

How, in the middle of a war, had she found her way from Luzon to Australia?

The box answered that question.

Chameleon had arranged it. No question about that. Twice before, the boxes had come. Inside each was his signature, a single chameleon. There had been no message in the first one, only a small snapshot of the boy standing in front of a Shinto temple in Tokyo. He looked terrified.

Hooker's intelligence people had devoted months trying to get a fix on Chameleon. Even their agents in Japan knew very little. He was head of a special branch of the Japanese secret service. Nobody had come up with his real name.

The second chameleon, a month or so later, had accompanied the first real message Hooker received. Typed neatly on a small piece of paper, it said simply: "The issue is negotiable."

Nothing more.

Then, after two more months of agonized waiting, she had come to verbally deliver the message to him.

The ultimate insult.

The snapshot was sadistic. Bobby, sitting in a child's coffin. The boy looked tired, possibly even drugged.

"What does he want?"

"It must be done quickly. In the next week."

"What does he *want*?" Hooker had demanded, angry to find himself negotiating with a Japanese officer and a concubine.

She closed her eyes and repeated, as if by rote, "He will exchange Molino for Admiral Asieda, whom the British are now holding prisoner here in Australia."

God, how he hated her. And yet, he was still attracted by her sensuality. He wondered if her body had changed through the years and he thought about her, lying naked beside him. For three years it had been a state secret. Only Garvey knew.

The general, only six months a widower, sleeping with a seventeen-year-old house girl and then sending her away after she bore his son. God, how the magpies at the Officers' Club would have chirped over that. And his superiors? They would have destroyed him.

Now he hated her all the more because, in his own weakness, he had lived a lie for three years and now it was coming back to haunt him. Staunchly Christian, he was needled by guilt as he stared at her. "You should be shot as an enemy agent," he told her.

"I want my son back alive," she said . . .

". . . plane crash," O'Hara was saying.

"I beg your pardon," Hooker said, snapping back to reality.

"I said Robertson, of The Stone Corporation, was killed in a private plane crash."

"Yes. Wasn't supposed to fly himself, y'know. Company policy. But when you're president of the corporation, who does the chastising, eh? That put us back a bit. We were close to an agreement with Stone when the accident occurred. There was also that chap in, uh, Dallas . . ."

"David Fiske Thurman, Alamo Oil."

Hooker looked at him, obviously surprised. "You've certainly done your homework, young fellow. Thurman always was a madman behind the wheel. Unless I'm mistaken, he had several close calls before that."

O'Hara pressed on, clarifying information before forcing the issue of Chameleon.

But the general began to slip again . . .

What nerve. To give him, the second highest ranking officer in the Pacific command, an ultimatum. He was infuriated.

"Here's what I think of that bastard," Hooker said to the woman. He grabbed the lizard, held it out with one hand and squeezed its writhing body until it was dead. The creature dangled from his fist. He threw it back in the box.

"Take that back to the son of a bitch with my compliments."

"You will let him kill Molino?"

"His name is Bobby."

"His name was Molino until you stole him from me. What a coward you are."

"Woman, you're pushing my patience beyond its limits."

She, too, had lost her composure. "I want that agreement. It is the least you can do. You left him once . . ."

"Left him! It was an act of fate. I didn't abandon the boy, I—"

"The boy. The *boy*. That's all he ever was to you, the boy. You took him away from me once. Unless you do this thing, I will tell them that you raped me in your house at Bastine, that you—"

"Raped you! I've never seen a pair of legs open faster in my life. He's my son and I'll call him what I want to call him. You have no claim on him. He's mine, adopted on record. All other records have been destroyed. You couldn't prove . . . anything."

"He is my son. They will kill him. You must do as—"

"Goddammit, woman, how dare you threaten me with lies and black-mail? Don't tell me what they will and won't do . . ."

Anger and guilt overwhelmed him. Images clouded rationality. Sins of the flesh. Calvin and his cane of lightning. The American flag. Images that catalyzed his hatred. Here she stood before him, an enemy consort, threatening blackmail. His rage burned uncontrollably.

"I don't know how you got here but it's the end of the line for you. I'm having you arrested and charged with high treason. I'll pull the trap on your gallows myself."

"And how do you propose to have me arrested without revealing that I am your son's mother?"

"No one will believe you. A Filipino whore turned Jap agent? Hah!"

Her dark, flashing eyes revealed her frenzied state. She threw back her head and spat across the desk into his face.

He got up slowly, walked around the desk and stood very close to her. "I'll teach you to repect what I stand for, you slant-eyed little bitch!"

She reared back again, growling with hate, and his own hatred erupted. He quite suddenly reached out and clamped his hands around her throat. His large bony hands first crushed her cries, then her windpipe, then her larynx. He kept squeezing, twisting . . .

He could still hear the sound of it, like the sound of twigs being twisted and broken.

"General?"

"Yes!"

"Are you all right?"

"Yes, yes, I . . . my mind, uh, drifted off there. It's been a difficult day for me."

"I'm sorry. I just have a couple more questions."

"I'll try to be more . . . uh, attentive."

"I'd like to get into another area," O'Hara said.

Here we go.

"Does the word 'Chameleon' mean anything to you?"

There was a glimmer in his eye, his lips moved, his jaw tightened. Color seemed to rise in his cheeks. "This really has nothing to do with the oil business."

"It has to do with your business."

"I really am feeling a bit low, Mr. O'Hara." He started to get up.

"Excuse me, General, but I know about Chameleon. We need to talk about it."

Hooker looked at him with annoyance. "Is that why you're really here?"

"Yes, sir, it is."

"And just what do you know?"

"That Chameleon is head of a very efficient intelligence agency for the private sector. That his agents have killed, stolen corporate secrets, sabotaged installations at the cost of more than a hundred lives. And for some reason, AMRAN and its partners seem be his favorite victims."

Hooker took time to dab the tobacco in the bowl of his pipe and light it. "Can we talk off the record for a few moments?"

O'Hara hesitated. A lot of good information had gone down the drain "off the record," but he had no choice.

"Chameleon is probably the most dangerous terrorist in the world today," Hooker said. "His methods are unpredictable and so is his choice of victims. Nothing is beyond him. Blackmail, kidnapping, robbery, murder, sabotage, nothing at all."

"Do you think your competitors are behind these acts?"

"They're not immune. Some of them have suffered too. Obviously companies are using Chameleon's unique . . . service. But I have no idea who or why."

"But AMRAN seems to be a particular target."

"I don't know—"

"Supposing I told you I believe Chameleon was responsible for the deaths of Simmons, Richman, Thurman . . . most of the executives connected with AMRAN who've died or been killed?"

"I would say strong talk with no backup."

"I know the man who killed them all," O'Hara said. "Or most of them."

"Then produce him. You have that kind of evidence, then perhaps your story will have credence."

"I don't think that's possible."

"Listen to me, O'Hara, nobody would be happier than myself if you were to turn up this . . . vampire and show the world what he is. But so far everything you've said or intimated would be comical without some way to substantiate it."

Hooker let the smoke from his pipe trail slowly from the corner of his mouth. He sat for almost a minute, staring across the room.

"Most of these men died of natural causes or in accidents. Heart attacks in a business where heart attacks are an occupational hazard. A high-stress business, oil is, and these were high-rolling gentlemen without exception, and all in their fifties and sixties."

"How about Bridges? He wasn't in the oil business."

"Red Bridges was a roustabout, a salvager, a gambler. Hell, for four or five years after the war he ran deepwater salvage off the Japanese coast. Shipbuilding is a very mean business. And Red had a bad weight problem on top of that. In his sixties, and a hundred pounds overweight. Prime candidate for a coronary. See what I mean, O'Hara? Without some proof, nobody'll believe you."

"That's why he can operate the way he does. Nobody's got guts enough to talk about it openly. Hell, we're off the goddamn record."

"Do you have some personal stake in this?" Hooker asked, surprised by his sudden outburst.

"I'm a journalist and I'm trying to do my job the best way there is. I know Chameleon exists. You know it. Apparently dozens of other powerful businessmen know it. And you're his chief target. Why?"

"We refuse to pay extortion. That's what it is, y'know, blackmail by fear."

"But why AMRAN? Why not Ampex or Blue Diamond?"

"I don't know. I suppose because we are the youngest of the oil conglomerates they think we're the most vulnerable."

He was sweating and he took out a handkerchief and patted his face. The pacemaker was ticking furiously. "I'm sorry. I . . . uh, I'm having a chill. Nothing to be concerned about. Blood's just too thin. One of the hazards of growing old."

O'Hara was genuinely concerned. The man seemed to have aged another year or two as they talked. His face was gray and his eyes had become listless.

"I'm sorry, I know this was an imposition," O'Hara said. "I'm grateful you took the time to talk with me."

Talking about Chameleon had at least cleared Hooker's mind. Now his concern was dealing with O'Hara. "Perhaps another time," he said.

"One last thing. Did Chameleon sabotage the *Thoreau* and the Aquila automobile?"

The general put his pipe aside and made a steeple of his fingers. He leaned forward, across his desk. "Mr. O'Hara, I told you before, nobody in the business wil discuss Chameleon. He's a profit-terrorist. People are afraid of him. He's vindictive. Most of my peers think that if they ignore him, he'll ignore them. Talking about him gives his actions a certain legitimacy. Nobody wants to do that."

"No guts, no glory, General."

"Chameleon is an apocalypse."

"Were you warned about the *Thoreau* or the Aquila? I mean, was there extortion involved or was it simply sabotage?"

Hooker was becoming frustrated. He said sternly, "You can't use any of this, young man, because none of it can be proven. The *Thoreau* lies in four hundred feet of Arctic sea. The Aquila's back on the drawing board."

"He's not going to stop, you know," O'Hara said. "He's got a good thing going. Give me a deposition to the effect that you suspect Chameleon was responsible for just one of these accidents, and it will lend credence to the story. It would be a start. Get it out in the open. This guy feeds on secrecy."

"Mr. O'Hara, do you know who Chameleon is? Where he lives, where he operates from? Anything about him at all?"

"Is he the same Chameleon who was on the list of war criminals in 1945?" O'Hara asked.

Hooker tapped the ash out of his pipe and tamped down the remaining tobacco.

"The man you refer to was killed at Hiroshima," he said. "His name was removed from the list in 1950."

"Do you know who he really was?"

"His name was Asieda. His identity was one of the most closely guarded secrets of the war. His specialty was espionage and he was accountable only to Tojo himself. He trained all the Japanese agents."

"Ironic, isn't it?"

"What?"

"That the Chameleon we're looking for and the war criminal should have the same code name."

"If there's an irony, it's that this fortress was once his headquarters. He trained his agents in these very buildings. And God knows what atrocities were committed in the three floors of dungeons below us. That's how I found out about the place. I came here with the Occupation Forces in 1945. But there was nothing here. All the records had been destroyed. In fact, there's no record anywhere of Chameleon's wartime activities. As far as the Army's concerned, he never existed. It's a closed book."

"Well, I think Chameleon's here in Japan, no matter who he is. And if he's here, I can find him."

Hooker stood up, a tall and intimidating presence, his back as straight as the day he graduated from West Point. He stuck out his hand. "Good day, Mr. O'Hara. We'll talk about depositions when you have more than suspicions and theories. Quite frankly, I think your guts are bigger than your brains. But I still wish you luck."

"One more thing," O'Hara said as the general led him toward the door. "Do you know anything about a big oil strike called Midas?"

The old man stood at the door with his back to O'Hara. Fury blazed in his eyes as O'Hara asked the question. The pacemaker began to clatter again. He coughed, to cover the telltale rattle of his man-altered heart.

" 'Midas' you say? An oil field." He turned back to O'Hara once he had regained his composure. "Never heard of it."

"Perhaps the biggest in the world."

Hooker chuckled. "And where would this be?"

"I don't know."

"Nor do I, sir, and oil is my business. Mr. O'Hara, I admire your imagination. But I think it's a bit far-fetched to think there is an oil field of the size you suggest and nobody knows about it."

"I know about it."

"Fine—then why don't you go find it. I'm afraid you'll have to excuse me now. It's time for my nap."

7

AFTER GARVEY HAD USHERED O'Hara out of Dragon's Nest, he returned to Hooker's office. The old man was sitting behind his desk, his face the color of clay, the pacemaker hammering in his chest.

Tick, tick, tick, tick, tick, tick . . .

"Take it easy, sir. I was monitoring the room, I heard it all."

"Did you hear him ask about Midas?" Hooker croaked.

Garvey nodded. "We'll just have to change our plans a little."

"How did he get all this information!" the old man roared suddenly. Blood flooded his face and the color changed to bright red.

"He's good, General. As good as they come. It was a calculated risk."

"Then we need a new goddamn calculator."

"We'll have him out in a couple of hours."

"And what about Chameleon?"

"General, we're that close to him," Garvey said. He held up a thumb and a forefinger, an inch apart.

"We've been that close to him for too long," Hooker said. He stood up and walked to a dark corner of the room, standing with his hands clenched behind his back, his tall frame outlined by the grow lights in the hothouse behind him. I should have been President instead of that son of a bitch Eisenhower," he went on. "I should have been a lot of things that I wasn't, thanks to that . . . that albatross around my neck. Damn it, man, *damn* it."

He fell silent, and the faulty metronome in his chest finally began to slow down.

"Kill them both," he said, and the venom seemed to linger on his lips like spit. "Kill them both tonight."

Fog whisked through the train station, urged by a chilly breeze. At one end of the station, a tall Caucasian sat smoking a Gitane. There was a phone booth next to him and when it rang the first time he ignored it. It rang only once. Then a few seconds later it started again. The second time he stood up and answered it.

"Higashiyama station," he said in a soft Gaelic accent.

"Excuse me, I must have the wrong number."

"Whom did you want?"

"The Italian gentleman."

"And the name?"

"Spettro."

"Good evening, Mr. Quill."

"Is your phone clean?"

"Public booth at the train station."

"Excellent. There is a change in plans."

"All right."

"O'Hara has become a problem. He's gone much further than we thought possible. And in the wrong direction. It is important that he be terminated immediately. Is he covered?"

"He's due here in three minutes."

"Do it as quickly as feasible, using your customary élan."

"How about the others?"

"Get this done first. Everything else is scrubbed."

"Affirmative."

"Sorry old man, you've done A-1. The man's smarter than we thought. It's a question of priorities."

"I understand."

"Let me know as soon as possible."

"Of course. *Komban wa.*"

"*Komban wa.*"

Tony Falmouth hung up the phone and sat back down to wait for the train.

O'Hara first noticed the woman when she got on the train at the Tofuki-ji station on the outskirts of Kyoto. He noticed her again as he got up to leave the train, three stops later, at the Higashiyama station.

He saw her reflection in the window, staring at him from the other side of the car. The doors opened and he hurried out, eager to get back to the house and discuss the Hooker meeting with Kimura.

The woman moved out behind him, scurried around other passengers and shuffled up beside him. "Please, follow me. I must talk to you," she whispered and hurried on.

O'Hara was preoccupied by the woman and paid little attention to the other passengers in the station. Tony Falmouth was sitting at the far end of the platform. He got up, walking quickly after O'Hara, side-stepping pools of street light.

O'Hara followed her through the marketplace, past the fish stalls, ignoring the vendors who shouted at him and shook eel and octopus in his face, to the edge of Maruyama Park. She was a tallish woman for an Oriental, and wore the gown and obi and the chalk-painted face and blood-red lips of a geisha. A jade hairpin protruded from the bun at the back of her head. It was dark, and fog drifted out of the park and swirled down into the market.

"It is dangerous for me to be here," she whispered. "Please, stand with your back to me. The bus will come soon. When it comes, please get on it and go a stop or two before you get off."

O'Hara hesitated for a moment. A dark street, fog, and he was standing with his back to her. Not smart. He stood very still, listening for sounds of movement from her. At first he heard only her breathing and then there was something else. It was not a sound as much as a feeling. He felt almost dizzy with excitement, and although he could not see the woman, he felt drawn to her, as if there were an electric current flowing between them.

He turned and looked up the street at the lights shimmering in the fog and the headlights of the bus, pinpoint halos in the distance.

"What do you want?" he asked.

"Was it not you who asked for information at the Kabuki-za in Tokyo?"

He hesitated again. The pull was so strong that he almost turned around. Fog swirled around them like flux.

"Yes," he said finally.

She spoke in a whisper. "You seek the one known as Chameleon?"

"Yes."

"Why?"

"To talk."

"Talk? Hah! You must kill him."

He wanted to turn again. His nerves were humming. He felt strangely in tune with her, but it was a feeling he could not interpret. He thought back to the previous night when he was doing his exercises and the presence of Chameleon had seemed overwhelming. Now he felt it again. It was as if the woman was marked with Chameleon's scent.

"I am not an assassin," he said.

"You will understand when you meet him."

"When will that be?"

She leaned closer. "Chameleon is here."

Now he felt almost elevated. His blood surged through his veins, and fuses of fire streaked down his arms and legs. He could almost reach out and touch the danger in the air but, oddly, he felt no immediate threat.

"You mean here in Japan?"

"In Kyoto."

"Where in Kyoto?"

"I have written the address—a house in the Shiga prefecture—on this piece of paper. He will return tonight at nine. And he will be alone."

"How do you know this?"

"I know. The why of it is not important. He will be there."

The bus lights swept over them.

"Why are you doing this?"

There was a pause. "Because I am a prisoner and I want to be free."

"A prisoner?"

"Yes. Here, take the paper, put it in your pocket. Quickly, he has spies everywhere."

Without turning, O'Hara said, "I must know . . . how did you know I was looking for Chameleon?"

The bus pulled up at the curb and stopped.

"Please, do not betray me," she said. "Go now. Nine o'clock. Do not be late."

There was no time left.

O'Hara jumped aboard the bus and heard the doors swish shut behind him.

8

A HUNDRED FEET AWAY, among the trees in the park, Tony Falmouth watched O'Hara board the bus. He twisted, from his ear, the small speaker attached to his long-range parabolic mike. He had heard every word perfectly. He made an instant decision to follow the woman and drop O'Hara for the moment. It would be no problem to pick up O'Hara's trail. But this woman held the key, he felt it. His pulse began to trip. He was close. The small listening device telescoped into a thin accordion-like rod. He put it in his pocket, and jogging from tree to tree, started to follow her.

He followed her away from the market, along the edge of sprawling Maruyama Park. She skirted the heart of the city and shuffled into a small suburban section, down through myriad quiet, high-fenced walkways that sheltered homes from which sequestered sounds segued as he passed from house to house: a baby crying, a radio playing elevator music, another soft rock, two women laughing softly, a man singing opera in pigeon Italian, a Coke TV commercial in Japanese. Lanterns swung idly overhead, moved by the gentle breeze, and cast Halloween shadows on the fences.

She was easy to follow; there were few people on the streets, and except for the muffled sounds from the houses, it was so quiet it was almost funereal. He could hear her sandals clopping on the cobblestones a block or so ahead of him.

Then she did the unexpected. She cut back to the main street and entered a small restaurant on Nijo-dori Street near the Hotel Fujita. Might she be a waitress? Or perhaps the manager? He did not want to lose her. She had given O'Hara an address, and Falmouth wanted that address.

He waited a few minutes and followed her in. It was not a fancy place, but it was serene and cool and very dark. It was so dark that it took him a moment to spot her, although the restaurant was almost empty. She was sitting alone near the back. The wall panels were open and there was a moss garden in the rear with a goldfish pond near the window. She was watching the enormous gold and black carp appraising the bottom for food. Falmouth walked to her table.

"Excuse me," he said. "Do you speak English?"

She shook her head.

Falmouth quickly switched to Japanese. "I am a visitor here," he said. "I have always heard Kyoto is the most beautiful city in the world. Then I saw you and I forgot Kyoto. I realize this is quite improper, to approach you this way, but there is a Zen phrase which says, 'Take time to enjoy the garden, you may pass it only once.' I . . . uh, I knew I probably would never see you again, so I followed you from the market. Please forgive my—"

She put her hand to his lips and silenced him. "I am not offended," she said in a low voice he could hardly hear. "I have lived in America. I understand Western ways."

She turned away and looked back at the fish.

So far, so good, Falmouth thought. Now for the big move. He played the flustered swain, sophisticated but with a touch of anxiety. "My name is John Willoughby. I'm from London. I really am taken with you. I could lie, of course, and tell you I am lonely and want some company. But the fact is, I would like to be with you. May I buy you dinner?"

She chuckled softly and looked back over her shoulder at him. The jade handle of her hairpin glowed green against the jet-black bun of hair, and he could see her eyes glittering in the dim light as she whispered, "Yes, John Willoughby from London, you may."

Kimura was away from the house when O'Hara returned, but Sammi was in the garden meditating. O'Hara waited for him to finish.

"I need to talk to Tokenrui-san," he said. "When will he be back?"

Sammi shrugged. "You know him, he moves with the spirit."

"An apt observation," Kimura said. They turned and saw the old man standing in the doorway. "And what is it that is so urgent, Kazuo?"

"I'll take a powder," Sammi said.

"It's okay, this concerns us all," said O'Hara.

"You seem sad," Kimura said.

"I need your help, Tokenrui-san. But in asking, I do not wish to offend you. You are as my father."

"I know that, Kazuo. And I can see from the trouble on your face that it concerns you deeply, asking me this. I understand it is something you must do. So . . .?"

"So—you knew Chameleon, didn't you, Tokenrui-san?"

Kimura pondered the question for a few moments. "The world is full of Chameleons," he said finally.

"Not the Chameleon I'm talking about. I know you trained the war chiefs of the Imperial Army in the Way of the Secret Warrior, before and during the war. Chameleon was head of a special branch of the secret service accountable only to Tojo himself. He had to be *higaru-dashi.*"

"That is a logical deduction. I am astounded no one has made it before this."

"Nobody cared before now."

"And what is different about now?"

"I care now. And a lot of innocent people have died because of this man. A lot more will die."

"You are sure it is the same Chameleon?"

"I'm not sure at all. But I think you know the answer. Tokenrui-san, is Chameleon still alive?"

Kimura looked straight into O'Hara's eyes. He shook his head. "No. The man you speak of as Chameleon is dead."

"But you did train him. He knew the Way of the Secret Warrior."

Kimura hesitated a moment and then nodded. "He is dead now. I can see no violation of confidence by telling you that."

"How long has he been dead?"

"The record says Yamuchi Asieda died in the holocaust at Hiroshima."

"I'm not interested in the records. Forget the damn records."

"I cannot do that, Kazuo. Nothing will be gained by changing things as they exist."

"I'm not interested in exposing some second-rate war criminal, I—"

"Wait. Before you go on: Yamuchi, the man you know as Chameleon, was loved by many people. He was not a war criminal to us, he was a man who sacrificed much for his country. To my knowledge, he committed no acts of atrocity. He trained the *kancho* and he directed them. There was none better. One reason he was so good is that people trusted him. He had a great empathy for people, that is why they were attracted to him. It is why he was number one. He was also very clever, a fly too fast for the spider's web."

"He must have done something. The government spent five years verifying his death."

"And why do you think they spent such time and money?"

"They must have wanted him real bad."

"They?"

"The Army, the CID, whoever . . ."

"Whoever, you say. One person, perhaps?"

O'Hara thought for a moment. "Yes, I suppose one person with enough clout."

"Ah, clout, the magic word . . ."

Clout, thought O'Hara. Enough clout to place a name on the list of war criminals.

"Like a general maybe?" O'Hara said.

"Ah, you begin to look beyond the obvious. Not 'they,' not some faceless organization. Him. One man."

"Hooker was military governor here for six years," O'Hara said. "From 1945 to 1951."

"Yes," Kimura said. "With a passionate hatred of Chameleon."

"Why?"

"An old wound. They were deadly enemies, remember."

"The war was over, Tokenrui-san, a lot of enemies were forgiven."

"Not all, however."

"But what did he do to Hooker, to kindle that kind of hatred?"

The old man pondered the question for a very long time, then said, "Perhaps he was frustrated because he could not identify Chameleon. There were no records. And no one ever betrayed the secret of his identity."

"You think Hooker had some kind of revenge motive?"

Kirmura nodded. "It is certainly a possibility."

"Hooker says Chameleon is a blackmailer, an extortionist, a terrorist. You name it. He implied that the whole industry uses Chameleon's services. Now they're his victims. They're terrified of him."

"I assure you, the Chameleon you know as Asieda is dead."

Kimura sat before the tea table and took out a flat box of cigarettes. "These are Shermans from New York. I understand they are superb." He took one out. It was pink with a gold-wrapped filter.

"I will have to think about the aesthetics of these," he said, holding up the cigarette and contemplating it; then he lit it, taking a deep drag and exhaling very slowly. "Five cigarettes a day. That's what the spirits permit me."

"How do you know that?" O'Hara said skeptically.

"I asked them."

"Tokenrui-san," O'Hara said. "You can solve the riddle of Chameleon for me. I am certain of it. If the man is dead, let me use your knowledge to put an end to this . . . this *guntai shi,* this death army."

"Kimura sat on the floor, crossing his legs in the lotus position. "Yamuchi Asieda was a wealthy importer in Tokyo, a man of royal blood and an honorable man," he said. "He was inducted into the *higaru-dashi* in 1939, a candidate for Tokenrui from the beginning. A man of consummate skill with the sword, as agile as a hummingbird, and a man who achieved the state of the seventh level with almost mystical persuasion.

"Yamuchi Asieda was not in favor of the war. His business took him all over the world and he knew how great the stakes were, how big the gamble. He was not a war lord, not an assassin. He was a man who loved jewelry, paintings, Dresden china. But the Emperor himself asked Asieda to take over the training of agents for the secret service. It was quite natural. Asieda had partners all over the world, so he set about building a network of spies. The Emperor in exchange agreed that his identity would never be revealed. He took the code name Chameleon and selected Dragon's Nest as his headquarters because it was remote and impenetrable.

"The only people who knew his true identity were four members of the War Council, and they all died at Hiroshima. When the war was over, Asieda became a nomad, wandering the islands, his identity lost forever in the ashes of the war. He died several years ago. So you see, this man was no terrorist, not an assassin. I can tell you no more, Kazuo —to do so would violate my word of honor."

O'Hara wanted to press him, but he knew better. Instead he took the slip of paper out of his pocket. "A woman who followed me on the train gave me this."

He handed it to Kimura. The old man looked at the slip without comment and handed it back.

"She says Chameleon will be there alone, tonight. Nine o'clock."

"And who was this woman?"

"I only saw her for a moment. She appeared to be a geisha. She followed me from the train. There was desperation in her voice. I asked her why she was turning him in and she said she was a prisoner, she wanted her freedom."

Kimura puffed on his pink cigarette and blew smoke rings in the air. "It seems too obvious for a trap. But then, what could be less obvious than the most obvious thing of all."

"Tokenrui-san . . ."

"Do not go tonight. Give me another day or two to sort this out."

"Tokenrui-san, I have not asked you to break your vow of silence.

Do not ask me to play a coward's game. She will lead me to him. I am certain of it."

"You know nothing of the woman. Nothing of the house. Nothing of Chameleon. And yet you would walk into this?"

"I will be prepared."

"If this Chameleon is as you think, are you prepared for a knife in the back? A wire around the throat? A silent bullet in the head?"

"I will be prepared."

"You try my faith in you."

"This is today. I live for today. You taught me that. If the spirit flies tomorrow, it will be as full as I can make it."

Kimura said nothing more. He stared past O'Hara at the wall. O'Hara finally got up.

"I respect and honor your silence, Tokenrui-san, I hope you understand why I must go."

"When the fool has enough scars, he becomes a wise man," said Kimura, still staring at the wall.

"*Arigato.*"

"Be careful." And as O'Hara started out the door, the old man looked up at him and smiled. "When you write this story of yours, remember, rhythm is the best measure of the latitude and opulence of a writer. If unskilled, he is at once detected by the poverty of his chimes."

"I'll remember that. Does the Tendai say that?"

"No, Ralph Waldo Emerson said it."

Laughing, O'Hara left the house.

"Shall I follow him?" Sammi asked.

"Of course."

She had been elusive throughout the meal, saying very little, eating her raw fish and sipping sake and making him talk about himself. He was a widower, he had told her, and was in the book business. It was his first vacation alone. He had dreamed of coming to Kyoto, but the trip had turned out to be lonelier than he had thought.

She had been sympathetic.

Now she led him down through more fenced walkways, past other sounds, into the quiet, almost fairylike residential section. She opened a gate in the high fence and led him through it. A large two-story house, unlike the others around it, sat fifty feet or so back from the street. Its tapered roof and carved columns told Falmouth it was the house of a wealthy person. The grounds were perfectly manicured and spotted with dwarf willows and pines. She held a finger to her mouth and led him around to the side of the place. A small creek trickled tunefully through the grounds and disappeared into the shadows, and somewhere in the back, wind chimes sang to the breeze.

Falmouth checked the place as carefully as he could without seeming obvious. The house was L-shaped. The only lights were at the far corner of the wing.

Deserted.

Beautiful. It might take some twisting to get the address. He didn't have time to woo the information out of the lady. It had to be quick.

She stopped in front of one of the chambers in the main wing of the house and quietly slid back its paneled door. It wasn't much of a step into the house, which was built on short, thick stilts, raising it no more than a foot or so above the ground.

When they were inside, she whispered, "My father lives in the back. No one else is here. We will leave the light off." She slid the panel shut, but light from the street filtered through the thin, opaque glass doors.

She unbuttoned his jacket and took it off, then his tie, then drew him down beside her. He thought, damn the luck. To walk into a tasty piece like this and it all has to be business.

She undid his gold watch and laid it gently on the floor beside the tatami.

It was nine o'clock.

She lay back and drew him down beside her. Her lips brushed his. She reached back and drew out the hairpin. Affixed to the jade handle was a stiletto six inches long.

Her hair tumbled down around her shoulders.

What the hell, Falmouth thought, a few more minutes more or less—

It was almost the last thought he ever had.

As he leaned over to kiss her, she held the dirk at arm's length and then plunged it into his ear.

Fire burned deep into the back of his throat, seared his brain and then erupted in pain.

His scream sliced the night like a hatchet. He rolled away from her, struggled to his knees, his trembling fingers touching the jade hilt, which stuck obscenely from the hole in his ear. The fire burned deeper and the pain of steel in his brain was unbearable.

He got to his feet but the room was already a blur, the pain frozen in his throat. He was growling like a fox in a trap. The floor tilted. He turned, tried to regain his balance and stumbled sideways and plunged headlong through the door. The glass shattered into hundreds of light blossoms. The frame cracked and the door crashed with him into the garden.

God, I'm losing it, he thought. Must . . . get . . . it out. And with all his strength he drew the stiletto from his head. Pain poured into the wound like burning oil. He staggered through the fish pond and fell face down into the rock garden. The knife dropped from his fingers into the creek.

Plump.

O'Hara found the address with little trouble. He tried the gate and found it unlocked. He looked at his watch. Nine o'clock. Perfect.

He had one leg through the gate when he heard the scream. It was unworldly, a man, shattering the night with anguish. He ran toward the scream, and as he rounded the corner of the house he saw a man plunge through a door. The man staggered into the fish pond, both hands clutching the side of his head, and then collapsed.

O'Hara ran to him and rolled him over on his back. "My God," he cried, "Tony!"

The woman stood in the shattered doorway of the house, a dark shape framed by the lights behind her, her black hair hanging in long strands about her shoulders.

"He is dead, or will be in a moment," she said in a harsh voice. "The blade was soaked in arsenic."

She reached up and grabbed the crown of her hair and pulled it and the thick black hair fell away.

A wig.

She threw it on the floor. She clutched her blouse with both hands and ripped it open. A padded shirt. She threw it aside also.

And suddenly she was no longer she.

She had become he.

A he, tattooed from waist to chest with intertwined chameleons, writhing across his belly, up his chest, between his pectorals, his left nipple forming an obscene eye in one of the vivid lizards. Each one was a different color, the vivid patterns along the slender, twisting bodies ranging from cobalt blue to lemon orange to flaming red, their eyes glittering venomously, forked tongues licking the man's hard stomach.

O'Hara was face to face with Chameleon.

9

HE WAS THE ULTIMATE CHAMELEON; the she-devil turned Satan.

What was it Danilov had said? "I know and I don't know. . . . Everybody, nobody. . . . The chameleon is never what it seems."

"So, Round-Eyes has finally met his match," the tattooed man said. "You should pray you are more fortunate than your friend."

O'Hara rolled Falmouth over on his back. His gray eyes looked up with terror, as though he were looking at the face of death. Blood trickled from his ears, his nose, his mouth. His lips moved, a sporadic tremble, like a butterfly flirting with a flower.

"Demon—"

"Tony, can you hear me?"

"Demon . . . Bradley, me . . . got us all. No bloody . . . wonder."

"Tony!"

His eyes cleared for a moment. He smiled up at O'Hara. "Owe me . . . hundred and twenty-five thou, Sailor," he said and died.

O'Hara looked back at the doorway. Chameleon was motionless, hands at his sides, fingers stretched out, legs slightly parted.

This was no old man; in fact, he was probably not much older than O'Hara. His body was hard and sinewed, his head shaved bald. O'Hara knew this man from somewhere.

"Okari," O'Hara said. "You are the kendo teacher, Okari."

"*Hai.* And you are the *beikoku* who is called Kazuo."

"That's right, I'm the American. You speak English well."

"I had a good teacher."

"Did he teach you how to kill helpless men?"

"Helpless. Hah! Look on his ankle. Up his sleeve. He would have done the same. An assassin has no honor."

"He was my friend."

"Then you need to be educated in the selection of friends. In fact, your education is about to begin. Is it true that you are a master of the sword?"

O'Hara said nothing. The garden was soundless except for the trickling of water across the rocks in the fish pond and the tinkle of wind chimes from somewhere in the back of the house.

O'Hara nodded. "I have worked with the sword," he said.

"You are too modest, *Marui-me*. Come, Round-Eyes, give me a lesson."

Chameleon backed slowly into the small room. O'Hara walked to the smashed doorway and looked in. It was a bedroom. The tatamis were laid out carefully in one end of the room. An obi lay at the head of the mats. There was a low table near the bed with a stick of incense smoldering in a holder. One overhead lantern shed an even but dim glow over the room. Chameleon slid back a panel in the wall and removed two samurai swords. The tattooed chameleons wrapped around his sides and across his back. Hardly an inch of skin had escaped the tattooist's needle. He turned around to face O'Hara.

He was a bizarre sight, his tattooed body glistening in the yellow light from the lantern, the eye shadow, rouge and lipstick still concealing his true features. He knelt in the center of the room and placed the swords on the floor, their hilts aimed toward O'Hara.

"It is your choice," Chameleon said.

"I did not come here to kill you," O'Hara said.

"Good, then we are of the same mind. I don't intend to let you."

"You should not have killed Falmouth."

"I have killed many like him. They come for blood and I give them blood."

"And did you kill all of them the same way, by hiding behind the skirts of a woman and striking when their eyes were closed?"

The muscles in Chameleon's jaw shimmered but he pressed his point. "You both came to kill me. He has failed. I am offering you a chance to avenge his death. Am I to believe that a son of the sword is afraid to lift the sword?"

"I prefer to follow the law."

Chameleon stood as O'Hara spoke. He took one of the swords and pulled it from its wooden scabbard and took several deliberate steps toward O'Hara, stopping perhaps three feet in front of him. He placed the point of his blade on O'Hara's throat and drew the sword slowly down to O'Hara's waist. It snipped off the buttons of his shirt, and they clattered to the floor. Chameleon flicked the shirt open with the point of his blade. There was a hairline cut from O'Hara's throat down to his navel.

"Take up the samurai, Round-Eyes," Chameleon ordered.

"No. I have taken a vow not to—"

"—defend yourself? This is an instrument of honor. To master it for play is an insult to my ancestors."

"If I lift the sword against you, I will dishonor it," O'Hara said. "You do not deserve honor. You kill from behind."

"You know the mark of *okubyo*, the coward? The cheek cut that brands those who are afraid to defend their own honor?" He put the point of the samurai sword against O'Hara's cheekbone. A pearl of blood appeared.

"I think you are the coward," O'Hara said.

Rage boiled up into Chameleon's face. He stared at O'Hara with the eyes of a reptile, beads of hate framed by his chalk-white painted face, scarlet-slashed lips and black-shadowed eyelids. He tightened his grip on the leather hilt of the sword. The sound of skin and leather feathered O'Hara's ears.

Chameleon stepped back six inches. He raised the sword over his head and then to the side. He was in a classic striking pose. One swipe could easily lop O'Hara's head off.

O'Hara's jaw muscles twitched. To permit Chameleon to provoke him into betraying his own honor was unthinkable.

Chameleon leaned slightly on his right foot. His arms were raised straight out from his shoulder, the sword tilted straight up. He shifted his weight and struck.

The shining blade sighed through the air and O'Hara saw it coming in slow motion, a blur of death.

He felt it nick his Adam's apple.

Chameleon's recovery was perfect. In a single move he returned to the strike position, the Position of the Ox.

O'Hara could feel the warmth of his blood trickling down his neck.

Chameleon shifted his weight to the right again. His eyes lost their expression. They became fixed. O'Hara knew the next swing would behead him.

It was now a matter of defense. Honor demanded that he respond.

He stepped away from Chameleon's sword and bowed.

He picked up the other sword. Chameleon returned to the standing position and lowered his blade.

O'Hara checked the weight of the sword, hefting it first in his right hand, then his left, weighing it by feel. It was heavier than he was accustomed to, but weighted toward the blade rather than the hilt, which was good. The hilt was scarred and old, but the cutting edge of the blade twinkled like a razor.

He knew the kendo teacher would probably favor the same death blows as the stick fighters. He would go for the chin-shoulder strike, or perhaps the hip cut.

Chameleon backed across the room and stood with his sword at his side. He began a very low chant, his eyes focused somewhere outside the room. Memories tumbled from his subconscious, bits and pieces to be flushed from his mind, purifying planes and reflexes; smoke and fire and stinking flesh and howling boluses coughing steel, and the raven-croaked gospel of death; angry-voiced silhouettes on paper screens and a woman's soft arms along dark streets; black, steam-spitting Goliath, chaotic pilgrims, earthquake tremor and volcano's roar, the agony-cry of iron against iron, wheel against rail, and a city, far enough behind, evaporating in boiling dust that rises to the brink of heaven.

Nightmares, congregated on the rim of his mind. Purged, they fled.

He was ready.

O'Hara fixed on the tinkle of the wind chimes, letting the sound cleanse his mind. He felt propelled out of his body, viewing the room from high above. His ears became the ears of a wolf. He could hear the air moving in the room and feel Chameleon's energy electrifying it. He became attuned to the space, could feel its currents, its molecules.

He faced Chameleon, spread his legs slightly, held his sword at arm's length in front of him and lowered it slowly to the ground. The attitude of the challenge.

Chameleon made the first move, a slashing drive straight for him, so quick that the sword was a silver blur singing through the air. O'Hara jumped back and parried the blow. The steel blades clashed, rang out in the tiny room, and his wrists felt the power of the attack.

Chameleon moved like the wind and O'Hara moved with him, two men pirouetting with death to the clashing rhythm of their weapons. The room bristled with silver flashes, the *shush* of steel slicing the air, the harsh cry of steel on steel.

To have tried to watch Chameleon would have been fatal; the tattooed man was much too fast. O'Hara sensed rather than saw his moves, feeling the air currents move with him, sensoring Chameleon's energy field. O'Hara's moves were classic defense moves, triggered by Chameleon's darts and twists. He heard the blade singing through the air with each of Chameleon's thrusts. He stepped out of time, moved mentally into the seventh level and every move was as if in slow motion. He felt the gleaming edge of Chameleon's blade slicing toward him from the left quadrant, center quadrant, then left again, then low, then thrust, and his own blade had time to parry, block, jab.

Chameleon, too, seemed possessed of an extra sense. His sword was like a specter, swallowed in movement. It was a dangerous and lethal presence, heard but not seen. Death sighed in the air of the small bedroom.

Chameleon was the ghost, silent and effortless. O'Hara was the dancer, his ears keened to each rustle of silk, each movement of air in the room, each whip of steel. His eyes seemed clouded over, almost transfixed, as he fought his defensive game against the tattooed man. He parried and countered, leaping this way and that, spinning, kicking, reacting instinctively to each of Chameleon's moves, drawing on twelve years of learning, practice and discipline.

The Japanese man was more self-assured, more aggressive. The sword moved fluidly in his hands. He deftly caught the low table in his path on the corner of his foot, and without missing a step, sent it spinning out of his way, crashing against the wall.

Their blades clashed constantly as they circled the room, each a dervish target for the other. The room crackled with their energy. Then Chameleon made a kill thrust, a spinning move followed by a leap, a false thrust and a charge. O'Hara side-stepped the plunge, caught Chameleon's sword near the hilt of his own as they spun past each other, and with a hard wrist reverse, he slashed Chameleon's shoulder.

It was a graze rather than a cut. A thin red streak appeared from Chameleon's shoulder to his collarbone. He stopped, poised, legs set perfectly, sweat-streaked muscles ridging his arms. The tattooed lizards on his chest seemed to move with each breath.

He stared at O'Hara, danger glittering in his irises.

O'Hara made a timid thrust, and another, and then, moving right to left to right, charged and slashed. Chameleon rolled sideways, dropped almost to his knee and then stood up and made his thrust. His samurai sword swept past O'Hara's, inside his thrust, and in slow motion, O'Hara saw the point of steel moving straight toward his eye. He moved his head slightly, felt its razor edge slice through his ear lobe, felt the harsh burn of the wound and dismissed it, and spun close to Chameleon, so close he could feel the heat of his body and once again, he tried a wrist reverse.

But the tattooed swordsman anticipated the move, twisting himself, regaining his balance, bringing the hilt of his weapon down and locking the two swords together for an instant, handle to handle, then twisting hard from the waist, feeling the surge of power up into his shoulders and down his arms into his wrists, twisting harder in that moment of contact.

O'Hara felt his sword wrench away and snap from his fingers, it soared out of his hand, and augering the air, it slashed into the wall and stayed there, its hilt gleaming with sweat, six feet away.

Chameleon landed on the side of one foot, a fault that almost snapped his ankle. He lost balance for the blink of an eye and O'Hara leaped past Chameleon, landing on his shoulder and rolling to the wall, coming out of the roll with his knees against his chest, surging up and yanking his weapon from its trap in time to catch Chameleon's next thrust on the flat side of the blade. They smacked together, weapons V-eed between them, and hit the wall with a shattering impact. O'Hara thrust his leg between Chameleon's, hooked it back and rolled away at the same time, flipping Chameleon's leg out behind him. Chameleon, thrown momentarily off balance, twisted as he turned and fell on his side as O'Hara leaped back to his feet. But Chameleon had lost it only for an instant, arching his back and hopping back on his feet and recovering with another offensive move. This time it was Chameleon's thrust, badly off mark, which O'Hara parried, twisting as he did. The move almost broke Chameleon's wrist, but he did not lose the sword. He reversed his move, spun on the ball of one foot and made a wide, sweeping slash at O'Hara's legs.

O'Hara leaped in the air and pulled his legs up, felt the cold scythe as it swished under his feet. Chameleon spun in midair like a twirler, brought the blade full around and made a second swipe. O'Hara caught it on his sword but the fierce power of the three-hundred-and-sixty-degree swing rang up the steel blade. Pain streaked into O'Hara's fingers, then his wrists, his arms, his biceps. The sword wrenched out of one hand but he held onto it with the other and rolled away, seeking a far corner of the room to regain his strength and composure.

But Chameleon gave no quarter. He charged again, a hopping move, bounding across the room, the sword held high over head.

As O'Hara straightened out of the roll and moved his feet under him, he sensed movement near the shattered panel of the room, and then heard the harsh order: *"Tomare!* Stop!"

They froze like statues, Chameleon poised with his sword overhead, O'Hara crouched, his sword in front of him.

Kimura entered the room. Sammi stood silent near the door.

Kimura stood like a referee between them, his right arm held straight out from the shoulder, the palm of his hand pointed toward the ground.

"To draw blood against each other is to dishonor the *higaru-dashi,*" he said quietly. "Whoever made this challenge must kill me before going on."

Okari stared at Kimura, the sword wavering in his two hands. "I do not understand," he said.

"Before you kill each other, you must kill me first," the old man repeated.

"Why do you stand between us?" Okari demanded. "This has nothing to do with the *higaru.* "

"Oh? You question the authority of the Tokenrui?"

"No!" cried Chameleon. "But this man is a *beikoku-jin,* he—"

"So he is an American. What difference? Would you attack an unarmed man?"

"Do not insult me, Tokenrui-san, I offered him his choice of weapons."

"And if he is not trained in the use of them, he might as well be unarmed."

"I know about O'Hara-san. He is the one they call Kazuo. He knows the way of the sword."

"I named him Kazuo. I have taken him as my son. And he, too, is *higaru-dashi.* "

Chameleon was shocked.

Kimura looked at both men. The muscles in his face were ridged, his eyes stern. "I thought both of you had gone beyond brawling. Do either of you think there is any honor to this duel? I fear if there is to be wisdom here, it must come from me. And if there is to be a challenge, it must be made properly and it must be approved by me."

"I made the proper challenge," O'Hara said.

Kimura looked at the thin scratch down O'Hara's chest, at the buttons on the floor. Turning to Chameleon, he said, "And you, Okari, provoked him."

"Hai. "

"You both insult me."

"Why?" demanded O'Hara.

"Because it is the way of *higaru-dashi.* Because we are all brothers, and an honorable man does not take up the sword against his brother. Because both of you are men of honor who have taken the oath of the Secret Warrior."

Okari and O'Hara stared hard at each other from opposite sides of the small room while the significance of Kimura's revelation sank in. Kimura stood between them, his arm still outstretched. Neither of them would challenge that gesture. To do so would mean to challenge Tokenrui.

Okari very precisely slid his sword into its sheath.

"*Arigato,*" Kimura said quietly.

"So, *Marui-me* has learned the Way of the Secret Warrior," Okari said.

"This man is your brother and yet you use your term 'Round-Eyes' as if it were an insult," Kimura said. "You, Okari, have you forgotten the fifth lesson of the Tendai? Your arrogance shocks me. For many years you have studied the discipline of humility and now you are about to throw it away in one foolish moment."

"He came to kill me!"

"You say that without fear of being wrong?" He walked to the far side of the room and turned, standing with his hands clasped before him. "I will remind you both, the purpose of our discipline is to make each man a competitor only with himself, for only when you have mastered that demon are you ready to challenge others."

O'Hara and Okari stood with heads lowered as Kimura chastised them, reminding them of their vows.

Okari said, "I never thought—"

"You never thought! For years you have been trained to look beyond what appears to be reality, to anticipate the unknown. Now you tell me you did not think. You are right—you did not think. Have you still to learn that one never trusts what seems obvious? Does the peacock joyously embrace the trap?"

He walked back to their side of the room and stood in front of them. "You have deceived yourselves by your failure to look beyond what seems to be. Both of you have achieved the mystery of the seventh level and yet neither of you has practiced it in this affair."

He stopped for a moment, watching the two men shuffling before him. "Could I be wrong? Perhaps neither of you is worthy to be a candidate for Tokenrui."

They both looked up with shock.

"Yes, one day I must select between you to take my place as Tokenrui. Now do you understand? I have watched and trained both of you since long before either of you achieved manhood. And at this moment, I could not choose between you."

"It never occurred to me that I might be considered," O'Hara said.

"Nor I," said Okari.

"Good. That is encouraging. Perhaps you are still in touch with humility."

"What about Sammi," O'Hara said, "isn't he a candidate?"

"Unfortunately, he will be number three. And whichever of you is not chosen as Tokenrui will be second to the one that is. I say 'unfortunately' only because Sammi is my grandson and he has trained as hard as either of you. But he has achieved only the state of the fifth level. Whatever the outcome, you three are brothers, and that can never change and if that bond is broken by either of you, you will be banished in dishonor from *higaru-dashi* forever."

"I am to call this *gaikoku no kancho* my brother?" Okari said.

"Does one tiger condemn the stripes of another?" said Kimura sternly to Okari.

The younger man flashed a look at O'Hara and then back at Kimura. "The *beikoku-jin* would have killed me," he said.

"Do you know for sure the American would kill you, or does the fear in your heart speak for you?"

Okari hesitated, staring hard at the green-eyed American.

"He is not a spy and he does not kill," said the old man. "And he is not one of them. He came back to expose them."

"He does not deny he is Chameleon," said O'Hara.

"Yes and no," said Kimura. "He is Chameleon and he is not."

"Yeah, the Chameleon is never what it appears," O'Hara said.

"This time it is quite true. The Chameleon is certainly not what you believe him to be. You both have much to learn. When you both have taken the Walk of a Thousand Days, and the special powers of Zen have been revealed to you, perhaps then your wisdom will be less cloudy. For now, we must decide on our next step. May I suggest we have some tea —all this talk has made me thirsty."

10

"THIS IS CHAMELEON, but not the Chameleon you seek," Kimura said, putting his hand on Okari's shoulder.

O'Hara had called the hotel. As planned, Eliza and the Magician had taken the late-afternoon train to Kyoto and they were in the bar waiting for him to return from Tanabe. He did not explain where he was and what had happened, he merely gave them the address. Now they were all seated in a square. O'Hara and Gunn faced Kimura and Okari. The Magician was seated at one end of the square and Sammi faced him. Tension still crackled between O'Hara and Okari, but they listened intently as Kimura spoke.

"Imagine that I have several boxes," he began. "Each is made of glass, so we can see through it, and in each box there is an event. In each box we have placed a moment of history. But to consider these moments in their proper order, we must suspend the boxes in air so we can see each in relationship to the others. Only then can we have a true understanding of what has happened and why. Only then can we see what lies behind each event. Only then will we understand everything. If there is something significant we don't know, it will become obvious in its absence.

"So, let us begin with the first box, the one we see most clearly. In it we will put what you have learned, Kazuo, so you must tell us what you *know*, not what you think.

"What we know is that a consortium of several petroleum companies was formed. It was conceived by General Alexander Hooker, who was president of Intercon Oil. During the three or four years Hooker was negotiating this deal, the heads of all of these companies either died of heart attacks or were killed in accidents. This includes Shichi Tomoro, the head of the Japanese combine San-San, which has just become a new member of AMRAN. An experimental oil rig was also sabotaged in Alaskan waters."

"Excuse me," Eliza said, "the same thing happened with the Aquila Milena, the car Marza was driving when he was killed. We don't know why yet. And the Aquila Motor Works is now part of AMRAN, and the consortium is financing work on the car."

"Don't forget the guy in Hawaii," said the Magician.

"Yes," said O'Hara. "A man was apparently murdered for some pictures that were taken aboard the oil rig. But all they wanted to do was destroy the film."

Kimura, like a mime describing a story with his hands, hung invisible glass boxes in the air each time they brought up a new point. "It is important to remember in what order these things occurred. The dates do not matter so much as the order," he said.

"Another element in the sequence is Red Bridges," Eliza went on. "He was a salvage man in Japan right after the war. He went from that to shipbuilding and then became involved in developing a large under-water living environment. It was designed by the scuba scientist Kaginakas. Both he and Bridges later died of heart attacks. The dish, as it was called, has since been completed and taken to . . . somewhere."

"He was also involved in refitting old Liberty ships, turning them into tankers," the Magician said.

"And we learned yesterday that Bridges was part of San-San, which is now part of the consortium," Eliza added.

More boxes in the air. Kimura leaned back, concentrating on the imaginary complex he was building. "A question: Is there any doubt in your minds that these corporation people who died were actually killed by the mad one with the umbrella?"

O'Hara, Eliza and the Magician all shook their heads.

"The accidental deaths were probably executed by someone other than Danilov," O'Hara said. "Falmouth, maybe, or a Frenchman named Le Croix, who is also a faceless one, although his reputation as a sadist is well documented. But the heart attacks were caused by Danilov, there is no question."

"And why has AMRAN been singled out as a victim of this terrorist you call Chameleon?" Okari said.

"Extortion," said O'Hara. "AMRAN refused to play ball."

"Play ball?" Okari asked.

"A *beikoku no* expression," Kimura explained. "It means they would not cooperate."

"There is another box we left out," Eliza said. "The oil consultant, Lavander. He had worked for all of these companies during the past year or so, including San-San, and he was murdered too, after they went to a lot of trouble to free him from a terrorist kidnapping in South America."

"Do you think there was a connection between the two terrorist groups, those who kidnapped Lavander and those who freed him?" Kimura asked.

"No," said O'Hara. "I think it was a genuine fluke. But it apparently scared one of these oil companies. They sent a man to test Lavander, and Lavander failed. He had become a security risk to someone."

"We recovered a ledger of his," Eliza said. "It contains highly confidential figures from all of the AMRAN oil companies, as well as others he worked for. The figures could be very damaging if they got out."

"Why?" Kimura asked.

"Because they prove that the companies have lied to the public about the amount of oil they have in reserve."

"And why would they do that?"

"To control the price of oil," O'Hara said. "The profit margins are staggering—four, five hundred percent a year. The public thinks it's because there's a shortage of oil, when actually there's a surplus."

"I see. Go on."

"There was also a notation about something called Midas," O'Hara said. "And Danilov mentioned Midas to me. He said, 'Midas is lost.' "

"And Midas is another question for which there is no obvious answer at this point," said Kimura. "So, now we have six questions unanswered. First, why was the man killed in Hawaii? Second, where was this dish of Bridges' taken and what is it for? Third, what is Midas? Fourth, why was this man Lavander assassinated? Fifth, why was the oil rig sabotaged? And finally, why was the Italian car blown up? Is that correct?"

"Right," said O'Hara.

"Is there anything else?"

"Yes," said O'Hara, "what was Tony Falmouth doing here?"

"Perhaps the most revealing question of all," said Kimura. "But we will hold it for a few more minutes. Do you still believe Chameleon is alive, Kazuo?"

"I'm looking at him," O'Hara said.

"And the Chameleon you seek was a Japanese agent in World War II, correct?"

O'Hara nodded. Kimura looked at Okari and asked, "Does this look like a man who served in World War II?"

O'Hara laughed. "No," he said.

"We can assume, then, that they are two different Chameleons?"

O'Hara nodded.

"So, we now have many boxes to peer through. But before we go any further, let us deal with this anger that is between you two."

"I didn't come here to kill anyone," O'Hara said to Okari. "I came to find the truth."

"And what is the truth?" Kimura demanded.

"That Chameleon is a monster who destroys without feeling, who kills for profit."

"My son, you have been chasing a name, not a person. You have both been tricked."

"Tricked? By whom?"

"The *eikoku-jin* outside, the dead one. He tricked you, Kazuo, into believing that Okari was your enemy. And you, Okari, were tricked into believing O'Hara had come to kill you. You both chose to believe what was obvious, and yet you both know that the truth often hides behind lies."

"Then what—"

"Tell me again, O'Hara, what was your purpose in pursuing Chameleon?"

"To destroy him with the truth."

"And you, Okari?"

"They have sent killers after me before. Why should this one be different?"

"Because Kazuo is not one of them. You both have the same objective. You both seek to destroy the same evil and yet you have permitted that evil to turn you into enemies."

"And Falmouth?" O'Hara said.

"An instrument. He follows you to Chameleon and kills both of you."

"How do you know that?"

"Because I listen with my brain, not my heart. Why else? You yourself have admitted to me that the *eikoku-jin* told you Chameleon was the head of these mercenary terrorists. It was he who sent you on the journey because he was not good enough to find Chameleon himself. For what other reason would he follow you?"

"I find it hard to believe, Tokenrui-san, that Falmouth was such a man."

"I admire your loyalty but not your perception. Why do you still trust him? He killed for money. Can such a man be honorable? Can he truly be a friend? And do you honestly believe that one who shares the Way with you is evil?"

"Perhaps my ego won't let me admit I was a sucker."

Kimura nodded sagely. "That is possible. But you had a difficult problem. He told you lies and painted them with truth. And then the mad one on the mountain confirmed them with his lunacy."

"So Falmouth shopped me to get to Chameleon?"

"That was his job, Kazuo, to eliminate a perpetual enemy."

"But why? If Chameleon is not one of them, why are they so desperate to eliminate him?"

"We will come to that. Let us stay with the subject. This *eikoku-jin* would then have killed you because you know too much. It was a risk they took, to reveal enough to put you on the scent but not tell you too much. You were better than they thought. You and Gunn-san."

"And then he would have killed Eliza and the Magician for the same reason."

"It is likely."

"You are right, Tokenrui-san, Falmouth could have killed me with ease. I wasn't expecting it."

Kimura nodded, but added, "Okari told me the *eikoku-jin* was behind you. He believed you were working together. It was when you told me you had not seen the Englishman since your meeting on the sea that I understood what he was up to."

"Great—now I owe Chameleon my life!" O'Hara said.

"Hai. A burden that is heavy to bear."

"I am in your debt, *nii-san,"* O'Hara said and bowed to Okari.

"And I owe you my apology, for drawing the sword against a brother."

"Ah, a beginning. Now we will have to endure the tests," Kimura said with a sigh.

"Tests?" Okari asked.

"Yes, you will test him, he will test you. Ultimately you will be true brothers, but before that, there will be this testing and it will be quite a bore, I think."

"The testing is over," said O'Hara.

"Yes," Okari agreed. "I have too heavy a burden to concern myself with such trivial matters."

"It has become a burden for all of us, Okari. We are all involved now," Kimura said.

"I still don't know why Master is so dedicated to killing Okari," Eliza said.

"Not Okari—Chameleon. It is important to remember that."

"Why?"

"To understand that, we must go back to the boxes. Now that you understand this Chameleon is not your enemy, what do the boxes tell you? Study the sequence of events. The men who were murdered all died before their companies were swallowed up by this AMRAN, is that not correct?"

"All but Bridges," said the Magician. "He was part of San-San almost from the beginning."

"But the others were," said O'Hara.

"The answer is in the boxes," said Kimura. "The Chameleon you seek wears the skin of a hero but has the heart of a weasel. He wears garlands when he should wear thorns. He used his military office to become rich. And he has fashioned an organization with its own assassins, thieves, destructors."

"Hooker," Eliza said. "You mean our war hero is the head of all this?"

"The true Chameleon," said O'Hara. "The question is, Why? Why did they have Falmouth set me off on a trail that would eventually lead back to them?"

"That's easy," said the Magician. "They had one of the best damn assassins in the world shopping you all the way. If you got outa line, they'd pull the plug."

"This man who followed me was really following you," said Okari. "I saw him at the station. I mistakenly thought that you were working as a team. And when he started to follow me, I was sure of it."

"Sumpin' happened," said the Magician. "You just came from your meetin' with Hooker. Falmouth musta known where you were goin' and when you were comin' back. He was waitin' at the train station, right? Then he musta changed his mind at the last minute, see, decided to follow Okari here instead."

A sad smile crossed O'Hara's face. "He told me he was getting too old for the Game, that he made mistakes. Sooner or later it had to be a big one."

"So—we look at the boxes and we see the general, Hooker, building his oil empire by murder. The reasons could be many. What is important now is that you must quickly destroy Hooker. He knows how dangerous you are. 'When you strike at a king, you must kill him.' "

"Anybody got any ideas?" asked the Magician.

Okari said, "It is written in the Tendai that truth kills faster than poison."

"Well spoken," Kimura agreed, "but what meaning does that bring to this problem?"

"Are not the Gunn-san and Kazuo voices of the truth?" he said.

"Yes," said Eliza, "but the truth requires proof, and so far we couldn't prove doodly-squat."

"Perhaps the final boxes will give us an answer," said Kimura. "But to put events in their proper place, we must go back to before the war. To the first Chameleon, Yamuchi Asieda.

"Asieda never married. His brother, an admiral in the Imperial Navy, was taken prisoner in the early days of the war. When the Philippines were about to fall, Hooker was ordered to leave his headquarters at Bastine by your President Roosevelt. Through an accident, Hooker's adopted son was left behind and ultimately fell into the hands of Asieda, who took him back to Japan.

"The boy, who was half Filipino, looked more Japanese than even his mother, so living here was not difficult for him. Asieda took him to Dragon's Nest, where he tried to arrange a trade. The boy for Asieda's brother. He communicated by sending Hooker a chameleon in a box and then he found the boy's mother and sent her to try to negotiate the trade. Hooker responded by murdering her. Asieda had no choice. Negotiation was out of the question. But what could he do with Hooker's son?

"Remember, this was a very kind man, not a war lord. And through the months of captivity, he had developed a great affection for Hooker's son. The boy ultimately felt secure with Asieda. They became inseparable. A true irony that Chameleon should adopt the son of his deadliest enemy.

"But as the war drew to its close, the members of the War Council panicked. The few who knew who Chameleon's son really was demanded a meeting, in Hiroshima. It was their plan to use the boy as a bargaining tool once the war was over. Asieda, of course, disagreed. They fought about it, and that night Chameleon, disguised as a woman, slipped away with his son and left at dawn by train two hours before the city was obliterated. Asieda and young Hooker watched from the train.

"He and the boy became nomads. They had two things in common: they loved each other and they hated Hooker. Ultimately they settled in Kushiro on the island of Hokkaido to the north. Asieda became a fisherman.

"Asieda had made a vow that he would never let Hooker rest. He knew Hooker had murdered his own mistress, Bobby's mother. He knew he was using his military position to set up new industries in Japan in which he was a silent partner. He learned all of the general's vulnerabilities, and there were many. Chameleon knew more about General Hooker than anyone alive. And he became like a conscience. When Hooker became military governor, he helped set up the conglomerate San-San and made Tomoro the head of it. In exchange, Tomoro tried for five years to track down Chameleon. But it was impossible. Chameleon's agents would never have revealed his identity—they were all members of the *higaru-dashi.* And those few members of the council who knew his true identity all died at Hiroshima."

"Asieda, too, was reported dead at Hiroshima," said Okari. "And so, for thirty years, Hooker was hounded by a ghost—Chameleon. Of course, it was no ghost, only one man, devoted to psychologically destroying his enemy. A simple fisherman who had taken a vow to wreak his revenge on a dishonorable man by becoming the voice of his conscience. His old agents provided him with information. So did his friends in the government. The vendetta worked both ways. Hooker sent assassin after assassin to find Chameleon. Some gave up. Some died. The last to come was your friend Falmouth. And although Asieda died peacefully in his sleep four years ago, Chameleon lives on. His son took up the vow. And it will go on until Hooker dies—or they kill me."

"So you're Bobby Hooker," Eliza said.

"I am Okari Asieda," the tattooed man said. "Bobby Hooker no longer exists."

He revealed to them private feelings which he could never share before, how he had hated and feared Asieda-san for months and how Asieda-san with patience and wisdom had finally won him over, had explained the meaning of the Tendai and the most ancient myths and how to live in the forest and fish the sea.

"And when the war was over and he set off on his Walk of a Thousand Days, I went with him, begging at doorways, walking from one end of Japan to the other, as he sought the wisdom of Zen. And always there was time for the lessons. He taught me the Way of the Secret Warrior, the Moves of the Sword, the Language of the Creatures. He taught me honor, respect and love. And finally, he revealed to me the seventh level of the *higaru-dashi.*"

"And he never attempted blackmail? Extortion?" the Magician asked.

"He never asked for anything after his brother died."

O'Hara leaned back, staring at the imaginary boxes hanging in the air before him, looking back through time. Slowly the pieces began to fall into place. The sequence became obvious to him.

What Hooker and his elitist friends needed was a power base of their own. From that, they could begin monopolizing other related companies. There was only one problem: monopolies were illegal. But an oil consortium of separately owned corporations, each with its own autonomy—that would be perfect. The key was AMRAN. They formed the consortium, then killed the key men in the member corporations and put their own people in. In effect, they owned every company. They owned Hensell, Alamo, Sunset, Intercom, Am Petro and San-San and all its subsidiaries. They even controlled a bank in Boston. The common thread was oil.

There were still a few empty boxes.

"I keep wondering why they blew up Marza's car," Eliza said.

"It made it easier to take over Aquila."

"And," the Magician said, "do you know what was so special about that car?" Eliza shook her head. "The fucker was supposed to get fifty, sixty miles to the gallon. It would have revolutionized the auto business. Do you realize how that would have cut into AMRAN's profits?"

"My God," Eliza said. "Are they that greedy?"

"Money's no longer the game," O'Hara said. "They've got all the money they need. Now the game is pure power."

"Then why did they sink the *Thoreau?*" Eliza asked. "If the AMRAN people were wooing Sunset Oil as a potential member of the consortium, they were destroying an eighty-million-dollar asset that might someday belong to them. Isn't that kinda cutting off your nose to spite your face?"

"Maybe it was a squeeze play," said the Magician. "Maybe Sunset was a holdout, and it couldn't afford to be a holdout anymore after the rig got knocked over."

"That's a good theory," said O'Hara. "But let's look beyond it for a minute. Why were the pictures lifted in Hawaii and then destroyed?"

"Because nobody needed them," the Magician said.

"Then why buy them?"

"So nobody else would!" Eliza said.

"That's what I think," said O'Hara. "Which indicates that whoever had the man killed had the details of something on the *Thoreau.*"

"The pumping station," said the Magician. "Gotta be!"

"If that's the case, there were two reasons for destroying the *Thoreau.* One was to put Sunset in a financial bind. The other was because AMRAN already had the plans for the pumping station. They wanted the pictures off the market. So AMRAN is probably using that pumping station itself."

"It's interesting," O'Hara said. "Hooker denies any knowledge of Midas."

"What is Midas?" asked Okiru.

"We think it's an oil field, maybe the largest in the world. But we don't know where it is."

"And I think I know why," Eliza said.

They all turned toward the tiny reporter, who was wearing one of her million-dollar smiles.

"Well?" O'Hara said.

"It's underwater. Kraft American said the underwater dish built by Bridges was called Midas. Midas is the heart of the oil field, it's the pumping station for the whole operation. And it's all under the sea, the perfect hiding place."

"But where is it?" the Magician asked.

"I think I can help there," Okiru said. "I have seen the room from which they direct everything. It is enormous, perhaps forty meters high. And there is a huge map with odd-shaped TV screens recessed in it."

"They're called diod screens," said the Magician. "Free form."

"These TV screens show their operations all over the world. They can watch everything that goes on in this empire of theirs. There is one in particular, near Bonin, which has this undersea dish you speak of. They have TV pictures inside and out. And there are also ships down there, it is like some great graveyard of old tankers."

"Beautiful," said the Magician. "That's the answer to the tankers. They sink them and store oil in them. I'll bet more than one skipper has vanished in that part of the ocean in the last few years."

"And Yumishawa has a new refinery on the Bonin Islands, less than a hundred miles away," said Okari.

"So they pump oil from their underwater storage ships to their refinery as they need it. Christ, what an ingenious operation," said O'Hara.

"They been on to this for—what, thirty years?" the Magician said. "Why didn't they start pumping oil back then? Why wait?"

"They couldn't do anything before this," Eliza said. "Not without revealing the existence of the strike. That's their ace in the hole. It gives them almost unlimited oil reserves. Just think what that means in the marketplace. The longer they keep it under wraps, the more powerful they become."

"Yes," Kimura reflected, "if one sells coconuts, the world knows one has a tree."

"Very patient men," Okari put in.

"Why not?" said the Magician. "Look at the payoff."

"And Lavander got it because he was hired to appraise the field when they started to make their big move," Eliza said. "It was in his book. He knew the potential. Hell, the poor fool just knew too much for his own good."

"They probably had plans to hit him even before he was lifted," the Magician said. "They only had one problem—Chameleon, who seemed to know everything they were doing."

O'Hara was deep in thought, trying to construct the abstract boxes in the air into basic realities. He was sure the answers to all their questions were there, now he had to clarify them. But he could not clear the image of Hooker from his mind. To dishonor the great wartime hero seemed almost like dishonoring history, besmirching America's victories—and that troubled him. Yet Hooker had dishonored himself. What hatreds, what frustrations, could have smoldered so deep inside him that they twisted his senses until he found relief in the dark side of his soul? He had betrayed his trust, designed a monolith of greed financed by elitists as dishonorable as he, and created a nightmare empire in which murder and robbery were taken for granted and executed by vipers: Hinge, Danilov, Le Croix, yes, even Falmouth. Hooker must be destroyed. But how? The answer was simple: with the truth.

How to do it was the problem.

"We need to get inside and get photographs of that board, particularly close-ups of the pumping station," O'Hara said. "The question is how."

"Why haven't you told anyone about this before?" the Magician asked Okari.

Okari smiled wistfully. "It was a personal matter," he said. "Besides, I did not understand the significance of all this, nor did Asieda-san. We had bits and pieces, scraps from their wastebaskets, memos on desks. They thought we knew much more than we did."

The Magician was humming "C-Jam Blues" and smiling. "I got an idea," he said. "This place is made out of stone, right?"

Okari nodded.

"No metal in the walls?"

Okiru shook his head. "Timber," he said.

"Perfect."

"You going to let us in on the secret?" asked O'Hara.

"They have security cameras scanning this room, right?" the Magician asked Okari.

"Yes, near the ceiling. Some are stationary, some sniff the room like ferrets."

"And we got the production truck. There's half a dozen videotape machines in there. All we gotta do, get us a coupla small microwave transmitters. Get inside, find the back of their monitors and hook the transmitters into their 'video out' lug. It'll change their scanner into cameras. We'll pick up the signal in the live news truck outside and videotape it. What we'll get is a continuous picture from inside the place."

"Where does one find such a transmitter?" asked Kimura.

"Oh, just about any radio shop," the piano player said, still grinning.

"How do you get into this place?" O'Hara asked Okan.

"Up through the great stone drains at the foot of the wall. They lead to the dungeons. Which are used only for storage. The grates are old. Once inside, I go to the locker room where the fixing men keep their uniforms. Once I have changed clothes, I come and go as I please. I rummage through wastebaskets, search Hooker's desk, find something to unnerve him, to make my presence known. And then I send the chameleon."

"And what are the risks, other than those which are obvious?" asked Kimura.

"The computers are in what were once the dungeons," Okari said. "It would be risky to linger down there too long. The guards are all sumo and their leader is a man who has the smell of an animal. I have seen him twice. He is very restless. He wanders the halls and dungeons at all hours of the night with a guard dog. I am always cautious that he does not get close enough to recognize me. I call him *Hitotsu-me.*"

O'Hara looked up sharply. "One-Eye?" he said. "Does he wear a patch?"

"Hai. With a very bad scar." Okari drew an imaginary line down the side of his face.

"I saw him today. I had the feeling he was watching me, and I also had the feeling I had met him before but I just—"

O'Hara paused, concentrating on the sketchy details of a face he had seen for only a few moments, isolating the vague details of that face in his mind and focusing totally on it. He said nothing for more than a minute, then: "No, I don't think I know him. And yet there's something familiar . . ." He tried to concentrate, tapping his memory. "A picture, perhaps . . . No, the face itself is not familiar." He went back to the beginning of it, to his conversation with Falmouth on the boat. The Players . . .

"Le Croix," he said.

"Who?" Okari asked.

"A Frenchman. Le Croix is his nickname. He lost an eye in Algiers and crucified a couple of dozen rebels to get even. It could be him. There are no photographs of him in existence, he had them all destroyed. If it is Le Croix, you're right—we're looking down a hundred miles of bad road. For the purposes of this junket we need to give him plenty of room. Any other problems?"

Okari shook his head.

"How did you figure all this out?" Eliza asked. "Going up through the drains and all that?"

"Very simple," said Okira; "you forget I lived there once. For three years it was my private playground. I know every stone in the place."

11

LE CROIX ENTERED THE DUNGEON STAIRWELL in Dragon's Nest and went down the wide stone staircase. The dog, an ugly mongrel, was expertly trained. It strode ahead of him, its nose first in the air, then along the ground, sniffing, alert.

Le Croix's instincts had been sending out warnings ever since he saw O'Hara at the fortress earlier in the day. It was the first time since he joined Master that he felt threatened. For three years everything had gone perfectly, not a slip-up. Then things started going a little haywire. First there was the job on the *Thoreau* when Thornley was killed. Then Lavander was snatched. Then Garvey and Hooker pulled him into Dragon's Nest to head up security. It seemed to him they were getting defensive, and Le Croix's game had always been an offensive one. Now this reporter, who was supposed to lead them to Chameleon, seemed to be getting closer to *them* instead.

He hated the dungeons. They were cold and dank and the wind, crying through cracks in the mortar, was unnerving. Even the dog got spooky down here.

When he was sure the place was secure, he retreated back upstairs to the warmth of the security office and sat watching the monitor screen as the camera scanned the dungeon stairwell. Something was in the air, he could feel it as surely as he felt the cold drafts down below. He would have some coffee and check again in thirty or forty minutes. He did not trust the electronic devices. He did not trust anything or anyone but himself.

The wall of Dragon's Nest rose out of the trees above them like an enormous gray shroud. They had climbed up the mountain from the road below and now they were at the mouth of a gaping water drain, its masoned stones green with centuries of moss. A trickle of water fell from its mouth and splattered on the rocks below. Red eyes glittered in the beam of O'Hara's flashlight. The creature squealed and scurried back into the opening. Vines cluttered the entrance.

"No wonder they've never paid any attention to this drain," O'Hara whispered. "You have to be crazy to do this."

"Welcome to madness," Chameleon said and slithered through the vines into the drain. O'Hara followed him, his hands slipping on the moss-covered rocks. The drain was four feet in diameter and long. It snaked out of light range. Far in the back, O'Hara could hear the steady trickle of a dozen streams echoing through the tunnel. Cold air moaned past them.

Chameleon moved on all fours, like a cat. And fast. They were both dressed in black pants and turtlenecks and black sneakers. Chameleon carried a rope with a small telescoping grappling hook on one end. They had four microwave transmitters, each wrapped in heavy Styrofoam, tucked in their sweaters. Nothing else but the flashlight.

They both crept along on all fours, their backs curved away from the top of the drain, past two feeder drains. At the third, Chameleon stopped. He pointed up and O'Hara flashed the light toward the ceiling. A shaft went straight up into the guts of the fortress. It was thirty or forty feet straight up to a grate at the far end. Chameleon put his back against one wall and his feet against the other and started shinnying up. It was a torturous ascent because the walls of the shaft were dripping wet. Foot by slippery foot he jerked his way up the narrow enclosure. When he reached the top he fastened the grappling hook to the grate and unwound the rope. It dangled down to O'Hara's fingertips. He climbed up it, hand over hand. He braced himself with feet and back while Chameleon very cautiously pushed up the grate and slid it aside.

The subterranean passage was grim. Only two lamps illuminated the low-ceilinged dungeons. What were once cells had been converted into storage bins, but the place still seemed to be permeated with soughs of torture and despair, as if history were whispering through its cold stone corridors. It was the wind, keening through cracks in the walls and down the stairways.

They quickly pulled themselves into the hall and replaced the grate. They hid the grappling hook and ran to an open winding stairway. Chameleon cautioned O'Hara to wait. They looked up and saw a camera shake its head back and forth, slowly scanning the staircase and the hall above. As it swept away, toward the hallway, Chameleon ran up the stairs and stopped directly under the camera. He stood with his back against the wall as it moved silently overhead, pointing back toward the stairwell. Then he ran the rest of the way down the hall to a fire door. The locker room was just inside. He had to make a move before the camera completed its swing back. If there was someone in the hallway on the other side of the door, they were in trouble.

He opened it and stepped through. The hallway was empty. Behind him, O'Hara dashed to the spot under the camera and waited until it swung back and then ran to the doorway.

They ran to the locker room and jumped through the door.

A man was standing in front of them.

Outside, Eliza and the Magician had driven to the top of the mountain to a point where the the road curved close to the edge of a precipice. Eliza pulled off to the side and parked. They could not see into Dragon's Nest from there, but the Magician was sure the reception would be excellent. He was sitting in the back of the van before three built-in videotape decks and monitors, twisting dials, looking for the signal. There was nothing but static.

"They're not in there yet," he said.

"I just hope when they do get in they get it done and get their fannies out of there," Eliza said.

"I just hope they don't run into one of those sumo wrestlers they have as guards. Four hundred pounds of bad news."

They had left a Toyota parked near the bottom of the mountain. If they were being chased when they left, Eliza would take the tapes and switch to the car. O'Hara, the Magician and Chameleon would stay with the truck and lead pursuers away from her.

It was O'Hara who had realized that they only needed to get some tape of the pumping system on Midas to prove that AMRAN had stolen the plans. That and the existence of the Midas field itself would be enough for them to justify blowing the AMRAN story wide open.

The Magician looked at his watch. They had been gone an hour. That's how long Chameleon had estimated it would take to get into the control-panel corridor behind the big map. The Magician would monitor the video screens in the truck and record anything that was shown. Each of the transmitters was set to beam its signal at a different frequency so the pictures would not overlap. He couldn't think of anything they had forgotten.

The man in the locker room appeared to be in his fifties. His eyes were faded, his skin was creased with age and his white hair was as thin as wisps of cotton.

"You're early," he said in Japanese.

"Yes," Chameleon said quickly, "there is a problem with one of the air conditioners."

"It takes two of you? My, times have changed. It is much too extravagant for a janitor like me. Good night. Don't work too late." He left.

"Close," said O'Hara.

"Let us hope he does not mention it to anyone on the way out."

"What next?"

"Check the open lockers. The fixing men usually leave their internal ID badges on their coveralls," Chameleon said. There were several, and the members of the maintenance crew obviously were not as large as those on the security force. They both found coveralls that fit.

Chameleon handed O'Hara a hardhat and said, "Put this on. Keep your head down so the cameras will not see your face. If you see anyone, just nod and go on. You will find there is little conversation up above. We will go to the top of the stairs and enter the main floor. The map room is immediately to your left, and the corridor leading behind the map is next to it. We are lucky. We do not have far to go."

"We hook up, check the map room to make sure the cameras are scanning what we want and then split," O'Hara said. "No hanging around rummaging through wastebaskets, okay?"

"I will try to control myself."

Getting behind the map was a piece of cake. The main corridor was empty and the door was unlocked. The wall was a myriad of TV monitors.

"It's going to be tough to find the monitors for the map room," O'Hara said.

"They are marked. See."

Each of the boxes had its location written on the frame with a felt-tip pen. Checking the inscriptions, O'Hara and Chameleon had no trouble locating the monitors for the two scanners in the map room. They hooked a tiny alligator clamp attached to a thin wire on the "video out" lug of each of the monitor boxes and plugged in the transmitters, which were three by five inches, and an inch thick. The wires connecting the clips to the transmitters were long enough to permit O'Hara to slide the boxes out of sight under the monitors.

Then O'Hara noticed another interesting monitor. It was for the scanner in Garvey's office. O'Hara hooked it up, too.

"Okay, let's check the game room once and get out of here. And let's hope they're picking up something outside."

In the news van, the Magician slowly twisted the small fine-tuning knob on one of the monitors. Suddenly the picture popped in. He was looking at the room Okari had described. The map was easily thirty feet high and twenty feet long. Recessed in it were a dozen diod screens. The camera was moving and the Magician watched it pan across the room and back. He tuned the other two. One of them was a stationary shot of an office. A small man with a waxed mustache was talking on the phone. The Magician recognized him from O'Hara's description. It had to be General Garvey.

"We got it, Lizzie. You're not gonna believe this. We got two different angles on the map."

"Can you see Midas?"

"Yeah—but the camera's still moving. O'Hara's got to get in there now and freeze it."

He tuned the sets as sharply as possible. The camera swept to the center of the room and then started back.

There it was. There were four screens on the Midas location. Two exterior and two interior.

"Incredible!" said the Magician.

"Do we have sound?"

Voices murmured in the map room.

"Yeah. And a million-dollar picture on all three—"

He stopped in mid-sentence. He was listening to Garvey.

"Quill. Nine twenty-five, April 8. 730-037-370. Red urgent. We have not heard from you for twenty-four hours. It is important you make contact immediately." He hung up.

"Well, I'll be damned. We just got a bonus," the Magician said.

"What?"

"We got Quill, on film. And guess who it is?"

"Hooker?"

"Garvey."

"How do we get to the cameras?" O'Hara asked. "Aren't they pretty high up?"

"There is a ladder with wheels in the map room. There will be four men there, five at the most, and they won't pay any attention—they'll be too busy. It is from this panel that all the machines on Midas are controlled."

"We just walk right in, that it?" O'Hara said.

Chameleon nodded. They entered the big room. O'Hara was stunned at the size. Then, on two of the diod screens, he saw Midas for the first time.

The exteriors were both eerie. Gray soundless pictures under the sea.

One was the dish, a saucer under water with its superstructure hanging down toward the bottom of the ocean.

The other was even more bizarre. A long line of rusted ships, settled deep in the sand, wavered before the camera. Powerful underwater searchlights peered through the murky water, etching the forms and shapes. One of the screens showed a close-up of the pumping station, the heart of the entire system.

There it was, the evidence they needed, in living color.

Four men were at work at the enormous console. One of them glanced back over his shoulder as they entered the room, then turned back to whatever he was doing. Chameleon rolled the eighteen-foot ladder in place under the cameras. Since there was no way for him to check the parameters of the two cameras, he wanted to make sure one of them was aimed at the crucial part of the map, the TV close-up of the pumping station. And there was no way for them to know for sure whether the transistors were working. At this point they were playing it by ear.

O'Hara went up the ladder. There was a small switch at the bottom of the camera which stopped it from scanning and froze it in place. Once O'Hara stopped the camera it would be only a matter of time until somebody in the security office noticed and came to check. They needed to get out fast once he threw the switch.

He was reaching for the switch when the door opened and Garvey came in. He was directly below O'Hara, who quickly looked away and started fiddling with the camera. Chameleon, too, turned his back to the jaunty little man.

"Everything okay?" Garvey asked as he passed them.

Chameleon nodded. "Just cleaning the lenses," he said.

But Garvey was much more interested in the console. "What's it look like?"

"We're about ready to bring in Number Seventeen," one of the operators said.

"Better get the general. You know how he loves to watch these new wells come in."

"Not much to see," the man at the console answered. "Just the on-line lights going and the digital counter clocking off the gallons."

"Ours not to reason why," Garvey sighed. He picked up a phone and pressed a number and waited. "General, we're about to punch in Seventeen . . . Very good, sir." He hung up. "He's coming in."

It was then O'Hara realized what was happening. They were getting ready to bring an oil well on-line.

They had to get out of there fast. O'Hara reached up and switched off the scanning button. The camera stopped roving. It was aimed directly at the Midas screens. He hurried back down the ladder and jerked his head toward the door.

Chameleon did not move. He was staring at the door. O'Hara grabbed his arm but Chameleon shook his head. He could not leave.

He had to see Hooker.

Just once, he had to be an arm's length away from the man he had hated since he was a child.

The general entered the room from his office.

O'Hara busied himself by returning the ladder to the corner, keeping his face away from Hooker and Garvey.

We have to get out of here fast, thought O'Hara. Everyone's in this room but Le Croix, and God know's where he is. If Hooker or Garvey spot me, the game's over. He turned back.

Chameleon was edging closer to the tall hawk-faced man.

Christ, O'Hara thought, he's blowing it.

But the small cluster of men at the console were all riveted to the instruments, to the action at the console.

The key operator said, "Okay, we're ready."

"Close-up on the valve," Garvey said.

The operator punched a key, and the camera, obviously equipped with a zoom lens, was triggered. The picture on the TV screen changed slowly as the lens zoomed in.

It was perfect. A close-up of the stolen pumping station actually in the process of switching on a new well. Now all he had to do was get Chameleon the hell out of there without being obvious. The tattooed man stood a few feet behind Hooker, transfixed, staring at the sharp profile.

His own father, a few feet away.

"On-line programmed," the operator said.

He punched some more keys.

"Counting down . . . five, four, three, two, one . . . and switch-in."

The TV screen told the story. On the console of the pumping valve, a bank of lights blinked on in sequence. Then the numbers on the digital counter began switching so fast that it was hard to read them.

"And we're in," the operator cried.

The general laughed and clapped his hands. "Well done, gentlemen," he said. "Congratulations. Jess, come on into the office, I've got champagne on ice."

"Right, sir, in a minute."

Hooker wheeled around and started back toward the office door. For a moment he came eye to eye with Chameleon. The general looked at him briefly, then nodded and marched off.

Chameleon was right behind him. Nobody else saw him but O'Hara. The others were still staring intently at the nerve center of Midas.

What the hell's he doing? O'Hara thought.

The general entered his office, and Chameleon, waiting until the door was almost closed, leaped through it sideways. The door clicked shut.

Well, I'll be damned, O'Hara thought. What now?

In the van, the Magician and Eliza were howling with glee. There it was, a close-up of what they needed, and in the process of bringing in a new well.

"We got it!" the Magician yelled.

"We'll get another minute or two, then we'll have to get rolling. They should be on their way out. We need to get back down the hill."

"Hey," the Magician cried, "something fucked up!"

Garvey was yelling, pointing off-screen, clawing at his belt. A machine pistol appeared in his hand. Then suddenly O'Hara leaped into the screen. He slapped Garvey's gun hand away, grabbed it, wrenched it backwards.

The pistol coughed a half-dozen times.

Bap, bap, bap, bap, bap, bap.

The bullets ripped into the sprawling glass map. A string of holes splattered across South America. The glass weakened and shattered. Behind it, the maze of wires that controlled the electronic marvel was sliced by falling glass. Sparks showered the room. Streaks of fire raced up the wall.

Inside the van, Eliza and the Magician were staring hypnotically at the tape recorders. They did not see the shadows at the edge of the road begin to vane, were not aware anyone was there until the side door slammed back and they turned to face the biggest human being they had ever seen. Four hundred pounds if an ounce, his neck bulging over the shirt collar, his eyes scowling out from a balloon face.

"Holy shit!" the Magician cried. He started looking for a weapon, a club, anything.

The guard reached in with a tire-sized arm and grabbed Eliza, lifting her out the door as if she were a doll. She did not utter a sound. She made a fist, stuck out her forefinger and little finger and thrust them into the guard's eyes. He roared with pain. She kept gouging, grinding the two fingers into his eyes. He dropped her, and she leaped back in the van and got behind the wheel.

The Magician jumped out, a lug wrench in hand, and hit the guard with a powerhouse swing. It made a flat smack as it smashed into the side of his head. The guard, temporarily blinded, shook off the blow as if it were a flea bite.

The Magician wound up and this time brought the steel wrench straight down on his head. The blow stung the Magician's hands.

The guard staggered and started toward him.

"Get in!" Eliza yelled as she pulled the gear shift into first.

The Magician took his third strike.

The tire iron flipped out of his hands. This time the wrestler went down like a stricken buffalo.

He dove into the van and Eliza whipped it in a tight circle and fishtailed down the road.

When Chameleon jumped into Hooker's office, he first stood flat against the wall, watching the general walk to his desk, lean over the champagne bucket and twist the bottle in the ice with the palms of his hands.

Then Chameleon moved slowly toward him. The old man looked up and glared at the maintenance man. "What is it, something wrong?" he asked.

The man did not answer. He walked slowly across the dark room toward Hooker and stood in front of the desk.

He was unbuttoning his shirt.

The room was deadly still except for the ticking in Hooker's chest. The clock began to run faster.

Tick . . . tick . . . tick . . . tick . . .

"What are you doing? What's the meaning of this?"

Still no answer. The man's eyes were filled with hatred. He opened the shirt.

Tick, tick, tick, tick . . .

Hooker's eyes bulged as he saw the tattoos. He was hypnotized by the specter standing before him. His brain was fumbling with a half-dozen disparate thoughts.

"Permit me, General. I am Chameleon," the man said.

Tickticktick . . .

The clock in Hooker's chest was frantic.

The ticking increased. It sounded like a Geiger counter.

"Y-y-y-you're too young," he croaked.

"Capice Military Hospital, September 23, 1933," he said.

It took a moment for the information to register.

"What do you mean?"

"The day I was born . . . Father."

The old man began to shake. The pacemaker went berserk.

"You're lying," he said. His voice was an echo squeezed from his chest.

From the map room he heard the muffled, staccato *bap, bap, bap, bap, bap, bap* of Garvey's machine pistol, but he barely paid any attention.

"Mother called me Molino, you called me Bobby. Would you like the date you murdered her in Australia? April—"

A tiny streak of fire crept across the ceiling. Hooker's eyes fled to it and then flicked back.

Hooker's "No-o-o-o!" was as anguished as the death cry of a wolf.

The old man snatched open a desk drawer and pulled out a Colt .45. He held it in both hands and pointed it straight between Chameleon's eyes.

The pacemaker was hammering.

And then it fell silent.

No more ticking.

What little blood was left in the general's face drained away. His lips began to shake. His trigger finger trembled.

The door flew open and O'Hara burst in. He stopped cold.

The general was pointing his pistol straight ahead. It was inches from Chameleon's nose, and yet he made no move toward Hooker.

The gun hand wavered. The general's eyes began to glaze over. He made one last effort to squeeze off the shot but there was no strength left.

"You're dead, General," Chameleon said.

Hooker's eyes crossed and he plunged face down across the desk.

"For God's sake, let's get outa here," O'Hara yelled. "All hell's breaking loose."

Behind him, half a dozen wires crossed and exploded in fireworks. Colored shards glittered in the air and turned the map room into a giant kaleidoscope.

Garvey stood in the middle of the room, staring in disbelief as the glass showered around him.

O'Hara and Chameleon ran for it.

Pandemonium.

Garvey was screaming orders.

Fire stitched the ceiling, snapped at the timbers. The short-circuited wires were like streaks of fire. Sparks showered around them as they ran through the map room and out the door. Security guards dashed past them with fire extinguishers.

They ran toward the stairs leading to the dungeons.

Behind them they could hear Garvey screaming, "Stop them! Stop them!"

They did not look back. They raced toward the stone staircase. As they turned the corner into the stairwell, a gun boomed behind them. Bullets chewed pieces out of the stones and they stung O'Hara's face. "Keep going," he yelled as he slammed the fire door leading to the dungeons and bolted it behind them.

They heard the dog before they turned around. It was a foot away. And behind it, Le Croix, a gun in his hand, had just reached the top of the stone stairway. He was not prepared for what happened next, for Chameleon moved instantly, dove over the dog and rolled past Le Croix.

"Keep going!" O'Hara yelled and Chameleon raced down the steps. Le Croix, distracted for a moment, shouted an order to the dog: *"Le cou!"* The neck. And as the dog went after Chameleon, Le Croix turned and fired at O'Hara. But Chameleon's diversion had given the reporter the instant he needed. Feinting first to the right, then the left, he leaped and kicked at the same moment, his eyes on Le Croix's gun hand. The pistol roared, bullets smacked the door behind O'Hara as his toe shattered Le Croix's wrist. The gun flipped out of his hand.

Chameleon jumped the last few steps to the floor of the dungeon and turned toward the grate. The dog was right behind him, its hackles trembling, its teeth bared. But it made no sound. As Chameleon turned to face it, the dog leaped toward his throat. Chameleon dropped in a crouch and rolled on his back. The dog landed behind him, paws scrambling as it twisted around.

At the top of the stairs O'Hara landed flat-footed, stepped in and snapped Le Croix's head back with the flat of his hand. The scarred man fell, but as O'Hara jumped over him. Le Croix tripped the reporter. O'Hara staggered but did not fall.

Behind him, Le Croix hesitated for a moment. A Leash dropped like a snake from his sleeve. It was attached by a small padded bracelet to his wrist. He whirled it like a lasso and it sang through the air as it flicked toward O'Hara's head, and O'Hara, hearing the *whoof* of the wire, turned for an instant, saw the deadly noose and ducked, raising his arm to ward it off. The noose snapped over his arm and tightened on his wrist, cutting into the skin. He jerked it and Le Croix fell forward into him. The two of them tumbled over each other down the stairway.

The second time the dog jumped, Chameleon was prepared. He dropped low again, and as the dog soared over him, he reached up and grabbed it by the throat with both hands, slamming it against the stone floor. The dog's claws slashed desperately at his arms, tearing away the sweater, drawing blood. Chameleon squeezed and twisted the dog in his powerful hands, got his feet under him, and standing, smashed its head against the wall. The dog shrieked once before it died.

"Kazuo!" he called.

"Drop the rope!" O'Hara yelled.

The fire door began to give as half a dozen sumo guards battered it.

Chameleon recovered the grappling hook from its hiding place and began to slide the grate back while halfway down the stairwell Le Croix and O'Hara grappled, connected together by the thin wire attached to their wrists. Le Croix was a brute, but fighting O'Hara was like fighting air. He slipped away, jumped to his feet, hauled Le Croix up by the wire and chopped him across the throat with his free hand. Le Croix fell backwards, dragging O'Hara with him. The patch fell away from his face, revealing a gruesome gray socket, split by the deep scar that ran the length of his face. The one-eyed assassin tried to twist the wire around O'Hara's throat, but once again the reporter moved too fast. He hopped over Le Croix, pulling his arm sideways. The wire wrapped around Le Croix's throat instead. O'Hara pulled the loop and Le Croix's hand was jerked against his neck. The wire bit into his flesh. His good eye swelled with fear. He grabbed for O'Hara with his free hand, but the reporter pulled his arm back and the noose tightened around Le Croix's throat. Le Croix thrashed, got his legs under him and lunged for his adversary's throat. O'Hara rolled nimbly, and Le Croix dove over him and skittered off the edge of the stairwell. He seemed to poise for a second, and then he dropped. O'Hara's hand was tugged violently by the weight of the falling body. And then he felt the wire snap taut and slice into his wrist.

And he heard Le Croix's neck break, like a dead branch.

The man's weight pulled him to the edge of the stairwell. Le Croix was dangling grotesquely on the wire, his feet dancing on air inches above the ground, his hand pulled tight against the side of his face, his tongue protruding obscenely, his good eye rolling wildly beside the barren socket. He jerked there for several seconds. The wire bit deeper into O'Hara's wrist, blood gushing from the torn skin. Then Le Croix's eye rolled up and he just hung there.

A moment later Chameleon appeared on the floor below and lifted up the dead man, easing the pressure. O'Hara released the ratchet and the wire noose fell off.

Splinters flew from the fire door. A crack appeared. O'Hara crawled to his feet and ran shakily down the rest of the stairs.

"Can you make it with just one hand?" Chameleon asked.

"I can try."

"Go," said Chameleon.

O'Hara didn't argue. He grabbed the rope and dropped into the black abyss.

The door burst from its frame and crashed to the floor. Three guards tumbled through the opening.

Chameleon started down the rope.

O'Hara was sliding down so fast that the rope scorched his hand. He could feel Chameleon on the rope above him. Then suddenly he wasn't going down anymore. He looked up. The grinning face of one of the sumo guards leered down at him. The man was pulling them back up as though they were puppets.

"Drop!" O'Hara yelled and let go.

He had no idea how high up he was. He plunged into the darkness, down into the main water tunnel, hit and rolled. Chameleon landed seconds later and rolled on top of him.

They shot down along the wet moss, end over end, like children in a funhouse, uncontrollably swept along by their momentum, and burst out of the tunnel, carrying vines with them as they continued tumbling down the mountainside until they were stopped by the undergrowth.

The van was ten feet away.

O'Hara's hands were rope-burned, his shoulder was skinned raw and blood streamed from his torn wrist. He tried to get to his feet, saw the Magician running toward him. "Chameleon . . .?" he asked.

"Right here, *tomodachi*," the tattooed man said, helping him up. It was the first time he had called O'Hara "friend."

They jumped in the van and fell on the floor.

"Get rolling!" the Magician ordered, and Eliza jammed the van into gear and headed down the rest of the hill.

"What the hell happened?" the Magician said.

"Shit hit the fan," O'Hara gasped.

"I am to blame," Chameleon said. "I lost it there for a few minutes. It was an emotional—"

O'Hara sat up. He laid his hand on Chameleon's arm. "Hey," he said, "who's complaining?" He turned to the Magician. "Did we get anything on tape?"

"The whole megillah."

O'Hara laughed and fell back on the floor of the van. "Is there a first-aid kit in the house?" he said. "I think I may be bleeding to death."

Eliza sped down the mountain and out into the flat at the edge of Tanabe. Behind them, yellow flames boiled up from Dragon's Nest. Chameleon watched through the rear window of the van and rubbed his aching arms.

"It is a cleansing fire," he said. "When it is over, the fortress will still be standing and we can restore it to what it once was, a nest for dragons, not weasels."

He leaned back and closed his eyes and the pain in his face was not from his cuts and bruises. Without opening his eyes, he said, "I am sorry, Kazuo, for violating my promise. I could have got you killed back there."

"But you didn't. The Tokenrui-san will say it was just an instant in time. The poets will pass it by."

"It was the sight of him, being that close to Hooker. It made me crazy. I needed to reveal the truth to him, just as you must reveal the truth about him to the world."

"Let it pass, Okira, let it pass," O'Hara sighed, and he slumped down to nurse his own aches and pains.

The Magician pulled the three tapes out of the recorders and wrapped a band around them as Eliza pulled into the clearing where they had left the Toyota.

"Maybe the Magician ought to go with—" O'Hara started to suggest, but she had slammed on the brakes and was already out of the van. As planned, she jumped in the car, started up and zoomed off.

"I'm gonna tell yuh sumpin, okay? I wouldn't drive back to Kyoto with her. She drove this van so fuckin' fast, half the time I wasn't sure if she was drivin' it or it was drivin' her."

They drove the three hours back to Kyoto without incident. The fire was apparently keeping Garvey and company too busy to bother with them.

As they reached the center of Kyoto, Chameleon asked to be dropped off. "It is better that I leave now." He reached out and took O'Hara's hand. "Whoever Kimura-san selects as Tokenrui will please me. If it is to be you, *tomodachi*, it will be my honor to serve you. If you ever need anything, this kendo master is at your service."

"I feel the same," O'Hara said. "*Arigato*, my friend." He watched Okira limp down a side street until the darkness swallowed him up. The reporter lay back on the floor of the van. It had been a long night filled with surprises, and despite his torn wrist and battered ribs, he felt suddenly refreshed. The truth was on the tapes. Howe would have his big story. Lizzie would get her shot at New York. A heavy burden had been lifted from Chameleon's shoulders. Yet to O'Hara, the victory seemed strangely empty. He thought instead about Falmouth, who had lied to him and betrayed him. It was a lesson that would stay with him forever. What was it Kimura-san said . . . "The wise man has many cuts." But he also said, "The happy man forgets his scars."

The Magician broke the spell. "Weird," he said.

"What's weird?"

"All those fuckin' tattoos."

They drove back to the hotel.

"We catch the first train out in the morning, the way I see it," the Magician said after they had parked the van. "We can be back in the States, shit, tomorra night this time."

O'Hara nodded slowly. "Let's hope Lizzie didn't kill herself driving back here."

He grabbed the first house phone he saw in the hotel lobby and dialed her number. It rang and the operator came on.

"Who please?"

"Eliza Gunn, U.S.A."

"Missa Gunn, she check out."

"Checked out!"

"*Hai.* Maybe twenty minutes."

"Thanks."

The note was in his box. It read: "I lucked out. Found a young pilot willing to fly me to Tokyo tonight. You get the big story, I get the tapes. Seems fair, doesn't it? By the way, would you mind returning the van to Howe/Tokyo. Thanks. See you in Boston. xxx E."

He handed it to the Magician.

"Well, I'll be goddamned," the Magician said, and he started laughing. "She scooped yuh, pal!"

12

CHARLES GORDON HOWE WHEELED HIMSELF into his spacious office overlooking the Haymarket. It had been a busy day, thanks to his two top reporters, and a fruitful one. The fire at Dragon's Nest had attracted news coverage, but Hooker's death got most of the space. All that did was whet everyone's appetite for the whole story, and they had it all. Eliza was coming on with a fifteen-minute news special. She had been editing it all night. He'd get a huge share on the news tonight. And O'Hara was on his way back with a front-page banner for the *Star*. All the fine details. The old man leaned back in his wheelchair and stroked his chin.

Excellent.

Eliza's bright face popped on the set, but it was wearing a serious expression. Nothing light.

"Good evening," she began, "this is Eliza Gunn, Six O'Clock News—"

"Don't worry, she'll do a helluva job."

Howe recognized the voice immediately. It came from a dark corner of the office, back among the plants.

O'Hara stepped out into the light.

"You scared the bedevil outa me there, Lieutenant. What the hell're you doing hiding back there among the goddamn shrubs?"

"I was hanging boxes in the air."

"What?"

"It's an old Zen trick. Really nothing more than logic."

"Is that right?" Howe said. He was watching the television set, almost leering as his star reporter described the operation known as Master and its perpetrators.

"There's a lot more to it than she has," O'Hara said.

"There's nothing wrong with the stuff she's got."

"Tip of the iceberg."

"Well, can it wait until this is over, sir?" Howe was getting annoyed.

"Every station in the country's gonna want to pick this up. How far along are you on your yarn?"

"It's finished."

"Great. Let's just see what she does with the story and then we'll talk about you—okay, m'boy?"

"I want to talk now."

"Goddammit, after the show, Lieutenant, after the show."

"It won't wait." He switched off the television set.

Howe looked up and scowled. "I beg your damn pardon?"

"It won't wait. You can watch this later, on tape. Garvey spilled his guts. In fact, he's probably still spilling them, only I've got enough to suit me. We can leave the rest to the historians."

"Garvey? Which one was he?"

"He was the man called Quill. He picked the assignments."

"Magnificent. Goddamn, man, you've broken one of the biggest stories of the century. Now can we just turn the damn TV—"

O'Hara cut him off. "Not we. Me. I've got the story."

"That's the way, lad. By God, we'll tear up the *Star* and give you the whole front page. Now, if you don't—"

"No. It isn't going to work that way."

Howe began to get interested. His mind shifted from the television set. "What do you mean?"

"I mean, you don't get it both ways."

"Both ways?" Howe was genuinely stumped.

"Sure. Look at the way it's sizing up. They can pin the takeovers on the little squids out in Texas who were in on the plan from the beginning. The ones that told them who to kill, who was strong and who was weak in the companies. It's called conspiracy, although they'll probably end up doing time in some government country club, like the Nixon bunch did."

Howe shook his head. "I still don't—"

"The way I figure it, Hooker's dead. Garvey and a couple of Texas millionaires are in for a lot of grief. One hell of a big cartel is going down the tubes. There's probably going to be several international murder trials. The whole intelligence community's going to be thrown for a loop. But the best part of the story will never be told."

"And why is that, Lieutenant?"

"Because nobody can prove it."

Howe leaned forward, eyes aglitter.

"But I have to deal with it," O'Hara went on, "for my own sake—do you understand what I'm saying? I have some feelings of my own about it."

"So?"

"So, I don't believe in coincidence. I don't believe Falmouth just came to you because he liked reading the Boston *Star*. I was set up from the start."

"I don't follow you, Lieutenant."

"Sure you do. You follow me just fine."

Howe's expression got cold. Anger tweaked the corners of his eyes. "You saying I had something to do with this?"

"No question about it."

"You're a bit smug."

"I feel smug." He moved some things off the corner of Howe's desk and sat down. "It was Quill, or Garvey, whichever you wish, who started me thinking. According to him, do you know who really started the whole thing? Poor old Red Bridges, only he didn't have any idea how it was going to turn out. In March 1945 a Japanese supply ship called the *Kira Maru* was limping toward Tokyo after our dive bombers crippled her. She foundered, and most of the crew made it to the Bonin Islands. Five years later an ex-sailor named Red Bridges was running a salvage operation off the coast of Japan. He signed on a couple of sailors that had been on the *Kira Maru*. They told him about the freighter, and they located her in shallow water off one of the Volcano Islands. He went down to take a look, and what he found was oil bubbling up through the ocean floor at less than twenty fathoms.

"Only Red knew about it. He didn't share the information with the crew, he shared it with one man, his old friend Alexander Hooker, who was military governor of southern Honshu. It made Red a rich man and it ultimately killed him. And it made Hooker one of two men in the world that knew the location of what turned out to be one of the richest oil strikes on earth.

"So Hooker started building his empire. He got his financing for it from wealthy friends. People who were elitists like himself. Who believe that the spoils go to the victor. Like the robber barons you admire, Mr. Howe. Fisk and Doheny and Morgan and all the rest of those pirates, people like some of your friends in the photographs on your boat. Hell, you even bought a yacht that once belonged to Doheny."

"Get to the point," Howe said.

"The point? The point is, you were one of them. You anted-up along with a bunch of other people in key places. I think you were one of the bankers on this merry-go-round. You used your clout to call off the Winter Man because you were all afraid of Chameleon. Hooker convinced you that Chameleon was a real threat, and Falmouth convinced Hooker that I was the man who could find him. Hooker was too close to pulling it off to have it blow up after all these years of planning—"

"Pulling *what* off?"

"A financial panic. First, drive up the price of oil and ruin the automobile industry. When it goes, the steel industry goes with it. Then keep pushing up the prime rate and wipe out the real estate business. Force the unions to their knees. Hell, right there's enough to start a wholesale panic. And when it's over, who's got the money? *You've* got the money. Prime stockholders in Master."

"Ridiculous oversimplification, Lieutenant. Not worthy of you."

"Hooker didn't think it was. He was going for broke. I don't know whether it would have worked or not, that depends on the numbers. And we'll never know who all the Players were because Hooker was the only one who knew, and he's dead."

Howe leaned back in his wheelchair. "Pie in the sky, m'boy."

"The bubble's busted, Howe. There's not going to be any more AMRAN. No more Master. No more Mr. Quill moving his assassins around the board."

"I was never involved in that."

"I believe it. I don't believe any of you knew what was really going on. All you wanted was results. But you did know Falmouth would kill me if I led him to Chameleon. You marked me, Mr. Howe."

The old man seemed to sag into his chair, to grow older as O'Hara watched him.

"I suppose you've got some kind of silly bug in your collar, recording all this rot."

O'Hara shook his head. "No bugs. Just you and me talking."

"I didn't know they planned to kill you. Not until Eliza told me this morning. All I did was get you and Falmouth together. Hooker was falling apart. It was important to put an end to this Chameleon thing."

"And you didn't know about the *Thoreau*? The Marza business?"

Howe did not answer.

"You walk out of this one clean, don't you, Mr. Howe? Only one thing—you don't get it both ways."

"What do you mean, both ways? That's the second time you said that."

"I mean, you're a newsman before anything else, Howe. Greed comes second. I think you figured no matter how it went, you couldn't lose. If I turned up Chameleon, Falmouth would take him out and either Gunn or I or both of us would have the story for you. If Falmouth killed me, too, Gunn would still have the story for you. Both ways—see what I mean?"

Howe chuckled. "Well, son, whatever I *thought* is known only to me. But it does look like it turned out that way—now, doesn't it?"

"Not quite."

"Oh," Howe said, raising his eyebrows, "and how's that?"

"I gave your story away."

Howe looked at him for several seconds, then said, "Gave it away?"

"I gave the story to an old pal of mine, Art Harris of the Washington *Post*. With enough to substantiate the story."

The realization slowly sank in. "What the hell are you talkin' about, O'Hara?"

"I gave the story to the Washington *Post*, Howe. But it's okay, I left you out of it completely. That's what you want, isn't it? Anonymity. That's what you got."

The expression on Howe's face turned from disbelief to doubt to realization to anger. "Goddamn, you can't—"

"Did it."

"I'll sue you until—"

"Not likely. Not without turning over a can of worms you can't afford to turn over."

"You're a thief. You gave away my goods."

"You don't own something you never had. Remember our deal out on Cape Cod? I could walk away from the story anytime I wanted and let somebody else finish it. Well, that's what I did, Mr. Howe. Except I picked the guy to finish it."

Howe shook his head. "You're crazy. You went through all that and what do you end up with?"

"I got even, Mr. Howe."

"And what do I get?"

"Anonymity. And a ninety-eight percent share, at least for tonight."

There were two messages in Eliza's typewriter when she returned to her office. One was to call Howe. The other was in an enevelope. She tore it open. The message was simple.

Dear Lizzie:
Caught your act. Terrific. You get the scoop-of-the-year award. I don't even get the girl. xxx O.

The shaggy mane of pines on Kinugasa-yama swayed before he west wind, which had brought rain with it earlier in the day. But by the time the sun began to fall behind the spire of Tofuku-ji, the rain was gone, and fog, painted with the dying sun, swirled across the verdant park. The park was always a lush green, even in winter.

He was bone-weary and sore when he entered the grounds. But there was still an hour or so before it got dark. Time enough to begin. When he came back to the house in Kyoto, it always seemed as though time had stopped while he was gone. Nothing had changed, no new flowers had blossomed, none had fallen. Everything was the same. What was it the Tokenrui had once said . . . "We are just a speck in the infinity of time. Nothing ever changes."

There were fresh flowers in the vase in his practice room. The dogs sat at his feet, looking up, waiting to be petted and reassured.

He opened the package and took out the *gogensei* he had just purchased. It was a gray tunic, bunched at the waist, made of rough cotton. He took off his clothes and put on the *gogensei*. It felt good against his skin. Then he heard the dogs bark and he knew she was coming.

She stopped in the doorway when she saw him, and then she looked at his clothes and back at his eyes.

"You are going again," she said.

He nodded.

"Now?"

He nodded again.

She came close to him, touched his lip with her fingertips, licked her lips.

"It is very late," she said. "Tomorrow is not that far away." And she moved against him. He stood for a moment and then slowly put his arms around her.

She was right. Tomorrow would be a better day to start the Walk of a Thousand Days.

ABOUT THE AUTHOR

WILLIAM DIEHL is a former reporter for the *Atlanta Constitution* and one-time managing editor of *Atlanta Magazine*. He is the author of *Sharky's Machine* and is currently at work on his third novel. He lives in Atlanta, Georgia.